John Je

C000299597

THE LEGACY C

AUSTIN MACAULEY PUBLISHERS™

LONDON * CAMBRIDGE * NEW YORK * SHARJAH

A CIP catalogue record for this title is available from the British Library.

ISBN 9781398466982 (Paperback)
ISBN 9781398466999 (ePub e-book)

www.austinmacauley.com

First Published 2023
Austin Macauley Publishers Ltd®
1 Canada Square
Canary Wharf
London
E14 5AA

I do not own a pc so I am grateful to the services of torfaen libraries cwmbran, pontypool and blaenavon for the use of their public computers and to the staff therein who assisted me many times when I came a cropper as I'm not techno minded. Hope they enjoy the fruits of my labours written on their machines.

Story Synopsis

Old man Joe Farr suffers a fatal heart attack at his home on the mountain, and his death sets off a chain of events that rocks the otherwise quiet village of Cwmhyfryd, which lies in the countryside of Mid-Wales. Immediately, a number of the villagers are in a celebrating mood, for Joe was a deeply unpopular figure—a hatred of long-standing. One villager however is considerably uneasy as she now has to prepare for the return of Joe's long estranged son, Jack, who has lived in the United States for twenty years. Susan Tanner, once Jack's soon-to-be betrothed, is now the principal estate agent who will be in charge of the sale of Joe's house on the mountain.

Once nothing more than a wooden and metal tumbledown shack, it is now a valuable hacienda-style abode. And in order to sell it, Susan must deal personally with Jack. The Vicar of the Parrish has to inform Jack of his father's death—and also tell him that Joe has left more than £5,000,000 in his will—the specific instruction being that Jack must return to Cwmhyfryd to deal with the Estate.

Flabbergasted by the news, Jack does return to his hometown—only to find he is as unpopular now as he was when he ran away from home. Home at last, he is dismayed to learn his father has made such an arrangement with his once fiancé regarding the sale of his home. It takes a delayed period of time before Jack eventually learns the truth behind the arrangement—and a truth about his father which colours his mind about staying home.

But just as Jack is slowly assimilating himself back into that life, two vicious murders occur—and he is the man accused of both. Someone—who?—is out to destroy him. Murder, love, betrayal and a horrific revelation on the mountain that surrounds the village are all a part of the confusion which encapsulates Jack as he returns to collect his father's legacy.

Chapter 1

The Old Enemy

In the small but growing ever larger village of Cwmhyfryd, situated in an isolated Mid-South Wales valley, all but four of its residents slumbered sweetly in the early morning. The four who laboured were local captains of local industry which served those slumbering residents. They were, respectively, Jones the Newsagent, Willis the Butcher, Graham the Dairy and the man who prided himself on being the community leader—self-proclaimed—Malcolm Fisher who ran the café-cum-bakery—the one shop contained in The Square which took the greatest custom of that township. Accordingly, Malcolm ran The Square as though he owned it. Bombastic and loud, especially when he laughed, he was tolerated and mostly ignored by the Cwmhyfryd residents and the younger residents who would just laugh behind his back as he paraded his opinions on "Community Spirit".

At exactly 6.30 am, Malcolm Fisher would prepare a small repast for the others by setting out a table and chairs, with a pot of tea and four plates of toast and cake for his colleagues. They would settle down, eat of the repast and engage in sentimental memories from previous decades—each of them being old enough to remember Cwmhyfryd when it was a smaller village, sparsely populated then mostly by farmers and farmworkers. Naturally, being the oldest of the group, the bulk of the talking came from Malcolm and his memories dominated the conversation, distorted as they frequently were.

The daily walk down the 'good-old-days' path never really settled with the others—but it kept him happy and they had a free breakfast. At 7 am, they each went back to their own labours. Malcolm would pack up the table and chairs and return to his shop. His habit was then to stare around The Square—and gaze around the sleeping village—smiling as the lights from the homes were being turned on and watching the slumbering residents who were beginning their day.

His final habit was to scan the four mountain ranges which almost surrounded the village. He smiled at their beauty and felt pride at nature's work which kept the village safe. Here, his bonhomie smile would fade. The last thing he would see was the house set just a few hundred yards below Mynydd Gabriel. He stared at this place—and thought about the man who lived there with undisguised hostility. He had performed this ritual every day for years as if he was praying for that man to die.

Today, in the oddest of ways, his prayer would come true.

*

A mile and quarter north of Cwmhyfryd Village and situated just a few hundred yards below the top range of Mynydd Gabriel, the subject of Malcolm Fisher's seething sat quietly in his own rocking chair, just lolling back and forth, drinking iced water from a half pint glass. Joe Farr—now 83 years of age—was deep in contemplation. Like those four captains of industry in the village below, he was an accustomed early riser—though not for any particular reason, just say it was a lifetime habit—and he was now thinking about life: his own and the lives of others. In particular, his late and beloved wife, Theresa, their three sons—Joseph Junior and his twin, James, and the youngest son, Jared, commonly called Jack by everyone except Joe himself.

The twins were long since dead and Jack was estranged from him and the village and now living in America. Joe hadn't seen or spoken to Jack since the day Theresa was buried in Cwmhyfryd cemetery—twenty years ago. Bad blood between father and son which had never been made good.

Joe contemplated other things as well—his poor health for instance. He had survived three heart attacks and had been reduced, by doctor's orders, to lead a now more sedentary lifestyle. Stop smoking, moderate alcohol, no more fatty foods, etc. Except, he had never smoked, hadn't touched alcohol in years and had prepared his own foods made from his own garden produce. Sedentary had never been in Joe Farr's dictionary and he wasn't going to let it into his life now. Damn a sedentary lifestyle.

Thinking about his lifestyle had prompted Joe to get certain things in order—and how to execute that order when the time came. In recent weeks, he had given his lawyer specific instructions to be acted upon after his death. He had also seen the local estate agent based in Cwmhyfryd regarding the sale of Greenacres—

the Farr family home since 1860 when Jared Farr, whom Jack had been named after, an itinerant farmer, was given leave to build his own home on this part of the mountain. That original tumbledown shack was now no more and in its place stood a Spanish styled hacienda—now worth £185,000—and the proceeds of the sale would go to his son, but only if certain conditions were met. This would be Joe's legacy to Jack—hopefully making amends to broken fences.

And now—the day he had aimed for had come. Everything was tied up and all legal arrangements had been made and settled. There was no need to drag this near worthless life around any longer. He had decided to end his life—and he had chosen the method. It was to be a battle. Against…

The old enemy.

Joe stood up, swallowed the last mouthful of the iced water and put the glass on the table. He wore an old furred hat—its side brim pinned up on the crown. When he'd worn it facing front, he looked almost piratical. He had stolen it 50 years ago in Africa from a dead African Bushman. He wore a sleeveless vest which hung around him loosely—once upon a time, it clung to him, snug-like, that's how much weight he'd lost. He wore a long pair of khaki shorts which he'd used during the North African campaign. He never used underwear or socks. The boots were old army and, though dilapidated from age through years of care, they functioned well enough.

He picked up the tools needed for the job—a pickaxe, a shovel and an axe. He strode down the front garden to confront the old enemy—a thick remains of an old oak tree which was rooted to the ground. Many years ago, he, the twins and young Jack had laid siege to this tree in a bid to wrench it out of the ground. They had hacked and dug around it all day and failed to uproot it. It was another failed attempt to dig this monster out of the ground which had brought about the first of his three heart attacks. Now, today, he was going to make another attempt. This time—succeed or bust.

He used the pickaxe to soften the fresh ground away from the roots and then he dug the loose soil away. This took just 20 minutes and by now, he was already breathing hard. A sizeable hole enabled him to climb down and using the axe, he chopped away at the roots. The effort had him pouring with sweat within half an hour of starting.

The sun rose and the day began to heat up. Three hours passed and he chopped and dug, getting rid of earth and roots as he progressed only to find more and thicker roots below the surface. Instead of stopping for a rest and rehydrating himself, Joe continued with his efforts. The sun was now above the forest tree range and was beating down on him and still he ploughed on. The sun burned into his flesh and sweat poured from beneath the Bushman's hat and into his eyes. He wiped the sweat away—only to fill his eyes with wet soil. He looked down at his feet and saw he was treading wet earth. Where the hell had water come from?

He stood back and looked down at himself and, to his disgust, saw that he had urinated down himself and he hadn't noticed. This had happened before and he was ashamed. The Doctor had told him the nerves in his bladder had ceased to function correctly and there would be times when he didn't know he needed to pass water. In the throes of hacking at the tree, he had failed to even notice he had peed down himself. The state of his disgust fuelled his temper and drove him on to hack at the tree.

By midday, Joe had been beaten by the trunk. Only his stubbornness kept him in that hole and thrashing away at the seemingly impenetrable roots. He was now swinging the axe and completely missing the tree trunk and its roots. His breathing was now a constant wheezing and his vision blurred. Soaking wet— from sweat and urine—Joe became enraged. He again screamed, raised the axe and brought it down on the thickest of the roots. It was as if he'd struck an electrical power line.

The axe bounced out of his hands and the pain shot up through his arms and wrenched him backwards. He screamed in agony. Having had three heart attacks already, he knew this was the big one but even he had not taken into consideration how hard this would be. The pain was worse than the first three combined.

'Oh God,' he whimpered. 'Oh sweet Jesus.'

He clambered out of the hole and tried to stand but his strength had finally left him. It was as much as he could do just to crawl, slowly, up to the veranda of the house and out of reach of the sun's burning rays. He used the rocking chair to stand up and leaned against the blessedly cool wall. Too late, he remembered, the front door was locked. It meant walking around the back of the house and getting to the kitchen through the back door, and to a phone. He had to call Doctor Pryce. He limped onwards and as he took a third step, another paroxysm

11

of pain cleaved through his chest and he was back on his belly. This time there was no chair to assist him back to his feet so he crawled across the boiling hot flagstones to get around to the back of the house.

He made it to the side wall where he was able to grab the hosepipe and turn it on. At first, warm water poured out but then it became a beautiful cold drenching. He gulped it down in his mouth and then ran it all down his face and body, clearing the soil from his eyes and the urine from his body. Dragging himself to his feet, he stood and leaned against the wall. Another shot of pain took his breath away and he knew he was seconds away from death. And in that knowledge, he stopped in his tracks. What the hell was he trying to do? This was what he had wanted. Damn calling Doctor Pryce.

He stared into the sun above him and smiled. Staggering into the lower half of his back garden, he stood still and raised his hands, as if beckoning death. A shaft of light beamed into his eyes and he lost all form of balance. He barely felt the sensation of falling backwards or the hard pain of landing heavily on the ground. He lay there for what seemed like an eternity but was in fact just seconds.

In his final moments, a myriad of thoughts raced through his mind. Christ, he thought, I've had a hell of a life. Didn't get it right on so many levels but I've known danger, excitement, true comradeship, the love of a beautiful woman and earned the enmity of nearly everyone living in the village below. Ha, he thought. Damn them all.

He raised his hands to the sun—*I'm done*, he thought, *come and get me*. The final thought which ran through his mind was how silent the mountain was right now—as if the creatures living there had all stopped what they were doing just to watch him die. *That was fine*, he thought. *They've been my neighbours nearly all my life and I have been happy to live with them.*

Another shaft of light burned into his eyes and he couldn't tell if it was the sun or if death had come to take him. His raised hands dropped to the ground and Joe Farr, 83 years old, died in the garden he had loved and tended for years.

An eerie silence ran around the forest as if every living creature was paying deference to the human who had just died. After some moments, life began again. Birdsong started and became a chorus, chirping sounds clicked and four-legged creatures screeched and yapped. The sun rose above the forest and beat down on life below. Joe's dead eyes stared directly at it. Slowly, insects of all varieties climbed onto the dead human and began to devour the proffered meal.

Joe Farr's body wasn't found until three days later and then only because an oversight at Doctor Pryce's surgery was noticed. She had attended a coroner's court hearing for three days in Cardiff and hadn't checked with her colleague, Doctor Sandler, of village progress. When he mentioned he hadn't seen Joe because the cantankerous old sod had missed yet another appointment, Doctor Pryce was angry. That "cantankerous old sod", she'd exclaimed, was 83 years of age and on his third heart attack—his case was important. And so, Doctor Sandler was despatched to find Joe and examine him, even if was just a cursory look-over at Greenacres.

Doctor Sandler drove up the long, winding road to Greenacres and was amazed to see the once rough pathway was now a smooth tarred over driveable road. He saw the house as he made his way up the final two hundred yards and his eyes widened. He had heard Greenacres had received a makeover… but this was extremely impressive. At the top of the road was a large circle designed for vehicles to turn around and go back down. He parked and got out of his car.

He entered through the wooden gates and the first thing he saw was the tree trunk and the hole around it. Then he saw the tools. He stared and groaned.

'Oh no, Joe—you haven't'. He went to the front door and pounded on it. He saw the empty glass tumbler by the rocking chair and it was filled with flies and other insects. He peered through the window and saw nothing moving inside. He walked around the side of the house and was about to go to the back door when he suddenly froze to the spot. His nose wrinkled in disgust. He sniffed the air— he had smelled that smell before. As he listened, the sounds of the forest around seemed to stop and listen also.

Out of the eerie silence, he heard a strange humming. He looked around— and saw a mound of earth moving. He took one step towards it and trod on a dry branch. The sound was like a whiplash—a loud cracking disturbing the near silence of the mountain.

What happened next was terrifying. Thousands of insects flew off the body of Joe Farr and completely surrounded Doctor Sandler. He screamed, his mouth so wide open that many of the insects entered inside. His arms flailed about, batting away the squadron of flies and God knows what else. He crashed against the wall, spitting out the damned things which had flown into his mouth. From this crouching position, he then saw the corpse of Joe Farr, his body scorched by the sun, his eyes wide open and, like much of his body, eaten away by the ravenous insect life. He screamed and, arms still flailing, ran out of the back garden towards his car. He dropped his keys, retrieved them, tears pouring out of his eyes as he spat the insects out of his mouth. He was still screaming when he got inside and started the car—and then vomited all over the steering wheel and dashboard. At the same time, he sneezed, so many of the damn insects had gone up inside his nose. Gooey insect-filled snot, tears and more vomiting interfered with his driving as he tried to reverse the car out and back down the driveway.

Any competent driver could have turned a bus in that space—but Doctor Sandler was not competent now. He smashed into the wooden gate, drove forward into the forest embankment, reversed into the wooden garden fence and again rammed back into the embankment as he sped—too fast—down the long drive. Even here, he managed to crash into the embankments of the forest as he tried to turn on a sharp bend.

An eerie silence returned to the forest. Nothing moved, no insects buzzed, no birds sang or yapped. After a few moments, life continued as normal—now that the human interference had left the scene. The life-forms which had flown from the gigantic meal returned and carried on with their eating. Birdsong resumed and in the distance, a fox led her cubs to this spot. Nothing would go to waste until there was nothing left to eat. And time passed.

Two weeks later, Joe Farr was buried in Cwmhyfryd Cemetery—in accordance with his instructions to his lawyer, he was lain next to his beloved wife, Theresa, and their two sons, Joseph Junior and James. On the day he was buried, it hammered down with rain as if Mother Nature herself was mourning the end of summer—and the loss of another of her children. Apart from Vicar John Redd and the professional team of undertakers brought in from outside, there was only a single mourner to send Joe Farr on to his next adventure.

Susan Tanner was escorted to her car by Vicar John Redd. The next few weeks, she knew, would be the worst she would experience in more than twenty years.

Chapter 2

Analysis and Rumour of a Dead Man

In general terms, life in Cwmhyfryd was very much like a sedate walk in the park. Not much happens beyond an occasional affray, say on a Saturday night when a resident would perhaps indulge a little too much of the beer and voice an unpopular opinion or maybe push someone around—and then be shown the door, half-roughly, by his neighbours. The next day, said resident would apologize to all who were offended—and end of story. The two professional police officers who patrolled the village barely had anything more serious than a minor difficulty to deal with and were scarcely challenged to rely upon their training to deal with whatever problem had been placed in front of them.

Until the day Joe Farr died.

It began when the residents—around a dozen or so—were engaged in their own personal businesses in The Square. They all heard it first—a roaring, screeching sound—added to by loud thuds. They all looked around and saw nothing in the village to answer their queries. Then the roaring was louder and the sound of mechanical crunching followed. Now they were able to pinpoint the source of direction. Everyone keened their eyes towards the edge of the village and the pathway leading up to the mountain. The sound was now more frequent and closer—and then, screeching around the bend of the pathway, they all saw the car crashing into the embankment, reversing and then setting off again. The driver was either drunk or insane because he or she sped down the pathway at a hell of a speed—and towards them.

The Square was a wide open space—big enough for large lorries to enter and turn around when they made their deliveries—but this driver managed to crash into the four cars parked in the bays and without stopping to check the damage, sped onwards and out of The Square, smoke billowing out of the back of the car which had clearly crashed into other things because it was smashed up on both sides.

They all stared. The shopkeepers who had also heard the noise came out of their workplaces and demanded to know what had happened. By now, the witnesses to the carnage had congregated and had easily identified the driver.

'That was Doctor Sandler,' said Mari Elis, 'I know him. That was him driving.'

Others agreed but Sion Tomos said, 'How could it be? He's a Doctor. Doctors don't drive like that.' And so the murmuring grew into a debate as to who the driver was and everyone pored over the damage on the cars.

'That's a write-off,' said Steffan Gryffydd, who knew about cars as he was the only car dealer in Cwmhyfryd and write-offs were his meat and drink. 'They all are write-offs,' he confirmed and saw a good day's business coming his way.

'What the hell was he doing, driving like that?' asked Hywel Parry, who had stood just a few feet away from the speeding Doctor as he passed. 'He could've killed someone.'

'Let's go ask him,' said Tyler Morris who was excited that something exciting had changed the day for him.

'You can't just go and ask him,' said Sian Llewelyn, 'he's a doctor. You have to have an appointment to ask a doctor anything.' And so the conversation raged between the residents and the shopkeepers and the four owners of the cars were called across and one of them cried as he saw his near brand-new second-hand car smashed to oblivion. Steffan Gryffydd offered him solace—and his business card—and pencilled him in for the first business of the day, after the police had completed their investigations.

But thirty minutes later, the same residents and many more who had come to view the excitement were all stunned when two speeding police cars, sirens blaring, sped past them and drove up the same pathway Doctor Sandler had come down—though with much more care and dexterity than the good Doctor had. Again, the congregation grouped and speculated.

'Did you see that?' shouted an excited Lewis Jones. 'PCs Harris and Taylor. Since when did our police ever come here in cars?' Never, were the general replies as both PCs Harris and Taylor were only mobility-active with pushbikes. Cutbacks, the South Wales Police told them.

The sirens blared until their sound died down and now the congregation grew larger until nearly everybody living in Cwmhyfryd, bar the young who were still at school, had arrived and set up camp. Many of them entered Malcolm Fisher's café and like the strident businessman he was, he cheerfully engaged them all by placing more tables and chairs outside the café and served more people in one hour than he would normally serve in a whole week. What interested him was where the police cars had gone to. He had already heard about Doctor Sandler coming *down* from the mountain—and now two police cars had gone *up* the mountain. There was only one reason to go up there—and that was Joe Farr. Whatever the reason, he played Mein Host with a broad smile and listened to the rumour-mongers who speculated on what was happening.

And then, to add to the day's excitement, twenty minutes after the police had sped through The Square, an ambulance did likewise. It slowed when it reached the first bend and the residents could hear its siren blaring for ages as it trawled up the long and winding mountain pathway. An ambulance, the residents cried. Something has happened and it must be bad, they all decided. Two cop cars and an ambulance. But what were they chasing? No, just no!

And the only answer aired out loud was…

The day went on, the sun glaring down over the residents and curiosity grew. As the afternoon came to its close, three more cars entered the Square— definitely official looking cars, the residents agreed—and then, which drew gasps from everybody, a hearse. 'They'll have fun taking that up there,' said Matthew Rees. 'Can barely get a bike up that damn path in places.'

The day grew old and in the early evening, all the vehicles which had sped up to the mountain came back down—a lot more slowly than they had done going up. The police cars first, then the ambulance, then the hearse with its windows curtained off and then the official looking cars. They filed out of the village in convoy and a slow morbid silence took over. Those who had sat in or just outside of the café came down to the promenade and now everyone was asking questions or offering opinions as to what had taken place that day.

And while everyone speculated, only one person stood still and silent, standing away from the melee, watching the congregated groups. She alone knew—*knew*—what had happened on the mountain and she alone knew what its immediate consequences would be. Susan Tanner turned away from the gabbing crowd and entered her own village office. She went to her chair and sat down. Her work partner—Sara Phillips—saw her face and wanted so much to ask what was wrong but didn't dare. Susan stared blankly ahead for a few minutes, then lowered her head and burst into tears.

*

Because of the nature of what had been seen on the mountain—the coroner had been informed and the process which followed was swift. Only the professionals who had seen Joe Farr's body were involved—the only outsider, and not a witness to that awful sight, was Doctor Pryce, who had relevant information pertaining to Joe Farr.

The coroner—Professor Morgan Davies—had listened to the very gory details of Joe Farr's death and asked principally if there were any suspicious circumstances which led to it. No, came the official reply. The answer was duly noted. Doctor Pryce—Joe's personal doctor at Cwmhyfryd—gave Professor Davies details surrounding Joe's last few years, the three previous heart attacks and confirmed it was a massive heart attack which ended his life. Duly noted.

'This business with the tree,' queried Professor Davies. 'Can you answer for that?'

'I believe Mr Farr was tired of living the life of a sick man, Sir,' said Doctor Pryce. 'It was the business of chopping down the tree which brought about the first heart attack a few years ago. I understand there was even a personal battle against that very tree which goes back more than four decades. I believe Mr Farr decided he wanted out—by waging a fight against that tree.'

'The tree won,' said Professor Davies dryly.

Professor Davies summed up. 'Joseph Farr, aged eighty-three and, by his own Doctor's testimony, a sick man, died of natural causes brought about by waging an exercise of energetic activity, namely the chopping down of a tree. Out of delicacy, and maintaining the gentleman's dignity, the final public report will not mention the urine-soaked clothing nor the burns and the bite injuries which were inflicted upon him post mortem. I believe there was a letter…?'

He looked up. The senior ranking police officer confirmed there was letter found in Joe Farr's kitchen addressed to a lawyer named Allan J. Gibney—a man who name and reputation was well known by the officials in this court. Mr Gibney was currently out of the country at present but had been informed of the death of Mr Farr. All business relating to Mr Farr's Last Will and Testament were being addressed by Gibney's Associates even as the coroner's court was in session.

Verdict: Death by natural causes.

Chapter 3

Post-Mortem Conversations in a Bar

On the day Joe died, and before anybody knew exactly what had happened, there was much activity down in the village as the curious gathered around and speculated. Many of them took their place inside, or outside Malcolm Fisher's café and ate and drank quite a sufficient amount—knowing only knowledge would sate their hunger and thirst. When the official vehicles drove slowly down the mountain and past the gawping crowd the word had already come back from the receptionist working at the surgery—Doctor Sandler had found Joe Farr dead in his garden. That word spread like a wildfire aided by wind and inflammable fuels. When it reached the café and Malcolm heard it, he punched the air and gloated, victoriously. '*YES,*' he shouted. 'There *IS* a God.' And with a smile which he beamed for Wales, he dived into the storeroom of his café and sat down.

At closing time, Malcolm saw his clientele drifting away and he cleared the café up in the fastest time. He locked up and made his way to his home. His normal practice was to go to his daughter's house and spend some time there before going to his own. Malcolm Fisher lived alone since his wife, Moira, had left him and he suffered for lack of company. Susan lived at one end of Bevan Road, he the other. Today, he wanted to do more than keep company—he wanted to *CELEBRATE!* So he went directly home, changed out of his day clothes, washed and changed into something more casual then headed out to the only pub in the village—The Night's Tail. There, he expected to see a number of like-minded haters of Joe Farr equally happy to have heard the news.

He stepped inside the pub—and saw it was rammed to the rafters with villagers. During the week, there would be a steady number of regulars who would attend the Tail—generally around thirty per evening. On Saturday, the number would double and that would give the pub around a three-quarters full environment. Tonight, midweek, in both bar and snug, the place was jammed. Every table was attended and every chair was almost doubling up, with people sitting on laps strong enough to take the weight. The atmosphere was loud and excited and Malcolm forced his way to the bar and ordered his usual half pint— which would last the entire evening.

Smiling as he paid his coin to the landlord who had been away for the day and hadn't the slightest idea of what was going on, and so was confused about the swelling numbers in his pub, he then made his way to where he would usually sit. After ten minutes, an occupied chair became unoccupied when its resident needed the small house. Malcolm leapt in and found himself in the company of three of the oldest men living in Cwmhyfryd. None of them were friends to Joe Farr and Malcolm gleamed his smile around the table. In the time it had taken him to make his way to the bar, then into the bar and ten minutes of standing around, he learned Joe Farr's death had been hard and brutal and it had traumatized the doctor. *Good, good*, thought Malcolm. This was good news.

He was about to raise his glass to wish Joe Farr a speedy journey to the place below when old man Rhodri got there before him.

'So,' he entombed, 'Joe Farr is dead.' The others raised their glasses. 'He was a boy, wasn't he?'

The second of the three, his glass still raised, said, 'Aye—and a bloody hard one as well.'

The third man said, 'Yes—and he did damn well to last as long as he did. Eighty-three is no easy age to get when you're on the mountain.'

The three then clinked their glasses together and chimed, 'Go well, old man—we'll follow you soon.' They then drank their glasses to the dregs and breathed out as they slammed them onto the table.

Malcolm wasn't expecting this exhortation. He was looking for condemnation comments and pleasure that the old fool was now out of their lives forever. He leaned back and listened to some more of the pub chat. There were many reminiscences of the late Joe Farr—mostly about the fights he had been in, the troubles he had caused in the village. He heard references to his two sons, James and Joseph and how much trouble they'd been. A few comments about the younger boy, Jack, and where was he now and would he be coming back? In general, the conversations were mostly affectionate and occasionally funny.

Malcolm sank his half pint and, disgusted, he scrambled past through the crowd and out of the pub. He was at least smart enough to know this tide wasn't flowing in his favour and chose not to contradict the fools doing the talking, for Malcolm Fisher, the well-known bombast and upright pillar of Cwmhyfryd society, was essentially a coward and he could not bear to suddenly be at odds with them—and certainly not over the likes of Joe Farr. He squeezed himself out of the Tail and made his way home.

If Malcolm was too cowardly to take his townspeople to task, he did not take the timid road where Susan was concerned. When he knocked the door and entered without permission, he saw David, his son-in-law getting dressed for an evening meal with the Bankers Association and in an argument with his wife.

'You talk to her,' he told Malcolm. 'I can't get through.' Malcolm stared at them and asked what the trouble was. When David told him, Malcolm turned beetroot and damn near exploded.

'You're going to his funeral?' he exploded. 'Joe Farr's funeral? Why?'

Susan was folding the clothes she had ironed that evening and had ignored both her husband and father. Without looking at either of them, she said, matter-of-factly, 'Because he asked me to.'

Malcolm ranted at her again. How, he demanded to know, would whatever Joe Farr requested make her to a damn stupid thing like this? Susan stopped her folding and explained that she was handling the sale of Greenacres and a part of that business deal was for her to attend his funeral and mourn him. Malcolm then spent five minutes reminding her that Joe Farr was the pariah of the Cwmhyfryd village, a deeply hated man. His twin sons, now dead in their graves, were apples who hadn't fallen far from the tree—and that she, Susan, had also made her own contribution of dislike of the Farr family some twenty years before.

Now this was the wrong thing to say to Susan and probably everyone else would have read the signs and shut up there and then—but Malcolm was blind to such a thing. David backed away some—*he* could see the demeanour in his wife's countenance had changed and he *did* read the signs. He wanted to warn Malcolm but his father-in-law did not recognize his boundaries. He continued his rant, condemning the father and the three sons—conveniently choosing to say nothing about Theresa—the woman he had loved all those years ago and had never come to terms with losing her to Joe.

Finally, he ended with, 'Well, I will not allow this. I absolutely forbid you to go to that man's funeral.' And that was the line he should not have crossed. David backed away to the door. Susan slowly turned to her father and stared him down, her voice never rising above conversational level.

'And what,' she said, 'makes you think that you have the right to forbid me anything? You… will not "*allow*"? Are you under some insane notion that you can treat me the way you treated my mother? Do you believe you have the same authority over me you had when I was a child?'

She advanced on him and Malcolm Fisher demonstrated his true nature by backing away from her—out of fear having forgotten her manner was more aggressive than his own but with the power to carry it through. Susan was her mother's daughter through and through—and she had the mettle to start and end a fight when he did not.

'I haven't needed, nor have I sought, your advice since I was sixteen. You will not treat me like I'm some kind of feeble-minded customer who is unable to decide on buying a coffee or a tea in the café. If you ever make this mistake again—I will turn you out. Now, get *OUT* of my house.'

She turned away from him—easily done as he was now out of the lounge—and slammed the door on them both. Shocked to his very core, he looked to David for assistance but all David could do was shrug his shoulders. Chastened, Malcolm Fisher slunk out of the Tanner house—though really it was Susan's alone—and slowly walked up the street to his own. He entered his home. It was cold and dark. Unwelcoming. No wife to greet him. No food prepared for him to eat and he now realized he was hungry. He slumped into his armchair and stared into the darkness of his cold and lonely sitting room.

This evening had not gone the way he thought it would. Not even the mental image of Joe Farr lying on a Mortician's cold slab could cheer him. At least that man was being attended upon. His body would be gently handled and respected by a person who had never even known him in life. Better than what I've had tonight, he thought.

He sat in silence and remained motionless for the rest of the evening.

Chapter 4

After the Funeral

To be truthful, Joe Farr had prepared practically everything leading to this moment—the day of his funeral. He had planned for the sale of his home, had set out his Last Will and Testament with the Gibney lawyer and had made a variety of stipulations which would be carried out after his burial. Of course, the best laid plans... It had been his intention for his body to be found *inside* Greenacres lying in his bed or sitting in his armchair. He knew, having missed the Doctor's appointment that very day, Doctor Pryce would make a personal call on his home and would then find him dead, or at least beyond any medical help.

But, as the politicians will say, "events, dear boy, events..." The attack had hit him earlier and harder than he planned and it took his life outside the house. Mercifully, he did not see what Mother Nature did to him after he fell.

The complication of how his body was found and would have been dealt with by the assigned team of undertakers—again, arranged by the Gibney lawyer—was dealt with in the most professional way. Once the attending physician had ascertained his death was of natural causes and nothing suspicious, the undertaker did the best he could with the material left to him. If not in a pristine condition, anyone viewing Joe's body laid out in the coffin would never have known how it had been ravaged in the three days after he died. But nobody came to see him.

So today, he would be buried. He had made stipulations about this—which would be conveyed to the Cwmhyfryd Vicar and would be carried out to the letter. And that letter was thus: No Church service, his coffin would not pass through the Church doors. Joe was no religious man in life and would not suffer hypocrisy in death. He had arranged for a single mourner to attend his burial. There would be no religious incantations read over his coffin as it was lowered into the ground and no mention of his life in any way. Joe had written what was to spoken and Vicar John Redd—by no means a conformist type of Preacher—was happy to carry out these instructions without challenging them.

'Today is a happy day,' Vicar Redd spoke as the rain hammered down on top of the giant umbrella he held aloft. 'Happy, because Joe is to be reunited with his beloved Theresa, his wife of twenty-seven years who lies here in this place of rest. Also in this same place are the twin sons of Joe and Theresa and Joe will see them again. A family united.' And that was it. Joe's final words.

The four undertakers, employed by Gibney, lowered Joe into the ground with sincere reverence and stood by as Vicar Redd moved across the path to join the service's only mourner—Susan Tanner. He barely knew her. She was not Christian and did not attend Church—unlike her father, Malcolm, who was very much a devout. He asked her if she wanted to say anything and she said no. He walked her back down the steep pathway and she placed her arm inside his for balance as he battled against the wind to maintain control of the umbrella.

With little conversation between them, she thanked him, got into her car and drove out of the cemetery, through the mist and then out of sight. Vicar Redd turned to see the four gravediggers—more Gibney appointees—filling the grave with careful and measured movements. The pounding rain had not driven them to get a move on. Satisfied he had played his part as was stipulated, Vicar Redd made for the Vicarage.

Blissfully, he had no other professional duties to perform that day so he paid grateful thanks to being a Vicar in a small Parish and relaxed. Immediately, he pulled off the wet, sodden through clothes and dumped them into the bathroom wash basket, filled the bath with hot and perfumed water and luxuriated there until the warmth permeated his body and he felt at peace. Then—dressed only in a gown, he indulged in his guilty pleasure—toasting a number of rolls over the roaring coal fire and spreading lashes of butter over them.

He had toasted and eaten three rolls and the doorbell rang when the door was knocked hard. Vicar Redd answered and was confronted by a man in a civil suit, drenched to the skin. He did not know the man who announced himself as Peter Eddy—'I work for Allan J Gibney,' he said. That was enough. Vicar Redd knew who the man was even though he had not met any of the Gibney Associates in person—everything had been handled by phone or E-mail.

'Dear fellow,' gushed the Vicar, a hot buttered roll in his hand and some of it in his mouth, 'Come in. Come in'.

Peter Eddy entered, was given a towel, a new set of clothes—left there by the previous Vicar—and within twenty minutes was joining the Vicar in the eating of hot buttered rolls toasted over a roaring coal fire.

'Haven't eaten them this way since I was a child,' Mr Eddy said. 'The only way to eat them,' replied the Vicar. The rolls were thus consumed—now—to business.

The Gibney Associate brought out a sheaf of paperwork from his briefcase and laid it out in front of Vicar Redd.

'I am happy to inform you, Mr Gibney was entirely satisfied with the service you delivered this day in relation to Mr Farr's burial,' said Mr Eddy. 'However, there is more work for you to do. I am here on Mr Gibney's behalf to instruct you.'

Now, Vicar Redd was perplexed. He had performed his assignment within the scope of his professional expertise as was set out by the late Mr Farr—what else was he expected to do? He had not known Joe Farr—he'd maybe seen him on the few occasions when the old man had visited Theresa's grave but had never even spoken to him. He informed Mr Eddy he had only been the Cwmhyfryd Vicar for eighteen months and only a small handful of the locals were Churchgoers—Mr Farr was not one of them.

'This is not a duty relating to the Church,' said Mr Eddy, 'This is something the late Mr Farr wants you to—concerning his estranged son—Jared—also referred to as Jack.'

'I don't know him either,' said the Vicar.

'Nevertheless,' said Mr Eddy, 'this is something that Mr Farr instructed us to do—to give to you. You are to contact Jack Farr—and tell him about his father'.

The Vicar protested. This was unfair. He did not know Jack, did not know where Jack was, what he was doing. Didn't even know if he had a family or a job? How could he, a total stranger, be called upon to convey such terrible news?

Here, Mr Eddy raised his hand and apologized. The fact was, he explained, that no-one at Gibney Associates had understood any of Mr Farr's requests—even down to the manner of his own funeral. Bearing in mind, he had been offered the services of one of the most powerful lawyers in the UK, it would have been the simplest of duties for them to pass on the sad news to the estranged son—a duty they would have been happy to perform. But no, Joe Farr wanted the news to come from the Vicar—for whatever reason—and it had to be tonight.

'Tonight?' exclaimed Vicar Redd. 'Why tonight?'

The business of Joe Farr was to be conducted at speed, said Mr Eddy—for his son's sake. This had been established by Joe to Mr Gibney at their very first meeting. Mr Eddy had attended that meeting. Mr Farr, he said, was very specific.

And now, the business of how Vicar Redd was to contact Jack Farr.

'He lives in Oklahoma, with long distance cousins of his late mother. Phelps their name is,' he said. 'The owner—Horace Phelps—is a rancher who also owns a small Vineyard. Jack works at the ranch. A latter-day Cowboy according to our research.'

Research, thought the Vicar. These people have already checked up on Jack—which made this instruction even more bizarre.

'You are to call him, on the phone—midnight tonight—and inform him of his father's death—and also to tell him of the worth of the Farr family home.'

'Which is what?' asked Vicar Redd who had heard of the Greenacres development from humble shack to grand Spanish-style hacienda.

The answer damn near floored him. '£185,000,' said Mr Eddy. 'Jack will be offered the options of claiming Greenacres as his own, or to rent it out, to sell it—or even to give it away. At any rate, the decision must be his—and he must come to Cwmhyfryd to sign his declaration. In person.'

Now here, Vicar Redd expressed his ignorance as to how the estrangement between father and son had come about. He wondered if Mr Eddy knew.

'Something which occurred about twenty years ago,' said Mr Eddy. 'It concerned a wedding which didn't take place and the sad death of Mrs Farr. I don't know the fuller details, except that the local estate agent—uhhh…Name?'

'Susan Tanner,' helped the Vicar.

'Ah yes. Mrs Tanner. Well—she and Jack were to be married—here in this very Church. And she jilted him. It led to a massive brawl and the same night, Mrs Farr passed away. Jack remained in the village long enough to bury her—then left. He hasn't been back since. Father and son have never communicated. I believe, and this is only my own take on the matter, that Mr Farr is attempting to redress that sadness.'

Susan Tanner—the single mourner at Joe's funeral—jilted Jack Farr twenty years ago. Had she attended the funeral out of guilt?

'Hold on,' said Vicar Redd. 'Are you telling me that the sale of Greenacres—is to be conducted by… Susan Tanner?'

'Yes,' confirmed Mr Eddy.

Vicar Redd breathed out—hard. What a mess—and what on Earth was Joe Farr doing by dumping this out on him—*and* Susan. Surely to God Jack would never contemplate coming back to do business with the very woman who had treated him in such a cruel way—which may have even led to the death of his mother. He said so out loud.

'There is another part of this business which must be told to him,' said Mr Eddy. 'Actually the most important part—a massive inducement you might say.'

Vicar Redd waited. He was already confused and didn't wish to invite more confusion in. 'Through Joe Farr's business deals—Jack is worth over £5,000,000.'

And now, the Vicar truly was defeated. Five million quid? Joe Farr was a millionaire? That old reprobate living in what used to be an isolated shack on a mountain—didn't even own a car, had barely joined the 21st century, was a millionaire?

'Bloody hell,' was his only response.

Mr Eddy did not know the finer details. Again, the only way Jack could claim this legacy was for him to return to Cwmhyfryd and speak to the relevant bodies, sign on the dotted lines and dispense with the riches in whatever way he chose. But there was a timescale. He had to return soonest—or the whole legacy would be dealt with by the Gibney Associates in a completely different way. Jack had to decide for himself.

The five minutes of silence which followed this bombshell was necessary. Vicar Redd felt poleaxed by the news and couldn't think of anything to say. In the silence, Mr Eddy passed over the full details of where Jack lived in Oklahoma—the phone number to call, when to make the call and who to speak with when the call was answered. The essential thing was that Jack must hear the news from him, the Vicar, and not from another party.

'Will you make that call, Vicar?'

At midnight that night, Vicar John Redd phoned the Oklahoma number given to him by Mr Eddy and asked to speak to Jack Farr.

Chapter 5

Jack Hears the News

At midnight in the UK, Vicar John Redd rang the Oklahoma number given to him by Peter Eddy—where it was six o'clock in the evening.

Horace Phelps—Hank to his peers and employees—took the call and ventured outside the main ranch home to find Jack Farr.

The Phelps family owned a number of industries which were land based. Two of them were vineyards and the others concerned livestock. This one—also home to the ten ranch-hands—dealt with equine and bovine produce. In another time, the ranch-hands had all slept together in a single hut which contained bunk-beds and the very basic living conditions. Today, after protest, each of the ranch-hands lived in their own private chalet. Again, basic conditions only but at least, now private, which the farm-owner felt was more dignified. It also saved on the furniture which was broken after frequent fighting. You can't put a group of men together and hope for a blissful union of friendship, she told her son—Horace.

Horace Phelps was forty nine, looked older, and was the de facto foreman of the farm but only served under sufferance. He hated the work and hated those who worked under him. He also hated his name—he, the third of that name. He changed it to Hank when he'd visited relatives in England as a child and read a British children's comic where one of the characters was called Horace the Wimp. His father—Horace Junior—a lover of Greek philosophy, told him about the Horace who'd fought at the Trojan wars and who was a heroic warrior but Horace III was not having it and changed it to something more masculine—Hank.

And so, Hank padded out of the ranch house, chomping on one his own family home-grown apples and scanned the area. The ranch-hands had finished work for the day and had just washed themselves in the communal shower unit outside their chalets. Jack was not amongst them. A single shower was still flowing inside the communal and so Hank padded—bare-footed—down to it. He poked his head around the doorway and saw Jack being engulfed by the flowing water.

He shouted through the flow of water. 'Jack,' his lazy voice sounded, 'some guy called Vic Red from England wants to talk to ya.' Without waiting for a reply or acknowledgement, Hank walked away back to the ranch.

Jack—his face turned upwards to the shower nozzle—had taken in a mouthful of cold water. He pulled the chain and the water flow stopped. He squirted the water out of his mouth and wondered if he'd heard someone speak.

'Who?' he asked.

Jack Farr—forty years of age—wearing only a pair of torn jeans which were soaked from the showering—stepped out from the communal and looked around—just in time to see Hank entering the ranch. He wiped the excess of water from his head with the towel and, still barefooted and topless, walked across the carefully laid paving stones which led up to the ranch. He was bronzed from the sun, broad shouldered and muscular from the farm work. As he was also known as being a relative of the Phelps family, he was also kept at a distance by the other ranch-hands who did not like the Phelps family—especially Horace.

He entered the ranch—the only one of the ranchers allowed to do so without permission—and found Hank in the air-conditioned kitchen now shovelling a yoghurt down his throat.

'Who?' Jack repeated the question.

'Vic Red, England. Wants you.'

'I don't know a Vic Red from England,' said Jack. He moved away and went to the small cubicle where the communal phone was kept. This was one of the few reasons any of the ranch-hands would have access to the ranch—phones were not installed inside the chalets and mobile communication was difficult in this geographical area.

He sat down, still confused, and said, 'Hullo—this is Jack Farr. Who's speaking please?' It was odd but given the length of time he had spent in the States—and in Oklahoma in particular—Jack had not gained the local accent by any depth.

'Jack,' the Vicar almost shouted, 'good to hear from you. Ah... my name is John Redd—I'm the Vicar at Cwmhyfryd.'

There was a pause while Jack let this sink in—and then he said, 'Excuse me for a few moments, Vicar.'

He walked down the passageway and poked his head around the kitchen door. 'How many times do I have to tell, you,' he scolded Hank, 'Wales is not a small province inside England.'

'Whatever,' replied Hank who then shovelled more yoghurt into his mouth without even looking up from reading the funnies in the newspaper. Jack left him and returned to the phone—although he had a good idea what this call was going to be about. He picked up the phone and said, 'Hullo Vicar... Redd? How may I help you?'

'First thing...' said the Vicar. 'Jack—can I establish for myself that you are Jack Farr, son of Joe and Theresa?' Yes, Jack affirmed. 'Good,' said the Vicar— and now his manner became audibly uncomfortable—a man given a sad duty to perform. 'Jack—I... uh... I have some sad news to tell you... uh...' Here, he dried up. He had done this kind of thing before on other occasions—but never over the phone. A bereaved soul needed the sight of the face of the bearer of bad tidings—if only to lean on that person for succour. Over the phone was distasteful.

Jack sensed the Vicar's discomfort and took the sad duty away from him. He delivered the news himself. 'My father is dead,' he said. There was a silence— and then, the sound of a man breathing out. A man relieved of a dirty job. Vicar Redd was grateful. 'Yes,' he said. 'I'm sorry, Jack.'

So there it was. The potential, though small likelihood that maybe one day, there would be rapprochement between father and son—gone. Years of silent estrangement would never be discussed but maybe a form of dialogue which would lead to a relationship, bearable to them and those around them. Now, that tiny likelihood was gone—for all time. Jack—who never felt at all guilty for stringing this silence out—sat in momentary silence as this realization washed over him. He dropped his arm and his breathing could be heard by the Vicar. After a few moments, he raised the phone and spoke.

'Thank you,' he said. 'How did he die?' The Vicar relayed the three heart attacks which had weakened Joe—and then the fourth, the fatal attack brought about by Joe's peculiar activity with the tree. Here, Jack laughed.

'The oak tree—in the front garden?' Yes, said the Vicar. And judging by the mess Joe had left behind, quite a vigorous set-to it was as well. Jack laughed again. 'The old enemy,' he said, almost under his breath. The Vicar did not challenge or ask him about that.

'Was he alone?'

'When he died? Oh, yes,' said the Vicar. 'Quite alone.'

'Right,' said Jack, 'are there any... outstanding debts I need to cover? Funeral stuff?'

Here, the Vicar was steady. He'd had the worst of this conversation taken away from him and was on safe ground from this moment—apart from one single issue which he had chosen not to mention.

'No,' he said. 'Joe took care of all of that some while before... he died. I think he knew his time was near and he prepared everything. He paid for his own funeral and the plot in the cemetery was his anyway. He actually built his own coffin—I found that out today. He... uh... also made arrangements with regards to the estate.'

'Estate?' asked Jack.

'Well, yes,' said Vicar Redd. 'The sale of Greenacres for instance.'

Jack laughed again. 'I doubt very much that old place will go up for sale. I'm surprised it's even still standing. I expect the Farmer's Association will pull it down. Nobody in their right mind would go and live there.'

There was a pause. Vicar Redd cleared his throat. 'It's been evaluated at £185,000,' he said.

Jack's response was loud and disbelieving. '*WHAT*?' Vicar Redd was equal to the task. 'The situation regarding your father's Last Will and Testament is... uh... convoluted, Jack. In fact, if you are to benefit from any of it, I am advised it is necessary for you to come home.'

'How the hell could that tumble-down shack be worth a hundred and eighty-five grand? It's corrugated iron, wood and mud. It was built in the 1800's.'

'And the home you knew was razed to the ground a while ago. What's standing there now is a house—a big house—and it is worth £185,000.'

'Where did he get the cash to build that?' asked Jack—his manner now testy.

'The truth is—no-one seems to know,' said the Vicar. 'I was told by the representative of the Law firm looking after the Farr estate, that the house is worth that amount—and...' He tailed off. How do you tell a stranger he is worth over £5,000,000? 'He also left—to you—five million pounds.'

The silence which followed was, paradoxically, loud and deafening. Vicar Redd could actually hear his own heart beating through the ear-piece of the phone. Jack was clearly smelling a rat. Was this call a joke? Has Joe died? Are you Vicar of Cwmhyfryd? He asked all these questions and Vicar Redd confirmed the truth of it all.

'Where the hell did he get five million quid?' demanded Jack. No-one knew said the Vicar. 'The thing is, Jack,' he continued. 'This estate can only be settled by your physical presence here at Cwmhyfryd.'

'Why,' demanded Jack. 'Why not E-mail or Fax?'

'Your father stipulated this method in his Will. The lawyers are intending to carry out his last wishes to the letter.'

God *DAMN* the man, thought Jack. The bastard is going to get to me even *AFTER* his death. But *FIVE MILLION QUID?* A house worth thousands? How?

More silence. Vicar Redd listened and silently approved of his not telling Jack who the estate agent Joe had appointed to deal with the sale of Greenacres. The prospect of Susan's involvement would have probably decided the matter there and then. Definitely not coming back then, he would have said.

Jack wavered. There was more to this than the Vicar was telling him (which was true) or even knew.

'Jack?' Vicar Redd asked. Silence. More intimidating than his anger.

Jack said, 'I'm here.'

'Are you coming home?'

Another silence. It was interminably long and the Vicar waited. He could hear Jack breathing out.

'Yes,' he said.

Chapter 6
Susan's Disturbed Night

On the day of Joe's funeral and after Susan had left the cemetery, she returned to her small office in the Village Square. Sara was sitting there tidying up the surplus mail they had received in the past few days when Susan was engaged in the City. Susan entered the office, clearly preoccupied with other matters in mind—the funeral being one of them which Sara still did not understand. Going to the funeral of a man who had been the village pariah for decades was a bizarre business. More so, coming from Susan, who had such a complicated relationship with the Farr family.

Susan slumped into her chair and stared out of the office window. The rain continued and had now filled the drains. Water was flowing down the street like a river. Sara moved from her position and went into the small kitchen and switched the kettle on. This was going to need a hot cup of solace, she thought.

But all she got out of Susan was how the funeral had gone. No-one else apart from her had turned up. Sara hadn't expected anyone to be there. If Joe himself hadn't requested Susan's presence, the Vicar would have taken the service alone.

Susan did not fill in the missing pieces and after an hour of absentmindedly sorting out the mail, she stood up and said, 'See you, Monday, Sara.'

She went home, made herself a cup of tea. Avoiding David when he came home at tea time who immediately went upstairs to shower and get changed for that evening's banquet with the Banker's Association (the third that month). Susan had been invited and had declined. She saw enough of those people during the week and loathed the internal politics contained within—which David relished. That's how people are promoted, he told her. And in his case, it was true. He was the senior Banking Advisor in three major areas surrounding Cardiff—all brought on by attending business banquets like this one.

He left her sitting alone and watching television. She sat still for hours and felt emotionally strung out. Physically worn down with today's efforts and burdened with the knowledge Joe had imparted to her months before, she cleaned up and retired to bed. She was hoping for at least one night of undisturbed sleep.

She was denied this hope.

Typically, when exhausted both physically and mentally, the mind suddenly becomes activated with thoughts just as the person would prefer to be thinking of nothing at all. The moment Susan's head hit the pillow the events of the past few months came at her like a tidal wave—no doubt exacerbated by today's burial of Joe Farr.

Again, she thought about the day he sauntered into her village office and stood there, looking at her. At first, she barely recognised him. The three heart attacks had taken their toll on his face and body. Gaunt in frame, a grey caste in his face, he did not resemble anything like the vigorous man she had known nearly all her life. Sara, however, had no problem in recognising him. Just a few days earlier, she had seen him taking on two of the village ruffians. In spite of his age and infirmity, Joe had seen the two men—from the Edwards' family— off with their backsides sore from the kicking he'd given them. Old and near decrepit, Joe Farr was still full of the old Harry and he could still give it out eagerly.

'I should like to speak with you, Susan,' he said. Now this took Susan by surprise. One, because he had spoken gently to her—not his most obvious manner. And two, because he had used her name. In all her time courting Jack from childhood and until her terrible act of jilting him at the Church, she couldn't ever remember a time when he addressed her with any kind of familial respect and he had never called her by name.

Confused—and not a little scared—she gestured him into the smaller office where private conversations could be held without interruption.

He wasted no time. 'Have you seen Greenacres recently?' he asked. She said she hadn't but was aware it had received a major redevelopment. This had happened while he was recovering from his third heart attack. Many Hyfridians—the local nickname for the villagers—had asked if he had in fact died and was it was being redeveloped for a new occupier?

'I would like you to come up and give me an evaluation on what you think the property is worth,' he said.

'You're thinking of selling Greenacres Mr Farr?' This was odd. That farm, that tumble-down shack had been built by Joe's grandfather in the 1800's and only the Farr's had ever occupied it.

'Well,' he said. 'Possibly. Depending on what Jared decides. It will be all his.'

This threw her completely. She asked, her voice trembling, if Jack was coming home. He paused, looked around to see if anyone else was listening. Then he leaned towards her, as if imparting a confidence.

'What it is, Susan is… I am dying. I don't have much time left and I don't want to hang around just waiting for my time to end. I am sorting out all my business and Greenacres is a major part of that. I want you to evaluate it so that when I am gone its worth can be added to the rest of my Estate. It's all going to Jared—what he does with what I've left will be up to him—I just want him to have that choice. But I don't want him on the back-foot and having to deal with this kind of business from scratch. If it's all done and sorted, all he will need to do is sign bits of paper.'

So—Joe Farr was dying and he knew it. And it sounded as though he even knew when that day would happen.

But there was more. He had already arranged the funeral service with his lawyer and how that service would be delivered. The Vicar would be told later, via an Emissary from the lawyer. What Joe wanted… was a single mourner to attend his burial. He paused. Susan waited—until she realized he was asking her to be that mourner. She sat back in her chair, horrified.

'Why?' she asked. 'Of all people—why me?'

'I know—because I've seen you doing it—that you are the person who has been tending my Theresa's grave. I never thanked you for that so I'm doing that now. I looked after it but with my illness even that effort is now beyond me. I went there one day and I saw the grave had been cleaned up and flowers and such. I saw you doing it one day—I watched you tend to it—and you were so loving and gentle. Theresa appreciated that, I know. She loved you very much—the daughter she never had.'

Susan's eyes welled up and it took a super-human effort not to burst into tears. It was true—she had always looked after Theresa Farr's grave after Jack had left home. Only basic maintenance but when Joe clearly couldn't manage, she took it upon herself to keep everything fresh and clean. The twins whose grave lay beside her were also maintained but Susan paid particular attention to the lady who became her mother after her own mother had abandoned Malcolm and her when Susan was sixteen. For Mr Farr to call her—'the daughter Theresa never had'—was heart-wrenching and it added to the guilt Susan had always felt for what she did that day. And for what followed.

But this request—mourner for his burial? She didn't understand. 'I only need one person,' he replied, 'and I don't have anyone else I can go to.' The simplicity of it all—the most basic need for a person to be acknowledged in death—Susan felt overwhelmed but saw he was being sincere.

'I will be at your funeral. I will mourn for you,' she told him.

His face changed. Momentarily, under the grey caste of impending death, it brightened up with a touch of flush red. 'Thank you,' he said.

The next day, she travelled up the mountain to perform this function of placing a value on Joe's home. When she saw it—two hundred yards away as she turned the corner, she gasped. My God, she thought, *I'd* live in that place. She parked the car and was greeted by Joe. He smiled and invited her into his home.

She walked all over the place. What a beautiful house, she told him. A bungalow domicile, built with care and pleasing aesthetics yet with a practical design. It contained a major lounge, a large kitchen, clean and practically un-used, two bedrooms (why?) and a large bathroom which contained both bath and shower unit. Above, there was large attic space. Outside, there was a storage room containing all the gardening implements Joe used for work. As she laid everything out in order to place a value on this desirable abode, he made her a cup of tea and they spent an amicable two hours together discussing everything except their own private histories. It was odd, she thought, that in the house, there was not a single photograph of any member of his family. Not even of Theresa. She did not make mention of it. He did not raise the subject of Jack—where he was living, what he was doing, was he married, children—the subject was not raised.

She gave Joe her evaluation. £185,000. He smiled and said, 'Yes, I thought it would be something in that area.' In fact, he knew the price already. The team who built it for him had already told him. It was gratifying to hear her confirm their evaluation. He knew she wouldn't stiff him on the sale—if it went on sale.

There was little communication between them after that. Confirmation by mail of the house's value. Her office's assurance that all would be done to in accordance of his wishes.

He didn't come back into the office and she had no reason to pay him a call at home.

The day when the villagers—the Hyfridians—saw the emergency vehicles speeding up the mountain alarmed Susan. They all speculated what might have happened to the man living up there but Susan knew for sure. When they came back down, this time slowly, with respect, she alone knew what the next steps would be. Joe's funeral—which she had promised she would attend—and the possible return of Jack to Cwmhyfryd. It was these thoughts, among others, which had kept sleep away from Susan this night.

She tossed and turned and never managed a wink of comfort. And for the umpteenth time, she asked herself if she had done the right thing in acceding to Joe Farr's request. So easy, she told herself, if another member of her Bank to have performed the evaluation of Greenacres—and this mourning business. What the hell was she thinking of? Sara's exchange was one of pure disbelief. 'You soft,' she chided. 'Soft in the bloody head if you go to mourn him.'

Her father's reaction was more predictable but she had long since ignored his protests. She knew the truth of his hatred of Joe Farr, the reason he had objected to her even talking to Jack never mind going out with him, the reason why Moira—her mother—had upped sticks and cleared off to London. The very idea that she—his daughter—was going out with the son of the woman he had pursued so hardily in his youth—and had been rebuffed by her many times—had rankled him. To marry a piece of work like Joe was too much for him to bear. Susan's relationship with Theresa's son was akin to committing incest.

So, disturbed by these thoughts, Susan moved about her bed as if she were on fire.

Nothing but time and knowledge of what Jack would do would give her peace.

And then there was David. Another problem which had been hanging over her. And, as if the thought had allowed it, at that moment, she heard a car arrive at her home. There was slamming of the door, laughter, bonhomie shouting, the beeping of the horn—at 2am for Pete's sake—and the car screeching away. That'll impress the neighbours.

David entered the house—and something smashed downstairs. Christ, she thought, he's drunk again.

He walked up the stairs—the careful walk drunks do when they are trying to prove to someone they are not drunk. He reached the landing top, breathing out and giggling. Bloody hell, thought Susan as she caught a whiff of cigar wafting into her room.

He was in the toilet. He had not closed the door and so she heard him piddling whatever he had drunk that night into the basin. And again, he laughed. This was followed by a long fart and him saying, 'Get out and walk you bugger'. More laughing. Susan was now running her hands through her hair.

He opened the door—not quietly—and saw by the light of the landing light that she was awake. 'Not asleep yet?' he asked, a stupid smiling expression on his face.

He entered the bedroom and tripped over the carpet. More laughing. He slumped onto the bed and began to undress. Then he laughed as if an invisible someone had just said something and he had to laugh just to earn yet another promotion.

Not reading the anger on her face with any accuracy, he decided to recount the night for her.

'Brilliant night,' he said, voice slurred. 'Saw Hogarth. Promotion suiting him down to the ground. Maybe getting a transfer back to London. Lucky bastard.'

He dragged on the last portion of the cigar and Susan seethed. She hated the smelly thing and wouldn't allow it in the house never mind her bedroom—*her* bedroom,

He laughed again. 'Tell you a joke Alwyn told me. These two bankers...'

And that was it for Susan. She threw off the duvet and erupted at him.

'Goddam it, David. It's two o'clock in the bloody morning, you're drunk and you stink of cigars and farts. I'm trying to sleep and you want to tell me more unfunny jokes from that half-wit at the bank. And what have I told you about blaring that bloody horn? Now put that damn thing out and get out of my bedroom. You'll be sleeping in the spare room tonight.'

She pushed him off the bed and he stood up, leaning on the wall for balance. Chastened—again—for this wasn't the first time she had pushed him out of the room—he picked up his discarded trousers and sloped out of the room. He slunk along the landing, ashamed—breaking wind with every step—and closed the spare room door very quietly.

Quiet in the bedroom was resumed. Susan pulled the duvet back and lay in the bed—listening to the night outside. It rained still. She thought of Joe Farr resting under the wet mud, his troubles were over and—if you believed that sort of thing,—he was reunited with his wife and sons. She wondered if he were better off than she was as she lay in a warm soft bed, protected from the harsh winds and pounding rain. She thought about Jack coming home, claiming his birth right. She closed her eyes and this time, she fell asleep.

Chapter 7

The Prodigal's Return

After the call to Jack in Oklahoma, Vicar Redd in Cwmhyfryd still had one more duty to perform. Peter Eddy had given him two phone numbers to use—one for confirmation of Jack's coming home and the second to confirm he was not. Vicar Redd looked at the two numbers—identical save for the final digit—and could see they were not conventional phone numbers. With each, he would have to speak clearly—"Jack Farr is coming home" or Jack Farr will not be returning to Cwmhyfryd". The wording was set out specifically so there would be no ambiguities about their meaning. He dialled the first number and was met with a metallic, robotic voice which instructed the caller to speak in clear tones. He spoke, very carefully, very directly, the message intended for this number. The response was a recording of his own voice and did he approve of the recording or would he need to make a second recording? He acknowledged the approval and the machine informed him the message was accepted.

His duties thus performed—he at last relaxed and breathed out slowly for clearly he was uncomfortable about what he had done. Not telling Jack about Susan's involvement weighed upon him and he knew it would come up again for the next part of his involvement was to meet Jack when he arrived in Cwmhyfryd. This had also been arranged by Peter Eddy acting upon his own instructions from whoever *he* was working for.

It was way past his usual bedtime and sleep would be a near impossibility at this time, so wound up was he. So he brought out six bread rolls and butter, stoked up the fire and indulged again in his guilty pleasure. As he ate, he thought about the man he had just spoken to and the journey ahead for him. He listened to the pouring rain as it beat down against the windows and doors and, for some reason, it was a comforting sound. At two o'clock, he retired to bed and laid his head upon the pillow. He drifted off to sleep around the same time Susan did in her own bed.

In Oklahoma, and about an hour after the phone call from the Vicar, Jack received a set of instructions on his E-mail from a group of lawyers called Gibney Associates. The instructions were how to make this journey back to Wales. It was very specific and the E-mail instructed him to follow the plan to the letter.

From Oklahoma, by plane, to Heathrow, from there, train to Cardiff, then a taxi to a small village ten miles south of Cwmhyfryd—Pentre Haf—from there by taxi to the outskirts of Cwmhyfryd and then from Cwmhyfryd village, a taxi up to his former home, Greenacres. He groaned at the prospect of such a journey.

Most of which was clear and simple—it was the final instruction which confused Jack. A taxi journey from Pentre Haf was understandable—the Railway did not yet extend to Cwmhyfryd and the local bus service was hardly regular. But to take a taxi from one village, ten miles in distance, to go to a place, and then to exchange that for another taxi to go just a further mile and half seemed odd. But those were the instructions and the E-mail was very clear on carrying out those instructions to the letter.

Jack did not simply accept these instructions blindly. He googled Gibney Associates and learned they had offices in Wales, Manchester and Cornwall. Their central office was based in London. The Associates had been in existence for over thirty years and it was no penny-ante operation. They were a large and powerful team of lawyers who would represent only the wealthy client. Again, Jack asked himself, how could Joe be involved in something this large? Back to the mysterious five million quid and the new Greenacres development. After spending a fruitless amount of time pondering on this issue, at which he could not even guess an answer he put it out of his mind. He informed Hank of Joe's death and what was expected of him (he did not mention the five million) and Hank gave his customary total-lack-of-interest-in-the-business nod of the head. Jack went to his chalet and began making the preparations to make the return journey to the village he had sworn he would never go back to. The best laid plans…

In the event, the journey back turned out to be more horrendous than he thought it would be. A mid-afternoon plane take-off delay at Oklahoma City, leading to a 14-hour trip across the Atlantic, a weather situation at Heathrow delaying the landing there, the Tube-way journey crossing London which got Jack to Paddington in time to see the GWR train to South Wales just pulling out of the station which meant another hour's wait. By now, his body clock had adjusted to UK time. It was nearly mid-day. He sat down, ate a burger, drank a fruit juice and watched life in an English city for the first time since he had left this station another lifetime ago.

The next train arrived and he struggled on amongst so many others to find a seat. Going past Reading, Swindon, Bristol, a flood delay at Severn Tunnel meant the journey took nearly four hours before he reached Cardiff Central. The journey from Cardiff to Pentre Haf which should have lasted an hour and a half lasted two hours. By the time Jack reached Pentre Haf, he had been travelling for more than twenty hours. And now he was sweating like an athlete. Typical British weather—it had moved from being a violent storm with powering rain and winds to now something quite sunny. He climbed into the back of the taxi and told the driver to go to Cwmhyfryd. The taxi driver was of Indian descent and spoke very little to Jack who was now on the verge of sleep and couldn't have engaged him anyway.

It was at this point in the journey where Jack made a deviation from the instructions laid out for him by the E-mail. He wasn't certain if this trip wasn't being witnessed by Gibney Associates and if he was being tested to see how obedient he behaved on the journey but he'd made this decision as far back as leaving Oklahoma. And the deviation wasn't purely out of funk or rebelliousness. He had a personal reason for doing what he was about to do. About a mile outside the entry road to Cwmhyfryd, Jack told the taxi driver to pull over. He would walk the rest of the journey. He had been awake now for nearly twenty-four hours in the planning and execution of this journey, during most of which he had been sat down. He needed to stretch his legs and get in a good lungful of air—clean Welsh air. To a Welshman, there is no pleasing sight than the beautiful countryside at the return of his home country. Even given his own personal feelings against making this trip, there was one thing he really missed from being home and that was the sight of the mountains, the rivers and the forestry of his home and surrounding areas.

Released from wheel travel, Jack stood still on solid ground and gained his bearings. From here on, the ground was familiar to him and his breathing was now racing. How much of it, he wondered, would have changed in twenty years? He picked up the three suitcases he had brought and began his walk to the entry road to Cwmhyfryd.

When he was just ten minutes away from the single point he had been looking for, he stopped and unloaded the small provisions he had prepared for this moment. A small round of chicken sandwiches, two fruits, banana and apple, a flask of tea—English tea—and his one concession to American culinary delight—three homemade pancakes from Auntie Phelps. He sat on a large rock and stared at the path in front of him. He was on an incline which led straight up onto Mynydd Haf, past three store farms, across the straight and levelled onto Mynydd Gabriel, past the Church and cemetery and then, another mile later, he would be standing just a few hundred yards over his old home. In his youth, he had taken this incline path many times returning from his work at the Brangwyn and Pentre Haf farms.

But in those days, he was a younger and vigorous man, unencumbered by heavy suitcases—nor had it been preceded by a long and tedious plane and taxi journey. He would then forgo, this time, to make that journey to his home. When he reached the point where the incline path divided, he would turn right and approach Cwmhyfryd at its entrance—as had been instructed by Gibney Associates.

As he ate his meal, two very beautiful girls came out from behind the trees. One of them clearly dressed for the summer spell which was beating down on them. She was dressed in a small white 'T' shirt which was tucked into a pair of cut-off jeans made to look like shorts. She was barelegged and wearing canvass shoes, no socks. The two girls were animated and talking fast. They passed him by, gave him a cursory glance and walked on, still laughing, as if he was something humorous to look at. Their conversations lasted until they were both out of his sight.

Jack smiled. It was the first time he'd heard a Welsh valley accent since he'd left home. He barely understood a word they said.

Refreshed by his small meal, he stood—and realized just how tired he was. From here, he was just a few minutes away from what he had stopped the taxi for to come and see. He picked up his case and walked, taking the right-hand path of the incline and a few minutes later, he turned a bend and there they were. Still untouched by human development and interference—Pedair Mynydd Cwmhyfryd—the four mountains of Cwmhyfryd. Nature in all her glory.

They were, respectfully, Mynydd Yr Haf—the Summer Mountain—so named because when dawn approached, this was the first of the four mountains to benefit. The second was Mynydd Gabriel—named after a mid-fifteenth century Baron who had assisted the King of England over a minor Welsh dispute. The third mountain—the most overpowering of the four—was Y Mynydd Carreg—the Stone Wall Mountain. It was the highest of the four mountains and the most intimidating because it rose above them, so high that sometimes, on foul wintry days, when the clouds were low, the top of the mountain would pierce those clouds. On the mountain itself, there was a wide plateau when once a community had lived. Jack wondered if the descendants—who were certainly still living there when he left—still lived on the plateau.

The fourth mountain—Y Mynydd Fach—was the least distinguished. It descended from the side of the Carreg and stretched three miles down to the base of the mountains which would then bend and join onto Mynydd Haf. There were no trees or rivers—just an old, possibly Roman-built path.

In its time and before the housing development companies had entered the valley, Cwmhyfryd had also been known as Dyffryn Pedol—the "Horseshoe Valley"—because of aerial pictures made of this area. Prior to the development, the valley was all but a circle. When the lower half of the mountain was excavated so an entrance could be made into the valley itself, someone noted it now looked like a horseshoe. There was even a suggestion that this should be the new name to replace its centuries old title—Y Pedwar Mynydd. Finally, common sense prevailed and "Cwmhyfryd"—Pleasant Valley—was chosen.

It was a beautiful sight and Jack had never tired of seeing it. How strange then, he thought, that he would experience that old feeling now. Picking up his cases, he walked on and within minutes, he was passing through the entrance which took him into Cwmhyfryd.

Chapter 8

To Hatred and Home

He saw the few changes the moment he entered through the stone gating which boasted a large plaque, announcing, in English and Welsh:

WELCOME TO CWMHYFRYD.
PLEASE RESPECT OUR VILLAGE

To his left, where once stood waste ground and ancient trees, there was now a small row of houses—quite like the chalets Jack and the other ranch hands lived in back at Phelps Farm. A street sign named the row as QUARTER HAVEN. He didn't know what it referred to. He scanned the village. Much of it hadn't changed beyond the odd development or house improvement. TV aerials and scanners on the sides of the houses, a house which had added another level to a bedroom, some houses had improved their driveways because if there was one thing this village had now that it didn't have all those years ago, it was a larger number of car owners.

On the sides of the mountains, a few larger domiciles had been erected but he doubted more would be built as the mountains from halfway up were very steep. The only way any more could be built would be to dig into the mountain sides themselves, to create roads and level the area—and Jack knew the villagers would prevent that. Otherwise, the village was pretty much the way it had been— if time hadn't stood still in Cwmhyfryd, it hadn't exactly moved along at a great pace either.

And so, back to the carefully laid out instructions as issued by Gibney Associates. The only confusing part of this journey. A taxi to the village—which he had cut short—and now the taxi ride up to Greenacres. He knew there must be a reason—and the only thing he could think of was someone—maybe his dad—wanted Jack to see the village from a pedestrian point of view—and maybe to be seen by the village pedestrians themselves. Whatever the reason was, he trawled past the houses, seeing curious faces who wondered who this stranger was, carrying three heavy suitcases through *their* private village. Twenty years ago, there was only one place where the only taxi stood and so he made for Grosmont Arch. The Arch had been constructed in the early 1920's in memory of a soldier who had served in the Great War—a native of Y Pedwar Mynydd— who had saved three soldiers in a gas attack on the trenches and who had died in that valiant attempt. His name was Ivor Grosmont.

Sure enough, the taxi rank was still there—and it had grown to three taxi's. Progress. As Cwmhyfryd was so small, there was little call for a larger taxi service, not for local trips anyway. On a Saturday night, it was used to ferry the drinkers back to their homes or for the more senior folk to get back and forth from visits and shopping. Mostly, back in the day, the taxi cab was used to take the early bird workers to their place of employment outside of the village and then back again for the bus service was most irregular. Twice in the week to outside villages and three times on the Saturday to include Cardiff.

When Jack arrived, one of the drivers was in dispute with another man, oddly dressed for the very warm day it was turning out to be. He wore a large, thick and dirty Parka coat, with, apparently no trousers that Jack could see and a pair of filthy plimsolls—no socks—and the hood covering his head. His legs were as dirty as the coat and the footwear and the taxi driver was extremely angry. He jabbed the man in the chest with his finger.

'You not getting in my taxi, butty,' he screamed. 'You stink the place out. Now BUGGER off.' The coat-laden man slunk backwards, glaring at the driver, and then he limped away from the rank.

Jack watched the argument as the other two drivers moved towards him. Apparently, there was no orderly queue as to which taxi driver drove who, so it was pretty much the first driver to see a customer who was the one to pocket the fare. The man who reached Jack first was the elderly Silas Hughes. Without waiting to be asked about the argument, he filled in the details.

'That's Dave the Sweat,' he explained. 'Bad body smells. You see his coat— the only thing he ever wears. We afraid to ask why just in case he shows us. He hasn't washed the coat—or his body—in years and the stench is incredible. He went to Pentre Haf library a while ago and he cleared the place in seconds. They had to leave the windows and doors open for days till they got a Fumigation

Service in. Teeth as green as the grass you standing on. Breath could kill a charging elephant at ten yards.' Welsh gossip in a microcosm.

The angry driver crossed over—still angry. The other two drivers now backed away. 'This one's mine,' he announced, 'to make up for that dirty boy.' The other two drivers were clearly intimidated by the angry driver—and with reason. He was tall, around 6'2", weighing around thirteen stone, a burly figure who clearly enjoyed throwing his weight about. Jack aged him about mid to late twenties. 'Get in. butty,' he ordered.

There was no dispute from the other two drivers—happy to see him gone from the rank. Jack climbed in after placing his suitcases into the car boot. The driver climbed in and sped the car away at a hell of a pace and Jack held his stomach. 'Where do you wanna go, butty?' he asked.

'Do you know where Greenacres is?' he asked the driver. From his position in the back seat, Jack could see a change in the fake joviality in the driver's face. His eyes narrowed and stared at Jack.

'What you wanna go there for?' An unpleasant tone, belligerent. 'The old man who lived there is dead.'

'That's where I want to go. Greenacres.' He laid his head against the headrest and watched the village from the speeding—too fast—car. As he had seen so far, little had changed in the village. When they passed The Square, Jack saw the same shops were still there and he wondered who was running them. The taxi passed them—and then through Bevan Road. Here, he held his hand up over his face. It went past that particular house without him seeing anyone—or anyone, he hoped—seeing him.

It was here where Jack saw the first major change. The pathway leading up to the mountain—and to his old home—had been given a big makeover. Once, a rocky track which only agricultural vehicles could successfully negotiate, it was a now a tar covered road, smooth and straight, no bumps, no heaving. The taxi glided across the road and it was a smooth journey for the whole one and a quarter miles upwards.

Jack wasn't just staring at the beautiful green and thick forestry—every now and then, he scanned the driver's eyes which had barely left his from the moment they'd moved off. The taxi turned a bend—and now they were approaching the straight path leading to Greenacres. And now Jack breathed out—completely taken aback by the sight of the house before him.

The Vicar had told him the house had been valued at £185,000—and he could see how that evaluation had been made. From the once iron corrugated, wood supported and mud cemented shack it once was, it was now a stunning Spanish-style hacienda—just as the Vicar had informed him—surrounded by a smart front and back garden which itself was surrounded by a small picket fence.

Ahead of them, he saw a large round space which had been constructed so any vehicle of size could park, reverse and drive out without causing the driver to move back and forth inch by inch.

The taxi stopped and Jack paid the fare. The driver did not get out of the taxi to assist him with the luggage so he took it all out himself. As he moved towards the house, the driver turned the car and then stopped. The passenger window slid down and he looked at Jack and said, 'You're Jack Farr, aren't you?' Jack confirmed he was. The taxi engine revved up. 'If I'd known that, I wouldn't have brought you up here. You not wanted here, Farr—go back home.' That comment was delivered by a look of pure hatred and the driver sped the taxi back down the path and skidded unnecessarily around the bend. Jack watched as it drove out of sight.

'I am home—*butty,*' he said.

He dropped his suitcases and stood in front of the house, looking over it from all the angles. The curtains were drawn so he couldn't see inside. The rocking chair—which his dad had made himself—rocked back and forth slightly, pushed by a gentle breeze.

Slowly, as if not wanting to see it, he turned and looked at the tree trunk. *The old enemy.* The cause of his father's death. An axe was buried into the trunk, a pick-axe and a shovel buried into the earth. What a damn silly way to die, he thought.

He had been given instructions on what to do next. Around the back of the house there was a garden—one which had clearly been tended carefully by Dad as it had vegetable produce planted. He took the luggage around and scanned the ground for a particular stone. A large stone with pink paint on it. He saw it, lifted it up and underneath there was an envelope and letter inside plus a door key. The letter was from Vicar Redd. He opened it and it said:

JACK—LEAVE THE LUGGAGE IN THE STOREROOM, COME OVER TO THE VICARAGE AND HAVE TEA.

It was signed, *Vic Redd.* He smiled. Vic Redd—Hank hadn't been far wrong then. He took the key and unlocked the storeroom. It was small, containing a few farming and wood-cutting implements, dusty from lack of use but otherwise clean—Dad wouldn't stand for clutter or dirtiness—not in the job he did. He put the luggage on a mat and was just about to leave when he saw that old hat his father wore every time he went out. After all this time, he had still held onto it.

Jack locked the door and then made his way up through the only path which would take him to the top of the mountain. Unlike the pathway leading up to the house, this one hadn't been touched. It was rocky, unstable and he had to forge his way through the overgrowth of tree limbs, thorny stalks and nettles. How often he had made this trek when he was a younger man. It ran for two hundred yards through a tunnel of trees which led him out and onto the mountain. He didn't pause, carrying on upwards on to the steep hill and eventually reaching the base level of the mountain. He stopped, breathing out hard for he was winded from the climb—and stared across the barren site before him. Untouched, wild and windy now, the sun was doing its job by warming him. Then, dramatically, he turned and looked down the valley and into the village.

It was as if twenty years hadn't happened. Beyond the small changes he had seen at ground level it was just as he had seen it on his final day.

'Home,' he said. And somewhere, buried in that single word, maybe a smile. Then he strode away and headed across Mynydd Gabriel and towards the Church.

49

Chapter 9

Reacquainting with Old and New Faces

The walk invigorated him—he needed it to keep awake. He knew if he'd rested at the house like he really wanted to, then he would've have slept for a long time. He'd been awake and active for more than thirty hours now. He resisted the sleep because he wanted to meet the Vicar and find out exactly what this inheritance business was really about. The mountain embraced him as the wind blew past and it stirred his walking on. So often, when as a child and teen, he had made this trek, walking to Pentre Haf or Brangwyn to work on the farms for the neighbouring Farmers in those villages. He saw there was little change in Gabriel—not much you can do to a mountain, he thought, but he had seen places where housing estates had been built on top of a peak overlooking a small town. He doubted it would ever happen here. He continued his strident walk. The Vicarage was a mile and a half from the point where he'd started—the only domicile on the mountain. The sun was declining and the warm breeze began to chill a little. He wore a short jacket now—prepared for the change in the climate which he remembered could fool people who were not used to mountain walking. As he walked, he turned back and stared at Stone Wall Mountain and again wondered if the old community still lived there. He remembered their name— the Fleminganese—named after the man who had founded their community centuries ago—Joshua Fleming.

He walked on—and then stopped when he heard a noise. A squeal of laughter. He looked around and saw nothing except the barren landscape. But then he stopped and stared and saw a peculiar thing—a bicycle, standing upright by one of the many dents which pitted the mountain range. Another squeal of laughter forced his curiosity to get the better of him and he walked to where the bicycle was parked. As he neared the area, he saw the rise—and fall—of a man's naked backside with just a pair of orange underpants and trousers around his lower legs. Another squeal of laughter—from a woman—told Jack that this was not his business and he should now walk back to the track.

He smiled. A breezy place to carry out a lover's assignation but each to their own. He saw the Vicarage. Now here, there had been a change. Twenty years ago, the Vicarage had been completely surrounded by a wire picket fence which stood around four feet in height. Now, it was a tall white stone wall with red brick around the top.

It was as if the place needed protection. There was a rear entrance into the cemetery, a massive gateway and passing through two large wooden doors. Jack entered. The Vicarage was a few hundred yards to his right—but he didn't go that way immediately. He needed to visit to his family first.

The residents of Cwmhyfryd cemetery were laid out in alphabetical order so finding them was an easy task. When he left here, his mother's grave was freshly dug. He remembered that day: nearly every Hyfridian had turned out to pay their respects to a woman they had especially cared for—despite being married to Joe. As the service ended, everybody left the graveside and made for the lower entrance. Before they had even reached it, Joe, James and Joseph had accused the villagers of being responsible for Theresa's death and a violent row broke out which led to a mass brawl—the second between the Farr's and the villagers in ten days. Jack watched and walked away towards the rear entrance, walked over the mountain, collected his meagre belongings from Greenacres and made for the village Square where he caught the Saturday bus going to Cardiff—and left behind the village which hated him and his kin—save for the precious Theresa.

And now, he was standing over three graves. His mother's—a neatly arranged monument. Next to her, the larger of the three graves which contained the twins, and—freshly dug—his father's grave. The twins' grave was maintained but nothing had been placed on it to signify the loss of loved ones. His father's grave was still wet with mud piled high. But his mother's grave? That was different. The grass was cut to a very neat level. It was surrounded by attractive stones, varying in colours and there was a freshly laid bouquet of flowers by the gravestone which read:

Theresa—taken too soon and placed into His good graces

Nothing more, no religious passages from the Bible or any kind of "Sadly missed" wording. Plain and simple. He wondered who was tending his mother's grave—and then he heard a noise behind him. He turned—and a surly chunk of flesh was staring at him—really staring, almost scowling. A belligerent stare, intended to scare the person being stared at. Jack was fairly certain he did not know the man and he ran up an appraisal of what he was looking at. Young, mid to late twenties, at least six foot three, around fifteen stone and not all of it flab. Red in the face, either from the sun or a complexion brought about by an energetic trek up the mountain to get to the Church. Jack waited. Any kind of talk would come from the surly man first, he knew.

'You're Jack Farr,' surly man said. Jack replied that he knew that already. The man stepped forward one pace. 'I'm Steffan Edmunds. You knew my dad. Sion Edmunds.' *Ah*, thought Jack, *this is a hangover from when I left*. Twenty years ago, he'd had a personal matter to deal with Mr Sion Edmunds. Clearly, father had told son what had happened and now the son wanted a bit of revenge. He expected there would be more of this kind of thing before he left Cwmhyfryd.

'You crippled my dad, you bastard,' said the surly Steffan and he took another step towards Jack and then the sun went out.

Something large—really very large—had interjected itself between Jack and Steffan. He couldn't see what it was—but then he heard the interjection speak.

'You're a long way from home, Steffan,' said the large interjection. 'Why you here, boy?'

Jack moved and saw the interjection was wearing a Vicar's collar. He also saw the look of fear on Steffan's face. His red face had paled, somewhat and he backed away.

'Community Service, Vicar,' said Steffan. 'Got to clear the mountain of rubbish.' Jack then realized Steffan was dressed in an orange set of dungarees—on the breastplate, it read *CWMHYFRYD COMMUNITY SERVICE BRIGADE*. It was similar to the kind of garb convicts were forced to wear in America when they were out in the community providing that community with a service—like clearing away debris from the side of the roads. Steffan had clearly been a naughty boy.

'Well, you won't need to serve this community, boy,' said the Vicar. 'They are already served. Now—*SCAT!*'

Chastened, Steffan slunk away down the hill and didn't look back. But Jack knew there would be another meeting between them.

Vicar John Redd turned to Jack—and his demeanour changed instantly. He stuck out his giant hand and beamed. 'Jack,' he announced, 'I'm Vicar John Redd. Welcome home, boy.'

Jack took the Vicar's hand. It was so big, it enveloped his own. The hand's texture was rough—like brickwork. The grip was strong. He shook it and Vicar John Redd then clamped his long arm around Jack's shoulder and marched him down to the Vicarage.

'Do you like hot buttered toasted rolls?' he said as they walked down the path. 'My guilty pleasure.'

They entered the Vicarage.

Chapter 10

The Worst News...

'Haven't eaten toasted rolls like this since I was a kid,' said Jack. In spite of it still being relatively warm outside, Jack was now being roasted in front of a roaring fire. There were no radiators or gas fires in the Vicarage. Apart from recent wallpaper decorating, the main room was still pretty much as he remembered it from the mid 1970's when he and Susan had spoken to Reverend Parminter in the days leading up to their doomed wedding day.

'The only way to eat 'em, Jack boy,' replied the Vicar who was squatting in front of this roaring fire as he toasted yet another large bread roll. Thankfully, the toasting fork was long enough for him not to get too close but even so he had to put his other hand up to his face to ward away the flames.

Jack did not bridle at the use of the word 'Boy'. People like John Redd will use such a word as either a term of affection or an admonishment without intending any kind of offence or of gaining superior ground for its own sake. When he called Steffan Edmunds 'Boy', it served as a dictate—meant as a distinction between them both—that the Vicar represented authority and the receiver was to respect that distinction—which clearly Steffan did because when Jack saw him, he was nearly quaking in his wellies. Something about Vicar Redd made that burly looking thug nervous enough to back down.

It was Jack's custom to make a study of new people in his life. Potential allies or possible combatants could be discerned swiftly with studied appraisals upon first meetings. So Jack studied Vicar John Redd. Big man—easily six foot six, weighed in around fifteen stone and at one time in his life, Jack surmised, that bulk would have been powerful muscle. The arms were still big enough to carry clout—physical as well as literal—in the need to calm down a tricky situation.

But it was the man's face which intrigued. It was marked, pitted with tiny scars and possible disfigurement. At some time in his past, Vicar Redd had been a fighter—a pugilist who had engaged in physical combat. The bulbous nose had clearly been broken on numerous occasions. Those enormous hands would have served him extremely well in such times. His manner—jovial now but combative when facing down young Steffan—may be bluff and humorous but he was not a man to be taken lightly or to be disrespected.

The toasts consumed, Vicar Redd got down to business straight away.

'What did you think of the house?' he asked.

'Well, I could see how its worth had shot up to £180,000 plus,' Jack replied. 'What I would love to know is how Dad was able to afford it.' He looked to the Vicar for the answer but the big man just shook his head.

'All happened before I arrived. I think, in fact, your father was in hospital at the time of my arrival. The second heart attack if memory serves. I am informed that the workers came in while he was recuperating and began work on both the house and the road leading up to it.'

'Did the Farmer's Association sanction it? Or the Forestry Commission? Dad worked for them for decades in the area. They own the land Greenacres stands on.'

But that didn't answer the £5,000,000 business. The FC and the FA wouldn't give such an amount to Joe for services rendered. Jack said so.

'Jack,' the Vicar said, quietly. 'I am telling you exactly what was told to me by this man Eddy. In fact, I'm not even convinced he knows the source of your father's good fortune. All I know is, during his second stay in hospital, the old house came down, the hacienda styled house went up and the road was turned into something people could actually walk on.'

Jack asked about Peter Eddy.

'He's a Solicitor, runs a small practice in Brangwyn. There aren't any Solicitors in Cwmhyfryd. Maybe his physical proximity to this village was the reason why Gibney Associates chose him to act as an Emissary in this business. What he told me was he received this sanction between the day of your father's death and the burial a short while later, along with these very specific instructions as to how the contact with you was to be made—by me, not him—and how you were to make the return trip home.'

'I checked on the Gibney Associates—they're a very high-priced law office, aren't they?'

The Vicar nodded. He had also checked on Gibney Associates. They had represented a sizeable number of... very active and dangerous individuals would be a fair way to describe many of their clientele. How Joe Farr came to their attention was a mystery. To Vicar Redd's knowledge, Joe—his local spats with the various Hyfridians over the years notwithstanding—was no criminal.

'Which leaves the sale of the house,' Jack said. 'When do I get to meet the estate agent?'

For the first time, Vicar Redd looked uneasy. He realized he would have to tell Jack exactly who the estate agent was—without it looking like it had been a *fait accompli*—which really it was but again, it was via Joe's very specific instruction that Jack would not know Susan Tanner was that agent.

'On that issue,' he began, 'I have to tell you something.'

Pause. He breathed. Then he breathed again.

'The estate agent is Susan,' he said, as flatly as possible. Jack didn't move, seeming not to comprehend what had just been told to him.

'And when can I meet this estate agent?' he asked. The Vicar moved off his seat and stood.

'No Jack,' he said. 'The estate agent... is... *Susan!*'

Jack stared at him, curious at the odd expression on the Vicar's face and then, the dollar dropped.

'Not... Susan... Fisher...' he breathed out. The Vicar paused—offered a weak smile and nodded his head. Here we go, he thought.

Jack's reaction was pretty much to be expected. He shouted out a curse word, questioned what he'd heard, demanded a confirmation and stalked around the room in protest. Vicar Redd felt he could not remonstrate with the reaction. He was reasonably convinced he would have reacted in a very similar manner had he been set up this way.

'Joe went to *HER?*' Jack yelled. 'What the hell did he do that for? Of all the people to go to—Susan bloody Fisher? Goddamn it—why?'

The Vicar calmed him down, made him sit back down on the sofa. Without going into an explanation straight away, he put his hands up as if to say 'Hold on now, boy'. He went to the kitchen and busied himself with making more tea and finding some old biscuits. Given the nature of the news, Jack's reaction was pretty calm taking into consideration the tragedy which surrounded Susan's jilting of him on the day of their wedding. He placed everything on the tray and returned to the main room. Jack was still seething but at least he was still there.

Tea poured and dispensed—the British balm to soothe all wounds—Vicar Redd set about putting the case for Susan Tanner so to dilute Jack's understandable ire.

'He went to her when he knew he didn't have long to live. I believe…' he paused on this and then breathed again… 'I believe he had decided to take this way out… this business with that tree…

'The old enemy,' Jack interrupted.

'Yes. You said that to me on the phone. What…?'

Jack explained. The tree was there when Great Grandfather Jared built the original Greenacres and he had cut the main bulk of it down. In time, over the years, he had attempted to remove the trunk—and failed. That duty was taken over by his son, James—and then by Joe and *his* sons—again, meeting with failure. Jack told the Vicar that the day Joe, Joseph, James and himself had laid siege to the tree was the only time he could remember when the whole family had worked and played together as a unit. While the men-folk laboured at the tree, Theresa provided the food and drink, the constant wash-downs and cheering noises whenever a branch or a root was severed and it looked like the trunk was near being pulled out of the ground.

By dusk, Joe, Joseph, James and himself were covered in sweat, dirt and cuts. That damn tree had not only resisted being yanked out of the ground, it had also attacked them with branches and thorns. Eventually, it was Theresa who called time on the three boys—the twins were then ten years of age and Jack was five— because they had to go to school the next day. She bathed their filthy bodies in two large tin baths, attended to their many scratches and bruises and put them to bed even as Joe continued his own personal battle against *the old enemy.*

Which he lost.

It hadn't surprised Jack when the Vicar had told him over the phone how his father had died. It was almost a fatalistic desire he would go out that way. The fact that he had done it at a time of physical weakness certainly signified to all he had chosen his own manner of death.

Vicar Redd listened, nodded his head and agreed. He felt heartened that Jack had not folded at the retelling of this amusing story or of how his father had brought about his own end and so he broached the subject of Mrs Tanner again.

'He arranged it with her evaluate the worth of the house—and to request her… to be the only mourner at his funeral. Which she duly attended.'

Pause. Jack stared at Vicar Redd. '*What?*' he breathed out.

'He requested her, she complied. I only found out… about you and Susan the night after I buried Joe. I read the Cwmhyfryd Diaries which my predecessors left behind. Big shock, I can tell you.'

He could see Jack had been taken aback—and so he ploughed on with the other piece of information regarding Susan.

'I didn't know who or why at first, until I saw her a few days later—but Susan has apparently been tending your mother's grave for years. I saw her cutting the grass. I know now it was she who arranged the ornamental stonework and there are fresh flowers every week.' He leaned back and drank his tea—a soggy biscuit was floating in the cup.

Jack couldn't speak. Susan's relationship with his mother was close—closer than her own to her mother who had abandoned Malcolm when Susan was only sixteen. Theresa took her in to their home as her daughter-to-be—which made what she did that day twenty years ago even harder for Theresa to understand. He was confused then—he was confused now. But he had no answers—or even questions.

He breathed out—resigned to what must happen next.

'So, now what?' he asked.

'First things first—you're home. That is the first box ticked. Next thing will be for you to make contact with Peter Eddy—I'll give you his phone number and E-mail. You'll need to call his office asap—on Monday, he won't be in the office today—and then you must declare to him exactly what your intentions are going to be.'

Jack look confused at this.

'It's all connected. Do you want to sell Greenacres or keep it, to live in, to rent out—uh... even demolish. Its future is entirely down to you. You decide. Tell Eddy what you've decided... he will then communicate your answer to Gibney Associates and depending on what you've decided the next step will then take place.'

'Which will be what?'

Vicar John Redd laughed, raised his hands as if he were praising whatever Deity he served and said, 'God knows, boy.'

And that was that. It was now late in the afternoon. Jack was exhausted from the trip, even more exhausted now he knew a little more about the next stage of the proceedings. Vicar Redd offered to drive him home going through the village, of course. Jack said he preferred to walk the way he had come. Vicar Redd told him he would join him. He wanted to know about Jack's adventures in America.

They put their coats on and left the Vicarage. Jack was silent all the way past the family graves. He didn't trust himself to speak—not without compromising himself.

'How do you feel, Jack?' There was a sizeable pause. Jack stopped walking and looked the Vicar in the face.

'It's the worst news,' he said. 'If I'd known she was to the main contact regarding the sale of the house, I would never have come back.'

Which validated the reason Vicar Redd had for not telling him. He kept that piece of information to himself.

They reached the top of the mountain and began to walk across it, making their way to Greenacres.

Chapter 11

The Fleminganese

Once again, the walk across the mountain invigorated him—and he needed it after what he had just learned from Vicar Redd. *Susan?* Of all people—in charge of selling his family home. What on Earth was Dad thinking of going to her? And why did she accept the commission? And this business about him asking her to be the solitary mourner at his funeral was bizarre. He had barely spoken two courteous words to her when they were courting back in the day—why then, would he use her office to provide this service—knowing full well it would be he, Jack, who would have to deal with it?

It was a curious business, he thought. For while his father was an acknowledged hard-case and a tough-nut to be sure, he was not generally vindictive or randomly malicious. If ever he did a thing, there would be a reason for it—but using Susan... and *him*... to conduct such a personal matter simply did not make sense. Any prospect of peaceful sleep after this news had evaporated.

Jack told Vicar Redd about his life in the States and how he had got there—through family connections in London—and how he had ended up working as a ranch hand on a farm. He had ridden trails, herded cattle and broke wild horses—they still did that in certain areas, Jack said. He was the only non-American on the ranch and there had been occasions when he had to swallow the insults from the ignorant rednecks who would comment on a 'Limey' related to the Boss working on the farm. But then there would come a point where the swallowing stopped, turning to fisticuffs and then they would leave him alone.

Jack and the Vicar talked about everything except the business at hand. As they spoke, Jack noticed a curious aspect of Vicar Redd's mode of speech. Somewhere in there, he guessed, there is a mid-European dialect—backed up with a twinge of Irish. An odd three way mix of speech and Jack was about to ask him where he came from when the Vicar noticed the same bicycle Jack had seen earlier standing up some distance away.

'Well really,' he said, 'why can't they book into a hotel or something? Honestly, those two are at it like alley cats all the time. They even came up to the Cemetery one night and congregated among some of the older graves.'

No sermonizing or pious preaching. Nothing more than a minor tut-tut from the Vicar of Cwmhyfryd. If John Redd was typical of the new religion, Joe could have made Pope.

They came into view of Stone Wall Mountain. Jack asked Vicar Redd if he'd ever gone up to the plateau.

'Ha ha,' laughed the man, 'I'm way past mountain climbing, Jack boy. You'd need to be a goat to get up there.'

Jack explained there was route up to the plateau on the Mynydd Fach side of the Mountain. The whole structure was pitted with caves and tracks leading in and around and up to the top. He asked the Vicar if he knew about the Fleminganese.

'The who?' asked the Vicar. And here, they halted their promenade and Jack told him about the Fleminganese community who had arrived in this area hundreds of years ago. They had travelled from Plymouth when this particular group were due to sail out with Myles Standish, the Captain of *The Mayflower* and the man who was to lead the Puritans to the Promised Land—the Americas— on The Mayflower. But Standish, Brewster and Carver had a big falling out with the leader of this group—Joshua Fleming—who felt that these men were not worthy or pious enough to be the Leaders of this venture. The result was—the group was denied entry to the Mayflower and the ship sailed away with them still standing on the harbour. Fleming stood watching until that ship had sailed out of sight beyond the horizon. Then he turned to his flock and announced he would take them to the real Promised Land.

From Plymouth, he led them across the west of the Kingdom and then northwards into South Wales, up into the wilds of the country and into Mid-Wales—travelling until they saw this huge circular ring of mountainous land. They camped below these mountains for three days while Joshua climbed the hills and entered the valley below.

He came out, three days later, carrying sacks of fruits and vegetable.

'I have found it, my children,' he shouted, 'I have found the Promised Land as the Great Maker has directed I would. Beyond those hills, there is a valley of growth and beauty—The Great Maker's own land—where we can begin our lives and live as he wishes.' It took the group two days to ascend the mountains for many were now ill or infirm—or just children who were limited in physical strength. No matter, there was food and cover aplenty in this region and once to the top they all looked down at the new Gethsemane. The valley was covered with trees bearing fruits, trees which could be used to build their homes, stone to support their foundations. There was a river which flowed from the tallest of the mountains surrounding the valley. The valley had everything the group had searched for. They did not need The Mayflower.

They began work immediately. They cut down certain trees which did not bear food and cultivated areas of ground to grow their own produce. It took over two years before the community was settled and then Joshua Fleming looked to the skies and saw the tallest of the mountains beckoning to him.

He climbed the smallest of the four mountains which led directly to the far side of the tallest and he found a cave which led directly through the mountains—holding vast caverns of pools and cover from the many violent weathers which they had endured since their arrival. He climbed through the labyrinthine tunnels and finally broke through the tree covered cave at the top of the plateau.

The area was immense. Flat ground, with one aspect leading upwards to a small pointed hill. Fleming stood and stared and knew that *this*—and not the valley below—was where the community should be living, eating and praying. So much nearer to God they were from this place. He climbed back down and told the community he had found their new—and their true—home. The wooden abodes were dismantled under his directions and carted up to the plateau. As one faction laboured on that task, another faction carved out a trail within the mountain itself—a trail which could be easily negotiated by horse and cart transporting the heaviest of their belongings in the shortest time.

The whole venture took five years and the new communal was built by the strongest of the community. During that time, many of them died from sickness, exhaustion or plain old age. Fleming drove the community hard—he working the hardest and longest of all—as they built their most humble homes and, on the small hill, their new Temple. By the finish of it all, only a third of those who had set out from Plymouth had survived—around two hundred people. But the community survived and thrived. When, as centuries passed, the valley below became occupied by new incomers farming the land for other the communities around the valley, the oldest of the original peoples—now named the

Fleminganese after the memory of Joshua—kept to their own world, their ways and away from those they considered unworthy of their company. From time to time, the living descendants of Joshua Fleming would direct the Fleminganese to venture further outward of the valley to barter—or even to convert those heathen peoples to their own true path.

Jack finished the story. The descendants of the original community had certainly still occupied that plateau when he was a child—he remembered seeing them coming down the hill, by horse and cart naturally—led by an ancient looking man, with long white hair and an even longer white beard. While the community bartered around the small village, the wild-haired man screamed his religion at the villagers and told them they were all destined for the burning fires of Hell if they did not join him and his people.

Vicar Redd assimilated all this with a curious expression on his face and Jack briefly wondered if he was in fact a former member of the Fleminganese. He didn't take his curiosity further than that though.

They arrived at the top of the mountain which overlooked Greenacres.

'Have you ever been inside the place? Jack asked. The Vicar shook his head and so Jack led him down the rocky path, negotiating away the brambles and branches as they stumbled down to the garden.

When they reached this point, Jack saw something he hadn't seen when he'd left earlier. A shape on the ground, coloured yellow amid the green grass. An odd shape. Like… human. 'Is that where Dad died?' he said. Vicar Redd did not answer. He didn't have to. The sombre expression on his face did it for him. He placed his huge hand on Jack's forearm and led him away. It was clear Jack hadn't been informed about how his father had been found. He wasn't going to volunteer that information and wild horses wouldn't drag it out of him. They made for the kitchen and Vicar Redd pulled out a set of keys…

Then they stopped and stared.

The kitchen window had a gaping and jagged hole in its middle. Jack moved to it and peered inside.

'That wasn't there when I arrived,' he said. Vicar Redd didn't flinch or speak—and yet Jack could feel the man's wrath even from where he stood. The sensation was palpable. His breathing became audible and his eyes were transfixed on the hole. Someone was going to answer for this outrage and Jack almost felt sorry for the luckless runt who had crashed the window.

They entered the house. They passed through a small section which contained a Fridge-Freezer and a washing machine. My God, Jack thought, Mam never saw any of those modern-day tools here. They entered the kitchen and looked around. Apart from the broken window, the kitchen was clean and spotless. Vicar Redd told Jack his personal Housekeeper came here to Greenacres every week to maintain its cleanliness.

Glass was on the draining board, the window sill and in the sink as well on the floor. Vicar Redd picked up a sizeable piece of stone around which was wrapped a piece of paper tied by string. He carefully unfolded it and held the paper so Jack could see it.

There was a message written on it which read:

YOR NOT WONTED YEAR FAR—GO HOME

No signature—but Jack didn't need one. 'That's what the Taxi Driver said to me,' he said. The Vicar turned to him, eyes blazing. 'Taxi Driver? Fat, curly hair?' Jack confirmed the description.

'Ryland Edmunds,' he said. 'Brother to Steffan—whom you met in the cemetery.' He screwed the paper up and put it and the stone inside his jacket pocket. He put his mighty hand on Jack's shoulder and squeezed.

'Now—don't be bothering about this, boy,' he said. 'You leave these people to me.'

Jack wasn't sure if he was the 'Boy' in that sentence or if the Vicar was referring to the man who threw the stone. At any rate, he demurred. This was the Vicar's parish—not his. He wanted peace and quiet, to get this inheritance sorted out as soon as possible and then to get back to Oklahoma post haste.

The Vicar had very kindly filled the Fridge with provisions which would last at least three days and so after clearing away the shards of glass, they sat at the table and partook of a cup of tea and biscuits.

Jack led the Vicar around the house—of course, learning about its interior at the same time. It was very well built—so spacious compared to its original model.

And again he asked himself: *How the hell did Dad afford this?*

The tour and tea ended, the Vicar took his leave and a very exhausted Jack stood by the main window and scanned the forest ahead. It had barely changed in all this time. His father's principle job was to maintain the forest, working for the Forest Commission and the Farmer's Association, both industries needing the mountain to remain as it was. Clearly, Dad had served the two official bodies well.

Finally, his eyes rested on the tree trunk. He could see where fresh cuts had been made on it and the deep hole surrounding it still had fresh dirt around the base of the trunk. That piece of wood killed my father, he told himself.

He thought: I will have to do something about that.

He downed the last gulp of tea and headed for the bedroom—not his father's but one which had probably never been used. He opened the windows and the room was filled with birdsong. That was fine. He'd frequently slept out at night on the trail herds and had heard wilder noises than birdsong. He kicked off his shoes and loosened his clothing. He then lay upon the single bed and thought about what had been told to him by the Vicar.

He would have to deal with Susan regarding the sale of the house. Dad had seen to that.

He gave consideration to the Edmunds brothers and thought: I might have to deal with them as well.

He closed his eyes and within seconds fell into a blissful sleep.

Chapter 12
Scenes from an Idyllic Small Welsh Village

And while Jack Farr, former resident of Cwmhyfryd Village, slept the "Sleep of the Just", other—more permanent residents of that village—congregated around a table in The Night's Tail public house and were discussing the return of that particular native.

The Chief Speaker of that group was Sion Edmunds, father of Steffan and Ryland, avowed enemy of the Farr family in general but of Jack in particular. In fact, it was Sion who had ordered his son, Ryland, to get back up to Greenacres and deliver the house-brick mail with the badly written and poorly spelt message. He also ordered his elder son, Steffan, who he knew was working near the Church, to get over there and find him. Sion correctly guessed Jack's first priority would be to make a visit to his mother's grave. Of course, he did not consider the intervention of Vicar Redd.

Here, in the safety of the pub and amongst friends, he waxed lyrical about how he would take his revenge against Jack.

The other drinkers listened with tired ears—Sion was an almighty blowhard and tonight he was blowing even harder. The group consisted of Adam Phillips, husband to Sara, his mates Tyler Davies, Ioan Lewis, Alun Jones, Sara's brother, Michael Morgan and Toni Pirelli. Each man had, in their time, been visited by Jack—and had paid a penance for the way they had treated him in the past—and in Sion's case, for a particularly nasty comment he made to Jack the day after his mother had died. That penance was high. Each man was still suffering even to this day from the wrath Jack had visited on them.

Sion still wanted revenge. 'I've already set my boys onto it,' he boasted, and told them about the broken window and the threat at the Cemetery. In truth, each of the men, hard boys in their day, really couldn't be bothered to listen to Sion's incessant yakking never mind actually taking up the cudgels twenty years after their day was long finished—ironically, by Jack himself. They listened—and waited for the blowhard to shut his blowing. Elsewhere in the village, other people had also heard the news. Different homes reacted in different ways.

Sara Phillips was telling her daughters, Catrin and Claire, and Claire's boyfriend Tommy Leeming, about Jack—she was obliged to as they had continually asked about him since practically everybody else in the village was talking about him. She told them he was the youngest son of the man who had died on the mountain a short while ago. In this talk, Sara had to relate very carefully what she said—because actions taken all those years ago did not put her—or Auntie Susan—or the Villagers—in a very positive light and both Catrin and Claire were very judgemental about what was proper.

Jack—along with his father and two twin brothers—were very unpopular troublemakers she told them, who had caused problems down here in the village. But—and this was where Sara had to tread very carefully—he had once been in a relationship with... Auntie Susan. 'But she's married to Uncle David,' said Claire. (To all the children and teens of the village, all adults over the age of their own parents were referred to as Aunts and Uncles) '

'Yes,' explained Sara, 'but back then, she wasn't. She and Jack... she and Jack were courting each other...' and Catrin stared at her mother. This story seemed to be very hard for her to relate and that was unusual for her mother who was usually most forthcoming in her speech.

'Courting?' she asked. 'You mean they were lovers.' Catrin had no such limitations on how she spoke. If it was there, she spoke it. Sara breathed out. There really was no soft way to break this so she took the plunge.

'Susan and Jack were to be married—but in the run up to their marriage, she... Auntie Susan—met—and fell in love with... Uncle David.'

'So she dropped Jack,' said Claire. 'Dumped him.'

'Yes,' said Sara, after a few moments—and again, her hesitation irritated Catrin. 'Well, that's okay,' she said. 'That sort of thing happens all the time. Why are people making such a fuss about it? I heard Olwen Berry asking if Auntie Susan knew Jack Farr was home. She sounded real worried.'

Another pause—and now Sara was visibly worried. Something in her face told Catrin something was not being said here.

'You might as well tell us, Mam, she said, 'we're only going to hear it from someone else anyway.'

And so, Sara breathed in and out, fronted it up and told her daughters of the day when Jack and Susan were to be married and how Susan—in front of everyone at the Church—friends and family—jilted him, run away from him and the Reverend Parminter and out of the Church—not to be seen again for another six months, during which time she actually did marry David Tanner somewhere else without telling anybody, including her father, what she had done.

The daughters' silence was almost screamingly loud.

Eventually, after what seemed a lifetime and in some despair, Claire spoke. 'I don't believe it,' she said. 'Auntie Susan would never do such a thing.'

But Catrin believed it. She stood up—all eighteen years of age of her and said, 'That is bloody disgusting. She jilted him? In front of everyone? Where was you?'

But Sara could speak no more. It was a bad memory she eventually got out to them and nobody in the village wanted to be reminded of it. But Catrin retained her anger and said, 'I'll never speak to Auntie Susan again. That's bloody wrong, that is. If she was in love with another man she should've said so. Bloody wait till they actually get to Church—and then drop that on him? Bloody wrong.'

She threw her magazine down and stormed out of the room.

Sara was disconsolate. Claire was also visibly upset because she loved Auntie Susan and saw her as a second mother. Uncle David was bit of a bore but then he *was* old—forty-seven years of age. Tommy listened and could say nothing about the incident, so he comforted Claire as best he could with soothing words instead. She was so young—sixteen.

*

In the Tanner household, Susan was working on her book-keeping when David sauntered in. He had been at The Night's Tail pub with Malcolm and he told her everyone in the village had heard about Jack's returning, that he had already been over to see the Vicar and asked her if she knew anything?

Susan said she'd heard he was back but nothing more. She carried on writing the figures in her books and David made his own supper. As he did so, he laughed a few times and wondered aloud how long Farr would be staying in Cwmhyfryd and how long it would be before he was causing trouble. Susan kept her head down. Then he pondered—again aloud—as to Jack's marital status and wondered where he'd been hiding since…

Susan looked up and David stopped talking. There were looks she would give that could stop a rhino from charging and normally he knew where the line was drawn. Unfortunately, and maybe because of the drink, David chose to ignore the line this evening.

'I expect he'll keep out of everyone's way,' he gabbed on, 'I doubt he'll want to engage with any of us in the village. I think he's smart enough to know where he's not wanted...'

The book was slammed shut and Susan stood up. Without speaking, she stormed out of the room and David stared— open-mouthed and uncomprehending.

The micro-wave tinged and he finished making his supper.

*

A mile away from The Night's Tail, by common accord between two "Keepers of the Inn" as it were, another drinking hole was being well attended. The *Blooz* was a small club where the over-18's-and-under-25's met and engaged with themselves away from their elders. In this club, they could drink, play snooker, eat at the café end and listen to a genuine 1950's Jukebox playing genuine 1980's music. The place was run by Geraint Morgan and he ruled it fairly well—with odd exceptions to his own rules. One of those exceptions was allowing both the Edmunds brothers onto the premises in spite of the age factor. Both were past twenty five—but, for services rendered, under-the-counter as it were—they were given house room. The *Blooz* existed in tandem with The Night's Tail so long as it did not intrude. Accordingly, it opened only three nights a week and was closed by ten o'clock each night.

Tonight, it was almost full to capacity which pleased Geraint Morgan even if he didn't know what the mass talk was all about. Unlike everyone else in the club, he was not from Cwmhyfryd and so did not know who Jack Farr was—nor any of the history contained therein.

Steffan was playing Euan Lloyd at snooker—for money—against the rules of the club but allowed by Geraint—and was winning a tidy pile. Ryland was lounging some yards away with a pint of beer in his hand. Every man there—there were a few girls but not many—was laughing, talking and drinking. Some were eating with their girls at the café end and trying to keep their romances away from those who were too loud.

Ryland had a half full glass—and he drank it all in one full gulp. After he had sank the whole lot, two hands grabbed him around the throat and hauled him out of his lounge chair. The whole room was thrown into silence. Even the jukebox suddenly shut down. Ryland was held aloft in mid-air and the owner of the hands was now shaking him by his throat, back and forth. Steffan made a move to protect his brother—but was pulled back by two other lads who knew better than to interfere when Vicar John Redd was on the rampage.

Ryland was then hurled back against the wall with such force he actually made a massive indentation in that wall. He slid to the floor, dazed, red-faced and spluttering to find a breath. Beer was spitting out of his mouth and his eyes were filled with tears.

Vicar Redd dropped down to his knee and took Ryland by the throat with one hand and held up the letter he had 'posted' in to Jack's kitchen window with the other. His face was a mask of undiluted fury and Ryland was now blubbering into his shirt.

'*YOU WRITE THIS?*' yelled the Vicar, pushing his face as close to Ryland's as their noses would allow. '*YOU WRITE THIS? YOU VICIOUS GUTLESS PIECE OF FILTH! YOU THROW THIS THROUGH HIS WINDOW—DID YOU?*'

He stood up and scanned the whole club—there wasn't anyone there who wasn't looking at him—many with abject fear on their faces for they had seen the Vicar at work in the past. He held the letter and the stone above his head. He turned around so that he could be seen by everybody.

'If you can't get along *with* Jack Farr—then get along without him. If I hear any more of…*THIS*… kind of *CRAP*… I'll be back.'

He screwed the letter up and threw it. It landed very neatly into a waste bin. Then he tossed the stone. It struck the green baize of the snooker table, hitting the white ball which then cannoned into the black ball and that ball was potted into the top corner pocket. 'Good shot, Sir,' said one player in the shadows.

Vicar Redd marched out of the club—and everyone breathed out. In the silence which followed, one witty wag said, 'More tea, Vicar?' A few people nervously laughed. Steffan and a few of his mates helped Ryland to his feet. The poor man was struggling to breathe amidst the crying and shame of what had just occurred. Nobody was laughing now.

Chapter 13

Revenge — A La Farr

It took Sion Edmunds an hour and a half to walk the quarter mile from The Night's Tail to his one-bedroomed apartment which he shared with Ryland and Steffan. Either one or both his sons should have been there at The Tail to pick him up and drive him home because any walk over 200 yards was near impossible for him to endure. His back and right leg were shot—the legacy of the beating given to him by Jack Farr twenty years before.

He cursed that man's name for every painful step he took. He stumbled and limped—partly from too much alcohol but mainly from his long-time injuries. He left some space for both his sons—and promised them in their absence that he would belt-strap both of them for failing in their duty to cart him home. Of course, such an action would never happen—he could barely remove his trouser belt in his condition much less wield it in anger—and certainly not against two men much bigger and more powerful than he.

He arrived at Brook Towers—the four-storeyed block of apartments he had lived in for 15 years. After his wife had run away with the carpenter who was refurbishing their original home, he refused to live in it and so was transferred to this temporary arrangement by the Village Community Council—a temporary arrangement which had lasted ever since. When both his sons had stepped out of favour with the Law, he had no choice but to house them there as well. This suited him—it meant he had 'gofers' to do his shopping and also drive him from one place to another. For them, it meant sharing a bedroom—Steffan one night, Ryland the next with a pull-out settee being used on the alternate nights while Sion had his own bed. In great pain—and it really was—he crawled up the two flights of steps and across the landing to let himself into his apartment.

But the apartment was empty, dark and cold. Neither son was there nor had they been all evening. The kettle was cold and the radiators hadn't been switched on. The arrangement was when The Blooz closed down one or both sons would come to The Tail and escort him home. But not tonight. Where the hell were they?

He slowly, gingerly, lowered himself into his own spacious armchair and laid his head against the cool head rest. As cold as it was outside and in the apartment, sweat poured from his head from the long arduous act of walking that quarter mile. He cursed again. All this pain because of…

And then he settled back. Inward reflection is a process most humans go through when they have arrived at a point of extreme emotions—happiness, sadness, misery—and then give consideration as to how they had travelled from wherever to here. There is no escaping the fact that Jack Farr was the man responsible for Sion Edmunds' present physical condition but it was he, Sion Edmunds himself, who had brought about the fight which resulted in such terrible injuries.

Here, in the cold solitude of his lounge apartment, Sion gave thought to that terrible day. In sequence, it ran thus: the Wedding between Jack and Susan— which resulted in a debacle still talked of today—a fight inside the Church, another fight outside the Church where father Joe and twins James and Joseph were eventually arrested, Jack walking his mother across the top of Mynydd Gabriel to Greenacres, then tragically, her death during the night, the emergency vehicles speeding through the village and up to the mountain home, her body being brought back down and the sight of so many people weeping when they learned about what happened. Every male who had loved and desired her, wept into their cups, chief of whom was Malcolm Fisher who now realized his passion for Theresa would now never see the light of day, and the many women of Theresa's age who mourned the loss of a beautiful friend.

It was the day after which led to the fight. Jack, still traumatized by the previous days' events wandered into the village looking confused and bewildered, making his way to the small Police Station intending to speak to Sergeant Brock to find out what had happened to his father and brothers—and asking if they knew about Theresa?

Jack passed Sion Edmunds and a small group of men—one of whom was Alun Jones—and Sion made an unforgiveable comment towards Jack. He stated that his mother's death was…" God's revenge on you for daring to marry one of our girls." Jack erupted.

There were no words, no demands for an apology or for Sion to repeat what he had said. Jack just launched himself at Sion and set about him with fists and

72

kicks. Now this scenario amused the small coterie around Sion Edmunds because in all the times when Jack had been insulted, chastised or even pushed around, he had never once retaliated with violence. To see him now, a man so unaccustomed to such an act and beating up against a man who was, looked quite comical.

At first.

The laughs stopped when they could see Jack's punches were now getting through to Sion and they were bloody hurting him. Sion attempted to retaliate but found he had no answer against Jack's speed and strength—or determination to do him a serious mischief. After a few moments of him delivering such a terrible barrage of blows, the group decided to intervene and pulled Jack away from his tormentor…

…and they suffered for this intervention.

Jack turned on all of them—five in number—and thrashed them all with some powerful punching. Two of them decided retreat was the safer part of valour and scarpered.

Alun Jones lay dazed as he watched Jack return to the floundering Sion Edmunds who by now had found his feet and was screaming blue murder. He raised his arms as if their wide scope would serve as intimidation against the smaller man—but Jack ducked past them, jumped to Sion's side—and then stamped hard at his knee. There was a God-awful crack sound and Sion collapsed in a heap. He screamed—a piercing scream which Alun told his sister much later he would never forget.

But Jack still wasn't done. He grabbed a handful of Sion's bushy curly hair and pulled him to his feet. Then he threw the big man backwards down a small flight of steps. Sion fell hard and awkward, clunking his head as he fell, landing on the edge of the steps on his back. Now the fight was over.

Breathless, Jack kept his hands up and turned around to see if anybody else was readying to continue the fight—but those who were there, remained on the ground either unconscious or too dazed to re-join.

Jack limped away from the area and headed up towards the mountain.

It was what Sion Edmunds did in the weeks that followed which effectively brought about his present-day situation. When the shouting and screaming was done, those who were there helped Sion to his feet and took him home. The first thing to be established, he commanded was—"No-one… *NO-ONE*… knows about this… It didn't happen. We did *NOT* get beat by Jack Farr."

All entreaties by his friends to get himself seen by the village Doctor or even go to a hospital to mend what was clearly a serious injury—or injuries for Sion was a bloody mess all over—fell on deaf ears. Sion insisted the injuries were slight and would mend.

After a fashion, he was proved right. Time and nature did mend the wounds—but not in the way a broken leg properly set by a hospital would have done—and what was a passable pain in a young vigorous man's day became a more difficult pain as his years passed. The leg break knitted badly, the damage to his vertebrae created more damage to his spine resulting in a crushed disc. When, eventually, he took his story to the Doctor, it was too many years too late and nothing beyond pain-killers would help him. There was one suggestion that breaking his leg and resetting it might improve his stance—but then again, it might not. He declined the offer.

And now, sitting in his empty, cold and dark apartment, Sion Edmunds ended his inward reflections and at least had the temerity to know that awful day was really down to him—saying such a thing to a bereaved boy.

Suddenly, the door opened and the lights were switched on. Ryland was being carried in by Steffan and Geraint Morgan. Not unconscious but certainly dazed. From his armchair, Sion read the riot act at them for abandoning him to a long walk home.

Steffan explained to his father what had happened at *The Blooz*—that Vicar Redd had turned up and in front of everybody had walloped the seven bells of hell out of Ryland, ending with the warning that *NOBODY* must go near Jack—or they would suffer more of his wrath. This revelation stunned Sion—going against Jack Farr was one thing—but against the Vicar? Why would *he* interfere—and in this way?

Ryland was placed in the bed, Geraint left the apartment and Steffan sat by his father—who had lapsed into a cold silence. Inward reflection ruled the night—for both of them.

*

Adam Phillips left The Night's Tail at the same time as Sion and the group—but had arrived at his home a good deal sooner. He had been home five minutes when he wished he hadn't come home at all.

Sara was crying, Claire was berating her for something, Tommy the boyfriend looked on in confusion and when Adam tried to calm matters down, in walked Catrin who continued the rampage she had left off earlier. Clair stamped off to bed, Tommy was sent to sleep in the basement—where he pretty much lived now—and Catrin told them she had been with Olwen Berry who had told her *EVERYTHING* about the wedding day between Jack and Susan. 'How could you?' she screamed. 'That poor man. Why?'

'Now hang on, Cat...' Adam began—and was met with a scowl from his eldest daughter.

'No Dad—not hang on. Both of you—Olwen told me—you conspired to stop that wedding and then laughed when it didn't happen. And Auntie Susan... God I'm going to give her one when I see her. *BLOODY DISGUSTING!'*

She slammed the door and stamped up the stairs, slamming her bedroom door, stamping across her bedroom floor before silence prevailed once more in the Phillips' household. The rest of the evening with Sara being calmed with a cup of hot chocolate and a cwtch from Adam. She eventually went to bed and Adam...

...began *his* own period of inward reflection.

The Wedding, his laughing at Jack's frightened dilemma, then preventing him from chasing after Susan as she bolted from the Church, his joining in the fight against the father and the twins, the joyful whooping when the three Farr's were arrested by the police at the Church gates... all came back to him now.

It was three days after that day when Adam had travelled to his place of work. He worked in a small Industrial Estate around five miles south of Cwmhyfryd. He travelled there with a dozen other workers from nearby Pentre Haf and Brangwyn on a works-provided bus. The work was easy, paid well and secure. He was always the life and soul of the bus party and there were laughs aplenty in the bus and on the work floor.

But not today.

The bus load arrived and the workers climbed out of the bus. Adam was making for his own particular Unit when he was confronted by Jack.

Jack, having walked home from the fight with Sion and awaited for the arrival of the police which did not come had clearly decided he may as well be hung as a wolf as a sheepdog, had then decided to target the next man who had offended him from the Wedding. Adam Phillips had prevented him from reaching Susan as she ran from the Church and had then laughed in his face before jumping into the melee which surrounded Jack and his mother.

Now it was time for *his* retribution.

Jack stood in front of him as he made his way to the Unit—and Adam moved to the side to avoid him. He had heard that Sion had been in a fight—Alun Jones had told him—but he didn't know it was Jack Farr who had inflicted those terrible injuries. When he reached Jack, Adam laughed again.

'What's the matter, Farr,' he sneered, 'you looking to get stood up again?'

Jack just stared—itself an un-nerving sight. Adam moved to go around him and Jack moved to stand in his way.

'You don't get out of my way, Farr—I'm gonna give you what I gave your father and brothers.' The threat was hard and he meant it. But Jack did not move. He did not take his eyes away from Adam's.

A number of other workers had now arrived—among them, Michael Morgan and Ioan Lewis—friends of Sion, Adam and Alun Jones.

Adam then pushed Jack aside—and this act was met by a hard thump to his gut. He fell back and rolled away. He scrambled to his feet and attacked Jack—and the fight was on. Like Sion before him, Adam, to his own disgust, found his own levels of strengths and skills were not the equal of Jack's—who was proving himself to be the son of Joe Farr after all. The fight was brutal and for Adam, mercifully short—until once again, it was interrupted by the onlookers who had decided Adam could take no more. Like those who had intervened at Sion's brawl, these men were also beaten down by Jack who then turned his attention to the wailing Adam.

Jack lifted the man up and threw him into the window of a passing workman's car. The window was smashed and Adam's skull cut open. The blow left him unconscious and he was attended by his workmates.

Jack walked the six and half miles back to Greenacres, taking the mountain road to avoid anyone in the village and, as he had done the day before, awaited the arrival from the Police Force.

It didn't come.

*

The third fight was the worst and has since passed into local lore—mainly because of who was involved and how it turned out.

76

Of the group who met at The Night's Tail, the only man not indigenous to Cwmhyfryd was Tyler Davies. He was Cardiff, born and bred in the small village of Bute prior to that area receiving a massive cosmetic make-over which resulted in it becoming known as Cardiff Bay. Once, it had been an industrialized area, with the shipping docks providing the main source of employment. Bute was one of the many drop-off points for much immigration and Tyler was descended from the people who had arrived in the UK in the 1950's on the ship *THE WINDRUSH* from Jamaica. His grandfather—Elijah—had been a farmer in his own country, a deeply religious and compassionate man who saw almost immediately the antipathy displayed by many UK residents to their arrival—in the words of the locals "here to steal our jobs and homes". Subsequently, compassion notwithstanding, Elijah raised his three sons to be fair and just—but to walk proud with an iron fist—just in case.

One of his sons—Oji—took that instruction literally and ventured into the noble sport—then—of boxing. He was only a partial success but he earned the respect of many of the locals and was placed into the sport's local training scheme for youngsters who found themselves at a loss to get on in the world and rather than turn their lives into lesser immoral wastes, they were given a purpose via the world of boxing where they were trained to defend themselves, to respect others and then make their way in the world without fear.

Oji trained his son, Tyler, in the same way. To respect others but not to be disrespected by those who found people of different cultures and skin colours alien to what they considered to be their own—better—way of life. When Tyler was of age, he added his mother's maiden—Davies—to his own, his own being too difficult to pronounce to his friends.

Tyler, it turned out, was a gifted young fighter and by the time he was in his late teens was being considered for greater things. He continued his training under his father's tutelage and was rewarded with a place on the Welsh Team going to the 1996 Olympics. He was cheated out of that grand accomplishment when, a week before the event, he went down ill with pleurisy and was taken off the team.

Words of consolation cannot replace such a trial and for a long time, Tyler walked a darker path using his skills and fists. One evening, he was visited by his old college friend, Tony Pirelli—son of Vincenzo Pirelli, Tyler's one time mentor in the ring. Tony told him of their friends from Cwmhyfryd all of whom Tyler had also been in college with, to tell him that a local thug from their village had exacted terrible scars and wounds on them. This man, Pirelli told him, was come from a bad lot and had been a renegade against the locals for some years. Tyler, not thinking with the same senses his grandfather had imparted to his sons, agreed to sort out this menace and restore peace and serenity for his friends and the place they lived in.

Consequently, one evening, Tyler, Tony, Ioan Lewis and a third man named Portman who had served alongside Tyler as a "Second" in the boxing ring, arrived at Greenacres to deal with this menace, named Jack Farr.

The ramshackle house was empty of life when they arrived so they waited. Tyler's view on how this potential scrap would turn out was decided upon the vision of the house itself. Anyone who lived in a metal cabin like this one could not possibly be of sound sense and mind and would be easily defeated.

In time, Jack suddenly appeared from the small walkway which was covered by a tunnel of trees. He saw them—was surprised by their presence. Tony he knew from the village, Ioan he knew as being a friend to Alun Jones. The burly Portman he did not know at all and the dark-skinned muscle-bound man he only thought he knew but wasn't certain.

There was no long talking or asking Jack why he had hurt his friends from Tyler. He merely announced that Jack had been identified as a menace who had hurt his friends and he, Tyler, had come to sort matters out.

Jack didn't speak or even attempt to defend himself. Clearly, this matter had already been decided by the visitors and he did not feel inclined to put his own case forward.

There was a brief pause—both men appeared to be sizing the other out. The "Seconds" moved back and became the boxing ring. The garden fence served as one perimeter, they the other.

And then, together, both Jack and Tyler raised their hands and adopted the orthodox stance of the boxer. It would appear Queensbury Rules would be in force. The fight began with both men moving slightly around their own standing area, then moving in towards each other—and then the first punch was thrown. A miss.

Once physical contact was made, it became the regular and not the rare. Both men landed hard blows against each other and within minutes, both were bloodied and bruised. The fight lasted a considerable time. For a man who had once eschewed physical violence, Jack was proving to be remarkably adept at this new regime. He gave a good representation of himself.

Tyler, however, paled by comparison. As strong as he was, as skilled as he had been in the boxing ring, despite the extensive training he had been given by Pirelli senior, the truth was Tyler had never been paired with another contender equal, or superior, to him. In every fight he had ever been in, he had never needed to see the fight out to the final round. Here, against Jack, the fight was not going the way he and his friends had envisaged. For one thing, this was not the three-minute bouts of combat, interspersed with thirty seconds of rest and liquid nourishment, there was no referee to prise them apart in the clinches and, more importantly for Tyler, he was not being hit by a man with padded gloves. Jack's punches were hard and there were more of them as the fight progressed.

Curiously, it was to his father that Jack owed this skill. Joe had never formally taught Jack such a way of defence but had set up his own area of boxing training. A large army-style bag filled with wet earth hung from a branch of the large oak tree in the forest and Joe set about it with an hour's worth of training every day. When as a young boy, Jack watched his father duck, weave, punch, duck, weave, punch, duck, weave-weave and punch and not really understanding why his father was doing this thing, and now he suddenly knew why. Lesson observed and it was now being put into practice.

He ducked and weaved and punched. As he did so, Tyler became less energized and his punches, when they made contact, had less effect as the fight progressed.

Jack ducked, weaved, and then from almost ground level, he straightened up and fetched Tyler a most devastating left hook which any pro-boxer would have been delighted to deliver upon an opponent and lifted this amateur boxer off his feet, sending him sprawling backward and crashing into this tree trunk in the middle of the garden.

Tyler staggered to keep his feet and Jack remained where he was, hoping the fight was over. He did not know this man and didn't have anything against him. It was the man's poor judgement which had led him to this business.

If it hadn't been for the intervention of the three "Seconds", the fight would probably have ended then. Portman screamed at Ioan and Tony to take Jack—which—a big mistake—they did. Portman, no mean boxer in his own right, incensed by the way his champion had been so convincingly defeated by this usurper, then launched into a tirade of punches which Jack, exhausted, had to take.

But then, maybe one punch too far, Jack grabbed the clothing of his two warders and used their body weight as leverage. His jumped up and booted Portman in the face—both heels from weighty army boots, connected with his eyes and nose. Portman was hurled backwards and landed in the long grass ten yards down the pathway. He was flat out and unconscious. Maintaining the momentum, Jack then jumped backwards, performing a somersault, landing on two feet and taking his two tormentors with him. He struck Pirelli in the throat and stamped on Ioan's groin. Both men screamed with piercing vocals and rolled around the ground.

Jack, furious he had been treated like this strode into his garden and towards Tyler. The man had bravely staggered to his feet and raised both hands to his face. Damn Queensbury Rules, thought Jack—the Right Honourable Marquess had never had to fight against four men at one time. Striding right up to Tyler's face, he head-butted the man in his forehead.

Tyler collapsed and that really was the close of the fight so Jack's next act of savagery could not be condoned. He picked Tyler off the ground and head-butted him a second time. But, whether, it was deliberate, badly timed or Tyler moving his head at the wrong moment, the head-butt connected with the skull just above Tyler's left eye. Tyler screamed and his body weight was too much for Jack. The man dropped like a stone to the ground, clutching his bleeding eye, screaming in agony and even crying.

Jack, truly exhausted, limped back up to the house and pushed his way through the heavy wooden door. He rushed to the large metal sink and vomited blood and whatever food he had eaten that night. He kept vomiting and washing his mouth out with water until he was just expelling air and the water was no longer red with blood.

He moved back into the small room where the family would spend time together each night and collapsed into his father's massive armchair. He closed his eyes and blacked out. Later, lights and noises woke him. In throbbing pain, he made his way to the window and he saw three men carrying Tyler to an open-ended van. They gently laid him on a mattress and covered his body with blankets. Portman was also placed in the back of the van—though with less grace. Nobody covered his body with anything.

A big man was arguing with Pirelli and Ioan and trying to make his way towards the house. Jack seized up, readying himself for yet another scrap. He heard Pirelli screaming 'Papa—Papa, no…' Then words in Italian followed. The big man then angrily pushed them away and he joined the others in the van. Slowly, it reversed down the rocky bumpy path, while Tony and Alun followed, taking them back through the village.

The night's noise ended.

A while later, Jack stripped his clothes off and scanned his body in the dim light of his parents' bedroom in front of a large mirror. Christ, he looked a mess.

Naked, he went out to the garden by the side of the house with a bucket and a bar of green carbolic soap. Using the tap fixed on the wall, he poured several buckets of freezing water over him until he was fully drenched. He rubbed the hard rough soap over his body until he was completely lathered and then repeated the bucket exercise until he was cleansed.

Numbed from the freezing icy mountain water and the cold night air, which to some extent assuaged his body pain, Jack, still naked went back inside the house, wrapped a huge towel around him, sunk into his father's armchair again and closed his eyes. In a few hours he would be attending his mother's funeral.

*

It was a curious affair. The four remaining Farr's stood silently as Theresa was lowered into the grave. Jack stood on one side, Joe, James and Joseph on the other. All of them were covered in bruises and swollen eyes. None of them spoke to each other to enquire about what had happened to them. What was really curious about this funeral was the fact that it had been arranged by an unidentified outsider—not by his father. Jack was told this by Sergeant Brock who had spoken to him as he was entering the cemetery gates from the Mynydd Gabriel end.

Even more curious was the size of the mourning party. Everyone who had attended the wedding was there, with the exception of Susan and her father, and many more besides. Quite a few of them carried their own bruises, collected from the fight at the wedding ten days ago. The men wept for the girl they had loved and never won and the women cried for the dear friend they had once held so close.

Amongst the mourners, four police officers from Cardiff Police were also in attendance. When the Service ended, Reverend Parminter rushed away. As the crowd dispersed, the four police officers came to Joe, James and Joseph and Jack believed they would be taking him away as well—but they ignored him. The officers placed them in handcuffs. Clearly, they were still being considered dangerous individuals. Police do not use handcuffs unless they consider a threat is imminent.

They led father and sons away down the path—and all was well until some idiot shouted 'You had it coming, Farr…' and then it all kicked off again. A melee erupted, the four officers were besieged and Jack saw the Reverend Parminter collapse to the ground for the second time—the first being at the wedding.

Jack waited till the Gravediggers, ignoring the fighting, began their work in filling the grave. He turned away, walked back to the top of the Cemetery and then through the gates.

He didn't even look back to see how the fight turned out. He already knew anyway.

*

It took him an age to undress himself from his suit—the same one he'd worn at the wedding, it was the only suit he owned—and his fingers were too swollen to undo the buttons. Finally, he just ripped the shirt away and tore the trousers off. He dressed in his more informal farming clothes, packed the most basic of his needs and left Greenacres. Initially, he had intended to leave the village across the mountain track—but funk seeped in and he wanted to walk through the village itself, defying all those who hated him and who would then be sanctimoniously pouring out their heartfelt sorrows for his mother.

He strode, as best he could, backpack loaded onto his shoulders and walked through the streets. The first street he had to negotiate of course is Bevan Road where Susan lived. He wondered if she was watching him as he went by.

He passed by the village Square where many people watched him limp through. No one spoke to him—not even to offer their condolences.

When he passed through the entry gate, he turned around and stared at the village. So picturesque to look at, the four mountains acting as silent sentinels over the village and he promised himself he would never come back to this place again. A promise he kept right up to the moment where John Redd, Vicar of Cwmhyfryd phoned him in his Oklahoman home to tell him his father had died.

*

And so, just a few hours after the return of Jack Farr, Susan, David, Sara, Malcolm as well if he were being honest, Sion, crippled for life, Adam, scarred across the face and neck, Tyler, blinded in one eye and informed by the BBBC that he would never step into a boxing ring ever again—and probably many others—reflected on their own personal parts they had played in the leading up to the terrible events of twenty years ago. Some swearing revenge, others just acknowledging their days were long gone from that dim and distant time.

And on the mountain overlooking them all, the man who was the focus of such reflections, was still lying on the bed, still sleeping the sleep of the Just, blissfully unaware that in some odd way, twenty years after those awful events had occurred, that he was still exacting his own revenge.

Chapter 14

Making Friends...and Enemies

He woke: his eyes slowly opened and he stared at the ceiling—and then they closed. He was still lying in the same position he had been in when he first lay on the bed. Now he turned over and lay on his left side. But his body was urgently telling him something and so his eyes opened again. Still drowsy—but now he was staring at a clock. Even in the thickness of sleep he knew he did not recognise the clock. His eyes closed again and he returned to his former position. And again, his body spoke to him—urging him to wake and stay awake. Again, he opened his eyes and this time kept them open.

Lying quite still, he stared at the ceiling, then at the open window above him, listening to the throng of bird talk outside. Now he looked around the room and he knew he didn't recognise it. He raised his head and tried to speak—but his throat was thick with sleep and so he just looked around instead. Nope, he thought, I do not recognise this room.

The first thought came to him. Either I've tied one on and I've been dumped here or those witty ranch hands have plugged me with a Mickey and left me behind for a joke. Such had happened.

After Jack had left the UK and made his way to the States via his relations' assistance in London, he took to the American mountains and walked for nearly two years before arriving at Auntie Phelps' farm and told her who he was. She already knew having been briefed by her English cousins and wondered why it had taken him so long to find them. In short time, he was installed at the Oklahoma farm and joined the ranks of other ranch hands who took an immediate dislike to him.

First, it was because he was an outsider—worse, a Limey outsider. Second, and more telling, it was because he was family to the Phelps. Auntie Phelps was a deeply dislikeable person and anyone rising to the top of the tree via blood was seen as a usurper and not to be included in the team.

84

Consequently, Jack found himself on the butt end of 'English' jokes, chaffing, chastisement and, occasionally, physical bullying. Having already endured for most of his life in Cwmhyfryd much of what was being thrust on him here on the farm, he was used to it—but having lately discovered that bullies bleed and can feel pain if you hit them back and hard enough, he quickly decided retaliation was the surest path to put a stop to it. The fights were short and brutal and he demonstrated enough ability to show the others he was not an easy man to mess with. Either he won or the combat were stopped when it was clear to the witnesses the fights might end in a death.

Which didn't stop the practical jokes. On occasions, rare for Jack, when he would go to town with the other ranch hands for a Saturday night 'relax', there would be some attempt to humiliate him or some idiot would be happy to push the boundary. One such night resulted in him being doped with a tablet in his drink and him waking up in a town two hundred and fifty miles from the farm. When he made his way back—a week later—he found the miscreant responsible and gave him the option of either leaving the farm or meeting him—no witnesses with this one—for a physical "sort-out". Upon advice from the other ranch hands, the poisoner left the farm. After that, Jack was pretty much left alone. Oddly, he did not seek to rise to attain any status of importance in the farm ranking and was seemingly content to put in his hours and take the pay.

Lying here on the bed, Jack wondered if he'd been doped again. He slowly swung his legs over the bed and stood. Still dulled with sleep, he made his way out of the room and wandered around whatever this place was. He came to a large room which had large front windows and it was only when he saw the tree trunk in the garden that he finally recollected where he was.

Home.

And then he realized what his body had been screaming at him to do. He needed the toilet.

It took him two doors and a few minutes to find what he needed—the bathroom. He stood, unsteady, over the lavatory and waited to evacuate his bladder but now the damned stream would not flow. Gently, he lowered himself onto the basin and waited until his body adjusted and nature took her course. In that time, he dropped his head and closed his eyes. Slowly, the memory of what he had been told by the Vicar came back to him. The vagueness of his father's Will and Testament; the funeral—and who attended it—and the fact that his father had commissioned his former fiancé to deal with the sale of the family home. That she had agreed to this arrangement and had been his father's sole mourner was a mystery to Jack. There was never a great deal of paternal affection from Joe to Susan when they were courting as children and teenagers. So—why?

Why, Dad? Of all the people to ask—why Susan?

His toilet complete—and now the fresh mountain air seeping through the opened windows refreshed his lungs—he cleaned his hands and left the bathroom going back to the main room where the sight of the forest appealed to him—it always did when he was a child. Something magical about the forest in front of him made his heart grow. He found his way back to the kitchen and the first thing he noticed was a foul smell. The broken window would need sorting out as soon as possible and Jack wondered how the Vicar intended to deal with the thug responsible. But the smell came from the carton of milk on the table. He lifted it to his nose—and it smelled of cheese which Jack always hated. He shook the carton—and the contents moved thickly as if it were sludge. He had forgotten to return the milk to the fridge after the Vicar had left the house—but still, to go off so soon...

He returned to the main room. He was amused by the sight of the television. Dad never wanted the damn thing in the house so the Farr family were probably the only people in Cwmhyfryd—probably in Wales to be honest—who never owned a TV set. It took him fifteen minutes how to figure out the remote control and to get a reception on the set. He channel hopped and eventually found the News Channel. He stared at the time and date.

It was Tuesday. Damn, he thought, I've been asleep since Saturday night. Two and a half days I've been on that bed. No wonder my bladder was in a hurry. And boy, am I hungry.

He watched the national News for ten minutes and then found the local BBC Wales News Channel which told him what was happening back home—'back home' he thought—I'm still on Oklahoman time. He returned to the kitchen and sifted through the fridge to find something he could eat and drink. The Vicar had been very generous and pretty well covered most of what he would normally eat. Forgoing a cup of tea, he settled for a fruit breakfast made of chunks of various fruits in a small tub which he washed down with half a glass of fresh orange juice. Feeling unclean, he then took his first Welsh shower in twenty years. He stood under a blasting cold stream of water and allowed himself to be drenched before taking to the soap—scented, not a green carbolic brick—another Dad concession. Again, still taking it slowly, he wrapped around himself a large thick flannel gown and sat in a large armchair and waited for time to dry him.

And now what? Oh yes—speak to Eddy—Peter Eddy, the Solicitor who was conducting the first part of the business relating to the sale of the house and the inheritance. Vicar Redd had furnished Jack with the Brangwyn Office number and he looked at the landline phone situated on top of the small table by the TV.

He dialled the number. The Secretary confirmed the location and told Jack Mr Eddy had waited for the call on Monday. Jack apologized and told her jet-lag had put him to sleep for longer than he'd planned. No problem, said the able Secretary and she would pass this message on to Mr Eddy who was currently in a Magistrates Court for this day. He would be notified of Mr Farr's call and physical presence in Cwmhyfryd immediately he returned to the office.

One job done.

This was 'bite-the-bullet' time. He knew, pragmatist that he was, he would need to go down to the village below to secure more provisions and the sour milk had upped the time schedule by a few days. Also, the provisions Vicar Redd had placed inside the fridge, as gracious as that deed was, did not altogether meet with Jack's dietary needs. So—some shopping was necessary.

He wondered how many more shops had opened up in Cwmhyfryd since his day.

He then noticed a red light beaming on and off by the telephone and saw it was recording machine. A message had been left for him. He played the message back.

It was from the Vicar.

Jack—I've been in touch with Jones the Glazier and they have assured me they will sort out the kitchen window within the next few days. They'll call you to let you know when they'll be up. Don't worry about the little sod who broke it—I dealt with him. Hope you're having a peaceful sleep. See you later, my friend.

"My friend"—nice to know he had one. He placed a board up against the window to secure it in case any wandering soul poked his head in to see if there was anything worth looking at. The doors locked—the windows secured—the house still a rather beautiful mystery to him as he stood next to the tree trunk and stared at it—Jack turned and strode into the forest to make his way into the village.

It was his custom never to go down the path to enter the village. It was a dull way to take a walk. Besides, he wanted to see his old second home again—which is how he thought of the forest. As a child, he spent much of his time in it, loving it the same way his father did when he went about his work in maintaining the integrity of the place. The old pathway was still there—though now covered with a multitude of branches, bushes and brambles. Summer had clearly been a boon to the plant life and left untouched, the growth was something to look at. He saw the great oak where he used to watch his father hang his old army carrier bag and use it as a boxer's punching bag. On this same tree, the letters 'J + S' had been inscribed by Susan when they were both sixteen—which earned her a minor rebuke from Joe for defacing the bark. Jack smiled when he recollected that moment.

He had walked through the forest for about half a mile when he heard a cough.

He made his way through the thickest part of the trees—wet from rain—and from a distance, he saw a young girl perched on a small concrete structure. She coughed again and then sneezed. Jack made his way towards her—taking great care to tread on as many twigs and break across branches as he could. He didn't want to frighten her unawares.

That ploy worked because she suddenly looked up and saw him approaching. He was at least one hundred yards away so if she'd wanted to, she could have run or moved away from where she was sitting. She remained seated where she was. The structure was colloquially known as the 'Death Well'—an actual water well which used to run the mountain spring water down to the village. It had been built by Jared Farr with his own hands. The legend behind it was quite tragic. Sometime in the 19th century, a young farmer's daughter had thrown herself down the well after she had learned her lover—an itinerant farm-worker—had eloped with her elder sister. Bereft of her love, she threw herself down this well when her father told her what had occurred. The well was closed down from that point—tainted by tragedy.

Jack wondered if this old folk lore had reached the younger generation yet. He was within twenty yards of her when she began to pay strong attention to him. He smiled, as though to comfort her and continued to walk where she sat.

'Good morning,' he shouted to her, with a pleasing tone which should not make her feel threatened.

'It's after two in the afternoon,' said Claire Phillips. 'After two thirty actually,' she continued.

Jack didn't have his watch on. 'Ah,' he said. 'Thank you. I've just arrived here from the States—I'm afraid my body clock is all over the place.'

He reached the well and gestured to her for her permission to sit. She inclined her head and he joined her.

'Hope you aren't thinking of throwing yourself down the well,' he said.

'Why would I do a stupid thing like that?' she queried.

'There is a Legend,' he explained. 'Around 1898, a young girl committed suicide by throwing herself down the well when her lover ran out on her.'

'Well, there's stupid, isn't it? Why didn't she just get another boyfriend?' From one so young. How wonderful to be that innocent, thought Jack.

And then—'You're Jack Farr, aren't you?' she said.

That unnerved him. He was certain he didn't know this girl—at her age— and she could have been only fifteen or sixteen—she wasn't even around when he lived here.

'Yes,' he said.

'You know my Mam and Dad. Sara and Adam Phillips.'

Crap, he said to himself. She knows who I am. I wonder if she knows what I did to her dad.

'Yes,' he said. 'I remember them.' Adam from the fights—Sara from the Wedding. Well, first person I see today and she's the daughter of two people I hate. Who both hate me.

'Everybody's talking about you in the village. You're famous.' She sneezed again.

'Bless you,' said Jack.

'Ta. I'm still suffering from bloody Hay Fever. I'm Claire Phillips.' And she offered her hand. Smiling, he shook it. Well—at least she didn't tell me to go back home.

They talked—about her, school, life in Cwmhyfryd for a teenager, then about him and his life in the States and on the farm which she thought sounded "Fantastic—all those horses," she exclaimed.

He talked happily to someone who was happy to let him talk—so they both were unaware that they were being scrutinized by a figure lurking behind a small clump of trees.

'Why are you waiting here, Claire?' asked Jack.

'Boyfriend. From Stone wall Mountain. He lives up there—but he won't allow me to go up there to see his family 'cos they're very religious and they don't like outsiders coming into their society unless they convert to their way of life. I ain't having that. You got to wear black all the time. I look disgusting in black. It's so final.'

Jack stared up towards Stone Wall Mountain which could just be seen through the forest because of its overwhelming size.

'The Fleminganese people are still up there?' he asked.

Claire explained. The name Fleminganese was no longer used as there were no more descendants of Joshua Fleming left. They didn't allow themselves to be called any name other than the Children of the Great Maker. It was enough for them to keep that society to themselves and away from all others. Jack queried how her boyfriend could be one of the "Children"—and yet be courting her.

'Well,' she said, 'it's on account of him working down in the village with Vicar Redd. He helps out in the Church 'cos most of the Children up there aren't exactly 'Children'—know what I'm saying?'

'They're old,' Jack said.

'Bloody ancient,' she replied. 'But Tommy isn't—he's nearly twenty—and he does some work in the village with locals and my dad—and also he used to work somewhere in Brangwyn I think. The previous Vicar got him a job there. Don't know what else he did but he used to work the Old Mill which is where I met him. He liked it.'

The lurking figure had advanced by some twenty yards. Stealthily was the way. They hadn't heard him moving through the soggy bracken. A hand lifted a branch away so they were now both in plain sight.

Their conversation passed quite pleasantly. Eventually, after fifteen minutes, Jack stood up and said he had to go into the village for food supplies. Here, her face turned dark.

'Well,' she said, 'watch yourself. Past few days since Saturday, a lot of people been talking about you and what I heard was they don't like you very much.'

Jack thanked her for the warning and walked away. She sneezed and coughed again.

'Bless you,' said Jack hitting his stride on the downwards path. 'Ta,' she called back.

Silence returned to this part of the forest and Claire hummed away. Two hundred yards further up into the forest, the lurking observant gently lowered a branch and watched as Jack walked out of sight. Claire sneezed again.

*

Beyond growth, nothing much in the forest had changed on this pleasing walk into the village. Jack paused here and there to sniff the clean air—so much cleaner than the constant smell of cattle and horse stock back at the Oklahoman farm. In truth though, he was just buying time to delay going back into the village—which now he was just yards away from—and more importantly, Bevan Road—where Susan had once lived. Then. He wondered if she still lived there now. Taking a deep breath, he brushed past another clump of trees and strode across concrete road.

Without stopping to look around, he strode through the street and made his way to The Square. When he arrived, he scanned the area. Fisher's Café was still the largest of the four shops—and the others still ran the same industries he remembered. He looked around further afield. Where once stood five old coal mining dwellings built in the 1920's which then later became ordinary dwellings in the 1960's there now stood four more shops. A clothing store—small but functional, a Chinese Take-away which was closed during the day, a computer store which sold games, phones and models and—best of all—a small Indian delicatessen. Wonderful. He made his way there and entered the shop.

He was mindful that a number of people around The Square had seen him and watched as he crossed the walkway. Inside the shop, another group of people stopped talking when he entered. They were the older generation from his day. No doubt, they either recognized him straight away or put the two plus two together and came up with 'son-of-Joe'. He made his way to the freezer unit…

…to find it was empty of milk. A young Indian girl was serving customers at the counter and he waited till she was free.

'Any milk?' he asked.

The delivery van was late and they were out of stock the young girl said to him. There would be some delivered by the end of the day—but Mr Fisher in the Café above The Square would probably have some in stock—which was not want Jack wanted to hear. The young girl confirmed there were no other shops in the village selling groceries and such.

He made for the door and was about to leave when three giggling girls entered. He stood back, holding the door and they passed through. He made a second attempt—and was delayed by the girls' parent or much older friend. He allowed her to enter. She did not even say 'Thank you'. Again, he made to leave, when… He froze.

Susan was standing there.

*

Jack walked aimlessly around the village, his mind milling in and out of a million useless notions which had taken control of his actions. He knew where he was going; to find the GP who had looked after his father. Uhhh…what was her name? Oh yes, Doctor Pryce, Vicar Redd had told him. She had paid particular attention to his needs in the last few months of his life and he wanted to at least thank her for her efforts.

The old surgery was not where it used to be—there was a big garage there now. He asked a few people and they gave him directions—but as his mind was on other things, he either hadn't listened to them or he was confused by the labyrinthine streets.

But the meeting with Susan (as brief as it was, they didn't even speak to each other) had unsettled him and he knew it. How odd, he thought, that even after all this time she had the same effect on him as she had when he knew her back then. He'd felt it from the very moment he'd laid eyes on her—when they were ten years of age. That disagreeable feeling one experiences when on a plane which has hit turbulence. It ducks under the airstream and the stomach lurches about, tosses up and over and one gasps from the sensation. He felt that sensation at ten—and then every other time when he saw her. His heart was in his mouth when—at eleven—he first asked her to talk to him, eat lunch at school on the same table, going for walks, meeting her father for the first time, she meeting *his* family for the first time, later on both learning there was some kind of feud between their fathers, becoming teens, him knowing she was constantly being advised, begged even, by her friends to drop his friendship and go with other boys instead and the joy he felt when she refused these entreaties and stayed with him, their sixteenth birthday (She was older than Jack by five days) and then the day he asked her to marry him—and her answer 'Yes!'

And so, after twenty years absence of seeing her and taking into consideration of how she and her friends had treated him and his family at the wedding, Jack found himself wandering the streets, wondering why his stomach was churning up just as it had done every time he'd seen her before.

He stopped and thought about what he had just experienced.

Her hair was no longer the fiery red it had once been. A shade darker and a bright-ish sort of brown. Her eyes were no longer the wide green pools he remembered, more paler now and—for some reason—sadder. Her face was not the round oval it had been, then fresh and unblemished from lines. There was something almost cynical about her now—hard and unsmiling, a woman who had nothing in her life except business and all other matters were placed somewhere else and could only be dealt with when she had time.

And time was never there for her.

But she was still Susan. She didn't speak so he didn't hear her voice which he remembered was rich in sound and cultured in delivery and she was stood next to him for only as long as it takes someone to walk by and then she was gone from his sight. Yet, his stomach lurched upon her vision and now he was walking about feeling the same dizziness he'd felt right from the first time he'd ever laid eyes on her.

'FARR!'

He turned. Someone shouting his name loud had shaken his reverie and his attention was drawn to a smart-suited man striding towards him, looking a little ruffled and red-faced. The man was approaching him at some speed and Jack saw he was not alone. The two Edmunds brothers were behind him along with a few other lads. Jack didn't need to wonder who or what they were—thugs waiting for a fight to happen. He stood still so the strident man in the smart suit could catch up with him. He stared at the approaching man and appraised him. Forty-ish, maybe older, a professional who was required to be smartly dressed at all times even in hot weather, balding on top, a man running to seed from too many business lunches. But that was it. He was fairly certain he did not know this man.

The angry man continued his strident walk and only slowed when he was just a few feet away from Jack. He breathed out, hard. Jack stared into the stranger's face. The man was clearly angry, had steeled himself into this confrontation with him—which meant he could possibly be dangerous—but, to Jack, he did not look like a man who was a natural fighter which made this situation unpredictable. Jack did not speak—he waited for this man to announce his intentions.

David Tanner almost tripped over his words. 'Stay away from my wife, Farr.' He demanded.'

Jack didn't respond. He was only curious about the man but was very aware that they were the focus of the other group's attentions. They were giggling—as if they knew what was about to happen. They were expecting violence.

'Did you hear me,' seethed David, 'I said stay away from my wife.'

Jack had to respond now. He was nonplussed by this man and clearly he needed more information. 'Who is your wife, exactly?' Gentle, not aggressive. Don't give the angry man reason to be angry.

'Don't give me that, Farr. You know damn fine who my wife is. And you know who I am.'

A pause—and then, for Jack, the dollar dropped. He was looking at the man who had royally screwed his life up. Jack's face changed from querulous curiosity to understanding. He relaxed.

'Tanner,' he said.

'That's it, Farr,' continued David. 'David Tanner. And my wife is Susan. You go upsetting her again and it'll be me you'll be dealing with.'

Jack wondered exactly what Susan had said to him. And then he stopped wondering. This man wasn't worth his time so he chose his words carefully.

'Grow up, Tanner,' were his parting words and he turned away.

But David, infused with a false anger, emboldened with poorly judged sense of bravado no doubt encouraged by the presence of the giggling idiots standing behind him, had come so far with this confrontation he felt he had to complete the journey. As Jack had almost turned his back on him, David grabbed his arm, whirled him around and struck him across the face.

It was hardly a crushing blow and maybe at any other time Jack could either have avoided it or parried it or just took it without too much pain. But today, still jet-lagged and suffering the after-effects of a long sleep, being slightly under-nourished and not looking for aggressive would-be fighters, Jack took the punch and fell back. He stumbled backwards over a loose slab in the pavement and then to the ground, striking his head as he landed.

Immediately, he heard cheering—a whooping of victorious joy and saw the group punching the air. He saw Tanner standing back, his hands were raised to his chest as if he were preparing for a retaliation from Jack and he felt an odd taste in his mouth—like iron. A brief image of a woman appeared in his memory—shouting and laughing at him. He knew he knew the woman but couldn't place her here. Then he blacked out.

But not yet unconscious. Dazed, his eyes half focused, he tried to move.

He heard more shouting and his eyes opened. Now—standing over him was a woman who was holding onto his face and shouting—'Jack—Jack—are you alright?' An Indian woman. He didn't know her.

To her left, he saw the huge bulky figure of Vicar John Redd, pinning a terrified David Tanner to the wall, his large hands around Tanner's face. Vicar Redd was also shouting, furious at what he had just seen.

'*WHAT THE HELL DO YOU THINK YOU'RE DOING?*' he screamed at Tanner. Jack, dazed, felt blood streaming down the right side of his face, saw the Edmunds brother and their mates looking equally scared of the wrathful Vicar and they moved away and then out of his sight.

Jack felt sick. His eyes closed again and this time they stayed shut.

Chapter 15

Dreaming of a Nightmare

He dreamt: The vision was hazy, unfocused, but he knew exactly where he was. He knew where—and when—and the image of that day was scorched into his mind maybe for all time. In recent years he had successfully suppressed it, burying it deep into his subconscious but now it was there, as fresh as the day it happened. Cwmhyfryd Church, twenty years ago, and a Wedding which did not take place—but instead ended in chaos.

On the one side of the Church, the Bride's side, the pews were filled with friends and two members of the family—her father and her Aunt Ruthie—her mother's elder sister. (Moira, still in bad odour with many Hyfridians for the abandonment of both husband and daughter, had wisely chosen not to attend, instead sending her elder sister, whom Susan had only ever met twice in her place.) The rest of the congregation were all her friends from her school days or workplace.

Susan was standing there—stunningly beautiful, resplendent in an all-white dress which contrasted greatly with her fiery red hair and the single red rose flower adornment pinned to the upper breast area of her Wedding Dress given to her by Theresa. Her father stood glued to the spot in the front pew—his face staring down at the floor, reddened with fury having lost yet another argument with her as to the wisdom of this day's proceedings. He begged her not to marry the Farr boy and she slammed every door in the house in his face. Ruthie smiled at her brother-in-law's impotence. She had never liked him and thought apart from giving birth to Susan, her younger sister had made a colossal mistake marrying such an oaf.

On the Groom's side of the Church there was just the Farr family. Joe, looking distinctly uncomfortable in his Morning attire. Joseph and James, equally out of sorts in their suits. And Theresa—like her soon-to-be daughter-in-law, stunningly beautiful, restrained so as not to steal Susan's light, smiling her bright smile at her youngest son's wonderful day, the proudest mother in all South Wales.

But something was wrong in the Church. Susan was crying—but they were not the tears of happiness and joy. They were sobs of misery and pain. She was backing away from him at the very moment she should have been saying "I do" to the Reverend Parminter who was looking very confused at this turn of events.

There were other noises—some encouraging her to see the ceremony through, others advocating Susan should run now while she had the chance.

Susan was hiding her face as she cried—the first time he had ever seen her cry in the entire time he had ever known her. She was begging for his forgiveness. He turned around to see anger from his father and brothers as the noise against him was rising from the so-called friends. He saw the distress on his mother's face—and that image had never left his memory. And then, it all kicked off.

Susan had reached the door and his attempt to get to her was now being deliberately blocked by her friends. A man—Adam Phillips—had blocked his path. This man was laughing hard into his face. And then, from behind, he heard a shout, 'My daughter isn't going to marry your son, Farr,' shouted a victorious Malcolm Fisher who now believed his protests had finally seeped through to Susan. This angry tirade was met with a straight right punch from Joe into Malcolm's eye and he was laid flat out in the pew.

Chaos reigned.

Those who were in the same pew now wanted out of the potential fists of fury which were guaranteed to follow. In order to get away from that situation, they all stamped over the prone Malcolm's body, leaving footprints which covered his grey suit.

Joseph and James jumped onto their pew and literally dived over it, crashing into a group of men who were still laughing at this Wedding debacle and at their younger brother's humiliation. Their heavy fall was sufficient to spread at least eight men flat on the ground. He made another attempt to reach Susan—but now a young girl whom he knew but only barely was in front of him and screaming into his face, furious laughter on her reddened face. Sara Jones ranted at him, 'She doesn't love you anymore, Farr. She's in love with David Tanner.' *David Tanner? Who the hell is David Tanner?*

He saw her exit the Church—but between where he stood and the heavy doors was a group of men and women scrambling to get out of the Church or who were engaged in battle with his brothers. He looked to his father who was now taking up the cudgels against other men who were trying to calm him down—fat chance, he thought—not when my dad is on a roll. Malcolm Fisher lay supine on the pew floor and Aunt Ruthie had taken Theresa aside and out of harm's way. The Reverend Parminter was spread-eagled at the base of his own lectern, a result of a stray blow or fainted just from the shock of watching what should have been a beautiful ceremony turning into a battle-zone.

The fight continued apace as he eventually succeeded in cutting through the melee and ran out of the Church entrance.

But of Susan, there was no sign.

In time, Ruthie had managed to bring Theresa out of the Church via the Vestry door. She assured him and his mother she would find Susan and this outrage would be addressed.

He took his mother up through the Cemetery and up onto Mynydd Gabriel, still listening to the screams and yells of pain behind them. She was continually asking him what had gone wrong, what had happened, why had this terrible thing occurred? He did not answer. In truth, because he genuinely did not know what the answer was, but also keeping some information to himself so as not to upset his mother even further. The idea that Susan could have been involved with another man was something he had never even suspected—and yet…

David Tanner!

Tanner! David Tanner! David… Tanner! Who the hell was…?

'TANNER!'

The name woke him—the face of the man who had struck him was now burned into his memory. He bolted upright and took in his bearings.

He was in a room. Small, white, the smell of cleanliness, anaesthetics, bottles, and signs on the wall which informed him he was in the Surgery. He had been lying, now sitting upright, on the trolley bed. He heard voices. A man and a woman. He knew both. And now, fully awake, the pounding in his head took over.

The door opened and the Indian woman he saw earlier entered. She was carrying a metal bowl of warm water with a large bobble of cotton wool in it in one hand and a mug of tea in the other.

'Easy, Jack,' said Doctor Jovinda Pryce. Her voice was soothing, calming. He needed to be calmed. She set the mug down and came to him with the bowl of water. She took the bobble of cotton wool and stood by him as she placed her free hand on his head and raised it to the light.

'Luckily, you have not suffered too much of a blow. There is bruising but no abrasion,' she told him as she gently wiped the cotton wool over the area which hurt him. The upper right side of his forehead ached. So did his right foot for some reason.

'You landed on this side of your head having tripped over a broken piece of flagstone paving', she told him still mopping his brow. 'Nothing serious and you will not need treatment. No stitches. How do you feel?' He nodded his head and gave her a thumbs up.

He sat still as she completed the wash then dried the area with a small towel. She moved away, smiled at him and then offered him the mug of tea. 'Drink,' she instructed. 'Always soothing after shock.'

He was not in shock but drank the warm tea anyway. Very nice. Had milk in it—the reason for his coming into the village in the first place.

The door opened and Vicar John Redd entered. 'How's the patient?' he enquired. 'Recovering nicely,' Doctor Pryce confirmed. 'Ready to go home, I think.'

A little more conversation followed and Jack stood up. Wobbling a little at first but then took strong hold of himself and also gave the Vicar the thumbs up when he looked at him, concerned. He thanked Doctor Pryce—once for what she had done for him and then again for the way she had helped his father. They all left the Surgery.

As they walked through the village, the Vicar wanted to know why Jack had come into the village. Jack updated him with all his movements from the moment the Vicar had left him on Saturday night.

'Two days?' he breathed out. 'My God, you must have been tired. And you only wanted milk?' And so Jack related to the Vicar exactly what had happened that day.

Jack told him that after he had left the delicatessen having briefly met Susan, he had attempted to buy milk at Fisher's café. The young girl working there—

Catrin was on her name badge—was about to serve him when Malcolm had come into the café and ordered Jack to leave or he would call the police and have him charged with trespass. This brief moment of Malcolm exercising his bombast was witnessed by Ryland Edmunds and a few of his friends—and they were highly amused at Jack's red-faced eviction from the café. The Vicar led him up towards The Square and told him he would take him either to the Vicarage or up to Greenacres if he so chose. Jack chose to stay a part of the evening with the Vicar but would spend the rest of his night at…

How odd—he actually thought of Greenacres part two as home.

As they walked, the Vicar enquired about any communication with Peter Eddy's office. Jack confirmed he had spoken to the Secretary and she would pass the news to Mr Eddy that he was now back in Cwmhyfryd and Mr Eddy would contact him as soon as was possible. The Vicar was pleased that the ball was rolling at last.

They reached The Square just as the shops were about to be locked up. The clientele inside Fisher's café were finishing off their teas and doughnuts—the staple diet of the uninformed. Ryland and Steffan were inside and Jack told Vicar Redd he did not want to see them again tonight.

Vicar John Redd entered the café and went to the counter. Catrin was cleaning cups and glasses and Malcolm was drying a glass tumbler.

'Vicar,' he beamed. 'How may I serve?'

Vicar John Redd looked about the store as if searching for the product he needed. His eyes lit on the tall freezer unit.

'I will have a carton of four pints, please,' he said. Malcolm attended the Vicar personally. The plebs he left to his staff—the upper gentry of Cwmhyfryd society he dealt with himself. It was a matter of propriety. He placed the carton on the counter and the Vicar paid for it. He placed the carton inside a plastic bag and thanked Malcolm and Catrin. He left the café and walked straight up to Jack and gave him the bag—and Malcolm Fisher's smile dropped from his face. This act was also witnessed by the Edmunds who decided, upon the Vicar's previous demonstration of fury against them, to say nothing.

Vicar John Redd entered the café again and went to the counter. He smiled at a now confused Malcolm Fisher who was again drying the glass tumbler in his hand.

'Malcolm,' he said. 'You're a twat.'

He turned and walked out of the café. Malcolm Fisher was frozen to the spot where he stood—and glass tumbler dropped out of his hands and rolled under the counter. The Edmunds brothers stared at him—open-mouthed.

It was left to eighteen-year-old Catrin Phillips to speak and break the deadlock.

'What did he just call you?' she asked.

But Malcolm Fisher was not disposed to speak to members of his staff under the age of twenty unless it was to give her an order to do something he felt was below him. Instead, he turned on his feet and stormed out of the café and into the back office.

She retrieved the glass tumbler and then told the Edmunds it was closing time and they should go now. They exited and she locked the front door, she saw the Vicar bring his car around at the bottom of The Square and Jack climbed in. She smiled.

Chapter 16

Events Leading Up To...

So exactly what actually happened after Jack had seen Susan outside the delicatessen? Well, as the Politician said—"Events, dear boy—events". Jack came out of the deli—almost physically bumping into Susan, they did not speak, barely even acknowledged each other before he stood aside and allowed her to pass by. Then he left the scene.

But this moment was witnessed by Steffan Edmunds who had just finished his day's work on the Community Scheme and was on his way to meet his brother, Ryland, at Fisher's café. He stopped and sat on a bench, finishing off the cigarette he would not be allowed to smoke once inside the café because that old git Fisher wouldn't have it. And while he was waiting, Susan came back out of the deli and sat on the small wall, her head in her hand and looking distressed. Steffan took that scene to be the result of her meeting Farr. In fact, Susan had been contacted by phone by her banking colleague in Cardiff who told her the sale of a house they had been working on for weeks had now been placed in jeopardy because one of the buyers had been thrown out of the family he was marrying in to. Susan was naturally distressed that their hard efforts looked as though they were about to collapse after what had been nearly two months of a difficult sell. She was now attempting to remedy this calamity and was understandably anxious.

What Steffan had seen was quickly passed onto his brother and their mates and they wondered if they could possibly make mischievous capital from it.

Then Jack entered the café and asked Catrin for a carton of milk. She was about to serve him when Mr Fisher entered the store and ordered him to leave or he would call the police. There was no objection from Jack—beyond a glare of resentment—and so he left the café. The yob entourage congratulated Mr Fisher on his command of the situation and he beamed back to those he would never usually even speak to and told them there was way he would allow a piece of scum like Jack Farr to eat, drink or purchase in *his* café—in spite of the fact the evidence of serving such people was sitting right there in front of him.

The yob element then left the café to collect Sion who had to place a Bet on a horse for the following day using the Newsagent's office. When they came down into the parade area, David Tanner arrived in his car. Steffan nodded to the group and wandered over to the man.

'Excuse me, Mr Tanner,' he spoke in his most solicitous manner which he was capable of doing when the moment required it. 'I don't know if you're aware that Jack Farr is back in Cwmhyfryd...' David confirmed he was and Steffan continued. 'Well, I just saw him have a go at your Missus... I mean, Mrs Tanner, and she was upset. I saw her crying over by the deli. I don't know what he said to her but she looked pretty upset.'

To David, merely speaking with a yob like Steffan was an affront to his delicacies—but now, to all intents and purposes, his masculinity had been challenged. The gauntlet had been placed in front of him. In a false sense of outrage, he demanded to know where Farr was—and the others said they would search him out. It took but a few minutes. Jack was wandering over near the Surgery. That was when David had called Jack by his name. After the brief skirmish resulting in Jack's fall and Vicar Redd sending David and the yobs scurrying away, they collected their father and returned to the café and ordered more teas and doughnuts, waiting for their father to do his business with Jones the Newsagent. A short while later, Vicar Redd entered the café, bought the carton of milk, insulted Mr Fisher and took Farr away in his car. They were then told to leave the café by the delicious Catrin—whom Ryland had already pencilled out for future amorous intentions—and they were on their way home when they saw Susan Tanner coming out of her estate agent's shop. Again, Steffan saw potential for a bit of mischief.

'Don't worry, Mrs T,' he yelled, 'your David sorted him out. He gave him a real hard walloping'

Susan, still engrossed in the problem of how to remedy the sale of an unattractive, dwelling heard her name being used and she looked up. Oh, she thought, it's the local plankton. But then she heard the other part of what he said. *Your David sorted him out?*

'Pardon?'

Steffan, now confident he had an audience, wandered over to her and repeated what he had said. David sorted *him* out. 'David sorted who out?' she asked.

'Farr,' said the smiling yob. 'Got him a right peach of a punch. Down in one. Never knew your hubby had it in him, Mrs T,' he crowed.

"Mrs T"—she hated being called that and only a lunkhead like Steffan Edmunds would use such a phrase. She demanded he repeat what he had just told her and what he was talking about? He repeated what he had told her, what he had seen at the deli and what had happened afterwards. David felled Jack with a single punch.

Susan's eyes widened slightly, her head lowered an inch and her voice dropped a tone.

'What?'

Moments later she was in the Surgery and speaking with Vicar Redd. He confirmed what the Edmunds boy had told her and that Jack was in the next room being attended by Doctor Pryce. Her face barely changed colour or expression but the Vicar could see the fury underlying her countenance. He asked if she would like to speak with Jack—and for a moment, it looked as though she would consider it but then she declined. She told him she would deal with her husband and set the matter straight.

As she left to go home, she saw Doctor Pryce take in a cup of tea when she heard Jack shout out. Vicar Redd wanted to know what had actually happened out there. He didn't get the answer from Susan so he waited to take Jack out of the Surgery and asked him.

Events.

Chapter 17

Confirmation of a Doomed Suspicion

At nine o'clock that evening, David Tanner came home, one glass of wine shy of being over the drink-drive limit and not caring one bit. His day had been one of pleasure and victory having scored twice in his own field of expertise and once in a field he didn't even know he was in. The separate events were sure to raise his profile professionally amongst those he considered his peers and socially amongst those he looked down on as being bodies of people one would normally walk around as if they were human versions of dog deposits.

He entered the house and slipped off his shoes and jacket—dropping the jacket when he tried twice to hang it up and then leaving it on the floor. The light was on in the main room so he knew Susan would be there and he contemplated on which of the three victories he would boast upon first.

Earlier that day, he had been involved in a crunch meeting at the Bank because of an individual's attempt to commit an act of embezzlement against his own Company. David had been sifting through documents and information supplied by the individual and something didn't pan out. So he scrutinized further and saw an inconsistency. Further investigation indicated an act of fraud was in the process of being committed and he took the matter to his immediate Superior and explained it to him. Phone calls to the Company were made and the fraudulent perpetrator was stopped in his tracks. The police were alerted and the would-be fraudulent arrested. Big thanks from the Company swept in, congratulations to the people responsible for the swift action taken preventing what would have been a considerable embarrassment to all concerned. David was back-slapped until his back was red with pain and he took it all with a broad smile.

The second prize of the day was when he was called in by his immediate Superior to deal with a rather wealthy client who had been engaged in a deal with the Bank over a two-month period and was now having doubts about an investment. It sent David travelling to Cwmhyfryd to pick up a Mr Clement, drive him to Swansea and speak with great persuasion to this doubting client and put him back on the right tracks.

Of course, David had arrived in Cwmhyfryd, was met by Steffan Edmunds and there was a minor diversion of his purpose for being there in the matter of dealing with Jack Farr. After the contretemps with Jack and then with the Vicar, David did pick up Mr Clement and they drove, at speed, to Swansea where they met with the obtrusive client and what followed was two hours of thorough explaining, mostly from David, and the client was saved from his own failings. Delighted by this victory, Mr Clement took David for a celebratory drink or six, passed on his effusive thanks to the Bank's Manager stating David's managerial skills had saved the day and should be promoted as soon as…

His star was in the ascendancy, his future pure gold. In two months, his immediate Superior told him, there would be a promotional run and his position would be strongly considered in that line-up. A move to an even bigger Bank, a pay rise of some considerable percentage. David's eyes lit up—a move up the ladder and in his bank balance would mean, he hoped, the leaving of Cwmhyfryd, something he had been working on with Susan, reluctant to leave, for some time now. This day could mean that day may actually dawn. And then of course, there was his victory against Jack Farr, and in front of witnesses who would not usually afford him such respect. They gave it to him today, with loud cheers and congratulations and applause. Only the Vicar's intervention spoiled the spoils. No matter. The word would be about tonight—Farr was beaten—by a Banker. How that rhyming word had constantly rankled him but maybe never again. Not after today.

So, smiling, drunk with glory if not from the actual amount of wine he had partaken in, he entered the main room and saw Susan sitting in her armchair.

The look on her face stopped him dead in his tracks.

Drunk or not, David was sober enough to know he'd seen that look before. It generally preceded a roasting of his character. He waited—not knowing what was about to happen.

She was dressed casually, a 'T' shirt, jeans, no footwear. She didn't often look so casual. Of recent times, he was more used to seeing her in her business arraignment and talking with her business head. It looked like it would be a different kind of business she would be talking tonight, he thought.

She stared at him for a few moments, and then she spoke. Her voice was level, calm—but steely. Scary even.

'I understand you have engaged in pugilism today,' she said.

That threw him. He didn't actually understand what she said. Maybe it was the too many wines. He opened his mouth but nothing intelligible came out so he closed it again.

'I have been told you have taken up fisticuffs,' she explained.

Ah, he thought. She knows.

'Would you care to explain to me what you did—and why.'

He was about to sit on his own chair—but felt he needed to remain standing if only to maintain an elevated advantage over her. He shuffled his feet and then breathed in.

'I decked Farr onto his ass,' was what he eventually said.

Now that *was* the wine talking. David was not prone to street-speak. Sober-ish, he would probably have said "I punched Jack Farr in the face and he fell down". He was that literal in his speech. Street-speak certainly did not suit him.

'And why?'

'Because he'd had a go at you and upset you.'

Pause. God, silence could be a real mindbender. She stared at him, more out of curiosity than scathing. The scathing was definitely on the cards, though—if he knew Susan.

'And who told you he'd upset me?'

Another pause. This answer would really not impress her. 'Steffan Edmunds,' he said, lamely.

She looked back and smiled. 'Ah, she said, 'And since when do we listen to the words of the Morons United team?

'He'd seen you and… Farr… at the delicatessen. He saw you coming out and you were crying. He said Farr had taken a pop at you. You were crying on the wall.' Lame again but it was all he had.

She stood up now and walked to him, stuffing her hands in her trouser pockets as if she was actively preventing herself from taking a 'pop' at him.

'First of all,' she told him, her eyes glaring into his—no mean feat, he was six foot four to her five foot six—'Jack didn't take a 'pop' at me. We didn't even speak. It was a meeting of micro seconds and then I was inside the deli and he was gone by the time I came out. The reason for my sitting on the wall and looking upset was because I'd received a phone call from Josephine in Cardiff who gave me some bad news. Jack had nothing to do with it.'

Now she folded her arms, Christ, he thought, here it comes.

'Secondly, the day hasn't dawned when I would allow anyone—even Jack Farr—to upset me. Jack is not—nor would he ever be—a threat to me.'

This is it, thought David. This is where I get caned.

'Thirdly,' she spoke and now her voice dropped a tone, always a bad sign. 'The day will…*never*… dawn when I will need *you* to protect me.'

There are some people who need to scream to intimidate others and there are other people who can scare the life out of people just by a whisper. Susan was of the second category.

Her arms still folded, she walked away from him, back to the far end of the room where she turned and leaned against the wall.

'I'm going to tell you something. It is information as well as sound advice so listen carefully. After Theresa died and before he left this village, Jack paid visits to some of the local hard knocks around here. You've seen Sion Edmunds, his injuries which keep him wheelchair bound. Adam Phillips, the scars on his neck and head. You know the boxer—Tyler… something—blinded in one eye. Those three and a few others, Jack fought against them all. We didn't find out any of this until Sara's brother got drunk one night and blabbed it. Adam filled in the rest of the truth. Those men were the so-called hard knocks—in the village and outside—and Jack took them all out.'

Arms still contained within her chest, she now walked slowly towards him. When she was face to face with him, she spoke slowly, softly and deliberately.

'In… your… *prime*… you would never have been a match for any of those thugs. In *their* prime… they proved they were not a match for Jack Farr. You are a long way from being a fighter, David. I recommend you don't do it again.'

He had to say something, if only to save face.

'I put Farr onto his back,' he protested.

'I spoke to Vicar Redd. He saw what happened. He told me. Jack had turned away from you and you struck him from behind. A sucker punch. As gutless as it was unnecessary. If he hadn't clunked his head on the concrete, I doubt you'd be standing here now. Look,' she said, this time, her voice was almost imploring him. 'Today, you got away with it. Hopefully, Jack will give you a pass. But ever stand in front of him again, and he will… kill you. You'll be sleeping in the spare bedroom tonight.'

And with that final remark, she walked around him and left the room.

David stood still in his stocking feet. Impotent, emasculated, redundant both as a husband and protector to his wife. And there, in those words, the final confirmation of something he had suspected for so long. That this unhappy marriage was indeed doomed to fail and end. He didn't know when it had failed, or why, but there were times when he felt it had ended the day after their so-called honeymoon. He'd wanted a trip abroad but Susan demanded they go nowhere. After her shameful exhibition at Cwmhyfryd Church, she felt they did not have the right to celebrate the happiest day of their lives. Instead, they spent the day in Cheshire where David originally came from.

What did she say? *The day will never dawn when I will need you to protect me.*

That was it. Confirmation, if confirmation were needed, that his long held suspicion of the state of his marriage was true. The three victories of the day— two genuine, the third just a wish, had now evaporated into nothing, shot down by his wife's carefully chosen and calmly delivered words.

Bereft of senses, really not knowing what to do, he remained standing in the middle of the room, unable to speak, not having any answer to what she had just told him. Silent, standing in the middle of the room, redundant. A perfect metaphor to the state of their marriage.

Chapter 18
Peter Eddy Calls

He woke: his eyes opened and he rolled over to look at the clock which read 08.40 hours. He lay quite still in bed—but this time he knew where he was and he knew how he'd arrived. There was no confusion and his body was now in time synch. Without any sense of urgency, he climbed out of the bed, conducted his toilet functions, examined the bruise on his forehead from the paving stone in the bathroom mirror which was now quite livid and the lesser bruise just under his left eye where Tanner had punched him. Nothing to worry about. No abrasions and not much discomfort. Two days had passed since that incident and he hadn't gone back to the village to see whatever consequences had followed. He washed his face and then went to the kitchen.

He set out his breakfast and stared across the kitchen. Vicar Redd had called him the night before to update him on the rumour mill which had been turning in the village after the fight incident.

The Edmunds brothers had been very lyrical in their own distorted version of the fight—according to their story David Tanner had confronted Jack Farr after the latter had publicly upset Mrs Tanner by the village deli. The two men had a verbal spat which resulted in Mr Tanner striking Mr Farr. A minor scuffle followed and the unwelcome visitor from the States was finally bested by the Cwmhyfryd Banker. All who drank at The Night's Tail sat engrossed. Ryland furthered the story when he told the drinkers Mr Fisher had thrown Farr out of the café after he had refused to serve him. Well done, Malcolm, went the cry.

Sion Edmunds celebrated with an extra pint, stating 'I've never liked that English ponce but for that piece of news I'll stand him a drink.' Adam Phillips was equally enthusiastic and told his wife when he went home that Farr had got his come-uppance at last—and from the right man as well.

It took the impartial witnesses just an evening to set things straight. First, it was Doctor Pryce at her Surgery when she heard her receptionist waxing about that "awful Farr man" being put down onto his back by a "Gentleman". The receptionist was sent packing with the correct version which she duly passed onto her neighbours.

Vicar Redd had also gone to the pub—later—and after the Edmunds family had left—and as soon as he heard the conversation of the night, soon put everybody in the real picture.

Sara Phillips got her correct version of the truth from Susan herself and wasted no time in passing it onto her husband. Catrin then corrected the other detail. The word that Mr Farr and Mr Fisher had a big verbal blow-out in the café and that Mr Fisher had thrown the intruder out was "crap." Not so, said Catrin. Certainly Mr Fisher had ordered Mr Farr out of the café but the man didn't even retaliate—he left quietly. There had been no fighting. Another fairy tale given out by the Edmunds brothers.

So, the Tanner/Farr battle was less than the Farr haters would have wished—but no less satisfying to them. The picture was still of Jack—prone on the ground and unconscious.

Vicar Redd duly reported all this to Jack who smiled. None of it really mattered. He expected nothing less from those people down there. He sat in the kitchen and looked at the wall clock. The previous evening, he received a call from the able Secretary of Peter Eddy who apologized to him on Mr Eddy's behalf stating the Court case he had been involved in had taken longer than was originally scheduled but now at last he was free and he would be calling Mr Farr when convenient. Jack told her any time was convenient and a call was booked from her to take place at 09.30 hours this very morning. Today, he would speak to the Solicitor and the next step to inherit this mysterious money from his father would be taken. Precisely at 09.30 hours, the phone rang and Jack spoke to Peter Eddy, who gave his own apologies and explained without going into great detail of the Court case which had delayed him. No problem answered Jack. What would be the next step relating to their own business he asked.

A meeting. It would be a face-to-face meeting—held in Peter Eddy's own law office in Brangwyn. No problem said Jack—except, Mr Eddy continued, it had to be conducted to the letter of his late father's wishes. The journey from Cwmhyfryd was to be taken by public transport—the bus to Pentre Haf—then a bus trip from that village to Brangwyn. The return journey would be by car provided by... Peter Eddy did not commit himself on that final piece of the journey.

Jack queried the journey—so complicated and fiddly. The bus journey to Pentre Haf was spasmodic during the week and would take over an hour to get there. Even longer to Brangwyn. Jack was prepared to hire a car and drive direct to Mr Eddy's office to expedite matters. But the instructions were set down by Joe—and demanded by the other party, the Gibney Associates, that the journey should be completed this way. Confused—and somehow, Jack felt Mr Eddy was equally in the dark—he consented and said he would make arrangements. He didn't know for a certainty how the bus service ran in the village anymore but he would find out and confirm the day and time of arrival.

So—one part of the return was now underway. Jack gave thought to how this trip had been planned out by his father. The journey across from America to the village was specifically laid out to the letter as to how he would make it—and now, it appeared, the same meticulous arrangements were being set out for his meeting with Peter Eddy.

He called Vicar Redd at the Vicarage and updated him. The Vicar was pleased there was now movement and sounded positive about the arrangement. He had the bus schedule in question and he would pass it onto Jack.

Two hours later Jack heard a noise at his front door. He went to it and saw the bus schedule had been dropped on the mat. He wondered why Vicar Redd hadn't knocked on the door, to come in for a talk or a cup of tea. Maybe he thought Jack was out—maybe he was in the forest where he'd spent the past two days or even back in the village, braving the ire of the Hyfridians.

The schedule he needed to take was ringed in red ink in regard to the times and which buses to take that would take him to Brangwyn. Jack studied the schedule, called Peter Eddy's office and spoke to the able Secretary. He confirmed he would attend Mr Eddy the following day. It was logged and confirmed by the Secretary and the meeting was set. Just one day to go—and then Jack would know for sure about the Joe Farr Legacy.

Chapter 19

A Satisfying End to a Confusing Day

On paper, it was a simple enough journey. The bus trip to Pentre Haf would take over an hour unless the route had changed a great deal. The same bus would then change its number and head West towards Brangwyn and then South towards Cardiff. A long journey which rarely carried more than a dozen passengers throughout the entire trip which was why it ran so limited a service. The hardest part of this journey would be negotiating his way through the village without some witty individual running up to him wanting to know what it was like to be decked by an over-weight tight suited Englishman—and a Banker at that.

While that scenario did not occur, Jack was aware he was the focus of much attention from the various people who lived near the bus terminal. His main fear was bumping into Susan again. He wondered what kind of story her husband had given her and if it actually married up to the truth of which she very much aware thanks to the good Vicar.

In the event, nothing harmful took place. Jack arrived at the terminal with ten minutes to spare and exactly on time, the bus arrived. To his relief, he was the only passenger to alight from Cwmhyfryd. This remained the case until five miles down the lanes two senior citizens joined the bus.

'Good morning,' sang the elderly lady to both Jack and the Driver. Her husband merely grunted. 'You have to talk to everyone?' he moaned. 'Lovely day,' sang the old lady again and Jack responded in the affirmative. The husband groaned again. 'Are you going far?' sang the old lady and now the husband clapped his head and gypped at her. 'You have to know everybody's business?' he asked, exasperated. So Jack said he was going to Brangwyn on business. This time, the husband glared at him and sidled up to his wife. 'Yank,' he said and Jack smiled.

The trip passed all the way to Pentre Haf without stopping and no more talking. The bus would stay in the station for twenty minutes before setting off to Brangwyn. It had been Jack's intention to pass over towards the Porter's Farm at which he learned his initial foray into farming work when still a teen but as the bus entered the village he saw the farm was no longer functioning as a farm. It looked as though redevelopment had transformed the large outbuildings into small blocks of apartments—plush looking they were as well. He walked around the bus station and inquired after the Porter family and was told father and son, Bill and Harry, had passed away years ago and the grandson sold up the week after their funeral. He was never cut out to be a farmer, he was told, and wasted no time hanging around the small provincial village either. Fairly well off now, the bus Inspector told him, and living in New York.

Back on the bus with another four passengers, it left the summer village and headed West. As a teen, Jack had also worked on farms in the surrounding areas of Brangwyn as well. He anticipated a wonderful journey. The countryside run between the two villages was splendid to see if you are a person who likes to gaze upon natural beauty, untouched by human development. And so it turned out to be—the mountains, the forestry and the rivers—all intact and would remain so for all time if the local populace had their say. And they would.

En route, he pondered over this arrangement of travelling to the law office. If it had been Dad's personal instruction that he should travel this way—and the trip from the States—then he must have had a reason. As he had noted in the past, Dad didn't do random—there was always purpose behind his every action.

Defeated by whatever the purpose was intended to be, Jack just sat back and enjoyed the sights of the journey. It was nearly midday by the time the bus arrived at Brangwyn and Jack got off and looked around. Like Cwmhyfryd, Brangwyn was a small village though larger than both Pentre Haf and Cwmhyfryd. Unlike both those provinces, however, Brangwyn was expanding. The area around it was flatter than the mountainous area Jack hailed from and there were less beauty spots to demolish. So Brangwyn was ripe for development—for one thing, advertising posters boasted of the impending new railway lines which would be in place within the next five years. No longer cut off from the principal City of Cardiff—there would now be a faster mode of communication between the Principality and its outlying provinces.

The village had grown in its own right as well. More buildings of a business nature had sprouted up and larger homes had been built around the former wasted edges of the village. Peter Eddy had given Jack directions to where the law office was based and he saw it just a few minutes after he left the bus station. He entered—his breathing slightly elevated. It was another fifteen minutes before he saw Peter Eddy—an interview which had gone beyond its one hour schedule. The client eventually left after a number of 'Goodbyes' had been made and Peter Eddy breathed out and smiled as he saw Jack in the reception room. 'Jack,' he said. 'At last.' His hand stretched out and Jack clasped the wettest hand-shake ever. Mr Eddy smiled, ordered two cups of tea from one of the receptionists and they entered his office.

Situated in a fairly well placed establishment—it was one of five different kinds of industry inside the building—Jack waited for Mr Eddy to bring out the files and documentations relating to Greenacres—and how it had been transformed into a hacienda, how did Dad pay for the transformation and where the hell did he get hold of £5,000,000?

All questions to which he received no kind of answer at all.

In fact, it transpired the whole point of this entire trip and Jack's physical presence in the office was to merely indicate exactly what his intentions were regarding the sale of Greenacres. Jack shrugged and said he probably would sell the place. In which case, said the Solicitor, closing the file, there would be no more further discussion today.

The look of utter bewilderment at the abrupt manner in which business was suddenly ended perhaps softened the Solicitor's hand. He smiled and sat back, opening his hands as though to indicate to Jack he had nothing to hide and what was being dealt now was a set of cards played by him but on behalf of another player in the game—thus far, unseen.

'Look, Jack,' he explained, 'I never met your father and I don't even know how these arrangements were made. I only came into this after he died and before he was buried. Everything about this deal—if you can call it that—had been prepared by him and Gibney Associates. How or why I came into the picture I do not know. I suspect they required, for some reason, a local intermediate who could liaise with your good self once you'd arrived in Cwmhyfryd and before meeting them once the appropriate conditions had been met—to whit, the sale or not, of Greenacres. And the first instruction I was given, by Gibney, was the prospect of Greenacres future. If you chose to sell, that would be the end of my involvement in this matter.'

'I don't understand,' said Jack. 'Is Greenacres mine or not?'

'I don't know. The little I do know is the original Greenacres was razed to the ground and replaced by the fine home you are currently residing in. Possibly, the people who built it, partly own it. If you had chosen to keep it, therefore taking it off the market, then it is yours—I'm only speculating now so don't quote me. But if you decide to sell, rent or even raze this version to the ground, the profits do not come to you and the rest of the Legacy becomes invalid. In order for you to receive your father's legacy, the first hurdle is to accept the house as yours.'

Jack stood up and walked the office floor. He needed to rethink his strategy. The sale of the house, the five million inheritance money was one thing—but the prospect of *living* there was definitely not in his long term game plan. The single week he had lived in the village had been quite enough and he couldn't envisage a longer period of time.

'Dad planned this?' he said.

'Apparently. Along with Gibney Associates because I can see there is a legal road here and unless your father was trained in such matters, I doubt he came to this method of passing this inheritance down to you without advice—and therein is another story—because Gibney doesn't come cheap.'

Jack paced a little more then sat down when the receptionist brought in a tray of tea, biscuits for both of them and for Mr Eddy a tray of sandwiches.

'Do you mind?' he asked, holding up one of the sandwiches. 'I won't get out of here before five and I am desperately hungry.'

'Go ahead. I need to think on what you just told me.'

He drank his tea, dunking the ginger biscuits into his cup while Eddy fairly gorged on the sandwiches. He looked like a man who barely ate, thought Jack—he needs more than a plateful of sandwiches. As he finished the small meal, Jack tried another route.

'Let's go the other way,' he said. 'I declare I have no intention of selling the place. What happens now?'

'I contact Gibney Associates—they draw up the necessary paper-work and you will be in their hands from that time on. Don't treat them lightly though—don't... uh... tell them you'll not sell the place and then sell the place behind their backs. I suspect the paper-work they'll create will be a legal obligation requiring you to live there—for a set period of time if not in perpetuity.'

Clever, Dad, thought Jack, very clever. For reasons Jack could not even guess at, he had been brought back to this place—the place he had sworn never to return to—by his father, and now he was being thrown a dodgy bone. To collect the five million pounds inheritance, he had to remain as a resident of Cwmhyfryd.

But why? Not out of malice, Dad wasn't that small-minded. And then there was the sale of Greenacres—which now he realized could only go ahead if *he* sanctioned it. How did this involve Susan? Did she even know?

'Again, I do not know. I know he visited her some time before he died and made this arrangement—and her involvement ties in with Gibney—because she would have had to sign up to it. It is certainly a peculiar piece of work.'

Silence fell between the two men. Jack was bereft of words. He had come here, he had assumed, just to sign whatever contracts were going to be laid out in front of him that would have expedited his return to Oklahoma in the fastest way possible, which he would have done joyfully, then back to the mountain, ready to pack his bags, wait for the money to be deposited into his Account and then—back to Oklahoma, or maybe a trip around the world. Oddly, he had not given the money angle much thought. People who have never had so much money to handle do not give serious consideration to what they would really do if such an unexpected windfall lands in their laps. Now—all thoughts of what he wanted to do would have be put on the back-burner. Just the simple refusal of living at Greenacres threatened everything.

'What do you intend to do, Jack,' asked the Solicitor.

*

An hour later, Jack Farr left Peter Eddy's office having signed the legal paper-work which had been given to Eddy by Gibney Associates confirming there would be a No-Sale of Greenacres until after the next stage of business had been discussed—this time between Jack and Gibney Associates themselves no less.

Eddy watched Jack get into the BMW supplied indeed by Gibney Associates. His journey *to* this office had to be taken via public transport, the return journey home by use of the company car. As soon as the car left the car-park, Peter Eddy picked up the phone and dialled the number given to him by the Gibney Official. He listened as the receiving end rang three times and then it was answered.

'Hullo,' he said. 'Peter Eddy from Brangwyn speaking. I have just had my meeting with Mr Jack Farr, in relation to the sale of Greenacres—and he has confirmed, by signed contract, that he has no intention of selling that property at this time. Please let me know if I can be of further use to you.' He ended the call after he heard the voice thank him for his work. A job well done, he thought. But he also gave thought to the future which had just been inflicted on to Jack Farr through his auspices.

*

The journey home was made in silence. The Driver had already opened the rear door for him, indicating he did not want Jack to sit next to him on this journey. The partition was already in place so there was no way Jack could converse with the Driver—so no inside information from an employee could be gleaned.

The Driver took a different route home. Not the bus route. Again, he saw more of the country he had left behind and, in truth, he pined for it. But that was silly sentiment and he had left that behind when the village killed his mother…

A bit strong, maybe. After he had left Cwmhyfryd and before he'd emigrated to the States, the official cause of her death was an aneurysm—something which could have happened any time under even the mildest of circumstances. He remembered his mother did suffer from constant headaches in the months leading up to the marriage. He'd put it down to nerves and a mother's natural reluctance to see her youngest son leaving home.

The journey took just under two hours and clearly, the Driver had been given a specific instruction as to how Jack should be returned home. Instead of going through the village and up the winding path, the Driver elected to drive up the Mynydd Haf pathway and across Mynydd Gabriel, passing by the Vicarage and then stopping at the precise point where Jack could walk the few hundred yards down the rocky path behind Greenacres.

He was unable to open the door from within the car so the Driver had to do it for him. Again, there was no talking. The door was opened, Jack got out and the Driver turned the car around, driving back down the path he had driven up. Jack stared at the registration plate.

GA 3

Gibney Associates.

He walked down the rocky path and entered the house through the kitchen entrance. The broken window had been repaired in his absence, courtesy of Vicar

Redd. A receipt was on the table with a calling card from the Glazier. He walked all over the house just to be certain he had not received any more visitors or bricks. The house was quiet and clean.

An hour later, as dusk approached, Jack sat on the front porch, a cup of tea in hand and giving serious thought about what had happened this day. It had definitely not gone the way he planned it. Again, he tried to think as if he were in his father's shoes—just what the hell was the old man playing at—but nothing came at him. Eddy told him a Gibney representative would call on him soon and the next stage would be arranged. Which gave nothing away and he was back to square one. Worse—not even on the first rung of the ladder. He'd signed that damned contract—effectively tying him to the house *and* the village—and immediately he regretted it. Even now, the prospect of becoming a millionaire five times over was just not worth the hell he would have to endure if he came back to live in this place.

And as he sat and mulled matters—he realized he was staring at the cause of his dilemma.

The old enemy.

You killed my Dad, he thought, which forced the Vicar to call me, he brought me back here to go through all this palaver—and that's not counting the insults of the locals and the humiliation of being punched out by the slob who had stolen his wife…

Susan.

He downed the tea and stood up. He pulled off the outer clothing he wore until all he had on was a pair of cut-off Jeans. He pulled on a pair of heavy boots, brought out the axe, pick and shovel and stood next to the trunk.

'Right,' he said, and he dug down into the roots of the trunk.

Using shovel, pick and axe, he worked on that trunk for over an hour. His body was bathed in sweat and then also covered in dirt. The sweat covered his face and entered his eyes. He used his forearm to wipe the sweat away and did the same thing his father did by filling his eyes with dirt. He cut with the axe, he dug with the shovel, picked at the rocks and went further down the hole than his father had and still he encountered more roots. Dear God, this bloody thing must have roots all the way to China. The night wore on, the air cooled and the swings became more laborious and out of focus. He breathed out hard and fell into the hole from loss of balance. Even the effort of lifting the axe was now too much for him—a child of five could lift this axe but he could barely raise it above his head.

'*Come on, Son,*' Joe shouted, '*you're almost there.*'

'I can't,' said Jack. 'I'm beat.

'*No—I can see the roots from here. A few more cracks and you'll sever them. Come on.*'

So Jack lifted the too heavy axe and smashed into the roots below the huge base of the trunk which itself, lay almost horizontal and level across the ground. Goddam, he thought, if that thing comes crashing down on top of me, I'm finished.

He chopped at the roots and still there were more below ground. He raised the axe, lost his balance and collapsed inside the hole.

'*No Jared,*' yelled Joe, '*don't stop now. You can do more. Come on, the roots are smaller now and there aren't many left. Now COME ON!*'

His father's admonishment lifted him to his feet and he continued the chopping.

'*Get under the trunk, Jared,*' shouted Joe. '*Get under it and lift it out of the ground. You can do it.*'

'Dad, I can barely stand.'

'*DO AS I SAY. YOU'RE ALMOST DONE*'

Jack threw the axe away and moved under the trunk. He grabbed the base and bent down so his knees touched the cold and wet earth below ground level. He strained at the lift and it barely shifted—damn thing must weigh a ton.

'*THAT'S IT—LIFT!*'

Jack lifted again—and this time there was movement. He heard a "crack" sound.

'THAT WAS A ROOT,' screamed Joe. *'YOU'RE LIFTING IT OUT OF THE GROUND! COME ON!'*

Again, he lifted, again, there was movement, another "crack" sound and this time the movement rocked back and forth. Joe was next to him and screaming in his ear...

'YOU'RE DOING IT! IT'S COMING OUT.'

'It's killing me, Dad,' Jack yelled back, almost in tears from the pain. But he lifted again... and this time...

SNNNNAAAAAAAAPPP!

The trunk suddenly became lighter to lift. Jack now found he was able to stand upright as he lifted the trunk which was now no longer held deep in the ground by its roots. A series of cracking sounds splintered the air and then...

'WE'RE DOING IT, SON,' yelled Joe. *'IT'S COMING OUT! WE'RE DOING IT!'*

Jack screamed—Joe screamed—and the trunk was pulled out of the deep hole it had lived in since the days of old Jared Farr. Out of the hole, out onto the garden and rolling down to the fence. It rested against the fence and lolled back and forth until it stopped moving. Father and son screamed their victory.

'WE DID IT, SON!' screamed the father.

'WE DID IT, DAD!' screamed the son.

They fell about the garden, drunk from excitement as well as exhaustion, punching the air, victoriously, punching the ground and screaming and laughing. The old enemy...

...was defeated.

Still laughing, Jack rubbed his face and realized he couldn't see any more because too much dirt was in his eyes. He crawled his way up the garden and across the porch, using the wall to guide his journey to the side of the house and found the water tap which the hose was still attached to. He turned it on and cold water gushed upwards. He lifted the hose and stood under the waterfall and he was drenched in freezing water. It cleansed his body and eyes and when his body became acclimatized to it, it wasn't cold any more. When he could see again, he put the hose down and leaned against the wall, still laughing, spitting the water out of his mouth.

'*WE DID IT, DAD!*' he shouted.

His voice echoed around the night forest. He shouted again. But this time there was no response. No one replied to his victory cry.

'Dad?' he looked around. He was alone in the back garden. Where the hell did his father go to? 'Dad,' he called again. But now the silence of the night caught up with him. As he spun around to find his father, his eyes fell upon the piece of ground just a few feet away from where he was standing. That odd shape in the ground—a human body shape. The grass had grown around it—but the shape stayed where it was as if it was as dead as the old man who had fallen upon it.

'Dad?' he called again—but this time, he knew there would be no reply. He turned to see where the trunk lay—and there it was—at the bottom of the garden, out of its hole which it had coveted for over a hundred years—longer even. It had really happened.

The truth seeped into his mind—but he knew what he had seen, what he had heard. He saw what he saw. He'd swear it on a stack of Vicar Redd's Bibles.

He turned the hose off and drenched, walked back to the porch and sank to the floor. He stared at the trunk. The garden, that damned shape, he stared at the bright Moon—an old friend. His breathing slowed and he wiped the water from his face. Silence followed.

He smiled.

'We did it, Dad,' he said.

*

An hour later, the phone rang and Jack, still half naked from the exertions, answered. One of the Gibney Associates confirmed the meeting with Peter Eddy had met with their approval and he would be contacted by a member of the Firm within a week to arrange another meeting—this time with a member of the Associates and possibly in Cardiff.

Well, he thought. Now I am on the first rung of the ladder and maybe I will get answers from these people. A satisfying end to what had turned out to be a confusing day.

Chapter 20

Reciprocity

But over a week passed by and Jack had heard nothing from the Gibney Associates. He raised the issue with Vicar Redd who expressed confusion at the Peter Eddy business—*he* hadn't expected *that*. The Vicar wondered aloud if maybe a meeting with Susan Tanner might be in order—if only to learn what *she* knew. Jack agreed it might be a good idea—but under the prevailing circumstances, regarding her husband's extreme behaviour, it might not be wise. Vicar Redd assured Jack there was no way he would allow the meeting to go ahead un-chaperoned and at any rate, David would not interfere again.

Jack nodded his approbation at the idea—but asked to hold the meeting back until it became absolutely necessary. He really didn't want to get into any deep business talks with Susan at this point. Vicar Redd agreed and that was the end of the subject. For now.

The problem was, the time had passed and now he found he needed more provisions. It meant another trip to the village, braving the insults or possible challenges to his person borne on the myth that he could be taken quite easily now. He considered asking the Vicar again—the previous experience of his defying the village's chief storekeeper had been widely circulated, Jack was now aware of. But then, this meant he would be acquiescing to the behaviour of the villager's attitudes and prejudices. Running from a confrontation which certainly wasn't in his mental make-up.

And so, he decided. Go into the village and damn those who would scorn or laugh. It would be a fast trip in, pick up what he needed and then back home. Even that felt like he was running—but it was enough to demonstrate to those people he would not be cowed—by anybody. He locked up the house, secured the windows, examined all within just to see if there had been any visitations in his absence—and then he strode through the forest and towards the village.

This time, there were no distractions en route. No young girl waiting for her beau to appear. No ramblers enjoying the mountain trek—of which he had seen many just in the week he had been back home. The walk through a thoroughly soaked forest lasted just over forty minutes and then he was on Bevan Road. Again, no pausing to see if anyone was staring, he made his way straight to the delicatessen to do his shopping and then back home.

There are days when one feels the fates are simply out to cause as much mischief as possible. Jack reached the deli—to be confronted with a sign on the door which read:

APOLOGIES TO OUR CUSTOMERS
UNFORSEEN CIRCUMSTANCES MEAN WE
CANNOT OPEN TODAY.
NORMAL SERVICE RESUMED ASAP

Well damn, he thought. And no other food store in the village. Again, he thought about spreading his net further afield but that would mean either catching the bus or a long walk to Pentre Haf. He had no choice. He made for Fisher's café.

He entered—and groaned the moment he saw who was sitting there. Steffan and his brother, Ryland. There were a few others sitting on the other side of the café but he didn't know them. The Edmunds looked up and laughed.

'Well well,' laughed Steffan, 'Look what the wind flew in. A loser.'

'Had any more boxing lessons from a Banker, Farr?' laughed Ryland, necking down a Cola liquid. Jack looked around. His principle adversary was not here. Malcolm Fisher, he hoped, would be serving somewhere else in the store next door or possibly purchasing his wares at the Cash & Carry situated a few miles south of the village. The young girl he'd seen before—Catrin was her name, he knew—stood at the counter—and suddenly, the smile fell off her face the moment she saw him. He went to her and took out his list of needs.

'Good morning,' he said, as mild as possible. Don't give the girl reason to think there's going to be trouble. The brothers had remained in their seats—don't get up lads, he thought, don't start something now. He was hoping the vision of an irate Vicar would be enough to keep the peace here today.

'Milk, butter, bread, uh… some ham. A packet of tea.' Out it came, voice calm, manner gentle. So far, so…

'Don't serve that man,' came the gruff voice from the doorway.

Jack looked to his left and saw Malcolm Fisher half in, half out of the café store. He was dressed in an apron and he carried a meat slicing knife. His expression left nobody in any doubt as to how this shopping excursion was going to proceed.

'Don't serve that man in here. Get out, Farr—or I'll be calling the police.'

'Or maybe you should call your son-in-law, Mr Fisher,' laughed Steffan.

Catrin moved back. Malcolm entered the café fully now. The two brothers moved in their seats to get a better view—and Jack remained still. He kept his eyes on Malcolm who now took up centre stage behind the counter.

'I said get out Farr—get out of my store.'

The silence which followed was oppressive. Within his own sound system, Jack could hear the pounding of his heart-beats inside his ears. He stood still. God Damn the hypocrite, he thought. This man, Fisher, who pontificated morality, espoused Christianity, love your neighbour and all that guff was threatening him over…

Milk, butter, bread, ham and tea.

Silence, when noise should be heard, is even more frightening than noise when it should be silent. The seconds felt like hours to Jack—but then he heard his voice.

'No,' he said, simply. The look on Malcolm's face moved from anger to total shock.

'What?' he spluttered.

'I wouldn't have come in here, Mr Fisher—except the only other shop selling food is closed. I need provisions—as simple as that. Now, either I do it—or I could ask the Vicar to do it for me but then I think that would be a nuisance for him, for me—and definitely for you, unless you're going to ban him as well. A few minutes here and then I'm gone. Hopefully, I won't have to come back. Hopefully, when my business with your daughter is completed, I can return to my home in America. Between now and then, I need to eat—so… milk, tea, butter, bread and ham, and I won't leave till it get what I came for. Either you sell it to me—or I'll take it.'

Well that was that, he thought. Challenge given and now accepted. Ball's in your court now, Fisher, he thought.

But it wasn't Malcolm who rose to the challenge—it was Steffan. He stood up, broadened his shoulders and stepped up to the counter.

'It's okay, Mr Fisher,' he said, trying to sound conciliatory, 'you don't need to deal with this trash. I'll sort him.'

Malcolm began to protest—but in fact, was grateful for the interruption. He hadn't given any kind of thought to what he would do if Jack had defied him.

Jack turned his attention to Steffan. He didn't want this—but he wasn't going to back down. Ryland was watching—an almost insane smile on his face in anticipation of watching his elder brother decking the man who'd crippled their father.

Steffan took one step towards Jack—and Jack did likewise. One step towards Steffan which un-nerved the man somewhat. He was expecting Farr to back away.

'Maybe you didn't hear the owner of this café, Farr. He said for you to get out. That means—you… get out. If you don't… get out… then someone's going to have to force you to… get out.'

Jack wondered where Steffan picked up his very TV language. Bad TV at that. As he looked up at the burly thug, an inner calm came over him. He measured the distance between him and Edmunds and then at the man himself. Big, bulky, he has weight and height to his advantage but he is arrogant enough to believe that is all which is needed.

Jack then made his own conciliatory speech.

'This is nothing to do with you, boy' he said—the same 'Boy' levelled at Edmunds as came from the Vicar—'leave it alone. I'm not looking for trouble—just back off and I'll be on my way.'

'I'll back off—when you have gone your way, Farr. You just don't get it, do you? You ain't welcome here—in this café, in the village, in South Wales—even in this entire country.

Now—you been told by the man who owns this place to get out. If you don't get out—I'll make you.'

Pause. Silence. You could have heard a pin drop in Swansea.

'Make me,' said Jack a lifetime later. The voice dropped a whole octave.

More laughs from the younger Edmunds. Steffan looked at him, an expression of pure but faked shock. 'It ain't like I didn't give him the chance, was it?' he mocked; his brother laughing again.

Steffan turned away from Jack and opened his hands as if to say "I tried".

But it was a feint—a move to suggest he'd had second thoughts about what he was about to do and maybe, nine men out of ten would have fallen for the feint and then be taken by surprise. But Jack Farr was not of the nine. He was an experienced man of too many fights and being forced to defend himself was something he had become accustomed to. He stood still—but didn't take his eyes of Steffan. He waited for the next move.

And there it was, the dropping of the right shoulder to gain distance and power—the delivery of the following punch aimed at his face intended to send the opponent backwards against the wall which by itself should be sufficient enough to end the fight at that point.

Steffan moved—his right fist curving around, aiming at Jack's left cheek. As it approached, Jack simply took one large stride backwards and he felt the 'whoosh' of air as the punch swept past the place where his face was a few seconds ago.

But now, Steffan was off-balance and his own bodily weight carried on the momentum of his forward movement—and straight into Jack's own response. A direct punch, squarely connecting to Steffan's nose sending the big man hurtling backwards as though somebody had lassoed him and pulled him back using a team of horses. He was sent crashing into the side wall and sunk to the floor. As he landed, there was a look of total astonishment on his face, a man wondering how such a finale had arrived from where it had started. He raised his hand and made a sound as if he were about to lodge a protest and then his head dropped and Steffan Edmunds was completely unconscious.

Ryland, outraged by this unexpected result, grabbed the bottle and raised it above his head. He stood up and brought it down over the table. But all he achieved was the breaking off of the table corner—the bottle remained intact. Clearly, Coca Cola Industries made their bottles from toughened glass. He stood there, momentarily transfixed—it didn't happen like that on TV—and he raised the bottle again. But this time, he was met by Jack's hand, the man's enclosed fist hovering just an inch away from his face, and the expression on Farr's face was enough to persuade Ryland to drop the bottle and scurry away—which he did.

And that was enough for Malcolm Fisher.

'*GET OUT OF MY CAFÉ, FARR OR I'LL HAVE THE POLICE ON... AAARRRGGHH!*'

Jack had jumped to the counter and had grabbed Malcolm's shirt to pull him over it—but he had not only taken the shirt, he had also grabbed Malcolm's fleshy pectorals. He yanked the flabby hypocrite towards him and was about to rant his own riot act at him when…

'Let my father go, Jack.'

The bark of authority was enough to end the aggression. Jack froze when he heard the voice. The scenario became a tableau.

'Let my father go, please Jack.' Less a barking order, more a plea but with no passion.

Catrin—who had moved a safe distance away—was never so glad to see Mrs Tanner. Mr Farr frozen to the spot, it seemed, then he pushed Mr Fisher away and into some of his shelf items, which shook the shelf and the items were spilled. Mr Fisher, his crimson coloured face in stark contrast to his white wavy hair, then screamed at Jack.

'THAT'S IT, FARR—THAT'S THE POLICE FOR YOU! YOU'LL GO THE SAME WAY YOUR SCUM FAMILY WENT—TO JAIL AND THEN TO DEATH!'

Jack didn't move. He was breathing hard and stared at Malcolm Fisher as if he were weighing up the possibility of inflicting another piece of harm on him.

Susan moved from the doorway and entered the café. She glanced around and saw the full picture. Ryland cowering behind a tall shelf, Steffan flat out on his back, the other customers looking a tad frightened for their own selves. She raised her hand to assure them that all was calm from here on.

Jack now calmed down. If he had a weakness, it was his anger but he always knew when to bring it to order once order had been restored. He didn't look at Susan—but was clearly addressing her.

'I just wanted… *MILK!'*

But now Malcolm, sensing the day was coming back to him, placed his hands on the counter and seethed at Jack. 'Get out, Farr—out of this café and go back to where you come from.' Which could have meant Greenacres on the mountain or the farm in Oklahoma. Jack didn't ask.

Susan took control. 'Serve Mr Farr, please Catrin.'

And now the silence seemed to go the other way. Malcolm froze—not quite believing what his daughter just said. *'WHAT?'* he spluttered.

Catrin stayed where she was. There is always a moment of confusion when the employee gets two contrasting orders from those who are the employers. At this moment, she was confused as to who was giving the order she was going to obey. She stayed still. This was between father and daughter.

'*WHAT?*' Mr Fisher repeated. 'Are you insane? I am not going to serve that man in my shop.'

Susan turned to him—again, her voice never rising above the conversational level.

'First, she told him, 'as I have made clear, this is *MY* shop—I bought it, I own it, you…are my employee. You… work for me. So does Catrin.'

All true. An arrangement made years earlier when the café was doing poor business and Malcolm was belabouring his lot to Susan who bought the whole store, reworked the café and the grocery end and turned it into a profitable business. Malcolm would continue as Manager—but it was established that Susan was the proprietor. His employer. He didn't like it, but it saved the business.

He turned on his daughter, his face an inch away from her nose.

'No, 'he screamed, 'there is no way I will serve that man in this shop. Either he goes—or I do.' Such an empty threat and it had no effect on Susan at all. Jack watched.

'Then leave,' she said and brushed past him. 'Serve Mr Farr, please Catrin.'

Bombast and genuine authority. Catrin, although only eighteen years of age, was able to tell the difference between the two and authority won over bombast every time. She turned to Jack and beamed her best smile.

'What do you need, Sir?' she asked and Jack repeated his order, keeping his voice low and calm so not to alarm the pretty counter-girl. The milk she brought from the freezer unit inside the café but the other items meant she had to go into the grocer shop which added more time for Jack and now the whole place became like a Court where a hanging Judge was about to sentence the guilty man to death by hanging and was taking his own sweet time about it.

Malcolm seethed—but now quietly. He stared as Catrin brought the items into the shop and placed them all into a plastic bag. Jack then remembered he had to pay for it all. He put his hands in his pocket and dragged out a small leather bag.

'It's alright, Jack,' said Susan, who gestured with her hand that he did not have to pay. 'For the inconvenience.' Another pause. He took the plastic bag in hand. He turned away—and then turned back. 'I just wanted things, you know. I didn't come looking for trouble.'

'It's okay, Jack—but please leave my shop now,' said Susan. Jack slowly walked to the door and exited. The danger was over, the other customers breathed out. No police, no more shouting.

Except, Malcom couldn't let it go at that. 'You served him? That man? Are you out of your mind?'

Susan addressed Ryland, still standing by the shelf. She nodded down to the unconscious Steffan.

'Pick that up and get it out of my café. And don't ever come back. You, your brother and your father are banned for life.'

With assistance from two of the other customers, Ryland was able to throw Steffan over his shoulder and carry him out of the café. Malcolm then slammed his fist on the counter.

'You serve Farr—and then you ban two of my customers? What the hell is wrong with you? I run this café—not you. I decide who gets banned—not you. If you don't like that—you know what you can do about it.'

Pause. Catrin waited for the inevitable.

'You're sacked. Get out.'

If someone had told Malcolm Fisher he had just won the biggest Lottery prize in the world, it is unlikely he would have exhibited a different expression of surprise on his face.

Impotent against his daughter's manner, he ripped away his apron and stormed out of the café.

Peace and order resumed and common sense prevailed. Susan went to a trembling Catrin.

'Look after this place for an hour. I'll find Olwen Berry to help you.' Catrin nodded. The quiet took over, they both walked to the front door.

'He hits hard, don't he?' said Catrin.

Susan smiled. She knew things Catrin didn't but she kept those secrets to herself.

'He always could, dear,' she said. Almost proud.

Chapter 21

A Near-Miss

Jack took the tarmac pathway back up to Greenacres. Going through the forest uphill was difficult enough without carting a bag of groceries especially when it had been drenched from constant rain. Besides, he needed peace and quiet to evaluate what had just happened. He didn't know which scenario had disturbed him the most, the brief skirmish with Steffan, the very public and loud spat with Malcolm or the exchange with Susan who had effectively saved the situation from turning into something more dangerous. There was no doubt in his mind he would have done Malcolm a serious mischief if he hadn't been stopped. The slow trawl up the pathway was just the means by which he could think without distraction about what had taken place.

Elsewhere in the village, the "word" was spreading at some speed. The bigger Edmunds thug was down and out, Mr Fisher had been threatened by Farr—and then sacked by his daughter and the two once-upon-a-time lovers had finally engaged in each other's company for longer than a few seconds. The deli incident had also circulated. Those who knew the history of each of these events would gossip for a long while. At least a two week stance on this one, the septuagenarians crowed. Glorious.

That word quickly found its way up to the Vicarage and as soon as Vicar Redd was able to complete his Church business, he was in his car and down to the village at hot speed. He first went to the café to find Olwen Berry standing in for Catrin. He received only the version she'd been made aware of so he left and went looking for Susan—or Malcolm. He would deal with Steffan and Ryland later.

But all this took longer than he'd wanted because the principals involved could not be found. He went to Susan's Estate Agency but found only Sara who had also been told—by Catrin—about the café incident. Not doubting her version, Vicar Redd still needed to hear the whole truth from someone who was actually there.

He returned to the café and ordered three rounds of hot buttered bap rolls. Duly delivered but toaster-made baps are never the same as if they'd been turned over by a roaring fire. He ate and waited, hoping Susan would return to the café—someone had to lock up.

But six o'clock came and Olwen cleared the tables and openly waved the keys about. No Susan. Clearly, an arrangement had been made between the two that Susan would not need to come back. Vicar Redd finished his guilty pleasure and left. He went by Bevan Road but her car wasn't there. Exhausted, he decided he'd call her and make an arrangement to see her. He got back into his car and returned to the Vicarage…

…only to find a near-tearful Susan waiting for him. She had gone there not long after completing Agency business and had missed his car coming into the village because it came via the South route.

Holding onto herself with some courage, she related the truth of the fight. She'd heard her father ranting because she had been in the back office working on his books, a task he'd recently let slide. When the second shout was raised, she had gone to the doorway and saw Jack stand his ground, deal with that thug Edmunds, and his brother, then grab her father and haul him over the counter. At that point, she intervened. She then told him of the consequences of the scrap and how she sacked her father. Listening patiently, he nodded and supported her decision. This animosity between her father and Jack had puzzled him and he didn't understand it, especially as her father was a full member of the Church where such behaviour would not be encouraged.

Susan explained the possible link between her father and Jack's mother so long ago, before Joe came back into the community from God knew where and then swept the village beauty up in his arms to the actual dismay of every male who fancied her and their chances—but especially of her father who bore such a betrayal of his affections very personally and very deeply. This feeling became even more intensified when he had mistakenly taken Moira to replace Theresa— a choice he regretted the first day after they were married.

Puzzle explained, thought Vicar Redd—but that didn't help Susan. Dealing with the Edmunds was a walk in the park—putting her father in his place was almost an everyday occurrence now—but having to be in the same environment as Jack she had found very difficult especially under such circumstances. A

133

public outrage against from Jack against her own father—and she had supported him by her own actions. It was that arena Susan had to contend with at this time.

Vicar Redd indulged in his personal guilty pleasure and was pleased Susan joined in. He offered solace and advice—but she already knew how it would all would transpire—such a small village with small-minded people.

She needed to get back to the village. Sara was alone and only Susan had the keys to lock the Agency up completely. She and the Vicar left together.

But things down below were also stirring. David Tanner was standing in the middle of his father-in-law's main room, aghast at what the man was telling him. Out of breath, talking at high octane speed, Malcolm Fisher had been liberal with the truth to say the least. Farr had barged into his place of work he claimed, had assaulted one of his customers and threatened him. His daughter was so confused because of the stress, she had inadvertently sacked him.

As before, David Tanner's fury was bravado-fuelled. Having said for so long he would like to meet Farr in a fair fight, and having demonstrated—however pathetically—his mettle in such an arena, he felt obliged, for familial reasons now, to engage in combat against Farr once more. With an odd visage of facial fury, he stormed out of the house and got into his car, reversing out of his father-in-law's driveway and speeding quite unnecessarily towards the tarred pathway leading up to the mountain. The distance between house and pathway was only a hundred yards and he would need to brake to turn the first corner.

But in that short distance, he sped past Susan coming down the other side of the mountain from the Church route and she saw David's car zipping past her at a hell of a pace.

'What the hell does he think he's doing?' she yelled to herself and came to an abrupt halt.

The surprise of what she had just seen forced her out of the car and Vicar Redd joined her—equally surprised.

'Was that David?' he asked.

But Susan was more interested in where the car was headed. In that direction there could only be one place. As she was thinking on that, she saw her father come out of his house and stare towards the mountain. He was smiling—so unlike her father.

Two and two make four.

She marched over to where Malcolm stood and confronted him.

'What the hell have you said to him?' But Malcolm stood defiant. His sneering look to her merely made her angry. She grabbed his shirt—not quite as physical as Jack's effort but just as telling. 'I said—what did you tell him? Where's he gone?'

'To do what you should have done. Sort Farr out. If you'd been thinking as a wife instead of God-knows-what, you'd've done that yourself today. Now your husband will do it instead.' He brushed her hand away and returned to his home.

Susan was, for once, out of answers. If it hadn't been for the presence of the Vicar, she would have remained standing there, transfixed with nowhere to turn. Her grief was evident. He came to her and put his hands on her shoulder. She lowered her head.

'David's going up to deal with Jack—Jack will kill him.'

Vicar Redd wasted no time. He pointed to his car and ordered her to get in. At that moment, Sara arrived. She was slightly miffed to say the least.

'I've locked up—I had to use the spare key… what's wrong?'

'Sara—get your car and follow us up to Greenacres—David's gone up to fight Jack.'

'Christ,' said Sara—and then looked to the Vicar with downcast eyes. She ran back into the village to get her own car which Adam had used to get to work. Susan got into Vicar Redd's car and he was already in first gear when she shut her door. With some speed and accuracy, the Vicar charged after the foolhardy David Tanner.

Jack drank the last gulp of his tea and breathed out heavily. Earlier that day, he had been famished—now it was as much as he could do just to force the one round of ham sandwich down him. The unpleasantness of the café incident had really stretched his nerves and he waited for the inevitable consequence—which he knew would come. It was just a question of whom came to dispense it. Malcolm Fisher probably would contact the local police and demand they serve Jack with some kind of restraining order—not to come anywhere near the village. Maybe the Edmunds family would claim assault in spite of the provocation Steffan had given Jack in front of witnesses. He rose from the table and put the cup and dinner plate on the side of the sink and turned the tap on to wash up— when he stopped and listened. He could hear the car coming up the mountain even from this distance. Whoever was driving it was going way too fast. There are only two stretches of straight road where the driver can go fast—right at the base of the mountain and at the last stretch leading towards Greenacres. Every part of the road between is short and winding. It makes no sense to gun the car at speed because you have to slow and turn. Go too fast and you stand the chance of crashing it into the banks—as Doctor Sandler found to his cost the day he saw Joe Farr's body being used as a mass insect barbecue. Jack went to the main room and looked out of the window.

Too fast, thought Jack—which means it can't be the police. In the approaching darkness he could see lights shining through the forest even before the car itself could be seen. Then he heard the hot water tap still running so he returned to the kitchen and as he turned it off he heard a screeching stop, a door being slammed and someone shouting. *'FARR!'* He'd heard that yell before.

Ah, thought Jack, the voice of an irate Banker. It didn't occur to him that Malcolm would send his son-in-law up to do the deed.

Jack left the house and stood on his porch. David was standing by the gate. Clearly he had come here as soon as he had arrived home—he was still dressed smartly—not completely in his Banker suit, he was minus the jacket and tie—but smart black trousers, smart black shoes and crisp white, ironed shirt. Not really dressed for a fight but here he was and ready to be aggressive. Jack waited for him to make the first move.

David stayed on the other side of the gate but his face was florid red and his breathing was erratic—a man who had steeled himself to do an unpleasant job.

'You just don't get it, do you, Farr?' asked David, trying to sound impressive. 'You wander back here, uninvited, unwelcome, a social pariah—you cause trouble when it moves you, you push yourself on people who would rather not want to see you again—like my wife, and yet you still come back for more.'

Jack doubted very much David had heard that from Susan—if he knew her at all, he would have bet David's Banking pension that Susan would have ripped him a new hole for what he had done that day. No—this was the Gospel according to Malcolm Fisher. Besides, there was the business of the house-sale to be considered. Susan would never have gone into that out of pure sentiment. Not with his father anyway.

Before he had a chance to reply, another car came up the hill. Driven much more carefully around the bends but, in the last stretch, with urgency. He recognised it. Vicar Redd, it seemed, was to join in the proceedings. The car was parked up behind David's and to Jack's surprise, Susan got out first.

She reached the gate just as David had passed through and walked up to where Jack was standing. He stood below the porch level but was still a few inches taller than Jack.

'David, what the hell do you think you're doing? Get back here now,' screamed Susan. Her usual self-control not as apparent as it had been earlier, thought Jack.

David turned to her and pointed his finger. 'I'm dealing with the man who assaulted your father, Susan,' he yelled back. 'The man who beat up a customer and intimidated everyone who was in your father's shop. Why you can't see that I do not know.'

'I was there, David. What happened was father's fault. Now stop being so bloody stupid and come away from there before you get thrashed.' Nice one, Susan, thought Jack.

But David would not be pulled away—not having come this far. His masculinity was on the line. It having already been diminished by his own wife—on the same issue—he felt he had no choice but to see this through. He jabbed his finger at Jack, the expression on his face was intended to frighten—but instead only made Jack smile.

'You stay away from the village, Farr. I know you have reason to come back and I know it involves my wife. God knows why she got herself involved in it but you stay away from her as well. You can sell this shit-pile using another estate agent.'

Not bad, thought Jack. A fairly good attempt at trying to be hard. He stood still. How easy it would be for him to sort the pontificating weasel who had ruined his life so long ago—and he smiled again. He decided to deflate the man simply by using calm words.

'Grow up, Tanner,' he said and he turned away.

And David did exactly the thing Jack had expected he would do. He grabbed Jack's arm and whirled him around, attempting to repeat the same physical action he had enjoyed partial success with a week earlier.

But Jack was not jet-lagged today. He was not tired and nor was he jaded by being back in a community which oppressed him. This time, he was ready.

David swung a punch at Jack's head—and Jack ducked, drove a punch into David's midriff which had the irate Banker doubled over, wheezing in pain. Then he delivered a hard straight punch right at David's nose which sent him hurtling backwards a few steps, tripping over a root and sliding down the soaked muddy garden on his back.

'Not this time, Tanner,' he said and turned away from the assembled group. He made to enter the house.

To Susan's relief, it was very much a scaled down punch he had used on Steffan—maybe for her sake—and so David was not spark out unconscious. But in a way, it was a crueller move. He was now covered in dirty soaking mud. To David, his clothes were the status he enjoyed in his work-place. He wore his Banking suit the way real heroes wear medals earned in war. His spectacles, which he had not removed before he had attacked Jack, were now askance on his face—giving him a comical appearance. There was blood running down the lower half of his face. Susan couldn't tell if it was from his nose or mouth but he spluttered the blood out. There was never a more confused expression on a man's face, she thought.

And that, she hoped would be that. David wasn't dead nor was he hospital case. Humiliated in front of the one person to whom he had sought to impress always, David had been reduced to something quite pathetic, losing any kind of lingering respect in her eyes, if any indeed still lingered. He saw the Vicar standing behind his wife, slowly shaking his head out of sympathy—but holding the view that this entire piece of drama was all David's own doing.

Susan breathed out, relieved. 'Right, David,' she said, a sound of shamed crowing in her voice, 'Congratulations. Now that you have proved you're not the Rocky Rambo of Cwmhyfryd you can return to the place where you belong… *JACK, LOOK OUT!'*

Without turning to her, without pause, Jack dropped to the porch floor, landing on his hands and tips of his toes. Susan would never have screamed such a warning if it weren't serious and Jack reacted accordingly. As he landed, he heard a 'thud' noise above him. He looked up—and there, embedded into the wooden frame of the door, his father's axe shook. David, as he clambered to his feet, had laid his hand upon the axe Jack had used to chop away the remaining roots of the tree trunk the day before. In his exhausted state, Jack had negligently forgotten to return the axe to its proper place—something his father would have raised hell over. David picked the axe up and hurled it at Jack's head. If it hadn't been for Susan's cry, it would have struck him in the head. There was an inch and a micro second in it between where Jack lay now and death.

'Dear God,' breathed out a shocked Vicar Redd. Susan didn't speak. Her hand was still at her mouth, her eyes widened in fear, for she knew exactly what was going to happen next.

Jack sprang to his feet and crouched—he stared at the hapless David who didn't know what was going to happen next. There was a look of absolute ferocity on Jack's face—he looked like a jungle cat about to pounce on an unsuspecting Okapi. He took two steps and leapt into the air. He dived at least six foot up and Vicar Redd would later swear Jack had cleared at least twelve feet across the garden. 'Oh Christ alive,' he breathed out again.

Jack landed on David—his hands landing on the man's shoulders and head-butted David squarely in his face. David squealed in pain and was thrown backwards over and through the small picket fence. He landed in the gully below the garden level, heavily on his feet and back with no sense of perspective. Jack's own momentum had also carried him over the fence—but his landing came with a forwards roll and then he was on his feet.

What followed was truly sickening for David had no response to the flurry of punches inflicted on him by a furious Jack Farr. As he smashed into the man, Jack could hear yells and screams behind exhorting him to stop what he was doing—but his fury was relentless. He rained down a series of blows even the hardest of men would find difficult to withstand—and David was a long way from being the hard man.

As Jack continued his violent tirade, he was grabbed from behind by the larger and equally powerful Vicar Redd who was now begging Jack to stop. *'YOU'RE KILLING HIM, JACK!'* yelled the Vicar but his pleas had no effect. Jack elbowed him in his belly and threw him aside.

At this interruption, David took advantage. He picked up a branch and swiped it across Jack's head which caused a bloody gash. Not only did this not stop Jack, it infuriated him even more and he continued with the beating. David, having attempted to crawl away on his back, was pinned to the ground, held in place by two trees on either side of him while Jack stood over him, his fists bloodied not only from David's wounds but also from his own. He had connected with David's teeth and even against the tree bark. But when Jack made facial contact David was being pulped into oblivion.

Suddenly, Jack was on the ground, his right hand pinned to the tree by another and a hand grabbing his face. He was about to throw his attacker off when Susan screamed at him. '*JACK PLEASE,*' she begged, '*YOU'RE KILLING HIM!*' Then, imploring, 'Please, Jack.'

Her voice—whether it was soothing as he remembered from way back when they were lovers, or when it was commanding as it had been in the café, was always something Jack would listen to. She lay over his body, her face just an inch from his, their noses almost touching, her eyes wet from fear of what he was doing to her husband. Jack stared up at her—his own eyes wide from now really seeing what he had done. She squeezed his face again. The scene seemed to freeze—he nodded to her and the brawl was over.

She released his hand, used his chest to push herself off his body and rushed from him. Vicar Redd was back on his feet and struggling to help David to his feet. But David was betwixt consciousness and being completely out of it. Susan reached them both and took up the strain. She moved under David's left armpit and supported his lax body. Between them, she and the Vicar carried David out of the gully. Jack did not attempt to get to his feet. This assault had exhausted him. He raised his head and saw, standing on the concrete pathway, another woman. He narrowed his eyes and saw her face.

It was the face of the woman who had screamed, victoriously, into his face telling him Susan was in love with David Tanner—the same face Jack remembered coming briefly to him when David had punched him last week before he lost consciousness. The look on her face was far from victorious now. Her hands were at her mouth, her eyes widened from the shock of seeing a fellow human being absolutely trashed and bloodied. David was almost beyond recognizable. Blood poured from his nose and mouth, and even at this primary glance, Sara could see he was not only spitting blood but teeth as well.

She was ordered to open the back of the Vicar's car and then to get her own car out of the drive. She told them she would ring for an Ambulance because, God knows, David needed one. But the Vicar said no—that he would transport David to the Heath Hospital in Cardiff. Getting an ambulance up here would take too long—and getting it up the winding mountain path would prove near impossible. He and Susan gently piled David into the back of his car and they climbed in.

Sara moved her car away from where it was parked so the Vicar could reverse out of the circle designed for this purpose. It took ten minutes for the three cars to be rearranged so the Vicar could drive down the hill but they did it. Susan then ordered Sara to follow them to the Hospital. The Vicar sped down the path with more urgency than he had used coming up.

Sara now managed to get her car onto the path and pointed down the hill. The last thing she saw before she drove away was the sight of Jack Farr standing by the path, drenched in mud and dirt, blood over his filthy top, hands clenched, covered in blood and mud. The expression on his face was one of total bewilderment. She then drove away, going too fast and was forced to brake as she reached the first bend.

Slowly, order took over the area. Silence resumed. Night noises started up again. The animals saw the human amble with uncomfortable movements towards his place of abode, with a confused gait, a look of pain on his face as if he did not really understand what had happened to him. They had seen such expressions on humans before.

He made it to the door and stared up at the axe. It looked to them as if he was about to remove it but instead entered the abode and the door closed.

Chapter 22

The Longest Night

'He has a fractured skull, a troubling swelling around both eyes. His nose will require constructive surgery as will his jaw lines. He has lost many teeth and he must have bitten his tongue during the assault. His ribs are either cracked or broken. His left wrist is broken as are both his ankles. He will be here for some time, Mrs Tanner.'

Doctor Ramjeh Singh had given her the news she had dreaded to hear but really it was nothing less than she had expected. He had asked her if he had been in a mob fight but she refused to answer.

It was now nearly two o'clock in the morning. The Vicar was still on the premises somewhere, in search for something for them both to eat. He had driven at some impressive speeds, taking the bends with expertise—which surprised Susan. It would have taken her at least half an hour longer to get to the City Hospital. He drove straight to the Ambulance Bay and, maybe it was because of his clerical garb, when he shouted for assistance, the two Ambulance crews ran to his aid. A stretcher was brought out when they saw what was in the car and David was taken away. Susan herself was almost on the verge of collapse and had to be helped in by the Vicar.

Sara waited with her for an hour before telling Susan there was nothing she could do and went home. Susan didn't mind. She couldn't face a talkative companion tonight—and Sara was never at a loss for something to say. There was no doubt what she would have been talking about had she remained. Susan thanked her for her help and Sara left. After that, it was a waiting game.

It took quite a few hours before they were finally seen by a Doctor who enquired as to who she was, was she related to the patient—what had happened to him etc. Nothing of any relevant importance was said beyond what the Hospital was doing for David at this moment. Susan and the Vicar sat in the reception room and waited for the news.

Hours later, Doctor Singh arrived and asked if Susan was the wife of the patient and once confirmed, he took her aside into an office and explained what was going to happen. The Vicar said he would go looking for something to eat. After outlining the extent of David's injuries the Doctor then told her David would be placed in an ICU and would be monitored throughout the night.

Exhausted, she sat in the office alone and her mind was a blank. She needed time alone to think but the office was not the place to do it so she left and went looking for the Vicar.

Instead, she saw her father. He was coming into the reception area, his face red with anger and striding towards her. They both walked towards each other, neither slowing down.

'Have you seen what that monster has done to your husband...?' he began—and was met with a powerful stinging slap across the face from Susan. It was loud enough to alert the few people who were in that area. Hospital Staff moved to a phone just in case they needed to call Security and relatives of other patients awaiting their own gloomy news watched as this couple had a vicious row in front of them.

'What is in that room is entirely down to you, you stupid man,' Susan seethed. 'What you told him about the business in the café—what the hell did you think he was going to do? He already believed he could take Jack in a fight. What did you think he was going to do? Have a bloody friendly "Let's-clear-the-air" conversation with him?'

Malcolm Fisher was in no mood to be berated by his own daughter and he tore back. 'Your husband is lying there—looking like he's been trampled on by a herd of bulls—and you're defending the man who put him there? What kind of wife are you?'

But Susan gave better than she had taken. 'David is lucky he's not going be charged with murder. He hurled an axe at Jack's head. One inch—one bloody second—and David would now be somewhere else talking to the Cops and facing prison. And that's down to you, you bloody arrogant old fool.'

For a moment, Malcolm was about to say "Good riddance" but he held back for fear of suffering his daughter's already demonstrated wrath. Also, Vicar Redd was now standing just a few feet away from them, holding onto two cups of tea and two bars of chocolate. The look on his face gave Malcolm the notion that he would not be supported here.

Susan backed away and took one of the cups. She sipped at it and Malcolm then let fly with another missile. 'We'll see what the police *do* have to say about this assault. Sara told me what she'd seen. They'll sort Farr out.'

Damn you, Sara, thought Susan—but walked back to her father.

'There won't be any police action, Father—I doubt David will be pressing charges—the whole thing was his fault anyway. He could've walked away any time. I told him to. The police won't be involved.'

'Oh yes they will be,' said Malcolm. 'I called them to go after Farr before I came here. They're already up there I expect—arresting him.'

Susan stood still—aghast at what she had just heard. Now her face had turned red with anger. 'You... *IDIOT!*' she yelled and threw her cup of hot tea at Malcolm's chest. He screamed and she walked away, past the shocked Nurses and relatives. 'Vicar,' she yelled as she strode away, 'I need you.'

And so, it was another heart racing speedy journey back to the village. Susan kept saying 'I don't believe it. Will this night ever bloody end?' He maintained his attention on the road which was absolutely necessary at the speed he was driving. On this road, there were no lines, no Cat's Eyes and no street lights. You had the car lights and your own eyes to do this trip and he was all attention. He desperately wanted Susan top calm down but said nothing.

They reached Cwmhyfryd at three thirty and he dropped Susan off at her house. She demanded she would deal with the police, if they were at Greenacres, alone. She got into her own car and drove. After just a hundred yards she stopped and wound the window down. She gulped down the cool night air and took time to breathe. No more panic, no more speeding. Let's take this last part of the journey in a calm way. So, accordingly, she drove the long and winding pathway in the prescribed manner.

When she turned the last corner and was on the final straight, she groaned. Ahead of her was a single police car, parked in the circle. She drove up and slowly climbed out, listening for any noises of protest. Nothing. Silence in the night. But not alone. Hidden in the trees just twenty yards from where she stood by her car, she was unaware that she was being watched. A figure pulled back a branch and saw her as she headed towards the house.

She walked to the doorway and saw the axe was still embedded into the door frame. She put her hand on it and tried to shake it. It was in deep and did not give any way at her hand. She entered the house—the door was partially open. She walked, almost on tiptoe to where she heard the voices. Finally, she came to the kitchen. When she looked across the kitchen, she saw a tall bald-headed police officer leaning against a wall unit—he had three stripes on his tunic. A Sergeant. They sent a Sergeant. She closed her eyes and entered.

The conversation she had eavesdropped on came to a stop. The Sergeant looked at her—surprised at this interruption. Jack was standing to her left, also leaning against a wall unit. He was dressed in a flimsy bath gown, barefooted, and had clearly taken a bath. His hair was still wet and he smelled freshly washed. She looked to the Sergeant and coughed.

'Good evening,' she stammered. 'Uh... I am Susan Tanner, uh... my husband... David...uh... started the fight you are investigating and I know my father gave the police the wrong idea of what happened here tonight and at the café earlier yesterday. I believe he intends to press charges against Mr Farr... uh... and I am here, on behalf of my husband and my father to tell you that no charges will indeed be made, or pressed.'

Silence followed. And then, the bald Sergeant picked up a mug of tea and said, 'Go on, Jack.'

Jack continued with his story about his first year working on the Oklahoman farm, riding horses and steering cattle. The conversation was friendly and the Police Sergeant then related his own story of how his four daughters were costing him a fortune with their own horse riding activities.

'Bloody stables, food, equipment. Dear God, they must think I'm the South Wales Police Commissioner the way they spend my money on those damn things. Badminton trials and everything. I'm working all the damn hours just to pay for horseshoes. You know how often those damn things need horseshoes?'

Jack laughed—and Susan felt she should join in as this wasn't quite the conversation she was expecting but if they were laughing, then maybe the charges would be set aside. The Sergeant drank his tea and then looked at Susan.

'Hullo Susan,' he said, 'How you doing?'

Now—*that* she hadn't expected. What was happening here? There was no anger from Jack. No threat from the police officer. And that voice... She stared at him—and he smiled. Hold on, she thought. I... know...

'Cenydd,' she blurted out. 'Cenydd Thomas.' She smiled, more out of relief than recognition. Cenydd Thomas—a fellow schoolmate of hers—and Jack's—and now he was here in police uniform and a Sergeant. 'Good God,' she continued, 'You're a Cop.'

'For twenty years, almost. Was promoted to Sergeant a year ago.'

The relief was now palpable from Susan. She laughed out loud. 'You're bald. What happened to your hair?' You had a mass of ginger curls the last time I saw you.'

He pointed to his head and laughed with her. 'Three marriages, four daughters and a stress-related job is what caused this,' he said. 'You'd go bald if you'd seen what I have to put up with.'

And so the conversation went. Him telling them what he had done in the twenty years absence and Susan—with certain restrictions telling him her story.

And then it was business.

*

'I was on my way home when the call went out—a fight of a serious nature had taken place in Cwmhyfryd—up the mountain—and a certain Jack Farr had damn near killed a man. Well, I thought, I remember a man called Jack Farr so I called my station and told them I would deal with it. Your father, it was, actually Susan, who gave us that version of events. I just got another side of it all from Jack—so what's your version?

Susan gave her version—the untarnished truth of the cafe incident involving her father, Steffan's contribution—and here, Sergeant Thomas laughed because he knew Steffan in a professional capacity—and then the scrap outside this house, including the axe-throwing stunt. He listened, with interest. Then he stood and folded his arms. Now he was back on duty.

'So, what you're telling me,' he intoned, 'is you're not pressing charges for what Mr Farr did to your husband. Mr Farr has already confirmed he won't be pressing charges against Mr Tanner for the axe business. A... let's see... a disagreement which got slightly out of hand but no more to it than that. Is that it?' Yes, said Susan.

'The injuries to your husband...'

'Were entirely of his own doing. It was his fault.'

And silence in the kitchen while Sergeant Thomas assimilated this information and wrote it down. He looked up, still smiling.

'So I can go back to the station and tell them no further action?' Yes, said Susan.

'Anything which doesn't require me to spend the night on writing up a report of this nature will suit me—and the station so...' He closed his notebook and smiled again. Then he placed his policeman's cap on his head. 'Time to go,' he said.

Jack and Susan walked him to the door and watched him get into his car—with Sergeant Thomas warning Jack to keep out of trouble. Jack walked with Sergeant Thomas to his car and a few more memories were shared en route and then he drove away, waving at them.

Susan smiled, waved back at Sergeant Thomas and breathed out with relief.

She leaned against the door, relieved it hadn't gone beyond where it was and no official action would be happening tonight. Not against Jack or her husband.

Jack stood where the axe protruded from the door frame. The proximity of head and axe confirmed just how close he had been to being killed. Her head lowered, from exhaustion, from shame.

'I am so… sorry,' she said and looked up at him. Such sadness in her voice. Such sincerity in the sadness, acknowledging the hurt and pain she had inflicted on Jack. Whether it was from the afternoon fight in the café earlier or her husband's insanity here later—or the tragedy from their shared past Jack didn't know—and he wouldn't ask—but it demanded a response. He moved towards her until they were almost face to face.

'Cup of tea?' he asked.

*

Twenty minutes later, they were both sitting on the swing sofa on the porch, covered by a thick warm blanket and drinking tea from Joe's work flask. It held at least six cup's worth. He also brought out some biscuits and a few cake rolls. In the cold night air, they were rather comfortably set up and relaxed.

Jack had told her about his days at the farm and how he'd learned to become a "Cowboy". Susan told him about how she had progressed through the Bank routes and had been asked to set up a couple of local Estate Agencies in the remote valleys of Cwmhyfryd, Pentre Haf and Brangwyn as those areas were being pencilled in for massive home expansions. Already in the past ten years, smaller Industrial Estates had sprung up nearer those villages and those with far sighted eyes could see a small booming arrangement of joining those places up.

Susan felt it necessary to tell Jack the extent of David's injuries and he nodded his head. Whether it was an acknowledgement of what she was telling him or his regretting how far he had taken the beating Susan couldn't tell—and she wouldn't ask. She could not sit in judgement of what he had done, not when the axe which nearly killed him was a just a few feet away from her, still embedded into the door-frame.

She turned her attention to the large rocking chair. She gently rocked it with her hand. 'Is this…?' she began and Jack laughed. 'Dad's,' he said. 'As far as I can make out it's the only thing he kept from the old place. He made it himself.'

'It's weather-worn a bit,' she said. Jack nodded and told her there was no way he could get it into the house—it was too big. He said probably his Dad had wanted it that way. He could see his Dad sitting in the thing at night even when the weather was hard rain or cold winter. Dad befriended all the elements.

And then there was silence between them.

Silence between friends is not uncomfortable if they are physically in each other's company. Over the phone it would be difficult as you can't see the other's face and you don't know what they are doing or thinking. Face to face, keeping company, it does not matter. Jack felt he had nothing more to say at this time and small talk is worse than silence. Susan, on the other hand, *did* want to say something—and was measuring just how far she could go in breaking this news to someone she had betrayed and had only just become reacquainted with.

'I'm going to divorce David,' she said.

He looked at her—and remained silent. This was her life and he had no right to enquire how happy she had been since… that day. Besides, it would simply rustle up the unpleasant memory and they had thus far avoided that.

She continued. 'It's not something I just decided—not because of what happened today or what he did last week. The truth is—I haven't loved David for a long time. We live almost separate lives now anyway. His life is all about promotions and status—having bloody business lunches and sucking up to the Bank Management.'

She paused. And then, 'He's a joke in the village. Everybody still calls him "the Englishman"—he's from Cheshire. He's never integrated with them and they don't want him to. The marriage hasn't…' and there she faltered.

Jack poured her yet another cup of tea and she gladly accepted it, grateful to Jack for not making her take this news any further. She dunked her oatmeal biscuit into the cup—the first time she had done so in years—not the sort of thing David approved of, you see, she told him, and the silliest laugh came from her.

The light was taking over the darkness of the night and she yawned. 'Thank God it's Sunday,' she said. 'I couldn't have gone into work today—not the way I feel.'

Another pause. 'I'll set Sara straight about last night and what has come from it. I think there have been enough wrong versions about it. By mid-day, everybody in the village will know what happened last night. They may as well know the real truth.'

She slowly moved the thick blanket away and stood up. She stretched and yawned. Jack watched her and knew… even after all this time… that he was in the company of the only girl he had ever loved and would ever love. No-one else had even come close. He moved his side of the blanket away and stood up next to her. Together, face to face, they just stared at each other.

Then they both walked into the house.

And in all the time they had been together, they were not aware of their being kept under close observation from the figure lurking in the forest just a hundred yards away from them. The figure did not move as they entered the house—but waited to see what would happen next. Would the Tanner woman come back out and drive away? Would they go to the main room and watch TV? The figure stared at the house.

All the lights from within the house were turned off and no-one came out.

So…

Chapter 23

Sara's Night at Home

It would be fair to say Sara Phillips had had a poor night, lying there next to a snoring Adam and her thinking about the events of the past few hours. It began with Susan not being at the Agency to lock up. There were spare keys for the outer doors but only Susan had the keys to lock everything inside the office up—and set the alarm system. So Sara locked the outer doors come shutdown and went over to Bevan Road to find Susan. She—Sara—had places to go and people to visit and was in a hurry. When she got to Bevan Road, she saw the spat between Susan and her father. Susan—in a flurry—ordered her to follow them up to Jack's house to stop David doing… well.

Susan and the Vicar sped away and Sara got into her car. And the damn thing wouldn't start. 'Bloody starting motor,' she screamed and Malcolm Fisher came back out. She got out of the car and opened up the bonnet. 'What's going on, Mr Fisher?' she asked. He gave her a reduced sketch of what had happened at the café. Farr had attacked him and a customer and now David was going to sort him out. He was fairly crowing at the sound of it.

Sara managed to get the car back to life and sped after Susan. Blimey, she thought, David against Farr—that won't end well. And her prognostication proved all too true. She arrived at Greenacres just as the fight was finished and David was being carried to the Vicar's car. If anybody looked as though he was standing on the porch of Death's Door, it was David. She had never seen a thrashing like it. From that point, everything happened so fast and the next thing she could remember she was on the country lane taking her to Cardiff City's Heath Hospital. The Vicar was already out of sight and she arrived almost an hour after they had. It took her half an hour to find Susan. Too late, she realized, she had left her phone at the Agency and wasn't able to use it to call Susan, Adam or the girls to let them know what the situation was.

Eventually, she found them both. Susan apprised her of what had happened at the fight—including the axe business—and waited with Susan for the medical report. But close to midnight, she decided she'd had enough and wanted to get home. Her family must be wondering what had happened to her. So she left and told Susan she'd call in the morning—and thinking "She'll be a widow by then if I don't miss my guess."

Sara drove home and came in after one thirty—only to find Claire, Tommy and Catrin were still watching TV and Adam hadn't even come home from the pub. He came in ten minutes after she did and he stunk of a boozy night with the lads. God knows where they had gone to but they had sunk more than a few pints and Adam was woozy, bumping into the furniture and laughing at nothing in particular.

The laughing stopped when Sara told them all about David Tanner being at Death's Door so be careful how you speak to Susan tomorrow. She may be grieving.

Adam breathed out. He shook his head and said, 'That man is a monster. He should be bloody locked up.'

It was Catrin who came to Jack's aid. No, she told them, it wasn't his fault. Mr Fisher had started it all by talking to Mr Farr in such a manner that he had to defend himself. Then that moron Steffan Edmunds butted in and Mr Farr had to deal with him. The pillock younger Edmunds brother tried to glass him but he mucked that up and Mr Farr only grabbed Mr Fisher because of how he spoke to him. But Auntie Susan then came to Mr Farr's aid by telling me to serve him and then throwing the Edmunds out of the café and banning them for life and then she sacked her father who walked off in a strop.

All in one breath.

And that tirade flavoured the discussion from then on. Catrin would not allow her father to diss Mr Farr as Mr Farr hadn't done anything wrong.

'You don't know, girl, you have no idea what he did,' said her father. Ah, replied his elder daughter, but she did. Auntie Susan told her about the fights Mr Farr had with Mr Edmunds senior, her own father, some boxer called Tyler and a bunch of other guys including her own Uncle. And he beat them all and that was why Mr Farr was so disliked by the so-called tough guys of Cwmhyfryd—because he was better than they were. And now Mr Tanner has found out exactly the same thing. Pillock, she ended the second tirade with.

And then the younger daughter told them all how she and Mr Farr spent a pleasant half hour having a conversation by the Death Well.

WHAT?

And he hadn't been nasty to her or to anybody in the village and she thought he was a nice man.

Well that went down like cold sick. Her mother remonstrated, her father shouted but then he was over the limit and he always shouted whenever he was over the limit. Catrin smiled. Tommy just stared, aghast at how the peaceful evening was turning into a war zone.

Adam Phillips ended the discussion with, 'Look at us—look at the village. We've had more bloody arguments and fights in the three weeks he's been here than we've had the entire time he's been away. He comes back and we're all at each other's throats. The man is a bloody monster. He should roast in Hell' And if he hadn't walked into the door when he was ending the discussion it might have made more of an impact—instead, it only made the girls laugh and Sara groan. God, she thought, I've got to sleep next to that tonight.

End of discussion, she said. They had Church tomorrow. She asked Tommy if he was performing any functions with Vicar Redd and he replied it was Jason's turn tomorrow but he would still be at the Church by ten o'clock ready for morning Worship. She then told them to turn the TV off and go to bed which they did. It had been a long night.

And so, lying next to the snoring Adam, Sara thought about what had happened up at Greenacres, thought about David Tanner and the absolute thrashing he'd walked into. About Mr Fisher and what would happen at the café if Susan didn't let him back in. She thought about Jack Farr—who, with the knockout blow delivered to the supposedly hardest man of the village suddenly put him far above anybody else's desire to take him on—and then, his treatment of an older man by hauling him over the counter and of how the girl who had once jilted him had come to his aid in front of witnesses.

This wasn't panning out the way she thought it would.

Adam snorted and shouted a name. God knows where he is now, wondered Sara. Eventually, she drowned out her husband's snoring with a pair of ear-muffs and found sleep waiting for her.

Chapter 24

Revelation Time

'You didn't,' exclaimed Sara when Susan told her where she had spent the night.

'Oh stop being so silly, Sara,' said Susan. 'I slept in the spare bedroom and Jack slept in his own bed. We had breakfast and then I came back down. We talked about nothing in particular except stuff that didn't count. Just banal stuff. I've already been onto the Hospital and they say David had a peaceful night—not surprised with the stuff they put into him but he was still out of it when I called so I'll call later today.'

'Are you going to visit him?' asked a still shocked Sara. She didn't like where this was going.

'Why should I? He is out of it like I said. Even if he were conscious he wouldn't be able to speak. And besides, the way I'm feeling about him now I don't really want to be near him.'

'Su—that man almost killed him. Your husband nearly died.'

'And if I hadn't shouted out, Jack would be dead now and David would be locked up in a police cell waiting to be charged with murder. He had no damn business doing what he did, Sara—it was Dad who put the fire into him and he's so far up his own backside over Jack he feels like he has to prove himself. Because of a lucky sucker punch, he thought he could do it again—this time face-to-face. Well look how that turned out. Idiot is lucky he's still alive.'

Susan poured herself another cup of tea. Sara had arrived at her house to enquire how David was faring and was fairly shocked to see Susan just coming down from the mountain in her car. They entered the house, Sara settled down and Susan put the kettle on. Her conversation about the previous night was so calm and steady, Sara wondered if Susan had actually grasped the seriousness of the situation and asked if she's gone up to the mountain house to sort Farr out. That was when Susan told her about the cosy conversation they'd had under a blanket and a bright moon, with tea and biscuits and then back inside to bed—

separate beds. Sara opened her mouth and it took quite a few seconds for her response to sound out.

And so an awkward silence came over the two friends. Sara was nervous of saying anything which would upset the apple cart of their friendship but she couldn't help the expression of judgement on her face when Susan told her about where she's spent the night. Especially as she seemed to be almost... jovial... about last night's incident.

Susan then brought Sergeant Cenydd Thomas into the story and how nobody was going to be arrested or charged—just formal warnings to all concerned—including her father whom she was going to talk to after tea break.

And then she told Sara she intended to divorce David.

You could have heard a pin drop in Tokyo.

'Because of *FARR?*' shouted Sara.

'No,' said Susan, quite calmly. 'Because of David.' She then spent some time outlining her personal grievances against her husband and his recent behaviour but then compounded it with the way their marriage had trawled out over the years. There was no love—at least, not from her—and David did not notice how low the state of their marriage had sunk. There was no point in holding onto something that she believed had never really been there from moment one, she told her friend. All of which shocked Sara.

So how had it come to this? The truth was, Susan confessed, the marriage was a mistake from the start and had only happened because of what she had done to Jack and she had felt "obliged" to do the thing she had more or less imposed on herself to prove that what she had done was the right thing. She knew the same week they married she had made a colossal mistake—but by then the deed was done and by the time they had returned to Cwmhyfryd, Jack had gone, Mrs Farr was dead and the father and twins were just about being spared jail because of mitigating circumstances.

And how did it all happen? Susan had progressed upwards in social status in her late teens by the company she had moved into at the Bank while Jack was working the farms at Pentre Haf and Brangwyn. By social comparison, he was a corn-chewing yokel while Susan was frequenting the society of older and much more sophisticated males. When the charming and more mature David Tanner came along—a man with charisma and personality—Susan was seeing a wider world beyond the borders of her home village. When Jack was baling hay and smelling of cattle, Susan was attending business meetings and being taken to

154

hotels for weekend parties. Socially, there was no comparison between Jack and the new world she had entered and now Susan was thinking above her own station.

The consequence of this new life had been witnessed by her friends and the inevitable attraction to David was of great interest to them. They waylaid her over the many plus points the dynamic young Banker possessed and for the first time in her life, Susan allowed herself to be swayed by other people's dictates. This pressure was riding over her right up to the day of the nearly wedding to Jack. Her own hen night was injected with how dull life would be with her chosen man while excitement was waiting for her just a few miles away in the City. Promotions, money, a new house, a family, no smelly animals, no dull conversations about the four seasons affecting the work on the farms—and Susan knew they were telling a truth of sorts. It was to her shame she had not discussed these matters with Jack who had already decided he was never going to be a farmer anyway. But the influence of her friends weighed on her and she did what she did.

And calamity followed.

The Tanner marriage, she finally conceded, was a brutal Karma for what she had done to the Farr family and she had been paying back ever since.

'That payment came to an end last night,' she finished. 'After what David did, I can't go on living this lie. We've more or less come to the end anyway—may as well make it official.'

'And then what?' asked Sara, her voice almost scathing, which was quite a brave thing for her to do. 'Marry Farr?'

Which was a mistake. She knew it the moment she had spoken.

For the first time, Susan looked at Sara and steeled her gaze. 'Look,' she said, keeping her anger controlled, 'that's the umpteenth time and it had better be the last that you've referred to him that way—by his surname and with venom in your voice. His name is Jack. If you can't use his first name, don't refer to him at all. And no, I won't be marrying him—Jack wouldn't take me back now if the future of Humanity depended upon it. I am divorcing David because the marriage is dead—it died a long time ago, long before Jack came home, long before this whole bloody mess with Joe Farr was going. I just didn't have the guts to admit it. But I won't tolerate it for another moment. When he regains enough of his senses for me to talk to him, I'll tell him what the situation is. Somehow, I don't think it will come as too much of a shock to him. Understood?'

Sara was defeated—and she felt the defeat personally because she out of all Susan's friends had campaigned on David's behalf—upon his exhortation—to begin the relationship with the beautiful flame-haired girl and Sara—herself envious of the beauty Susan possessed and felt she was sacrificing it to a man whose idea of fashion was whatever gumboots were in vogue that year—wanted so much to be a part of Susan's new world, and maybe, by proxy, to even pick up her own dashing, charismatic and soon-to-be-wealthy man in a three-piece suit, living in a four-bedroomed house, a swimming pool and two cars in the driveway. Such dreams. And what did she get? Adam bloody Phillips and that was only because a baby was on the way.

Sara was so shocked she did not attend Church that morning and called Vicar Redd to apologize, telling him she had gone down with a migraine—not so far from the truth actually.

But then she had to tell Adam, Catrin, Clair and Tommy what Susan had told her. Their reactions were mixed to say the least. Adam swore in front of the girls, expletives he would have walloped another man for had they been spoken in front of his daughters.

'You see?' he ranted at them all. 'Just three bloody weeks back in the village and all hell has been let loose. Fights. Arguments—and now a divorce between two people who have been happily married for twenty years.' Sara did not tell them Susan's own version of that marriage. It would only lead to more outraged rambling. Tommy claimed Susan could not divorce David because she had sworn to be faithful to him—"Till death do you part" he said—and Catrin said that was only true if they had made those vows in Church and Auntie Susan and David had married in a Registry Office. Claire said she thought it was romantic. Adam spat his tea out and said he was going to the pub.

Another sunny day in the Phillips' household, thought Sara. She thought: I wonder what else will happen.

*

In the early part of the same evening, a man living in Brangwyn received a phone call from someone with a peculiar voice asking if he wanted to earn a thousand pounds.

'Sure,' said the man. 'What do I have to do?'

'I want you to kill a man,' said the voice. There was a pause.

'Sure,' said the man. 'Who's the man?'

'Jack Farr,' said the voice.

There was a pause.

'Sure,' said the man.

Chapter 25

The Clay Twins

Andrew and Sean McGregor were colloquially known as the *Clay Twins* to all who knew them. In fact, not only were they were not twins, they weren't even brothers. They were first cousins, born in a blaze of publicity to two sets of twins—twin brothers marrying twin sisters. To add to that wonderful story, both their sons were born on the same day within twenty minutes of each other at the same Hospital and in the same ward. They were the focus of front page tabloids—local and national—and even appeared on a BBC WALES TV morning programme. They were both raised in the same street and when they first attended school, they were dressed in the same clothes and walked into the school holding hands and waving at the many journalists who photographed them.

And their fame lasted for years afterwards as they grew older and found they were famous amongst their own peers. The McGregors were physically bigger than their age group and they were the boys that other boys looked to for local leadership and the girls for boyfriend material—gold status on both counts and the McGregors relished every conscious moment of their notoriety.

The problem of being elevated into such a position where your peers either idolize or adore you is the vanity which attaches itself to that status. The McGregors could handle trouble if it was smaller or at least their equal—but they failed miserably when trouble came in larger sizes or greater numbers and when they were just a year from leaving their hated Comprehensive School, both Andrew and Sean saw their mini-Empire come crashing down when newcomers moved into the area and swiftly took over the area the McGregors lived in. This transferred to their school and their admirers watched, miserably, as both Andrew and Sean were soundly challenged and then thrashed in front of all their mates. Loyalty has a short-life value when that which you have been loyal to for so long loses face and body after one beating. When information relating to their later notorious behaviour was made known to the authorities and the respective parents, they suddenly found themselves out of favour everywhere by everyone. When both Andrew and Sean left school without a single qualification to their names—and with an unsavoury reputation to match—they were cast out into a bigger and badder world where the truth of small fish swimming in bigger ponds suddenly became very relevant.

What made their domestic situation even harder to bear was the destruction of their parents' marriages. One brother ran away with the other brother's wife and the remaining twins refused ever to speak to each other ever again and left the small village of Brangwyn where they had lived for so long. Bereft of family and reputation, both Andrew and Sean decided to fight back. They launched a number of abortive attempts to resurrect their previous status of local "tough guys" and run a criminal Empire based on the successes of their idols—Ronnie and Reggie Kray. In these attempts, both of them proved to be entirely useless. Every attempt failed and was more often than not, dealt with by the local law. For a number of years, post school, every venture resulted in financial loss and even more loss of face. The McGregors were now becoming a local laughing stock.

Until Hywel Parry found them and introduced them to a new, more successful, venture.

The Parry operation was very simple. It simply involved the transport or transference of certain products from one area to another. The operation was successful because Parry ran it spasmodically—not regular enough for any Police Force to notice a pattern—and the geography changed from one location to another. A city, a town, sometimes even just a street if the product was small enough. And it worked because Hywel Parry was careful, methodical and he didn't boast in words or in appearance the nature of his enterprises signalling to anyone in authority that this was a man who was clearly successful in life because he drives a big expensive car or lives in a big expensive house. To all intents and appearances, Hywel Parry was a man living on sickness benefits brought about from working down the mines for so long. He did not live like a man who actually had more than £150,000 squirreled away in a foreign Bank. But that was the truth. Parry estimated another year of this particular enterprise and he would then be able to move away to another country and live the rest of his days in comfort and splendour. Not bad for a man who was still only in his early fifties.

What had complicated the newest Parry operation was the loss of two of his sons who had been caught up in another criminal matter unrelated to the area and the family. They were both sentenced to long terms in jail—and Parry was short of two men who could do the physical work of what was involved. His youngest son—Edgar—knew the McGregors from school—in fact, he was one of those who had idolized them—and he suggested them to his father. Hywel Parry was in an immediate bind as an operation was due to be conducted in Swansea and he needed two extra bodies to assist him. Andrew and Sean were brought in and they proved useful. It was thrust into their minds that their financial gain in this matter was to be kept an absolute secret so no-one would notice the difference in their lives—which currently had them signing on at the Jobcentre in Cardiff. This arrangement suited Andrew and Sean down to the ground.

Three years and a number of successful operations later, the McGregors were now living very comfortable lives—and no-one who mattered—the police or the Benefits Office—were even looking in their directions.

But there came the major operation where more than just two physical activists were required and Hywel Parry had to cast his net wider. The names of Joseph and James Farr was brought to his attention.

Now this was unfortunate timing for the real twins—recently, their mother had tragically died and their father had seemingly given up on life altogether. Their younger brother had run away from home and no-one knew where he had gone and they were both themselves in tricky situations resulting from the fights at the Cwmhyfryd Church. The Judge had accepted the mitigating circumstances of the first fight—the brawl following the marriage debacle and then again when they buried their mother. For some reason, not made known to the public, Joe Farr was completely exonerated from the Court proceedings and both twins were treated lightly by the Court—they were fined a considerable amount of money—which was paid by an outside source—and then released. The problem for them was employment. As a consequence of these fights and the publicity which resulted from them, both twins were sacked from their day jobs and were not allowed to claim any kind of Social Benefits as they were deemed to have been responsible for their own actions. They were jobless, friendless and broke. It had come to a point where they had no choice but to entertain another way to earn money. And—via Hywel Parry—that choice was to enter the world of crime.

Their mother had represented the moral compass which all three sons were raised on—their father represented the physical authority—get it wrong and you will be punished was the dictate. And rarely did the three sons get it wrong. Bereft now of both those parental dictates, James and Joseph felt they had no choice but to spread their considerable wings just to keep themselves alive. When Edgar Parry approached them with a venture 'not altogether legal', both twins decided to jump in. It was to end in tragedy.

Edgar introduced James and Joseph to his father and the McGregors and the plan was set up. This was, in fact, to be the final operation conducted by Hywel Parry which would lead to his official 'retirement'. The operation was more involved than previous operations because it contained materials of a more sensitive nature—involving more than three separate groups and placed in locations over England and Wales. Parry's attention to detail was now well known and his discretion was assured. He planned it, arranged the participations of those who would actively be involved and he set the time and place. Everything was set. It would run over three days and three different locations— no pattern to follow by anyone of a suspicious nature—and away from all domestic and prying eyes. The eventual transfer of these sensitive materials would take place in a small boat factory situated between Brangwyn and Pentre Haf—the nearest drop-off point to his home any of the operations had ever been.

It was that final choice of location which undid the whole deal.

Unbeknownst to Hywel Parry—his very first mistake in all these ventures— the owner of the boat factory had placed inside the unit, motion cameras which picked up everything moving from the smallest rodent running across the work floor to the occasional bird flying across the rafters. This equipment would alert the owner who also had a receiving monitor unit at his home—and so when the operation began with both the Farr twins and the McGregors entering the factory—by key—and walked about the place to ensure all was well, the system alerted the factory owner. He naturally assumed it would be more animal activity—so when he saw these humans—strangers to him—parading around in his factory, he alerted the police who were on to it immediately.

A further complication of that night was the delay on the visiting customers—not from the UK—who had gotten lost on their trip to this backwater place in the Welsh countryside—and were observing travel plans insisted upon by the ever careful Hywel Parry. It gave the police the time and the opportunity to arrange a team ready to go into action.

The deal was still in action when the police arrived—and who were not witnessed arriving by the two McGregors who had been posted to keep watch. It was raining hard that night and both Sean and Andrew decided that as nothing could possibly go wrong, they kept their heads down inside a small tin shack hut and so did not see the rather large team of police officers as they stealthily made their way across muddy land to the factory.

The police struck and pandemonium followed. The visitors had brought with them their own reinforcements, in case of local trouble, all of whom were armed. A team of eighteen police officers, unarmed and not expecting trouble of this magnitude, were fired upon and three were killed, four wounded. Hywel Parry attempted to run. He successfully eluded the invading Police Force from inside the factory and had safely reached the exterior gate when both James and Joseph came crashing out of the factory on their large motor bike. Unable to maintain balance because of the rush exit and slipping on the muddy embankment, the bike careered into Hywel Parry and took him to the bridge wall. He was pinned against the bike and the wall and when they reversed away, he was left behind, screaming in agony. Two police cars gave chase to the Farr's and it ended when James attempted to crash through what he thought was a wooden fence—but was in fact a wall made of solid stone. Both twins were killed instantly.

When it was over, the McGregors were found shivering from cold and cowering from fear in their tin shack and were arrested.

The eventual result of the very long trial which followed months after the showdown was confused as far as the principle actors were concerned—mainly because of how the facts were presented in the Court. Simply put, there was so little to go on apart from what materials which were seized at the scene—the ownership of which was denied by those who were there. Hywel Parry was crippled from the neck down—he would never again function as a normal human being. He was found guilty but because of his physical situation, the Court deemed it unnecessary to jail him. No prison sentence could hurt him the way he had hurt himself in this venture. He was placed in a secure abode, cared for by his son, Edgar, who had been given a suspended sentence. The foreign visitors pleaded ignorance of the entire proceedings and told the authorities they had been asked to visit a mutual friend, not knowing what the meeting was really all about. Because of their poor English, it took weeks to get an appropriate interpreter to negotiate the interrogations. They were all found guilty and sentenced to life in prison—to be deported from the UK when their sentence was served in, probably, eight years.

The precise roles of the two men who had been killed on the motor bike could not be ascertained and their deaths, though regrettable, were put down as "Misadventure". Their personal histories were known to the Court and their father had been informed.

Because Hywel Parry had been very meticulous about this and previous operations, there was nothing consigned to paper as far as detail was concerned. Therefore, there was nothing to tie the McGregors in with anything else which may have occurred before. Their own Brief stated they had been employed by the man Parry to act as lookout on this one-off operation and had not known of the seriousness of their involvement. The Judge was aware of the previous records against the two accused and they were sentenced to two years. This was the longest sentence they had ever received and it proved almost catastrophic for Andrew.

Andrew was the toughest out of the two cousins—or so he claimed—and he attempted to assert his position inside jail. It took just four fights for him to rethink his claims and from there serve the rest of his sentence in near solitude. By the time they came out of prison, Andrew bore small facial resemblance to the man he was when they were sent inside. His nose had been broken twice, his jaw once, he had developed a cauliflower ear and his left eye was damaged.

The problem was the experience and the time they both served had still not proved to them that crime was not their forte and they continued along the lines of trying to prove to the populace they really were the local versions of hard-line criminals. Every single criminal venture failed and when they were finally caught on yet another abortive run, photographs of them showing them in the same posed styles as the notorious pictures of the Kray twins were circulated in the media. This time, there was no sympathetic Judge or Court to let them off— the crime itself was not so serious but their constant attempts to walk this life had annoyed those who had to continually deal with it.

Judge Alun McCartney at Cardiff Crown Court was scathing in his summing up about the career choices made by the McGregors and the fact they had been so pathetically disastrous at it. He drew particular attention to the submitted photographs and the link they had tried to forge between them and the more successful Krays.

'You are useless at crime,' he told them. 'Every venture you have engaged upon has ended in disaster and yet again, we find you in this Court, wasting tax-payers money, my time, the Court's time and the sterling efforts made on your behalf by others to keep you both on the straight and narrow. We see from these photographs that you have modelled yourselves on two other notorious individuals who were, for a measure of time, more successful in their careers than you have been. Such role models you have chosen to emulate. They failed and died in prison—it would appear you are attempting to do the same thing. From such a wonderful start...' and the Judge held up the old newspaper clippings submitted by the McGregor Solicitors of when Andrew and Sean were born and seen as loveable infants, 'to see you in this Court again—having failed—*again*—in your ill-chosen career. Well, gentlemen, you are not true gangsters, you are palpably not the Kray twins—you are a poor copy of those two evil men—more like the "Clay Twins" to be more accurate'... And here, the Court erupted in laughter at Judge McCartney's knife-sharp humour—and the media reported it word for word. The picture of Andrew and Sean, in black and white, one cousin standing behind the other looking over his shoulder, dressed in black suits, white shirts and black ties was featured with a drawing of puny bodies beneath their faces and the headline—*THE CLAY TWINS*—and the reported whole sordid history of their complete failures in the life of crime.

Humiliated beyond description, the McGregors served eight years for their latest failed adventure and came out of prison, on parole, greatly changed and beaten down. Both of them had been subjected to beatings from the other inmates and they were left in no doubt as to the reality of their situation.

Now aged forty seven, unemployed and unemployable, the cousins were separated under a new scheme for criminals who were deemed to be a nuisance rather than a serious threat to the communities they lived in. In an experiment created by the Welsh Labour Government, Halfway Houses were constructed—within communities—though situated slightly away from their nearest neighbour—for small-time criminals to reassert themselves back into the community they had been placed in. To be able to walk the streets and serve as "volunteers" in local activities under the watchful gaze of whoever presided over these activities. These "Watchers" were ex-Prison Warders or police officers and were no milksop fools to be easily taken advantage of. Each of the released criminals had to perform certain functions to serve out their time if released early—before they were given full licence to live away from the Halfway Houses without their guards.

Certain restrictions were enforced. There would be no communication with fellow criminals with whom a crime had been committed, there was a curfew to be observed, a ban from certain establishments such as Public Houses or Off-licenses—in fact no alcohol was allowed at all. Each in-mate would give a blood test or breath test at the end of each day. Any breaking of these infringements would mean being sent back to prison to complete the rest of the original sentence.

This meant Andrew and Sean were, for the first time in their lives, kept separated from each other. Sean was held in Pentre Haf and Andrew in Brangwyn. This was the worst period of their lives.

A single concession was made for the Cousins on their birthday. Their record on the new system was proving to be effective and so they were allowed to join up at Andrew's halfway House in Brangwyn to celebrate their forty eighth birthday. As per the rule, the society was limited—just the one evening which would be ended by nine thirty and Sean would then be transported back to Pentre Haf.

Halfway Houses are purpose built for the incumbents, designed for simplistic use rather than comfort. Each house had three levels and each level contained six rooms in a dormitory styled corridor. There was a communal kitchen, a communal TV room, a small room which held a snooker table, a card table and books. On the first level, there was a protected room inhabited by the Warden who oversaw all activities inside the House. Not quite home—but a definite step up from the restrictions of prison life. In each corridor, there was a small alcove with a phone. They could receive—but not make—phone calls, privacy guaranteed. This system had thus far, proved to be successful. In the two year period of the experiment, no in-mate had ever been returned to their prison.

One night, Andrew received a phone call. The Warden alerted him—and added curfew was just ten minutes away so keep it short—and Andrew took the call. This was the same night Sean had been allowed to join his cousin for their birthday celebration. Each cousin had bought the other a small cake, one candle each.

'Hullo?' said Andrew. He was not expecting a call—the only person he really knew on a social level now was Sean—and he was here in the House with him.

What came back was a strange, tinny voice—almost robotic.

'Andrew McGregor?' it asked.

'Aye,' said Andrew—slightly confused. 'Who is this?' He waved at Sean who was standing in the doorway, eating his cake. Sean went to him and listened in.

The tinny voice returned after a few moments. 'It doesn't matter who I am. I wish to make you a proposition. A small job for money.'

Silence followed. Andrew's ears lifted. He and Sean were flat broke and living on State Benefits with no chance of real employment and good wages to make their lives a little easier as long as they remained in this position.

'Would you like to earn a thousand pounds?' the voice continued. Now this was better, thought Andrew. But it sounded odd so he kept his voice calm and low.

'Sure,' he said. 'What do I have to do?'

'I want you to kill a man.'

And this is where Andrew turned his face down. The crimes the Cousins had committed had thus far been victimless-free as far as violence was concerned. They had proved to themselves how inept they were at the physical stuff and killing anyone had really never entered their Modus Operandi. Andrew gave something which sounded somewhere between a laugh and a cry of despair.

'Ah,' he said, 'I don't think so. Not my thing.' He was about to hang up the phone when the voice came back.

'Not literally kill the man—more like...' he paused, 'I want you to kill his reputation.'

The caller then went on to tell Andrew of this man who had come to a village not far from Brangwyn and had caused an immense amount of trouble and disruption for the locals and he had to be dealt with. His reputation had already carried fear amongst those he had invaded and he needed to be brought down— preferably in front of those he had transgressed against...

'Transgressed...?' mouthed Sean, his eyebrows lifting. Andrew shrugged his shoulder and continued the conversation.

'Sure,' he said. 'Who's the man?'

'Farr,' came back the reply. 'Jack Farr.'

Andrew had to wait a moment before he could reply. Farr? *Farr!* Where had he heard that name...? *Ohhh... yes!* This was going to be sweet.

'Sure,' he said. 'Give me the details.'

Chapter 26

Bloody Milk

Another week passed before Jack finally received the phone call he'd been waiting for. It came from one of the Gibney Associates' Secretaries who told him there would be a meet between him and one of the actual Gibney's—probably Mr Allan J Gibney himself the Secretary said—and he implied it would be a high profile meeting because unless the client was of a certain social status and Mr Gibney did not usually bother with any kind of business he considered could be dealt with at an ordinary level. Jack listened—slightly confused—and then waited for the confirmation of date and venue—which didn't come. Mr Gibney would make that particular arrangement himself the Secretary told him. And that was that. End of call—with Jack still slightly confused.

He called Vicar Redd and told him of the very small progress with the Gibney side of things and wondered why there was such a slow trawl of making this kind of arrangement.

He then opined it fitted with everything else that had been arranged regarding the inheritance and asked the Vicar if the whole business was just some kind of scam. Too many people had been involved with the matter ever since the Coroner's Court proceedings, the Vicar told him. Allan J Gibney himself had been involved, the Brangwyn Solicitor Peter Eddy was well known and could not possible be part of a scam. No, said the Vicar, all was happening the way his father had set things out. Quite exactly why Joe had set things out this way remained to be seen, said the Vicar and that left Jack in the same state of confusion he'd been in when he'd called the Vicar.

What next? Well—he thought Susan should know as she was indirectly going to be involved one way or the other even if the sale of Greenacres was temporarily on hold. He looked up his food storage and decided it needed replenishing—even if only for a hopefully short period. Jack had stayed away from the village since the fight with David Tanner just to keep out of everyone's way. Enough damage had been done and he didn't want some gutless wonder attempting revenge—probably from behind—to reinstate the false honour of Cwmhyfryd's Bank Manager.

But food is food and his larder was near empty. If he could get to the village and speak to Susan—bring her up to date with the information he had been given and then arrange for food to be bought without being seen by such as the Edmunds brothers—then he could get back up to the house and wait for Mr Gibney to call. Having decided upon that action, his first actual action was to call Auntie Phelps in Oklahoma to inform her there would be yet another further delay but hopefully he would be back home in the next two weeks or so. Auntie Phelps was recovering from an alcoholic bender and told him in no uncertain terms that nephew or not, if he ever called in the small hours again to tell her nothing in particular, she would geld him.

Everybody who needed to know—barring Susan—had been told and so he made his way from Greenacres to the village.

(So engrossed in the morning's phone call and what the Secretary told him, Jack completely failed to notice his father's axe had been removed from the door frame)

He travelled through the soggy forestry and entered the village.

The Tanner house was empty—he could see that. David was still receiving Hospital treatment and Susan's car was gone. This meant she was out of the village on either café business or House selling business—she wouldn't drive it to her shop. He made his way to the Estate Agency and entered. The only person inside, sitting at her desk and working on the computer, was Sara. He came into the shop and saw her. When she saw him, she damn near jumped out of her chair. He raised his hand and indicated he was here not on an aggressive mission but one of peace. He gestured towards Susan's desk and said, 'Where…?'

Sara—still jittery—told him Susan had gone to the Deri Farm Cash & Carry to stock up for the café. He asked her if she was okay—she shrugged and said, 'yes'—he asked if both her daughters were well and happy. Again, a jittery 'yes'. He didn't ask about Adam. No point in pushing your luck. So he left the shop and made his way towards the café.

Slightly un-nerving for him was the sight of so many villagers who were milling about and staring at him. It was obvious from the whispering comments of many and the finger-pointing that the rumours Susan had intended to dampen down had travelled throughout the village. They stared at Jack as if he were

Public Enemy Numero Uno and the biggest villain of the country had just descended upon their sleepy village to do more mischief.

He climbed the steps leading up to The Square and as he headed towards the café, a man stopped him.

'Your Jack Farr, aren't you?' the man said. Jack stopped and took a half step back. As was his customary habit, he stared at the man's face and evaluated it. The man was in his mid to late forties—big but running to seed, was clearly an unsuccessful fighter as his face was pretty much smashed in. He could be either friend of foe. Nevertheless, the man's manner was threatening and Jack was immediately on his guard.

'Yes,' he replied to the man's question. The man smiled.

'Thought so,' he said. 'I knew your brothers. I did a job with them once.' This told Jack nothing. James and Joseph had worked in a small unit factory a few miles south of Cwmhyfryd and it was staffed full of men and this character could well have been any of them.

'I always believed it was them that got me and my Cousin sent down,' he continued and now his smiling manner was replaced by a look of pure hatred and Jack stiffened, ready for an attack...

...which came—but not from the man in front of him. Sean McGregor had been standing in the shop side of Fisher's Café and hadn't even given Jack a glance. Now he had stepped up behind him and wrapped his arms around Jack's body, pinning his arms to his waist and holding him firm. Jack couldn't move and Andrew McGregor stepped closer.

'Me and my Cousin was doing a job and your brothers were s'posed to be guarding us—but the Cops raided us and it ended in a bloody mess. The man we was working for got crippled for life on account of them and we got sent down for eight bloody years. We would've killed them when we got out of prison 'cept they was already dead. But now we can have a bit of revenge by working on you.'

Jack's senses assailed the environment. People were staring at this new fight. Some of them were in the village street and others were actually standing on The Square itself. In fact, he could see the girl who worked inside the café banging on the café window.

Andrew launched his first punch. He struck Jack in the gut just below where the other man's arms were holding him. The punch was enough to hurt him and he reacted with such a jerking movement that the second man had to readjust his

169

hold on Jack. He slid his arms away from the torso and grabbed Jack's own arms. The second punch was delivered to the left side of his face. That did hurt him and Jack knew he couldn't take too many of those.

'We bin waiting years for this, Farr,' said the first man and he drew his arm back for a third strike. Again, he aimed it at the torso and he struck at that part of the body—but this time, Jack raised his knee and the man's punch connected with his kneecap. The man screamed as his bones crunched against a much harder target and he fell slightly back, holding onto his crunched knuckles and swearing blue murder. Jack used the other man's body weight as ballast and jumped up, striking out with both legs, his boot heels connecting with his adversary's nose and eyes. The man screamed again and was hurled backwards, crashing against the railing fence. The kick held enough momentum to push both Jack and his gaoler backwards and they hit against a brick wall. Jack lowered his head a few inches—then brought it back fast and hard. The back of his head connected with the man's nose and now it was he who screamed. It was enough to make the pinning arms release Jack from the hold and he then dug his elbow into the man's midriff, causing the man to wheeze air. Jack brought his elbow up and struck the man across the face. The man was dazed and flailing about the pavement. He tried to defend himself by raising his arms but he wasn't looking where he was going or watching Jack who now ran at him, jumped up and kicked him off the steps and over. Sean McGregor was kicked into the air with such force he cleared six steps before he landed on the seventh on his back and tumbled backwards on the remaining five before landing unceremoniously on the path below. One down.

Jack heard a click. He turned and saw the first man—now bleeding from the mouth and nose and looking somewhat comical as there were two dark heel prints on his face just below his eyes. He looked like an anaemic panda bear. But now the threat was more dangerous because now he held a flick-knife up towards Jack. He groggily got to his feet and waved the knife at Jack.

'I'm gonna gut you, Farr…' and was then taken completely by surprise by a milk bottle which struck him on his left temple. The bottle smashed and milk poured across his face and down his clothing. Jack turned and saw a furious Susan standing in the café doorway, another milk bottle in hand. He turned towards his attacker who looked so pathetically out of it, he dropped the knife. The white milk had now turned pink—blood from the side of his head had mixed in with it. Jack moved towards him but the man had had enough for one scrap.

Andrew gripped the top of the railing and hurled himself off with one bound. Maybe it had been his intention to land on two feet—or maybe all four of his limb points—feet and hands—but the drop from this point would have been at least twelve feet and the fall would certainly have hurt him.

There was a scream—and a yell—and the sound of metal crashing. Jack and Susan both rushed to the railing and looked over. What they saw was, for them anyway, an amusing end to this scrap. Andrew had landed on top of passing cyclist below the railing and had crashed on top of both him and his bike. The victim raised hell and brimstone against the unexpected interloper and used language learned from his days in the Navy and building sites. He attacked Andrew with some considerable vigour before removing his safety helmet and proceeded to bash the man across his defending hands and head. What amazed Jack was that the man was clearly elderly—he was near bald with wisps of white hair sprouting around the sides. He looked to Susan who told him, 'Ianto Evans'. *Ianto Evans?* Jack remembered the man back in the day. He'd been a Union Firebrand in the sixties and he clearly had never lost the taste for a damn good scrap. He was giving Andrew an example of that attitude right now. The second man ran across the road and screamed for them to get the hell away from this bloody place and Andrew, who was pleading for the old man to stop hitting him, turned tail and they both scarpered as fast their legs would take them, followed by a still furious Ianto Evans who demanded payment for his crushed bike.

Silence returned to the village—though everyone was now staring up at The Square to see what other atrocity this man Farr would visit upon them.

He turned to Susan who was still glaringly angry. She looked at him and said, 'Can't you stay out of trouble?' He raised his hands as if to say this wasn't his fault. She grabbed him and dragged him into the café.

Chapter 27

Learning

'Honestly, this village has seen more blood on its paths in the few weeks since you've been back than it has in the entire time it's existed. And stop your whining.'

Catrin had to suppress the urge to laugh as she listened to Auntie Susan berating Mr Farr because of what happened outside. After Ianto Evans had chased the two men away with his bike helmet, Susan had taken Jack by the arm and brought him into the café, plonking him onto a chair then disappearing into the back of the store to find some liniment to clean Jack's facial wound while yakking at him because of the fight. The attacker must have been wearing a ring or some kind of adornment because there was a small gash which had drawn blood on the upper cheek of Jack's face. Susan cleaned it and dabbed it with cotton wool while giving him a lecture about the violence which had occurred since his return. Catrin knew it was more out of relief that Jack was unharmed than a serious telling off. He protested each comment and was shut up each time.

But who were the two men?

'I don't know,' said Susan. 'They aren't from this village. I know every man and woman here and unless they're newbies, they aren't from around here. What did they say to you?'

'They knew me—one of them called me by my name before they attacked. They said they'd worked with my brothers—and the puncher claimed they had done time because of them.'

'Is that likely?' asked Susan.

'I don't know. James and Joseph had a few jobs outside the village—but they never said anything about having trouble with any of their workmates. Certainly not sending anybody to prison.'

And then, Sara rushed into the café, laughing.

'Oh my God,' she panted. 'I just saw the funniest sight. Ianto Evans chasing the Clay twins down of the village high street. He was walloping one of them with his bike helmet. They were both begging him to stop.'

The Clay Twins?

Susan looked shocked. 'They weren't the Clay twins,' she said in disbelief. But Sara was adamant—she knew them from Adam's family connections and friends and she recognized their faces from recent newspaper photographs.

Who are the Clay Twins?

'My God, said Susan, 'I never would have recognized them. They looked really beat up. I remember them from when we were at school. They were all the girls used to talk about.'

The Clay Twins—anybody?

There was a brief trip down memory lane between Susan and Sara—while Jack and Catrin looked on and listened, not being part of this new conversation. Jack put his hand up twice and was ignored. 'Who are the Clay twins?' he asked—twice. Eventually, they stopped their reminiscing and looked at them.

'Andrew and Sean McGregor,' Susan and Sara chorused together. Jack looked at them, nonplussed and shrugged his shoulders. Susan and Sara, alternating the telling between them, then gave him the full story of the Clay twins, from birth to present day with Susan including their most recent defeat at the hands of Jack and herself. That last bit amused Sara.

Jack listened—with a curious interest. This was the first time he had heard exactly how his elder brothers had died.

There was a pause. Then Sara piped up. She held up a photograph. 'I found this out there,' she said. She gave the picture to Jack. He stared at it, now even more confused. Susan joined him.

It was a picture of him. Head and shoulders.

'Where did you get this?' she asked Sara.

'Found it at the foot of the steps outside. It isn't wet or dirty so it couldn't have been there long.'

Jack stood up and wiped his face dry. 'I just kicked one of them down those steps. They must have had it to recognize me. They'd never seen me before.'

'Somebody gave them a picture of you?' asked Susan.

Jack studied the picture. It was a close up—head and shoulders and he was wearing a 'T' shirt. But in the background…

'This was taken at the house. See that thing in the background…?'

He showed them the picture. A large dark object occupied the upper right corner of the picture. It was next to a gaping hole. The tree trunk.

'I dug the tree out of the hole last week. This would have been taken since then. In the past few days.'

Susan studied the picture. 'The old enemy,' she breathed quietly and Jack smiled. She remembered the "old enemy".

'Someone photographed you—and passed the picture onto the Clay twins? Why?' asked Sara.

They all sat down. Susan brought out a cup of tea for each of them and biscuits. Initially, there was silence and then a few opinions were passed around the table. Catrin kept quiet. She didn't know the Clay twins or their history. She didn't really know much about Mr Farr's elder brothers apart from what had come out in the weeks since Mr Farr had come home. After a few comments, Mam, Auntie Susan and Mr Farr all arrived at the same conclusion. The Clay twins had been paid—by someone here in the village—to attack Mr Farr and work him over.

But who?

'Mr Lewis takes a lot of photographs,' said Catrin, adding her own contribution to the conversation. But Mr Lewis was not an original Hyfridian and hadn't lived in the village when… those things happened, said Sara.

And then Sara piped up again. 'Hywel Parry,' she said.

'Who?' asked Jack and Catrin.

'For God's sake, the man we just been talking about. The one your brothers and the Clay twins were working for the night they got… uh… killed.' She paused on any subject relating to Jack's family—she wasn't sure how he'd react if anything said which wasn't… respectful.

But Jack had no such feelings about his elder brothers. He knew them and how they'd behaved. Respect wasn't a thing they demanded—or gave. 'What about Hywel Parry?' he asked.

'Well,' said Sara, 'he lives here.'

'In Cwmhyfryd?' asked a shocked Susan. 'Where?'

'Quarter Haven,' said Sara. 'He's been there since three years ago. He lives with his son.'

Chapter 28

The Man Living to Die

Jack rapped on number 12 Quarter Haven, having rung the bell and knocked the door a number of times already. He now knew what this small enclave of chalet-style buildings were, having already seen them on his first day back in Cwmhyfryd. The small row of buildings were in fact the first row of four such rows numbering up to 48. Originally built for people of a 'No-Fixed-Abode' status, Quarter Haven had descended into a mini-ghetto for the unwashed and un-inclined, people who had dealt in illegal activities which the law had chosen to turn blind eyes to. There were genuine cases in this small allotment and the Parry clan were of that breed. Hywel Parry had never recovered from the devastating injuries he'd received from the Farr twins when they crashed into him on their bike—and though his life had been saved by the skills of the surgeons, the general desire, from him at least, was to be allowed to die. His son, Edgar, the only other survivor from that terrible night, had kept himself within arm's reach to ensure his father did not die. The other members of the Parry clan had fallen on the wayside either by natural causes—or not so natural causes.

Jack rapped the door again and was just about to turn away from it when it was opened. He, Susan and Sara were then engulfed in a cloud of smoke which blew at them from within the small apartment. Both Susan and Jack retched on the stink which came with the smoke.

'Bloody hell,' said Susan.

'What the hell is that?' Jack gasped.

'Skunk,' said Sara whose husband had occasionally indulged in that foul smelling extension of the cannabis weed. All three of them put their hands to their noses as Edgar Parry peered at them. A small, clearly unhappy man whose life was nought but misery in the taking care of a man who wanted nothing more than to just slip away from his own life.

'Yes?' barked an angry man—mid fifties, thought Jack, though he looked older mainly through adversity and life's pitfalls. A man not disposed to small talk nor of kind words so he bit the bullet and jumped in.

'I'd like to speak with Hywel Parry,' he said. 'I believe he lives here.'

'Who are you?' barked the unhappy Edgar again and before Jack could give his name, a bell from inside the house sounded and Edgar turned away, his intention was to close the door behind him without even checking to wait to see if it closed. As the door reached the jamb, Jack put his hand out and stopped it closing. He waited to see if Edgar came back but he heard voices from inside the apartment and he gently pushed the door ajar. The stench of skunk enveloped them again.

'Dear God,' said Susan, hand clasped to her face, 'how does he breathe with that muck in the air?' Sara said nothing. She was used to Adam's filthy habit.

Jack took a step inside and stood in the reception area.

'Uh, Jack…' said Susan. 'We weren't invited in.' but he moved through the reception and towards the closed door in front of him.

In the main room of the apartment, Edgar wiped his father's face of slippery snot from which he had just drooled a sneeze. Hywel Parry lay supine on a large armchair, a man whose body was emaciated from lack of food and had the facial pallor of an anaemic ghost. His arms were barely more than bone covered with scrawny flesh, made even more repulsive to look upon by the profusion of hair growing on his forearms. His face was sunken and the eyes darkened which gave the skull effect even more prominence. To use Sara's colourful phrase, if ever there was a man standing on the Welcome Mat of Death's Door, Hywel Parry was that man—he had one foot firmly inside the door and the other about to jump in after it. Edgar cleaned his father's face and stood up—he himself was a man waiting at the approaching gate of defeat as he watched his father dying in front of him while stubbornly insisting on taking yet another breath. Anyone else would have given up by now. As he stood upright, he became aware that he was no longer the only person standing upright in the room. He turned and saw the three intruders from outside. Rightfully, he was angry at this intrusion.

'Who are you?' he demanded. 'How dare you enter my home?'

Jack stood quite still, his hands still covering his face as he was bereft of a hankie. Both Susan and Sara had fortunately come prepared and their faces were thus covered. The stench of stale cannabis and whatever else the old and dying Hywel Parry had sucked into his lungs floated in the air like a thick smoke. The walls, painted white when they had moved in, were now a dirty sickly yellow and brown. Worse, the radiator heating was on full and in such a small environment, the heat was oppressive to anyone who possessed an ability to move more than a few steps in a few seconds. It felt to Jack, Susan and Sara that the apartment was a furniture version of a sauna and water dribbled down the dirty brown walls.

Jack could only look on with sadness. This man—a criminal in his day to be sure—was now living the end of his days in a near-death condition because of what his twin brothers did on their bike. He was not responsible for this man's condition in any way but he felt the guilt nonetheless.

Edgar was a puny man by Jack's standards but even a man's dirty castle is still his home and he took umbrage. He confronted Jack with as much courage as his puny frame would allow.

'I said, who are you? What do you want?'

'My name is Jack... Farr. I wanted to speak with your father... about something which happened to me a short while ago.'

And Edgar shot right back. 'Well, Mr Farr—as you can see, my father is in no condition to speak with...' He stopped and drew back. He stared at Jack with some venom. 'Farr?' he enquired. 'Your name is... Farr?'

'Jack Farr—and yes, James and Joseph were my brothers. But I had very little to do with them when they were alive and I'd already left this village when... your father...' He left it unsaid. Truthfully, no words could explain it.

But Edgar was in no mood to commune with any member of the family who had destroyed his. Maybe, because of the presence of the two females, he found some courage and was able to talk tough to Jack—but the fear mixed uneasily with the anger. His face was turning crimson red and the trembling of the voice signified he had spurred up the guts to speak—but he was still scared.

'Well—what did you want to talk to my Dad about? If it's about doing a job I think I can safely say on his behalf he isn't quite the man he was twenty years ago and anything heavier than a brick might prove difficult.' Not bad. Courage through sarcasm.

Jack's stance wobbled slightly, as did Susan's and Sara's who were now using the walls to stay upright. Sara may have been used to this kind of aroma but not to this heavy extent and Susan—a non-smoker—was not used to it at all. Jack was getting the worst of the stench as he had nothing to cover his face. He was having to take breaths and explain his arrival in one sentence.

'Two men attacked me an hour ago Mr Parry and I am informed they used to work for your father and I came here to find out if he had employed them to work me over.' He moved to Susan who took a deep breath and offered him her hankie. He took quite a few deep breaths before giving it back to her. Perfumed. Nice. In the meantime, Edgar gazed at all three with some amusement. His father made a noise and more watery snot was oozing out of his nose and down over his mouth. He bent down and wiped his father's face again.

'Are you accusing my father of setting these men onto you, Farr? Is that what you're saying? In his condition?'

'Asking,' Jack said. 'I didn't know he was in… this condition.'

Edgar stood upright again and this time faced Jack directly—a smile on his face. He nodded to his father. His voice was now reduced to a rasping hiss.

'You think this pathetic husk of a man could conduct such a business? He hasn't moved from that chair since we came to this pissant hole three years ago. Or spoken to me. Before then, his last words to me were spoken when he came out of hospital and he begged me to let him die. I been letting him die ever since—but the old bastard won't stop breathing. He can't barely move. He's dead from the neck down apart from his one arm which he uses to smoke his brain into oblivion. The stink you and your bitch friends are breathing in is the only thing that keeps him from feeling any pain. He can't eat unless I shovel the stuff into his mouth and I have to wipe his dirty arse five times a day. My father died, Mr Farr—the night your brothers ran him down on their bike. What's left is this—an unfunny joke dressed up like a human being.'

Another noise from Hywel Parry and Edgar rolled his eyes.

'On cue, as it were. I now have to undress my father and clean away his shit. Would you all like to stay and watch? We haven't had an audience for so long. I'm sure my father would love for you to stay and chat to him while I clean his filthy crack-hole.'

He bent down and began to untie the cord around his father's pyjama trousers. Then he laughed.

'Who were the two men?' he asked.

This time, because Jack looked like he was about to fall, Susan answered. 'Sean and Andrew McGregor—they are called the Clay twins by most people.'

Edgar laughed again. 'Those two?' he said. 'Jesus. What a pair of tossers they turned out to be.' He stood upright again and moved one step towards Jack.

'Look, Farr—even if me or my Dad wanted to work you over—which we don't—and besides I didn't even know you even existed—we sure as hell wouldn't use those pricks. They were on guard duty that night and they must have watched over a dozen Cops simply walk across the field and into our place of business and they didn't see a damn thing.'

There were tears in his eyes now and Jack wanted nothing more now than to get out of this pit and out into the fresh air. Edgar allowed him that opportunity.

'Whatever happened today, Farr—I promise you, it had nothing to do with me or my Dad. Now—if you don't mind...' He raised his hand which held a large nappy. Jack nodded and he gestured to Susan and Sara to leave the room. He took one last look at the pathetic Hywel Parry—a man who had once ran a small but successful Empire and had been on the verge of retirement to be able to spend the fruits of his criminal labours.

'I am sorry for the intrusion, Mr Parry,' he said. But Edgar was now attending to his father's needs and gave no sign he had heard the comment—which could have been meant for his father as well. The door closed and Edgar slipped the filthy pyjama bottoms out from underneath his father's backside—the dirty brown slime of his defecation now spreading on the plastic covering of his armchair. Edgar lowered his head and cried.

'Die,' he begged. 'Please die.'

*

Jack, Susan and Sara stumbled out of 12 Quarter Haven and took massive gulps of fresh air before making their way to a small wall where they sat down and regained their balance and bearings. Five minutes passed before they could speak.

'Not Hywel Parry, then,' said Susan.

'No,' said Jack. 'Not Hywel Parry. Nor his son. I believed him when he said he didn't know about me. I saw the look on his face.'

Eventually, refreshed by clean country air, all three stood and—though still slightly wobbling—they ventured back towards the café.

Two hundred yards away, secreted behind a tree, a figure moved, having watched the three people entering and leaving the Parry home, their every movement observed, their every word overheard. When they were out of sight, the figure came out from behind the tree and stared at the Parry home. After a few moments, the figure moved back into the outlying forestry.

Chapter 29

The Meeting

Three days passed without incident for Jack Farr—so he walked into town with a bright cheery mood inside and around him and went straight to the café. Susan was cleaning the tables with Catrin at the sink, washing the cups and saucers. After six o'clock, Catrin was given her marching orders and she left the café—smiling at Auntie Susan as though she knew a secret that even the people the secret involved didn't know.

Susan poured a cup of tea for Jack and they sat at the table. Update: The attack upon him by the McGregors had been reported to the local police, the knife used by Andrew handed in, carefully wrapped in a plastic bag so no other fingerprints were on the handle. This report then went out to the two Halfway Houses and from there to the Probation Service as the McGregors had broken the boundaries of their Probationary Time. Neither of the two McGregors returned to their respective Halfway House and so a call for their arrest was put out to the local police. Jack was interviewed by the two police officers based in Cwmhyfryd and his statement sent to South Wales Police. It was easy for all concerned to see why he had been attacked by the McGregors—revenge for their time in prison which they blamed on James and Joseph…

But it was that photograph of Jack which placed it in another category. Who took it—and when?

The photograph was copied, the original logged and placed in evidence. The copy was given to Jack.

The good news which Jack had brought with him was the meeting between him and the Gibney's was imminent. He had been called that day by the Gibney Secretary that he would be picked up the next day and taken to the place where he would learn about the inheritance and how he would collect on it. Jack asked if Susan Tanner would be involved citing the sale of Greenacres—but the Secretary said she would not be involved in this area of the discussion at this time.

'So, you're going to meet them at last,' Susan said. 'About time. They've kept you dangling long enough.' True—what should have been a relatively simple task conducted in a small period of time had developed into something complicated and over a longer time—much longer than Jack would have wanted. And in that time, he had been in too much involvement with the locals. Too much physical contact.

And on that issue…

'I'll be going to the Heath later,' she told him when he asked about David. 'He's conscious but unable to speak. Now that he is at least aware of his situation, the Doctors wish to begin surgery on his jaw. He can't barely move yet.' She did not chide Jack as David's situation was completely of his own making. As for her father, he had taken to remaining inside his home unless it was necessary for him to venture out. He was still very much aware of what was going on in the village. He knew about the McGregor attack—Olwen Berry had informed him. He would have had plenty to say about that as well if Olwen hadn't told him about the part Susan played in that particular scrap.

The Gibney pick-up would be the next day, Jack told her, and early in the morning so he wouldn't see her before he left and he wasn't sure what time he would be back home. Where was he to be taken, Susan enquired and Jack assumed it would probably be in the Gibney Cardiff office. He left the café—this time unharmed and without argument. He took a bath at home and had an early night, ready for the next morning.

*

At seven the next morning, he heard the car driving up the path. A Daimler. He locked the house—making sure all the doors were secured along with the windows and walked out. The man standing by the car was not dressed as a Chauffeur and he didn't look like a man who would be employed by a lawyer. Jack moved towards him—wary of the man.

The man was huge—at least six feet seven, weighing in about fourteen stone and hard with it. He may have been in his mid-fifties or older—slightly balding on top but with a heavy swarthy shade around his face—a man who would need to shave every few hours to look clean shaven. He was dressed very smartly in a suit which must have cost hundreds of pounds. As Jack approached, he broke out into a wide smile.

'Jack Farr,' his voice boomed, 'I'm Allan Gibney.'

*

The big man himself, thought Jack. He was expecting an intermediary, a representative of the Gibney Firm—but no, he got the big man himself. They had been in the car for about ten minutes after leaving the quiet village of Cwmhyfryd before Gibney spoke.

'You used to live there, I'm told.'

'Born there, at the original Greenacres, raised and worked. Almost married there and then I left it behind twenty years ago,' Jack replied. He wondered how much Gibney knew about him and if any questions were genuinely looking for unknown information or was he just fishing. The conversation then turned around and Gibney spoke about himself, his own life and how he had ventured into the Law profession. It was quite a revelation.

Allan J Gibney, it had to be said, was not... *quite*... the most legal man Jack had ever known. In fact, a sizeable portion of his life had seen him operating on the other side of the law—not exactly breaking it but certainly not living within its constrictions. The Gibney's relationship with the law had been contrary for at least three generations and it seemed to this latest generation—Allan in particular—that a sound working knowledge of how the law worked and operated would be of sound benefit to them—and to those they represented, many of whom were definitely of the criminal fraternity. He gave Jack chapter and verse of how his family had ventured into the legal world and how they had prospered from it. It felt surreal to Jack—himself a man not disposed to contravening the law out of funk or malice—and yet he could see exactly why this man had chosen to become a lawyer.

It would be fair to say—and Jack knew this—that not all aspects of the Law are... how do we say this... are not *right*. Legal, maybe—but not *right*. There is a world of difference, Gibney told him, citing differences between what is legal and illegal and what is right and wrong. And it was those distinctions which instructed Allan J Gibney.

'Give me right and wrong any day,' Gibney said. Innocent people sent to prison for crimes the law knows they haven't committed—and guilty people walking free when their crimes were blindingly obvious—but unproven. Allan J Gibney had witnessed countless incidents where the law had failed the communities they are meant to serve and had been persuaded by his own father to remedy the matter. And so, Gibney Associates was created—the necessary lessons learned at University, the exams passed and at least six sons and one daughter were fully experienced lawyers doing just what their father had instructed them to do—remedying the matter. And they had remedied many matters in the decades their company had existed. Not completely on the side of the Angels—but handy to have when a person—a known felon—was being persecuted for a crime he or she had not committed.

Gibney told Jack of a number of legal incidents he had been involved in and every one of them a colourful story. Had it not been for the fact that he was now aware of where the car was being driven, Jack would have been more curious about Gibney's life—and of his own personal involvement in this inheritance business. But they weren't heading towards Cardiff that was for sure. In fact, they were cutting across country—heading East.

'Where are we headed/' he asked. 'England?'

'Yep,' said the burly lawyer. 'England.'

And that effectively ended all conversation. Jack sat in silence and Gibney ventured no more family anecdotes about the law and criminality. From Cwmhyfryd, the journey took two hours before they even saw another town. They drove over the Heads of the Valleys by-pass, through Abergavenny and then towards the M50. Jack had very little experience in these sights—like many of the Hyfridians, he had ventured outwards of his home village very rarely and had not visited other places. For a man who had travelled a sizeable chunk of the American mid-west, it seemed peculiar to him—now—that he had seen so little of his own home country.

They left the M50 and travelled southwards down the M5. They left the M5 at the Stroud Junction and were heading still east through the Cotswold countryside which Jack marvelled at. Such beautiful countryside and very well taken care of. He was particularly impressed by the stonework of many of the houses there.

'You have an office here?' Jack asked. Gibney said 'no'—one in Cardiff, a central office in London and they were optioning for one in Swansea. But no— nothing in this area.

Jack wondered how his father's inheritance merited this journey and after an hour of relentless travel, he asked out loud how this journey was relevant.

Gibney stopped the car and smiled. He explained that he was not privy to the whole story—but represented the man who was. And in less than ten minutes, they would be arriving at the man's own domain. So, Jack was to be patient and don't worry.

Sure enough, ten minutes later, arriving through a small forested area, the car stopped on a country lane—and in front of a large building which did not look like anything belonging to the beautiful Cotswold countryside. There was a big sign behind a hedge which read:

ELLISON PHARMACEUTICALS
PRIVATE

There was large stoned wall arch—which Gibney drove through and was then stopped by a security guard. The guard saw Gibney and waved him through. Another drive up a lane—at least half a mile—and surrounding the lane were rolling fields populated by cattle and sheep. Ahead of them and behind a huge building of glass and stone a large Stately Home stood. The car drove up to the large house and parked in a large stone chipped area in front of the house. Gibney got out of the car and stretched his arms upwards emitting a loud groan as he did so.

'That is a long drive,' he said, a cheery tone in his voice. 'A long time to be cooped up in a car. Out you come, Jack.'

Jack sat still, wary of this development.

He got out of the car and not for the first time, wondered if he hadn't been set up for some kind of trick. He had expected a meeting between himself and the Gibney lawyers in Cardiff—not this lovely but mysterious grand tour around some of England's finest countryside.

He was about to protest when a man came outside and spoke to Gibney— who then gestured towards Jack. 'There's your man,' he told the man. The man then came to Jack—smiling—and asked him to enter the house. Still uneasy, Jack felt he had no choice but to do as he was directed. He had come this far…

The man walked through the house and Jack saw the wealth contained within. Wealth. Ah, now maybe *this* was the place which connected his father to the five million plus. They ascended the stairs and walked through corridors until they came to one door. The man opened it and entered, bidding Jack to follow.

Inside, it was almost an empty room. A table in the middle of the room, three comfy chairs and around the four walls photographs—all black and white—of soldiers, dressed in the older army uniforms of yesteryear. The man left the room and Jack stood still. He gazed upon the photographs and wondered if there was anything relevant to learn from them.

Well—in nearly all the photographs one man was clearly shown. A handsome looking man, early to mid-twenties, in a Captain's ranking, some posed, looking directly at the cameraman and some taken whilst he was engaged in activities.

It was the largest photograph in the room which drew Jack's attention. A huge piece of work, eight feet by four in diameter—a picture of a group of soldiers all sat around, some of them looking towards the camera and others looking away to each other or down at some other object. In the middle of this picture was the same man who was the main focus of this room—but there was something else which had alerted Jack—something he couldn't immediately put his finger on just by looking at the picture. So he scrutinized it closely, one man at a time, until he saw… *That was it!*

It was that bloody hat. That damned bloody hat his father always wore when he dug in the garden or walked in the blaring sunshine. The one he claimed he had stolen from a dead African soldier.

And underneath that hat—sat next to the handsome Colonel—laughing at something he was holding and not posing for the camera—was Joe Farr. In army uniform.

The voice came from behind.

'See anyone you recognize, Jack?'

Chapter 30

Fathers

Jack whirled. So transfixed was his gaze upon the large photograph, he had not heard the man enter the room. He was still in surprise mode when he saw the man. After a few seconds he looked at the other principle photograph in the room, of the man who looked directly at the camera. Either it wasn't as old as it looked or the man standing before him was remarkably well-preserved. Or...

'My father,' the man said, giving Jack his third option. 'Sir Walter Ellison. I am Arthur Ellison,' and he smiled broadly at Jack before stretching out his hand to shake the visitor's. 'Jack Farr,' he said, with delight in his tone, 'a pleasure to meet you after all this time.'

Arthur Ellison was fifty years of age and was possessed of a jovial demeanour so Jack was now completely relaxed as he sat at the table alongside him. The physical resemblance between him and Sir Walter was quite astounding and Jack said so.

'Only facially,' said Arthur. 'He was much taller and very much a man of action when he was serving the British Army. As was yours I am informed. I am not so inclined'

The confusion on Jack's face told Arthur that he had not known Joe had served in the Army. Certainly there were no pictures or stories of his time spent in service. Arthur nodded.

'Actually, Father rarely spoke of his time there. The most I could get out of him was that he'd lost many friends in combat and he kept the rest of it to himself. Jack,' he said, another broad smile filling the atmosphere, 'this is a curious thing but both you and I are here because of your father.'

Now this confused Jack even more so Arthur relaxed back in his chair and told the story of just how Joe Farr had been responsible for their meeting.

'See that photograph,' and he pointed up to the huge picture. 'Just twenty four hours after it was taken, all but your father and mine were dead. My father was a Captain in a specially constructed elite Commando Unit which had been formed to deal with a particular problem in the Gambian District. They were to track down a gang of Slavers, who were smuggling these poor men across the desert and out of the country for which they were paid a lot of money for the time. Anyway, my father selected this bunch because of their own specialized talents and they were set out to destroy the slavers and put an end to their operation.'

Arthur rose from the chair as the man Jack had seen earlier entered the room with a tray of food and drink. Left alone to serve themselves, Arthur continued with the story.

'Don't know what went wrong—neither did father—but this Unit was bowled out almost as soon as they entered the jungle. A four hour gun battle ensued and everybody was hit with an absolute barrage of bullets and bombs, killing them all. The slavers then went through the whole group and what they did to the dead men defies explanation. Somehow—by your father's skills—the slavers missed both our fathers. After a few hours of no noise, your father carried mine miles through the swamp infested jungle and back to Base Camp. It took him two days.'

Another pause and another cup of tea with sandwiches and biscuits. Arthur by now was clearly recalling this part of the story with anxiety. The room was cool and yet there was a bead of sweat across his brow.

'The medics did what they could with father and it took three days before he was transferred back to Alexandria. He was in Hospital for a week with the wounds giving him much pain. Eventually, they had to remove his right leg as it had been shattered by mortar bombs. he had lost a lot of blood in the jungle—if it hadn't been for your father, he would still be there.'

Jack sat silently, drinking his tea and dunking his chocolate biscuit, not quite believing what he had just been told. Though he and Joe were never intimately close as father and son, he could not understand why he had never heard this story before. He wondered if James and Joseph had ever been told—or even his mother.

'Father was transferred back to Britain and from there to the family clinic—the Ellison's have been involved in pharmacology for many decades—the family business you might say. He was laid up in a Surrey Hospital for many months, during which time,' and now, Arthur smiled again and opened his hands out wide,' he met a young Nurse. They fell in love and Father married the Nurse. A year later,' again he opened out his hands as if presenting himself, 'I was born. I also have two brothers and a sister. And all of us are here because...' and now he relaxed back in his chair, still smiling, 'because your father carried mine out of that damned jungle and back to safety.' He was almost in tears when he spoke those words and Jack looked at him—the same confused expression on his face as he again shook the outstretched hand from Arthur Ellison.

'I was practically weaned on that story. It really is a pleasure to meet you, Jack. I am happy to say I knew your father in the final years of his life. And we have this to share...'

He took out a large A4 envelope and opened it. Inside was a photograph and Arthur gave it to Jack.

The picture was of Joe and very clearly the much older Sir Walter Ellison, sitting next to each other on a plush looking sofa, both men laughing, each holding the other's hand and giving the cameraperson a thumbs up with their spare hands.

'It was taken by my mother, uh, two months before my father died. Maybe two years ago now. My mother passed away shortly afterwards and I was given the strictest instruction that I was to personally take care of your father's medical situation—which I did.'

Arthur then gave Jack the full story behind Joe's final years and how they had met. After his first heart attack, Joe had been taken to the Heath Hospital in Cardiff and by luck, his name had been noticed by the youngest offspring of Sir Walter who was a practising Doctor there. This information was passed onto Sir Walter who visited Joe the very next day. A reunion was made though both men had remained in mail contact on and off for many years. As soon as Joe was strong enough, Sir Walter arranged for him to be transferred to the Hospital wing of this establishment, although mainly a clinic for drug experimentation, the Ellison Foundation also ran it as a Private Hospital. Joe was installed and, in time, recovered.

When Joe suffered his second heart attack, and the writing was clearly on the wall in relation to his mortality, he and Sir Walter began to make preparations for what would happen later. To begin with, Sir Walter sent a team of architects to view the place Joe lived in—and what they came with was an amazement that an old man had lived in such conditions for so long. And so, the destruction of the original Greenacres was arranged and the house built by Jared Farr in the late eighteenth century finally was torn down and the new version constructed. Of course, Joe objected to this intrusion but his arguments were shot down in metaphorical flames by Sir Walter who wanted his friend and saviour to live the last years of his life in comparative luxury. The fact that Joe remained in this new house was a testament to its architects skills and the persuasive voice of Sir Walter.

The third attack proved to Joe his days were numbered and, ever the pragmatist, it was then he went back to Sir Walter and told him he wanted to remedy the estrangement between himself and his son, Jared. Joe, truthful to the end, did not stint on how this estrangement had come about. He confessed it was mostly his fault—though mitigating factors also played their part. Sir Walter then made arrangements for Joe to become a major shareholder in the Ellison Companies list. He bought the shares for Joe and they were placed in perpetuity for his heirs to inherit upon his death. His only heir, as far as he was aware at this time, was Jack though by now, the Gibney Associates had been brought in and private detective work had confirmed that Jack was alive, well and working at the Phelps farm in Oklahoma, unmarried and without issue.

And so, between them, Joe and Sir Walter prepared the Joe Farr Legacy to be inherited by Jack upon his father's death. Sadly, Sir Walter did not live to see this arrangement come to fruition but Arthur took over his father's mantle and worked with Joe to see out his dream.

Here, Arthur took a breath. Clearly the memory of the past few years was now catching up with him and emotion was now affecting his voice. So Jack took advantage of the silence and asked why the whole business had been constructed with so many delays.

'To be honest,' he lied, 'I don't know. But he was very specific about how you would be alerted to his death—by using the local Vicar—and exactly how you were to journey home. Very specific. In fact, I wouldn't be at all surprised if your journey hadn't been... let me see... observed? By the very able Gibney people. But why he was so fixed on the method...'

Again, he opened his hands out wide.

Jack then related the part Susan Tanner played in this business—bearing in mind it was Joe who had brought her in. Did Arthur know of their shared history? Arthur confirmed he did and again, it was Joe's idea. Again, he was puzzled as it had been arranged by Joe with absolutely no malice in mind. Jack paused. Yes, he confirmed, Dad would never have done such a thing out of malice. But the way this business had been conducted had ensured his time back in Cwmhyfryd had been for a much longer period of time than he would have wanted.

And then, the light dawned on Jack. The exact intention behind Joe's actions were laid out in front of him. It was all deliberate. These arrangements had been designed, by Joe, in order *to keep* him in Cwmhyfryd for as long as possible before deciding to return to the States.

'But why?' asked Arthur.

Jack stood up and walked about the room. He extemporized the intention behind Joe's actions.

'He deliberately kept me here so that I would inevitably become involved with the village and its people. He brought Susan in to sell the house so that I would have to meet her and do that house business with her—all of which would... reintegrate me back into the village.'

'And again—why?' asked Arthur.

Jack sat back down. 'One way or another, this return trip would serve... as a means to an end of the unfinished business of what happened twenty years ago. It would end... that part of my life... one way or the other. Obviously he couldn't have predicted some of the things which have happened, like the fights—and obviously I don't know what he knew of the state of the Tanner marriage—but he was topping and tailing my part of that story—which maybe I should have done myself long before now. Maybe from guilt as he seems to have recognized his own part in the proceedings from those days. Making it happen this way has just reminded me... of what I left behind when I ran away from Cwmhyfryd. Now—when I leave, all matters will have been resolved... and no thinking about the past.'

Clever man, thought Arthur. He understands *exactly* what his father did. I didn't even have to prompt him.

'So what will you do once this matter has been finalized, Jack?'

Jack paused. Up to this point his desire had all about sorting the inheritance out—confirming it to be real for one thing—and then hightailing it back to Oklahoma. But things had changed and for the first time, he was unsure of what he would decide. Sensing the dilemma within him, Arthur stood up.

'Look,' he said, 'there's no rush on your part. The inheritance is unconditional. You can sell the shares or keep them for your children's future if that happens, sell the house, rent it or keep it, go wherever you want whenever you want and whatever is yours is yours. Take some time to think about things and then let me know. Whatever you decide will be quite acceptable to all. There will be some paperwork for you to sign depending upon which path you decide to take.'

He smiled and left the room. Jack sat back in the chair and stared out—at nothing at first but then at the large photograph and mainly at his father whom he had never seen looking this young before. Joe had never lived on sentimentality and so pictures of his past had not adorned the Farr home. Jack had never even seen a photograph of his parents' wedding. He looked up at the smiling Joe and his Commanding Officer and their comrades in arms. And how tragic this picture was when taken into consideration that twelve of the fourteen men were already dead probably even before this picture had been developed.

He stared for over an hour as the room slowly darkened.

He looked up at the clock and saw it was after five in the evening. Time to go. He had paperwork to sign.

He had decided.

Chapter 31

The Gibney Connection

By the time all the paperwork had been signed—quite a lengthy process—and all small conversations and pleasantries spoken, it was after six in the evening before Jack and Mr Gibney left Ellison Pharmaceuticals. The journey back was not as instructive as the talk with Arthur Ellison but it was at least informative.

En route to Wales, Gibney pulled in to a Public House called the Air Balloon. He needed to use the toilet and also to eat something. His own business at the medical farm had prevented him from eating anything beyond the same sandwich fare Jack had been given and his physical constitution demanded a much bigger meal. By now it was seven o'clock in the evening. Jack didn't mind as the day's event would require him to indulge in some quiet time. The Air Balloon was well situated and comfortable. Gibney ordered a steak meal and as soon as Jack smelled the wonderful aroma emanating from within the pub kitchen, his own taste buds salivated and he ordered the same.

It was eating the meal where Gibney told Jack about his own family connection to Joe Farr. The Gibney family—starting with Allan J's father, Adam, had ties with the Ellison family for many years—going back to when Sir Walter was still in the Army. An odd combination between two men—one who was descended from belted aristocracy and one who had risen from the back streets of old London when that place was run by mobsters.

Gibney told Jack that the first family connection between them began when Theresa had died. When the police informed Joe—who was still an incumbent at a Cardiff Police Cell from the wedding scrap—that his wife had died, Joe was bereft, to the point where it took him hours to make a communication to the Sergeant at that Station. And that communication was sent directly to Sir Walter Ellison. From there, Adam Gibney met Joe and the funeral business was dealt with there at the Station whilst Joe was still held in the cell. Neither James or Joseph played any part of it—they themselves too emotionally broken up to think

194

things straight. An instruction was sent out to Adam's younger Associates that Jack was not to be involved, his own emotional situation probably being even more precarious than Joe's.

And so it was the Gibney connection which dealt with all of Theresa's funeral arrangements. Adam was placed by Sir Walter to represent the Farr family when their case came to court. All was going smoothly until the day of the funeral when the second scrap broke out and this time, there were not only hospital cases but four police officers were seriously injured as well. Adam Gibney pointed out that it would be next to impossible for anyone to be able to claim which member of the Farr family—or Hyfridian villager—had inflicted the injuries on the police officers and so those claims were left on file. Gibney explained the details of the wedding and the funeral to Mr Justice Orgrand and claimed mitigating circumstances should be considered. And his argument worked. Joe was released without charge and the twins were sentenced to a month in jail, already served. Of course, by the time Joe and the twins returned home, Jack had left—without letters of explanation to explain why or where he was headed.

Again, the Gibney connection served Joe Farr. It took some time but good detective work eventually learned that Jack had gone to London to stay with relatives on his mother's side of the family and from there—to the States where he backpacked across the States for eighteen months before finding the Phelps farm and settling down there. Through surreptitious means, Joe learned that Jack had disowned the family he came from and had sworn never to return to his home village. Joe was happy to let that situation lie for the interim while Jack worked the grief out of his system—and had it not been for the Hywel Parry incident, Joe would probably have sent missives out to Jack if only to find out the boy's long-term intentions. But when James and Joseph were killed, Joe's life went in a downwards spiral and from which he never really recovered. To lose his beloved Theresa and his three sons in such a short period of time was too much even for someone as tough as him and he became the recluse that everybody knew about right up until his death. Only those who were more intimately attached to him knew the fuller truth.

And so, Jack finally discovered practically everything there was to know about his father in one whole day. He ate his meal and then sat in silence while Allan Gibney finished his. You think you know a person just because of many years association but then you discover there was a whole life lived before you had even been born. The Army, the saving of a man who was then to have such an important part to play in Jack's own life so many years later. He only knew his father from what he had grown up with. He wondered if his mother had known any of these things—had she ever met Sir Walter—and was that a part of why she had fallen for a man so obviously unsuited to a woman of her gentleness and refinement. How much of this man's life was known by the elder peers of Joe in Cwmhyfryd and could they possibly had done the same things his father had done and was that the reason Malcolm Fisher was so jealous of Joe Farr?

He wondered how much of this new discovery he should tell Susan. He would definitely need to see her as soon as possible if only to tell her the decision he had made at Ellison House.

The meal eaten and enjoyed, Jack and Gibney left the Air Balloon and headed back to the home village. How odd that Jack would now think of that place in such terms.

It was after ten thirty when they arrived at Cwmhyfryd and Jack requested to be let out at the end of Bevan Road. He wanted to speak with Susan and he fancied the walk up to Greenacres would be a pleasing way to end the day. Thanks were spoken by both men and Allan J Gibney drove away—his role in these proceedings ostensibly at an end unless there were any glitches at which point he knew he would be employed to sort them out. Jack watched the Daimler drive out of sight before he went to Susan's home and knocked the door. The lights were on and her car was in the driveway so she must be home. It was a neighbour who informed him that she was still at the Hospital with her husband, having been taken there by the woman who worked at the Estate Agency.

Disappointed, Jack walked up the long path to his house. No matter. He would pass on the news to Susan and the Vicar tomorrow. He began his long walk, enjoying the near silence of the night. The only sounds he heard were his own footsteps and the animal noises in the forest. He did not hear the silent creeping of the shadowy figure who was matching his steps from the village and all the way right up to the house.

From a distance of a hundred yards, the figure watched Jack enter the house—and then it crouched down and waited.

Chapter 32

To Home and Death

Jack entered the house and immediately knew something was not right. He stood still and sniffed the air. There was an aroma floating about which did not come from him. A perfume. A woman's perfume. He stood still and listened but the house was silent. He closed the door quietly and held his breath. Still the silence. He flicked the light switch on—but nothing happened. Right. A perfumed aroma and no light—I've been visited, he thought. His coat was cumbersome so he removed it, never taking his eyes away from what little he could see in the darkness. His mind raced—what was different to this place compared to how it looked when he left it? From the doorway reception, he could see across the floor and through the door leading into the kitchen. It at least offered him some light which came from the moon's glow outside. Once his eyes had become acclimatized to the dark, he was able to make out shapes. But they were shapes which belonged to the house. No movement, no sound, nothing for him to latch onto. He slowly and carefully pushed the main room's door and his hand crept around the doorway towards the light switch there.

And again—no light came on. He paused awhile. It was possible the electrics were out. The old Greenacres was often subject to electricity blackouts—the old house had barely entered the 20th century even by the time Jack lived there and for a long time Joe used an old generator to maintain power. But Jack doubted the builders of the new version would leave that antiquated system in place. No, something else was happening here and he was in the middle of it.

He pushed the door all the way open and waited to hear it bang against the wall. If somebody was in the house and they were waiting for him to enter—say, behind the door—it would have banged up against something soft. But no, it hit the wall, no-one was waiting for him there. He entered the room and stood still, his heart thumping loudly in his ears. His movement was quick and he stood with his back to the door.

But now he knew something was definitely wrong. He couldn't immediately put his finger on it but there was something about the room which did not gel. Again, he paused and listened. He listened to hear breathing apart from his own. The main room was so dark, anybody could be hiding here, behind the sofa, the chair, hiding in the shadows. They could not be seen—but their breathing would be heard. But no—just silence. He fully entered the room…

…and his foot collided with something hard and unmoving on the floor. He was propelled forwards. He did not attempt to check the lurch forwards but instead performed a head-roll over whatever he had tripped on. He landed quite neatly on his feet and crouched down. What had tripped him up?

Again, his mind raced. When he had left the house this morning, had he left something in the middle of the room? No—the only thing which could be moved that was of a low level height was the footstool and his hand was already resting upon that piece of furniture. He strained his eyes to see what he had tripped over…

…and that was when he realized what was wrong with the room. That it was so dark he could *not* see. Why? Because the curtains had been drawn tight shut. He never closed the curtains—in any room he occupied. He hated closure and wanted to see life happening outside wherever he was. Even at night and just staring out at the forest was good enough for him. Someone had been in the house during the day and they had closed the curtains. Why? Because that someone did not want Jack to see as he entered into the room—and that would explained the lights failure. Either the bulbs had been removed or they had been broken. Moving carefully, still listening for any intruder, Jack shifted to the curtain rod and slowly pulled the cord. The curtains drew back—slowly—and the moon's glow began to enter the room until, even though still dark, the room became lit. And then, Jack saw what he had tripped over.

It was a shape. In the middle of the room, long, and of enough height and weight to unbalance him without it itself moving. He moved back to his former position, still straining his ears to hear movements or sounds but if there was anybody in the house they were keeping perfectly still.

The ceiling lights not working put Jack in a disadvantage but he wondered if the intruder had put out the lamp light which stood over the sofa where Joe would have read at night. That light was covered by a plastic casing and not so easily removed. He stretched out his hand, found the switch and turned the light on. The main room was alive with light now.

There, lying in the middle of the room, to his eyes, was a woman, her back facing him. He studied the body for a few moments. She was dressed all in black, a blazer with skirt, black stockings and black high heeled shoes. He crawled to where she lay, and gently shoved her in the back. No movement came back to him. Either she was unconscious or she was dead. He gently pulled her shoulder over so he could see her face. What he saw sickened him. The woman was bruised around the eyes which were also swollen, her broken nose covered in dried blood. Her lipstick was smeared across her face and the mascara was streaked down her cheeks. Somebody had given this girl a real pounding.

As he gently lifted her dyed black hair away from her face, he could see a series of bruises across her throat and neck. She had been beaten and then choked to death. He let her go and her body resumed its former position.

Jack moved back to where the landline phone stood on the small table. He took the phone of its cradle and dialled 999. The Operator asked him which service he required and he said 'Police'. One moment passed which seemed like an eternity—and Jack thought about Doctor Einstein's comment on how fast or how slow Time passes depending on what you are doing at the time, invoking handling Marilyn Monroe's posterior as a demonstration. The call was answered and Jack spoke very carefully.

'My name is Jack Farr,' he said. 'I live on Cwmhyfryd mountain in a house called Greenacres. I am calling to report a fatality. There is a dead woman in my house.'

Chapter 33
Chaos

From what had been a quiet and retrospective day which had been both pleasing and educational, Jack had now descended into a chaotic nightmare. It had taken the police almost two hours to reach him and that included two phone calls from the police still in transit in their cars who couldn't figure out where he lived. For some odd reason, Greenacres did not have a postcode so they could not punch that information into their Sat-Navs. Eventually, Jack gave them Susan's postcode and told them to then drive up the mountain path that began near her house—but please to take the journey carefully because of the narrowness of the road and the bends they would encounter.

Once one police car arrived it was only a small period of time before the entire mountain became festooned with others. Their blue lights flashing on and off filled the dark mountain and must have been seen by everybody in the village who would no doubt have been woken by the many sirens blaring through their village disturbing their slumber.

By the time the police were there in force, it was three in the morning. Scores of white suited SOCO's swarmed about the place sifting for evidence. Also in attendance was an Ambulance standing by ready to transport the dead body. The Pathologist was already inside the house conducting her examination of the dead woman.

Jack sat in the kitchen, accompanied by one of the two officers from Cwmhyfryd—Officer Harris. The second Cwmhyfryd Officer Taylor was outside assisting the police officers from Cardiff with local information—mostly about Jack.

In the immediate aftermath of finding the dead woman and then calling the police, Jack sat in the main room for just a few moments before moving out of it. Initially, he went to open the door because he desperately needed fresh air—he felt woozy from both the sight of the badly beaten victim and the pungent

200

perfume the woman used to decorate herself. But as his hand went to the door, he paused. It dawned on him that he had been used—set up—that he was to be implicated in this murder and he entertained the notion that person who had taken the photograph, who passed it on to the McGregors, had maybe upped their game when they saw how that particular venture had failed. Then possibly, his mind was still racing, that someone may well be watching him now. What would they expect him to do? What do most people do when they receive such a shock? Well, most people go for a drink—whiskey, brandy or some such potent libation to calm their nerves. In this environment, a natural thing to do would be to do what Jack had just attempted—fling open the door and breathe in the air.

And so he didn't do any of these things. If the killer was out there, in the forest, watching to see his reaction, he would stay his hand. Confound the enemy and not do the predictable. He knew nobody could see into the house at the point where he now stood—it was too late to go back into the main room and redraw the curtains—but he made a mental note of what he had done in there and would pass that on to the police when they asked him to relay his movements of the day.

To that end, what he did do was to take out a sheet of paper from the store room and a pen and he sat at the kitchen table ready to write everything he had done and had observed. It occurred to him that the killer may now be hiding behind the back of the house so he made one concession to not doing the predictable and he slowly closed the kitchen blinds, noting the dark of the outside, maybe hoping he could see someone hiding behind a tree or something.

Another thing he did was to locate the photograph which had been taken of him in the garden and he attached it to the sheet of paper ready for viewing. He had touched it, Sara had touched it, Susan—the McGregors—but maybe there was some kind of DNA evidence on it of whoever took the thing which may be useful to this investigation. He was glad now, that Susan had insisted upon taking the photograph to the Cwmhyfryd Police along with the story of the fight with the McGregors and the subsequent visit to the Parry home at Quarter Haven. Everything was written down on the paper, from the day of his arrival to Cwmhyfryd, the many discussions relating to the inheritance, the fights and the principle actors in this drama which had now moved from comedy to tragedy.

And now he sat in the kitchen. His clothes had been taken from him and had been "bagged" and he was wearing a set of white overalls similar to the ones worn by the SOCO Forensics. He was waiting for the arrival of the more senior police officers who would speak with him before moving him out of the house and… go where? Cardiff City Police Station he supposed. It was a long wait.

Detective Sergeant Stone cursed every step she took leading up to Greenacres. She had been forced to park her car at the base of the mountain and had to walk up the path to get to the house as there were so many cars and other Emergency vehicles up there her own car would never have made it through the bends.

'I'm the Investigating Officer,' she bleated to Detective Constable Morgan. 'I'm supposed to be the first person on the scene after the plods have done their preliminaries. There at the scene of the crime—not bloody walking miles up a steep path in the dead of night in these shoes.' She moaned all the way up to the house and DC Morgan listened to every syllable without speaking.

'Where's the Governor?' he eventually did ask when they were in the final straits leading to the house. A reference to their DCI who should also have been there with them.

'Swansea,' said DS Stone. 'Possible abduction of a teen held by a man who was teaching her Maths at home. He'll love this.' And after that, she made no more references about a man she clearly had no respect for and privately hoped she could solve this murder before he became involved—a feather in her cap and a possible inroad to promotion.

They reached the house and peered around the area. Dawn was breaking behind the mountain and DS Stone shivered. 'Christ,' she said. 'What a place to live in.' They entered the house and were met by the Pathologist, Doctor Swain, who was just coming out of the main room, piling her notes into her briefcase.

'What have you got for me, Liz?' asked DS Stone.

'Definite murder, throttled but only after she had taken a hell of a beating. A real powerful set of hands did this—and maybe in some frenzy to help out. She's been dead some time—maybe at least four days. And she wasn't killed here. As soon as I get her on the table I'll give you more. Where's…?

But DS Stone walked past her and left her DC to answer as to where 'he' was. She saw the local PC standing by the kitchen door who had heard her voice when she came in. She stopped at the doorway and peered inside. The owner of the house was sitting at the table and there was a sheet of paper laid out in front of him.

'Has he said anything?' she asked.

'Not spoken anyway—but he has written out a sizeable chunk of stuff he's been involved with since coming back to the village.'

'Coming back?'

Officer Harris then gave DS Stone a brief historical telling of Jack Farr, his family, the wedding farce, the death of his father, this supposed inheritance and Jack's recent adventures including the scrap with the McGregors. 'There's also a photograph which he says may be of some interest to you.'

DS Stone entered the kitchen and pulled out a chair, sitting diagonally to Jack who didn't take his eyes off her. Again, he made his usual mental customary though cursory appraisal of a newcomer in his vision. Female, mid-thirties, looks hungry to get on in her chosen career. If she were in a hurry to solve this case, she may rush to the wrong conclusion. He hoped he was wrong.

'Why did you kill her?' she said blankly.

Nope.

Chapter 34

To Add to the Misery

DS Stone and DC Morgan stood on the mountain range just above Greenacres and scanned the area, looking for track and road and how it would be possible to bring any kind of vehicle up into this area undetected. To their left, the mountain ran straight across then bent towards the Vicarage sloping downwards to the main roadway a mile away. To their right, the huge escarpment of Stone Mountain rose high into the clouds which were low enough to obscure the plateau. There was no apparent way around the range to get to Mynydd Fach. The road track they were looking at could certainly accept any strong vehicle as long as care was taken to traverse it. Any agricultural style vehicle would make this road quite easy.

DS Stone held a map which had been given to her by PC Taylor—the map contained all details of Cwmhyfryd—the valley itself as well as the village—and the surrounding mountains. The morning wind and light rain made the viewing difficult but it was necessary to get everything down so that when their DCI became involved, they would not be floundering to answer any questions—and he would be asking questions.

DC Morgan had asked DS Stone why she had mucked up the questioning session almost immediately when she spoke to Farr—the session ending immediately she asked the 'Killer' question. Jack looked at her, a surprised expression on his face, and he just shook his head. After that he refused to speak. The interrogation came to a premature end when Morgan asked her to step out. Stone did not feel disposed to answer the DC's question on her method of interrogating Farr.

Dr Swain had completed as much as she could with the body as she could and wanted it to be removed to the laboratory for further and more detailed examination which Stone acceded to. Morgan took Stone into Jack's bedroom and there, spread out on his bed, were items of clothing. They were made of rubber, a fetishist version of a Nun's garb.

'Ah,' said DS Stone, a look of prurient delight lit up her face.

Inside a leather case dropped onto the bedroom floor, there were details of what the dead girl's profession may have been. A notebook which had written names—or non-deplumes—of potential clients and addresses.

'She was a prozzy,' said DS Stone. 'And Farr was her client for tonight.'

Morgan doubted that but said nothing. The notebook was examined for the woman's last client. "The Preacher" it stated. No details about the client—real name, age or address. Other references had similar titles—"The Teacher", "The Cop", another odd inclusion read "Margaret Thatcher". The assignation for "The Preacher" was timed for the fifth of the month and at 9.30pm for that night. That put her intended movements the night before Farr claimed he was at this mysterious meeting relating to this inheritance business. So what did he do next—pick up a prostitute and have a bit of fun to spend his future inheritance? Morgan doubted that as well but Stone was delighted. She returned to the kitchen as the dead woman was being transported out of the house. She sat back in the same chair and leaned towards Jack, elbows on the table.

She asked him if he knew the woman but this time he said nothing, choosing instead to just stare at her. After a few more questions and getting no replies, Stone asked him if he was going to answer any questions at all.

'After what you just said—no chance,' said Jack. And that was that. Stone ordered the uniforms to transport Mr Farr to Cardiff Police Station and the questioning would be continued there, under caution and from the DCI himself. The sheet of paper and the photograph he had provided was bagged as evidence and Jack was placed into the back of a police car and driven away from the area.

Which left those who remained behind to explore how the girl would have been brought up here—if the written statement Jack had provided was to be believed.

Local knowledge is always useful in such cases and PC's Taylor and Harris were brought in to talk about local geography. How many ways are there to get to this place? Answer—two, if you're coming by car. There is also the trek through the forest.

'From the village by car—the way we all came up here,' said PC Taylor...

'And across the mountain range behind us—Mynydd Haf from the main road at the bottom of the valley. You would have passed it on the way to enter the village,' said PC Harris. 'It is possible to drive a vehicle across the mountain and up to the spot just above this house. I can get a map if you want.'

PC Taylor was despatched back to the village Constabulary to collect the map as he knew exactly where it was. SOCO continued with the examination of the house though there was little to find. There were only a few fingerprints and most of those would definitely belong to the owner of the house. Jack had stated the house had only been visited by the Vicar and Susan Tanner while he had been located here and this would mean getting their fingerprints just to eliminate them from the enquiry. The main bedroom was clearly used but the others had not been used at all.

DS Stone then received a phone call—from her DCI—who wanted to know how the preliminaries were progressing. She briefed him on the murder—the fact that the murdered woman was possibly a prostitute—and then she opined the death had possibly been brought about by the owner of the house, a Mr Jack Farr, which had DS Morgan rolling his eyes in despair. The DCI told her he was just finishing a report on the case he had been involved with and he would join her later. She ended the call by saying the case would probably be solved by the time he came up and the signal went dead. She smiled. Promotion, here I come. The sooner she was out of his eye-line the better.

She and Morgan then trawled up the rocky path to get a view of the mountain. PC Taylor rushed up, breathless, and gave her the map and she thanked him without actually looking at him and they scoured the map, matching it up with what part of the mountain they could see.

'There's the Vicarage,' said Morgan—pointing towards the tops of the building. 'Not much else to look at around here.'

'There are CCTV cameras in the village,' said Stone. 'Around those shops we saw. Farr says he left here early yesterday morning. I want all video footage of any vehicle that went through… what was that road?'

'Bevan Road,' said Morgan.

'Bevan Road. Any vehicle going past that road, going up the path we climbed and up to the house. Uh… right… head over to the Vicarage and ask the Vicar… whatsis name?'

'Redd,' said Morgan. 'John Redd. Hasn't been here long, apparently.'

'Okay—ask him if there are any cameras at the Vicarage pointed towards the mountain that may have picked up any vehicles driving across. That woman was brought up here and I don't think she was carried a mile and a half up the road we walked up. Going through the forest would also be difficult. And somehow,' she keened her eyes towards the escarpment and its near impossible terrain, 'I don't think anything could have come from that direction.' As they studied the map for any other possibilities, PC Taylor came back rushing up the rocky path, red-faced and out of breath.

'Sir—Ma'am—ohhh, me guts… there's… there's…'

'For God's sake, Constable—get it out and stop prattling,' ordered Stone.

'…been a murder,' said the exhausted Taylor.

'Yes, Constable,' said a now very irritated Stone. 'We know. That's why we're here—investigating the murder.'

PC Taylor put his hands up to her face while be bowed down to get his breath back. 'No, Ma'am—in the village. There's been another murder.'

Chapter 35

A Grisly End

DC Morgan leaned against the wall in the small apartment of 12 Quarter Haven and clamped a hankie to his face. He breathed in and out which made him feel more dizzy than he'd felt when he'd entered the place. It was necessary to open both the back door and window—which he did with gloves so as not to add his own fingerprints to the new crime scene. He was in the company of one of the two Cwmhyfryd police officers—the other one had had to carry DS Stone out of the place because, quite comically, she had almost fainted at the sight of what Morgan was looking at now.

Hywel Parry was seated in the same chair, in practically the position as he had been when Jack, Susan and Sara had seen him a few days earlier in the week. Only now he was dead. In the middle of the top of his cranium, an axe had been embedded into his head. There was a look of mild surprise on his face—both his eyes were open—and his mouth appeared to be getting ready to say something. In his left hand, were the remains of whatever Hywel Parry had been smoking when he was struck. Perhaps it was the sight of this man's grisly death or maybe it was the overly pungent stench of the house itself that had caused DS Stone to collapse—both were strong contenders. At any rate, DC Morgan felt compelled by duty not to show any kind of weakness in front of the uniformed Cops and so stayed his ground. Given the option, he would have walked out with DS Stone. Whoever had done this thing had really meant business. It was clear, even to a non-Forensic Officer like himself, that the dead man had been struck more than once with the axe—a completely un-necessary thing to do—the first blow would have been enough to kill the man.

DS Stone stumbled back into the room—a hankie covering most of her face. There were tears in her eyes—unusual for her to be so emotionally compromised by a murder and she had seen many.

'Call him,' she breathed out to Morgan. 'Tell him we need him asap. Call Swain as well. Call the whole…' and only the movement to vomit prevented her from swearing her head off. This was a bad 'un. She made it to the sink just in time.

Chapter 36
Enter Taffe

By mid-morning, Cwmhyfryd was a village under siege. The main entrance had been cordoned off and two police cars had been placed either side of the entrance wall. Nobody could get in, nobody could get out. Delivery drivers were told either to come back and make their deliveries to the shops or park up and wait. As the produce on their vans were placed in order of delivery, they couldn't drop any produce off to other customers until the first drops were made and so they were forced to call their customers to explain the situation and just park their vans on the road. Shift workers from the factories outside the valley were also kept out of the village for fear their cars and physical presence would contaminate a crime scene—already compromised by the comings and goings of the Police Force attending the murder at Greenacres.

The pathway leading up the Church was also cordoned off and two police officers stationed there to ensure nobody went to the Vicarage—or came down from it. Likewise, the path leading up to Greenacres was also cordoned off and guarded by police officers. At the house itself, a small coterie of officers kept patrol to make sure nobody inadvertently wandered up or down through the forest, unaware of the circumstances of what had taken place.

Cwmhyfryd had essentially been contained from the world outside.

Susan woke to the sound of her mobile ringing. The visit to David at the Hospital last night had largely been a waste of time as he was still sedated and the Doctors were engaged in other matters, too busy to give her much attention. The tedium of the night was increased when she and Sara got back to the car and, once again, it stalled on them. Sara cussed the damn thing and occasionally kicked at it as if that would improve matters—and then, an hour of using varying languages, it simply started up. After promising Susan she would really now do something about the car, they drove away. They got back to the village late and Susan went straight to bed. The good news was, she had no early meetings the following morning—her first client was at 11.30—so she said she was going to treat herself to a lie-in. She went to bed, using the spare room situated at the back of the house—and so did not see or hear the speeding police cars, their blue lights flashing on and off, as they passed her house to attend the call made by Jack. Nor did she hear the rest of the police convoy which followed afterwards.

It was Sara ringing her at nine in the morning telling her what was happening in the village, mostly at Quarter Haven. Susan dressed quickly and ran out of the house—and the first thing she saw was the police cordon at the end of her road—plus the two stationary police officers. She ran to them and demanded to know what was going on—and did it have anything to do with Jack Farr? They were particularly interested in her association with Jack Farr but stated they were not allowed to tell her anything relating to whatever may have happened up on the mountain. They did, however, log her name and protest.

Sara arrived—her car still steaming but driveable—and they both headed over to the Quarter Haven area to see what was happening.

If it wasn't pandemonium it was only just a notch below. Practically all the Hyfridians were there, crowding around the largely blocked off bunting which surrounded nearly all the first row of houses there. There were too many police officers to count—but they were heavily engaged in making sure none of the 'rubberneckers' breached the bunting cordon and crossed over to what was now the established crime scene.

While they observed the event, Susan used her own mobile to call Jack—but there was no answer. Which may have meant nothing as his day yesterday was bound to have been long and possibly emotional—after all, it involved learning the truth behind the inheritance and maybe something about his father.

But what the hell had happened here?

It took them a while to figure out exactly which house was being used by the police before they saw it was Hywel Parry's. Sara stared at Susan—coincidence or…?

They asked many of the residents if they knew what was going on but most of them shrugged their shoulders and didn't take their eyes off the house. A number of residents were now bringing out folding chairs and picnic baskets—and others used their phones to film any kind of activity either side of the bunting.

'I heard a lot of screaming, around seven this morning,' said Huw Jones—a resident of Quarter Haven. 'Screaming and doors banging. God knows what was happening.'

211

Rumour and counter-rumour scattered about the crowd and time passed with blue-suited Forensic SOCO's coming and going from within the house. Susan noted the many police cars and a single Ambulance parked away from the area. Whatever this was, it was very serious—but did it connect with Jack?

Her phone rang and she practically pounced on it. 'Jack?' she yelled—but it was the Vicar. He told her that the Vicarage was being cut off from the village and two police officers had enquired as to whether or not there were any CCTV cameras facing the mountain behind. There weren't. He was told he could not leave the Vicarage until given permission. Did she know where Jack was because he'd called a few times and there was no answer. He wanted to know how yesterday had gone for him. Susan confirmed no to each of his enquiries, told him about the drama going on down in the village and the call ended.

And then…

She saw the police officers moving the two cars away from the entrance wall and pull the cordon away. A car entered through the entrance and the cordon was put back up immediately. No-one else was allowed in. The car was driven the few yards across to Quarter Haven and then it parked, its occupant remaining inside the car.

She also noted that many of the police officers were milling around each other and nodding towards the car—or its occupant—as if a message concerning the occupant was being passed around by stealth.

Five minutes passed—and then the occupant got out of the car. A man, aged maybe mid to late forties, dressed completely in black which made him look positively criminal. Not a big man—medium sized—but there was something about his demeanour which exuded authority and power. He stared around the mass of people and gave a small shake of his head. Then he walked up the path towards number 12—and the three police officer who were posted outside the entrance to the house moved away—as if to make sure they did not come into physical contact with this new stranger.

PC Taylor was standing next to his village colleague and were both part of the holding force preventing any incursion from the inquisitive villagers.

'Is that him?' he breathed out, his voice almost a whisper. 'Is that Taffe?'

Before PC Harris had a chance to reply, a head popped into the space between them.

'Do you have a problem with the Inspector, Constable?' asked Sergeant Cenydd Thomas. The young PC shook his head and said, 'No Sarge—it's just that I never saw him before.'

'Well now you have—so keep your voice down—the Inspector doesn't like people talking about him behind his back.'

Chastened, the PC nodded—and looked back to where the Inspector was standing—still at the front door of number 12—seeming to debate as to whether or not he should enter. And then, rather unnervingly, he looked across the crowd and directly at PC Taylor. It shook the young PC quite a bit. 'Jesus,' he whispered, again, under his breath. And then he watched the man enter the house. He breathed out. There must have been a distance of at least 150 yards between him and where the Inspector stood. There was no way he could have heard...

Susan noted the officers who had moved away from the man's path had now resumed their former stations. Who the hell was he? And why did they look at him as if he were something to be feared...?

Detective Chief Inspector Owen Taffe did indeed generate a feeling of anxiety between all the officers performing their duties here. There wasn't one who didn't know him—either personally or by reputation—and all of them deeply distrusted him and disliked him. For DCI Taffe was notorious within the Police Force—not just of the South Wales Force but in other Forces around the UK. A man not given to gentility—many criminals, hardened as well as amateurs, feared him when they heard he was involved in any investigation relating to their ventures. He was a known puncher and had been subject to a number of IPCC inquiries over the years—all of which cleared him as a police officer acting within the boundaries of his investigations. But above all, and the reason why his colleagues in the Force didn't trust him was that Detective Chief Inspector Owen Taffe was a cop-killer.

He entered the house and saw the situation as it was. To his right, in the kitchen, DS Stone and DC Morgan, both drinking tea and eating biscuits obviously belonging to the house they were in. They immediately saw him—they hadn't seen him arrive outside because the kitchen blinds were closed—and put their cups down, standing almost to attention. He popped his head into the kitchen and said, 'Tea, two sugars, milk—and three chocolate biscuits.' DC Morgan complied immediately. Then Taffe turned his attention to the living room where he saw the dead Hywel Parry sitting on the armchair, the axe still embedded in his head and Dr Swain kneeling down beside him.

She looked up and saw him—and though her Department had no personal connection with specific members of the Police Force, she, like other officers, looked unhappy when he stood there.

He didn't speak—not even to wish her a 'Good morning'—and he watched her as she examined the late Hywel Parry. He observed the immediate surroundings. It was very warm in the room and he put his hand on the radiator. Warm, but off. The walls were a yellowy brown with streaks of … what…? sweat…? running down them. The ceiling was the same colour. He then looked at the hands of the corpse. Right hand was slightly stained but the left hand was almost black with cigarette stains—clearly the hand he used to hold his cigarettes with. The yellowing of the walls and ceiling were the result of long term smoking of cigarettes. Without entering the room—he wasn't wearing the standard coverings—he noted the small container at the dead man's side. Filled with rolled up… not cigarettes… very long spliffs. He sniffed the air around the room. Skunk, cannabis, marijuana and possibly a heavy mix of other more exotic drugs indulged in by the dead man. He looked at the axe. Not new. Old, in fact, the handle was long and weathered. From what he could see of the axe-head itself, it was of an older style.

Then he spoke.

'How many times?' he asked. Dr Swain looked up from what she doing and stared at the injury. 'Five, maybe six times,' she said. 'The first one would have been enough. The other blows were for effect. Somebody sending somebody a message, maybe.' She continued with her work and Taffe moved away from the room and went to the kitchen where he was handed the mug of tea and two chocolate biscuits. 'Only two left, Guv, sorry,' said DC Morgan. DCI Taffe dunked the biscuit into the mug and said, 'Don't call me Guv—we aren't "The Sweeney." And thank you.'

He turned his attention to DS Stone. 'Maybe I heard it wrong when I received the message but that dead man in there doesn't look remotely like a dead female prostitute.'

'The prostitute is the murder victim up on the mountain, Sir,' DS Stone said. 'This came afterwards. We were already on scene as it were and now there two murder investigations.'

'Do we have a suspect?' asked Taffe, and half the biscuit dropped into his tea. 'Damn,' he said.

'Yes. A man named Jack Farr—lives on the mountain—a rather posh looking place. He didn't answer any of my questions so he's now in Cardiff.'

'Who called that one in?'

She paused. Her "suspect" theory, all of a sudden, was about to scrutinized by the Chief Inspector. God, she hated the man. She said, 'Jack Farr.'

Another pause while Taffe used a spoon to dig out the half of the biscuit he'd lost to the tea. While he did that, he continued talking to her. 'Your suspect... is the man who called the police? To report the murder?'

'Yes Sir.' Damn.

He dragged out the biscuit and wolfed it down in one gulp.

'Do we know anything about the dead prostitute?'

This time, it DC Morgan who stepped up to the plate. 'We found items of clothing—of a... uh... sexual nature in her carrier bag, Sir. No ID, no money, no keys... nothing to tell us who she was. But there was notebook with... uh... names... not people-type names, uh... more like references to her clientele. Uh... nicknames if you like. To indicate who she was attending that night.'

'And who was she attending that night, Constable? What was the reference?'

'"The Preacher", Sir. And the costume she had with her was like a porny version of a Nun. Rubber and... and... short... in the dress part of it.'

Taffe wondered if the DC had a problem when it came to describing matters of a sexual nature. He drank his tea in one gulp and put the mug down.

'And this one... what happened here?'

And now Stone took up the story. 'It's a little more straight-forward. The neighbour to this place—uh... number 13 I think—heard a lot of banging and muffled screaming so he came out to see what was going on. That was about... uh seven this morning, I think. Anyway, he saw the front door was open—which he said was unusual 'cos the man who lives here, the son of the dead man, always keeps that door locked. Anyway, the neighbour and his wife comes in and sees the dead man—and the wife runs out screaming blue bloody murder to everyone who'll listen—and the hubby goes to where he hears the banging—in the utility room next to the living room. And there, he finds the son—what's his name, Morgan...?'

'Edgar,' said the helpful DC.

'Edgar Parry—bound and gagged inside the store cupboard. All the towels and clothes are on the floor and he's hog-tied and curled up inside. The neighbour frees him and when Edgar sees his Dad—dead—he throws up everywhere and then runs out screaming blue bloody murder as well. By that time, nearly every neighbour had heard the wife screaming her head off—and they all come rushing out to see what the hell's going on. And then they see Edgar doing the same thing and the Hubby also staggering out, gasping for breath—which is why…'

She paused. There was a lilt of embarrassment on her face. Taffe didn't take his eyes off her—almost smiling… not in a nice way.

'When we got here, this place was like a bloody sauna. Every damned radiator was turned on full so we got blasted by the heat straight away. And the stink… Jesus God Almighty damn near wiped me out and…' She looked up at Taffe. 'Well, I fainted.'

There was a pause. It was almost as if she had confessed a great guilty secret. Bad enough it happened at all, but it had happened in front of subordinates—and now she had to confess it again to the one man she would rather not have told it to.

Instead of the expected rebuke, Taffe looked at her and said, 'Don't apologize, Sergeant. This place could take out anyone with a nose. It still stinks. Who opened the doors and windows?'

'The neighbour, Sir,' said DC Morgan. 'Probably thought he was doing the right thing.'

'And how many of the neighbours trawled in and out of the place before you lot arrived?'

'Practically the whole of this housing arrangement, Sir. As you can see, it's set slightly apart from the rest of the village. This place is… uh… mainly for people who have either been evicted from other homes or have… uh…records of… anti-social behaviour. I think the local Committee who put this arrangement into practice kind of thought if all the troublemakers lived next to each other—they would get to know what it's like to live next door to a troublemaker.'

'And the Parrys are troublemakers?'

'Not now—but in his day, the Father—the one in there—was a big deal in the criminal fraternity. It was committing some kind of offence that got him seriously injured and why he's a…or was… a cripple.'

Dr Swain popped her head around the door. 'There's a name on the handle of the axe.'

'Whose is it?' asked DS Stone, hoping for an easier day.

'Greenacres. I know I've heard that word recently…'

And Stone pounced on it. 'Greenacres. Farr. That's his house. That ties him in with both murders.'

She punched the air. Case sorted.

Chapter 37

Aftermath of a Death

In the hours following DCI Taffe's arrival, a few facts or pretty close conclusions had been established. Dr Swain estimated Hywel Parry had been murdered at least 48 hours earlier—it was difficult to put a more firm time on it because of the heating condition of the house. All the radiators were on full term and had been between the attack on Edgar Parry and the duration of the discovery of the body which complicated the measure of rigor mortis. Only a full examination in the pathology laboratory would confirm time of death.

It was the situation regarding Edgar's attack which sparked Taffe's curiosity. Why go to the trouble of rendering one man unconscious to the point of spending time tying and gagging him, then hiding him inside a store room and then murder another man in such a grisly manner and who could not possibly have offered any kind of defence or fight?

SOCO found a wallet near the dead man's armchair. Only £75 inside it but it signified robbery was not a motive. There was a comprehensive selection of exotic recreational drugs in a box which were designed to put the user into a near comatose state—such was Hywel Parry's physical condition DCI Taffe could easily understand the man's need and addiction to what was in the box. But robbing the victim of his supply was also ruled out as a motive.

It was DC Morgan who made a comment which really interested Taffe regarding Edgar Parry.

'I am sure I smelt Chloroform on his clothes as we were putting him into the Ambulance, Sir. I got a whiff of it when we carried him out.'

Chloroform? It suggested the killer had come armed specifically to do the thing which had been done. To get Edgar out of the way whilst dealing with his father—but again, why such a method of killing the man? And why was the axe left embedded inside the head?

The vision of Hywel Parry being carried out into the street in public—even inside the bag—was too much to be contemplated as the axe could not be removed until the body was at the Path Lab and so Taffe ordered the Ambulance to be brought up right to the front door. The movement from the armchair had already presented some difficulty for the people picking him up as there had been an evacuation from his bowels either before his death and before the son had the opportunity to clean him up or just after his death when his body would have completely relaxed. The faeces had filled his nappy and was now dried and crusted around his rear end and lower back. One of the undertakers remarked that this had been one of the smelliest jobs he had ever worked on. Eventually, the corpse was bagged and placed very carefully inside the Ambulance and then driven away.

DS Stone wanted to get to the City Station so she could get on with questioning Farr—Taffe was happy to see the back of her but ordered no questioning was to be made on Jack Farr until *he* had returned to the Station. This angered DS Stone who immediately asked him if he believed Farr hadn't committed the murders.

'I won't know 'till I speak with him. Make sure he is looked after, Sergeant—but don't speak to him until I get there.' He paused—then looked her directly in the eye. 'Understood?' There was no point protesting against the DCI as Stone knew Taffe well enough to keep quiet from this moment on. She left—in an angry huff—and DC Morgan went with her.

SOCO continued with their search and Taffe decided he wanted to see the other crime scene. Up to this other place then—Greenacres.

Chapter 38

The First Interview

DCI Taffe left the house and was about to get into his car when his arm was pulled back. He turned—to see a distressed Susan Tanner standing by.

'Inspector? You're the Inspector?' she said, her voice thick with worry.

He turned to her and smiled. So far, no-one had expressed any kind of upset at the death of the man inside—and she didn't look like someone who would worry about an old man out of neighbourly concern.

'I am Detective Chief Inspector Owen Taffe, Mrs...?'

'Tanner. Susan Tanner. Uh... I want to ask you something about a friend of mine. The road to his home had been cordoned off by the police and I can't get him on the phone. Even the Vicar has tried and he can't get him either. I need to know... I need to know if he's...'

Her voice broke again. Ah, thought Taffe. This will be a friend of Mr Farr.

'What's your friend's name?' he asked.

'Jack. Jack Farr. He lives on the mountain and it looks like his place has been sealed off by the police.'

DCI Taffe suggested they go somewhere to speak and she took him to her house in his car.

*

'I don't know what condition your friend is in, Mrs Tanner—except to say he is still alive. He is now at Cardiff City Police Station awaiting an interview from myself. I can't tell you exactly what has happened at the house up there but there has been an incident. As far as I am aware, he is unharmed. What exactly is Mr Farr to you?'

They were in Susan's house, drinking tea and having biscuits—again. DCI Taffe had not eaten properly for some time and was inclined to get any kind of food down him until lunch break—should he get the opportunity.

And so, answering the DCI's question, Susan gave chapter and verse of her life with Jack Farr—their childhood romance, their engagement, the animosity from the Hyfridians against Jack's family, the wedding debacle, his fights with the local ne'er do wells—she left nothing out—everything right up to and including the inheritance following his father's death and the mysterious meeting with his benefactor at some so far undisclosed place with people thus far unidentified. Well, that will come up when I question him later, thought Taffe. But it was very interesting information. Mr Farr appeared to be a man in a hurry to return to his place in Oklahoma and resume his life there a now richer man than he had been when he left.

Taffe did as much as he could to reassure Mrs Tanner that her friend was safe and well—but obviously couldn't give her much more than that concerning the two murders.

And then Sara burst in to the house and filled in those details.

'I just heard—Jack's been arrested for murdering a prostitute up at the house...' She stopped abruptly when she saw the DCI—about whom she had heard quite a lot while rubbernecking the Parry house. 'Oops,' she said, hand on mouth. 'Sorry.'

DCI Taffe smiled and nodded to her—then left the house.

Susan felt her own senses leaving her and she slowly sunk into the armchair. Sara, big-mouth that she was—sat on the arm of the chair and put her hand around Susan's shoulder.

'Sorry, Sue,' she said, soothingly, 'did I screw up?'

221

Chapter 39

Crime Scene Number One

DCI Taffe drove up the now empty pathway leading to Greenacres and saw the patrolling police officers as he approached the house. Nice house, he thought. A little ostentatious for this kind of area but this was also a part of the information given to him by Mrs Tanner. It was once little more than a metal and wooden shack, built in the late 1800's by a Farr ancestor, and had remained such until it was demolished and then rebuilt by… whom and why remained a local mystery.

He got out of his car and the police officers—like those below in the village moved out of his way. They resumed their positions once he was inside the house. He didn't speak to them nor they to him.

He entered the reception area and stood still. Last night, Jack Farr had done exactly the same thing—this he had got from DC Morgan who had confirmed this much from Jack the previous night. He flicked on the light switch—and nothing happened. He looked up into the light fitting—and there was no light bulb. He pushed open the main room door and remained standing the doorway. Again, he flicked on the room light switch—and again nothing happened. Again, no light bulb in the fitting. A lined-out shape had been made on the carpet where the poor unfortunate girl had been found. He stared at it.

No blood.

Speaking to Dr Swain at the Parry crime scene, she said it was her opinion the girl had been murdered somewhere else and had been brought to the house.

How? Up the mountain pathway? Across the mountain track behind the house?

There was no sign of the doors being forced open—just like the doors at the Parry house. Either they were already open or the killer had access to each house. It was too much to consider there were two killers—killing the girl and the old man separately with no obvious connection to either—so Taffe, though keeping his options open—concluded the killer of both was just one person.

But why use Jack Farr as the fall-guy? There was no doubt of the intended implication. The Farr house for the dead girl and the Farr axe on the old man. Both meant to look as though Jack had committed both murders. But why? Maybe Jack knew.

There was nothing to keep him here now. SOCO had done their job—and had found practically nothing in the house apart from what the girl had brought.

He left the house and drove back to the City, going past the still rubbernecking viewers at the Parry scene all being held back by the ever thin Blue Line of the police officers.

He had to interview Jack Farr—but before that, he had some homework to do.

Chapter 40

Profiling the Accused

En route back to the Station, DCI Taffe called ahead to get the ball rolling. He wanted all and any filed reports on Jack Farr, his father and brothers—Mrs Tanner had been quite candid about Jack's forays into the aggressive arena and he wanted to see if there'd been any police actions taken against him. Also, everything on Sean and Andrew McGregor—AKA 'The Clay twins'—their criminal history, their most recent offence and its subsequent punishment and their whereabouts at this time. It may be necessary he told the Duty Officer, to put out an All Ports on the McGregors as it was likely they would go on the run having broken their parole bonds. What else, oh yes—everything on Hywel and Edgar Parry—Father and son, the former now deceased—and their criminal history. Mrs Tanner had included the fight between Jack and the McGregors which led up to the visit to the Parry house and he wanted that information passed onto DS Stone who was preparing the interrogation of Jack Farr. Had she seen or spoken to him since his incarceration? No, replied the D.O.—and Mr Farr was quite comfortable where he was. Had he asked for anything? A cup of tea and something to eat was all he asked for which the D.O. had prepared for him—a bacon sandwich. He was sat in the waiting room either exercising or meditating.

Accused of murder after finding a brutalized body on his living room floor—and he was drinking tea, eating a bacon sandwich, exercising and meditating—a cool man.

Taffe requested a full aerial map of the village to be on his desk by the time he got there.

He sped through the lanes and gave the matter some thought relating to Jack Farr. Inwardly, he wanted the killer *not* to be Jack but his old Teacher had always instructed him to maintain an open mind until the moment when there was no longer any doubt about the accused's innocence or guilt. Thank you, Dad.

He received a phone call from the D.O. which forced him to stop the car. A woman from Swansea had filed a missing person report on her girlfriend—she'd been missing over a day and hadn't kept the girlfriend updated on her movements which was something they regularly did. The description of the missing girl fitted the details of the woman found at the murder scene up on Cwmhyfryd mountain. Taffe ordered the D.O. to get full details and a possible identification arranged. What was confirmed here was that both the woman from Swansea and the missing woman were in the prostitution profession and were both known to the police.

He arrived in Cardiff and was about to enter the Station when he received a phone call from the D.O. telling him to report to the Pathology Lab immediately as Dr Swain had important information for him. Diverted, Taffe made for the Path Lab.

*

He entered the lab and Dr Swain was washing her hands. The corpse of Hywel Parry was now lying on the table, cleansed of all bodily wastes and the axe lay on the Doctor's table wrapped inside a plastic evidence bag.

'I've got something for you,' she said when he came in and she led him to her table. She showed him the report forms on what she had learned from her examinations at Greenacres and Quarter Haven.

'When I was at the man's house—Quarter Haven—I saw two areas of blood splattering. One around the chair where he was sat and the other some distance away and on the carpet. The second splattering area was more concentrated and in one place. I couldn't understand why there was so little blood from the dead man considering the extent of his injuries—and then I entertained a possible reason why.'

'It sprayed onto the killer,' said DCI Taffe.

'That's it, and given the amount of blood loss from the man's head, I'd say the killer's clothes would be fairly drenched in blood. Now—I ask myself—this killer has already come prepared with chloroform to deal with the son and he brought an axe with him—the attack on the old man was deliberate and well executed—there is no sign of frenzy in this attack, Inspector, each blow carefully aimed and struck—and then, the killer has to retract the axe from within the cranium, no easy task, as each blow is deep inside the head which means the killer had to place their hand on the man's head to gently pull the axe out—and then strike him again. With me?'

'All the way,' said DCI Taffe.

'And so I think the killer entered the house—*prepared* for blood splatter. But that amount of blood on clothing would raise questions if seen by other people. So—I think he went in wearing something similar to what our SOCO use. Some kind of coverall which can easily be disposed of. '

Taffe nodded. Good deduction, he thought—I probably would have got to that conclusion myself. Is this why you called to speak to me, he asked.

She then showed Taff the second report—the one from Greenacres—the dead woman.

'It's the blood group. The second blood group I found at Quarter Haven. It's from the dead woman. But I found it at the scene… of the second murder.'

This took Taffe by surprise. He wasn't expecting there to be such a direct connection to the two murders.

'The dead woman—was killed—at the *Parry* house?'

'Yep. Not only that—but like the son—she had also been chloroformed. I'd even go so far as to claim she was probably unconscious when the killer beat her and killed her.'

He paused. He had to get this in order and relating to when it happened—and where Jack Farr might have been at the time. Time of death?

'At least forty eight hours for the girl—probably the same for the man—I'll confirm that when I've examined him—but I'll bet your pension both the deaths occurred at the same time since they happened at the same location.' She then showed Taffe the woman's clothes.

'Blood under the trousers behind the knee area and smears of blood across the left side of her blazer. This is how the killer carried her out.'

She stretched her arms out in the fashion of someone carrying someone. The carried person's left arm would be placed around the killer's neck. The Doctor said she would confirm the blood group on the woman's clothing by the end of the day but the bets were on it being Hywel Parry's blood being transferred to the woman's clothing. Taffe thanked the Doctor and then he left the Lab.

It was a SOCO report which confirmed the Doctor's words—a shiny, silvery false fingernail had been found at the Parry House—identical to the false nails on the dead woman's fingers. The question for Taffe now was: how did the killer transport the dead woman up to Jack Farr's house without being seen?

He enquired within the police station—any coppers who have some kind of intimate geographical knowledge of the Cwmhyfryd village would need to report to him asap.

He entered his own office. On the table was the requested map of Cwmhyfryd. He studied it for ten minutes and the only modes of entry to Greenacres were the main pathway starting from the base of the village at Bevan Road and the surrounding track at Mynydd Haf before entering the village. But it is possible there is another route to the mountain not sketched on the map and he needed someone with local knowledge. He called the D.O. and asked again for someone to assist him. The D.O. confirmed there was a man and he was already making his way back to the Station—a Sergeant Cenydd Thomas from Swansea. Taffe ordered him to be brought into his office immediately he arrived.

He poured himself a cup of tea and brought out his own sandwiches, prepared by himself the night before when he had been called to go to Swansea to attend the abduction case—which he solved twenty minutes after getting to the father's home. An accusation by the girl's father, accusing a Private Teacher having a relationship with his daughter. Taffe read the girl's diary, saw the notes she had written on the luckless Tutor and had worked out exactly what had happened and where the girl was. The girl was found within three hours and the Tutor walked free—traumatized but free. Taffe was about to eat his sandwiches when he was notified about something much more serious—a dead woman in a small village. He hadn't eaten since that call and now he was ravenous.

On his table there were the other filed reports besides the Farr family: the McGregors, the Parry criminal family and information about the two deceased.

With interest he read about the many conflicts engaged in by the Farr's—and he noted that none of them had ever been started by them. Mostly, they had been provoked by other people who had wanted to assert their own authority and territory over them—which had been met with opposition by either Joe or the twins—and settled then. On occasions, the police had become involved but no actions were ever taken. The worst of these incidents revolved around the wedding debacle and the funeral day—again provocation from the villagers was recorded by the attending police officers against the Farr's and no action was taken against Joe—just a token response against the twins and nothing of any kind against Jack. Taffe noted that the police weren't even brought in regarding the fights Jack had in during the period after his mother's death. He was clean. So far. Don't forget Dad's advice.

The McGregors file read like a comedy script—there wasn't one thing they'd been involved in which hadn't turned out farcical. The Judge's comments about their being so unsuited to a life of crime just added to the humour. He made a mental note of Mrs Tanner's assertion that they may have been hired to take a strike at Jack. On that issue, he noticed the paper which had been written by Jack Farr at Greenacres was not here. He called the D.O. and requested to receive it.

The Parry file was a little more fulsome. Such a clever man when he was operating all those years ago—and never to even raise a suspicion from the local police. It was the final job which lead to his serious and life debilitating injury which made Taffe's eyes light up—the Farr twins had been responsible for that. Well.

The D.O. brought in the paper which Jack had written at the house.

'Where is he now?' asked Taffe.

'I looked in on him just before I came up, Sir. Still exercising and he says he's okay.' Taffe thanked him and carried on reading. There was really nothing in the files to add to the cases before him—but the background information was useful.

Then he took up the paper Jack had worked on. A sheet of A4—and a photograph of himself stapled at the corner. It was a detailed list of his movements from the moment he'd received the phone call from Vicar Redd right up to the moment of writing the information down—which was timed at three in the morning. He even offered an explanation relating to the photograph. That it had been taken by someone who had hired the McGregors to work him over and had been taken outside when he was in his garden sometime last week—the photographer had probably been hidden by the great oak tree which dominated the forest embankment. Taffe made a mental note to get that area visited to see if anybody had been standing in that ground behind the tree.

At the end of Jack's detailed report was a list of all the people he had met— old and new—since his return to Cwmhyfryd and the exact nature of his relationship to them. The most interesting name was Allan J Gibney—a lawyer, he knew, of some notorious repute and apparently representing the Farr family name. Well.

All the names would have to be interviewed. How many on that list still hated Jack—and who would be desperate enough to commit such extreme offences to get him jailed?

A knock on the door ended the reading session and Sergeant Thomas entered. In just five minutes, Sergeant Thomas answered the most important question of how the killer could have taken the dead woman up to Greenacres. Taffe called the D.O. and asked for DC Morgan to come to his office.

DC Morgan arrived and Taffe showed him the map with the now new red-lined diagram which had been provided by Sergeant Thomas. A path leading away from the Parry house through the Quarter Haven Estate, which did not have any kind of street lighting at all. A public footpath leading up to the mountain on the west side of the village, and directly to the Church. Over a gate, walk up a quarter of a mile ahead, there is another gate, which then leads onto yet another public footpath not officially recognized by the Community Council—which leads directly into the forest surrounding Jack Farr's home.

'I want you to return to that place,' said Taffe, 'with the Sergeant, go up this pathway, and follow the route through to the forest. You're looking for heavy indentations—not actual footprints because the killer may have been wearing covers on his footwear. The killer may have been carrying a nine stone woman. Look for a path and head towards the house. Any sign of footprints—and I doubt there'd be many—and get the Forensics people up there immediately. Also, find the big oak tree and see if there are any footprints around it. Farr says this picture may have been taken from that point. Off you go.' He gave Morgan the picture. DS Morgan and Sergeant Thomas trawled out of the office and out of the Station and headed towards Cwmhyfryd for the second time that day.

Taffe continued with his reading and digested every single word of Jack Farr's mini diary which also included a question as to how any intruder could have gained access to his home so easily and who, out of those he had offended against, could have killed a girl. Taffe noted there was no mention of any other attack so he would keep the second murder to himself until it was time to come out for a walk. He called the D.O. again.

'I want Farr placed in an Interview Room and let DS Stone know I will be speaking with him in ten minutes. Tell her I want her there with me.'

Taffe picked up the plastic evidence bag containing the axe. There was dried blood on its axe-head. He placed it on the table so the name Greenacres, written in green marker ink was face down. It would be interesting to see how Farr reacted when he saw both the blood and the word.

Chapter 41

Interview

Jack was seated at the table when DCI Taffe entered the room. DS Stone was already there setting up the tape recorder for the interview. Constable Roberts stood by the door—ready to intervene in case of any adverse reaction from the person being interviewed. Taffe took his place at the table, the item he was carrying buried under a large cloth which he laid on the far side the table away from curious eyes. He placed a notebook in front of him and laid a pencil by its side—all of this he did while looking at Jack's face to see how this experience was affecting him. Eventually, he settled, put his fingers together and bent them sending out a cracking noise which echoed around the large room. He smiled at Jack.

'How you feeling, Mr Farr?' he asked.

'Tired and confused but otherwise fine, thank you.' Voice firm and confident. Good, thought DCI Taffe. This will not be an aggressive accusation or denial kind of interview and he felt much could be accomplished here provided everything was kept to an acceptable level of decibels—which meant all he had to be worried about was the interruptions from DS Stone who was still convinced the killer of the girl and Hywel Parry was sat in this room. He kept his principle playing card under wraps—and its possible revelation could tell him a great deal about Jack Farr.

Taffe begun his spiel. 'For the purpose of the recording—I am Detective Chief Inspector Owen Taffe, in this room with me are Detective Sergeant Stone, Constable Roberts and Mr Jack Farr, all in relation to the incident at the village of Cwmhyfryd.

Incident—not incidents, not murders. Taffe noted Stone's look of surprise when he referred to it in the singular tense and not the plural. Jack didn't flinch.

'I am aware—thanks to a written statement given to us by Mr Farr—of how Mr Farr, a former resident of Cwmhyfryd, has recently returned to it, coming from Oklahoma in America in order to deal with his late father's Estate. He has been in the village for just over a month. In the statement he has referred to incidents and has named a variety of people with whom he has come into contact. Included in the statement is a photograph taken of him by someone as yet unidentified—which he maintains led to a violent incident—which we will address later in this interview. I will state now that Mr Farr is being interviewed as a witness and not as a murder suspect—this reference pertaining to the dead female found by Mr Farr in his home last night at around the 10.30 time—yes, Mr Farr?'

'I came home at that time, yes. I found the body a short time later and called the police immediately.'

'In fact, that call is timed at 10.50, which marries up to what Mr Farr has just said.'

Taffe heard a wearisome sigh from DS Stone—her way of saying she did not agree that Mr Farr should not be described as a "suspect". Taffe did not respond in any way—she had to learn not to be so impulsive. He smiled again.

'Whilst I am aware of this inheritance bequeathed to you, Mr Farr—I am not aware of the details of the journey you took yesterday to learn of its origin. Are you able to tell us anything about that?'

For the next ten minutes, Jack laid out in very specific details, times and even the roads, of the journey he and Allan J Gibney took to get to Ellison Pharmaceuticals. When the name Gibney was mentioned, DS Stone suddenly looked up. How was this man Farr mixed up with one of the country's most powerful lawyers? She looked at Taffe who hadn't flinched at the mention of Gibney—but then, DCI Taffe had read the statement written by Jack at the house which mentioned him—so he *was* prepared.

Jack then recounted the day and time he'd spent with Arthur Ellison—and what he'd learned about his father, his war, his friendship with the late Sir Walter Ellison and the origin and nature of the inheritance. Then the journey back to Cwmhyfryd and their mini break at the Air Balloon pub and the meal they had eaten. Very specific with the time and again, which roads they had taken.

Finally, the end of the journey at Bevan Road where Jack had left Mr Gibney—his intention to inform Mrs Tanner of how his day had gone but only to be told where she was—at the hospital in Cardiff attending her husband.

'And that was that—I walked up to my house, went in and found the dead woman.'

'A little more than that, actually,' said Taffe. 'After you went in, you also found…'

Jack paused. Oh yes, he said, the lights weren't working, the curtains had been drawn, something he would never do—then the dead woman.

'I'm interested in how she was in your house, Mr Farr,' said Taffe. 'You stated you were certain you'd locked the house up. And yet—there were no signs of a break-in—no damage to the doors or windows. How could this person have gained access to you home?'

Here, Jack paused. He had given thought to it, he said. So many people had the keys to the house before he'd even stepped foot back on UK soil. The Estate Agency—which meant Susan—the Vicar, possibly Peter Eddy the Brangwyn Solicitor, and maybe even Gibney Associates as they were the bodies of people representing both parties of Farr and Ellison. Anybody could have used either the main key or copied it for their own use whenever they wanted to.

Taffe made a note of that—*keys to Greenacres and who had access?*

'Regarding your day yesterday—who knew you'd be away for such a long time?'

'Mrs Tanner, uh…Vicar Redd. Of course, the people I went to see would have known. And I didn't know exactly how long I would be there—I thought I was going to Cardiff—not to Gloucester. Who they all told I don't know.' Taffe noted that as well. Everybody on that short list Jack had written out was going to have to be questioned.

'Did you look at the girl's face?'

'I saw enough to see she'd been beaten, there were bruises around her eyes, dry blood on her face and heavy bruising around her throat.'

'Did you recognize her?' asked DS Stone.

'No. I could see she was young so she would have been a child when I left Cwmhyfryd. I haven't seen her around the village since coming back.'

'Presuming her to be a… how do they call themselves? "Hyfridians"?' asked DCI Taffe.

'That's the word. Their own coinage. Makes them sound special—or unique.' And then he looked at Taffe. 'Ah, you mean she might not have been from the village.'

And on cue, the door was knocked and a policewoman entered.

'For the tape—Officer Lambert has entered the room with…?'

The officer handed Taffe a handwritten note which read:

DCI Taffe—a woman named Lynda Bennet has positively IDed the dead woman as Yvonne Shepherd—both prostitutes from Swansea area. It is urgent you speak with this woman ASAP. D.O.

Taffe read it twice and nodded to the officer. 'As soon as I am done here,' he said. She nodded back and left the room.

'Officer Lambert has left the room.' He paused. 'When was the last time you went to Swansea, Mr Farr?'

'I've never been to Swansea. Not even when I lived here.'

'Don't know what you're missing. Okay—you come home, you literally fell over the woman—yes?' Jack nodded. 'And then you call the police. Uh... what did you do next?'

'I checked around the house to see if anybody was still there. Only the lights in the reception and main living room weren't working. The police arrived— uh... some while later and I sat in the kitchen while they did their work. They took my clothes off me and put me in this outfit.' He gestured down to the white coveralls he was still wearing.

'To check for any kind of DNA evidence—and on that issue, do we have any updates...?' asked Taffe and he turned to DS Stone who still looked at Jack as if he were the Cwmhyfryd Ripper.

'Forensics are still working on Mr Farr's suit, Sir.'

Taffe looked to Jack who nodded. Moving on. Now for the big one. He took the bagged article from under the cloth and placed it in front of Jack.

'I am showing Mr Farr an axe. Can you identify it, please?'

First, a look of confusion from Jack. What the hell was this all about? Why was his father's axe here? To be absolutely certain, he peered at it closely but there was no doubt what it was and to whom it belonged.

'That is my Dad's axe,' he said.

'And when was the last time you saw it?'

Jack breathed out. He hadn't wanted to talk about this because it would involve Susan and her husband in the axe-throwing incident which almost decapitated Jack. How this involved the dead woman he couldn't figure but...

'Right. Uh... I had a small disagreement with a Mr David Tanner—and he...uh...threw this at me. It missed by a mile and it ended up in my doorframe. That was over a week ago—and I haven't used it since. Actually, the last time I saw it, it was still in the doorframe.' Jack presumed one of the SOCO Unit must

233

have prised it out of the doorframe and bagged it as evidence assuming it was related to the dead woman's demise.

'So—you've used it?' Jack nodded. 'Obviously, your father used it—and Mr Tanner. Is he related to… Uh…Susan?' Jack confirmed it.

A pause—and now DCI Taffe paid close attention to Jack. 'Turn it over, Mr Farr,' he said. Another pause—with Jack now looking at both Taffe and DS Stone with some confusion on his face. He did as instructed. He turned the axe over and saw the word Greenacres written in green ink on the handle. His facial reaction intimated more confusion.

'Well—it is definitely my Dad's axe—but he didn't write that on it.'

'You're certain?'

'Dad wasn't a child, Inspector—he wouldn't write something on his clothes or property to prove he owned it. Not words or names. Anyway, I would've seen it when I used it. This is new. It's a bit childish actually.'

Taffe nodded. He had come to that conclusion as well. And then Jack suddenly stared at the axe-head.

'Is that blood?' he asked—with more than a little shock in his voice.

'It is indeed blood,' said Taffe. This is it. How will he react to this?

'But there wasn't any large amounts of blood on her. Not from this kind of weapon. I checked her carefully.'

'This isn't her blood. This was used on someone else.'

Pause. Jack stared at Taffe. '*What?*' he said—his voice rising a tone.

'You knew a man named Hywel Parry,' said Taffe. 'How did that come about?'

Jack didn't respond to *knew*—not immediately. 'A few days ago, I was attacked by two men. This was witnessed by… Susan Tanner. It was from that attack we found the photograph. Uh… Sara Phillips, a friend of Mrs Tanner, told us the two men were…oh hell, I've forgotten their names. They are known as the "Clay twins".'

'Sean and Andrew McGregor, Sir.' This came from Officer Roberts at the door. 'They are known to us.'

'Thank you, Officer Roberts. So you were attacked by the McGregors. And how does this involve Mr Parry?'

'Well—that's when I learned the McGregors had worked for Hywel Parry— and that he was a resident in the village. He lives at a place called Quarter Haven.

I went to speak with him—to see if he's hired the McGregors to work me over. But I found...'

Now it was Taffe's turn to stare. "*He lives...*" Jack said. Not lived.

'The man is a cripple. Practically dead from the neck down and... well, I learned it was my twin brothers who'd crippled him. I thought it might be revenge but his son, Edgar, put me straight on that. My being with the Parry's lasted just a few minutes. I haven't seen them since.' He paused there—and then realized. 'Hold on—*Knew* Hywel Parry?'

Taffe leaned forward, both hands raised to his mouth and clasped. 'Jack,' he said, 'I have to tell you now that Hywel Parry has been murdered—and he was killed with your father's axe.'

The atmosphere in the room turned suddenly cold. Jack visibly blanched and he looked as if he were about to fall. Had he been standing upright he probably would have done. DS Stone studied him as did DCI Taffe.

After a few moments, Jack whimpered 'No,' in disbelief. His voice was little more than a breath and for Taffe, who frequently made studies of people's reactions to shock news, it told the truth. Jack's stunned face was too genuine for it to be role-play. There was no way he killed Hywel Parry—but, as his own father had instructed him, keep that mind open.

Jack looked away and now his mind was racing. The girl's death—well, maybe that could have passed off as an isolated and possibly unconnected incident. But this—with Parry—and his father's axe? No. Someone had gone to extraordinary lengths to implicate him in this vile business and he needed something to be able to give to Inspector Taffe—because DS Stone was already convinced of his guilt in the girl's murder. This—and the fact that he not only knew Parry but also they had a shared history—put him right in the centre of it.

But who? Who would commit such an atrocity in such a manner just to get to him? Someone in the village? Jack's mind sped through all the principle participants—Fisher, Edmunds, Phillips, the Boxer, Tyler something or other—it just didn't seem possible, not even from those people who hated him. Impotent of information, he lowered his head and kept silent.

After a few moments of that enforced silence, he looked up again. 'How did Parry die?' he asked.

Stone was about to say something but Taffe got there before her. There was no point in hiding the full truth and it might tell him something if he brought it out.

'The axe was used to crush the late Mr Parry's skull. My colleague in Pathology says the killer used it maybe six or seven times—and then left it inside his head which was where we found it.'

'Edgar—the son,' said Jack. His voice returning to its original confident stride.

'Traumatized but unharmed. We're looking into that. The killer left the son alive but kept him captive inside the house.' No details. Let Jack do the walking. Taffe never took his eyes off his man. Colour was now flushing back into his face and shock was being replaced by fury. Taffe recollected exactly what Mrs Tanner had told him about Jack's foray into violence in the period following his mother's death. A man quite capable of serious harm to be sure—but those fights were in the nature of self-defence. This was different. If Taffe knew his man, Farr would now be on the metaphorical scout for the killer himself—and if the information given to him by Mrs Tanner was anything like close to accurate, Taffe would have to move fast because if Jack Farr got to the killer before he did, there would be nothing left for him to arrest.

Taffe looked at the note given to him earlier. The word *URGENT* concerned him—the D.O. wouldn't flower a thing like this up so he decided to end this session. 'Interview with Mr Jack Farr suspended at 13.10 hours.' He turned the tape recorder off—much to the disgust of DS Stone whom, he knew, would question the soft-pedalling he had given Farr. Tough, Sergeant. This man didn't kill those people and I have other important business to attend to.

'Right, Jack,' Taffe adopted a more formal approach now, 'Forensics are still examining your suit of clothes but I know they'll be finished soon. And then we can take you to wherever you need to go. But—you cannot return to your home as it is still a crime scene. And, this is only advice but if I were you I would avoid Cwmhyfryd Village. If the killer is a resident there and they see you walking about as a free man, they may take another stab—either at you or maybe someone close to you. Is there anywhere you can go?'

The problem was the only people who could help Jack in this matter were both suspects. Susan—highly unlikely—and Vicar Redd—again, unlikely but...

'Do you mind if I speak with Mrs Tanner? She runs an Estate Agency and she may have an empty house I can reside in while...' He left the sentence where it was. Taffe would understand his situation.

'Absolutely. Just be sure to keep us informed as to where you do go and any movements in or around the village. And Jack—I am aware of your abilities in

236

the fighting department—I would advise, very strongly, for you *NOT* to undertake any kind of vigilante work. I can appreciate how you're feeling—but let's not muddy the situation any more than it already is—okay? I am certain your friend Mr Gibney would advise you in the same way.'

There it was again—Gibney—*Friend?*

'Deal,' said Jack and he stood. He knew he was in luck here—and he saw the scowl on DS Stone's face. Officer Roberts led him out of the interview room and back to his cell. Taffe heard them speak and Jack saying loudly—'A cup of tea would be very welcome, thank you.' Taffe smiled. Not bad. An almighty shock to the system and he had borne it well.

He turned to DS Stone who stood there with her left hand on her left hip. The look was intended to intimidate.

'I can't believe you let him off the hook so easy,' she said.

'You still think he did it?' asked DCI Taffe.

'The evidence says so,' she said, with a steeliness in her voice which came with the disappointment of seeing her only suspect being set free by this interfering Inspector. He turned to her and faced her down.

'Look,' he said. 'You have here a man who ran away from this village and its people twenty years ago because of the way they treated him and his family. He didn't just leave empty-handed either—he had blood on his hands then. He hasn't communicated with any of them—including his father—in that time since. The only reason he came back was because of the father's inheritance, the conditions of which stipulated he had to deal with the matter—personally—face to face—with those people who were acting in his father's interests. It is his intention, Sergeant, that the moment this business in completed, he is going to skedaddle back out of this village and return to the States. Do you honestly believe—that he would engage in any kind of activity that would have him kept in this country a minute longer than was necessary? Do you honestly think that this man would first murder a girl—in a very brutal way—inside the house of a man he had already spoken with, *then* murder the man—*with his own father's axe?*—leave the axe inside the dead man's head, cart the dead woman a mile and half up the mountain, dump her on his own living room floor—and then call the police?'

Bereft of explanation, DS Stone just scowled at him. Taffe moved away and left her standing to deal with the tape recording. He had to speak with the girl's friend, partner or whatever. And according to the D.O. it was urgent.

237

Chapter 42

The Partner

DCI Taffe stood outside the waiting room for at least five minutes before entering. He looked at the woman sitting at the table, a cup of steaming tea in front of her. She was, he guessed, in her mid-forties, and had at one time in her life been an attractive woman but had turned blousy and was now out of shape. Her face was deeply lined and the mouth downturned as if in permanent angst. Possibly, the girl's death—and the manner in which she had met her death—was making a huge contribution to her appearance but Taffe guessed her beauty days had long since sailed past and she was now heading towards her senior years in a poor way.

He looked closer at the face which was streaked with black mascara running down her cheeks and the tears had been flowing for some time. Officer Lambert was inside the room with her but standing at the other side of the room and she did not speak with the woman.

Taffe entered. Officer Lambert stood and looked at him. He nodded and she exited the room. He went to the woman—Lynda Bennet was her name he remembered now—and sat at the table next to her. This woman was in deep grief. There had been love between this woman and the dead girl and she was feeling its loss very greatly. Taffe—who had only had ever experienced one major love in his life, unrequited—knew the pain of loss. He placed his hand upon hers—itself an infraction of rules—and spoke gently.

'I am Detective Chief Inspector Owen Taffe—I am the officer heading the investigation relating to the young lady's death…'

'Yvonne,' said the woman, grief croaking in her throat. 'Her name was Yvonne. I called her Vonna—she called me Lyndy. She was my girlfriend.' And then she lowered her head and howled into her scarf. Her head and shoulders appeared to collapse and she rested her head on the table and continued her howling.

The sound of a person grieving is too painful for an outsider to listen to and most people would probably leave the room and allow the griever to cry the pain out of their system—but Taffe had a job to do and he needed to get through this while at the same time not being insensitive to the person in pain.

He squeezed her hand and again, spoke gently. 'Lynda, Mrs Bennet, I am sorry for your loss—but I need to find Vonna's killer—there is another aspect to this case and I need to find the killer before he strikes again.'

She looked up at him. Her face was thick with black streaks, red in the cheeks, saliva dribbling out of her mouth, eyes swollen with emotional pain.

'I was told you already had the killer,' her voice was strangled and it jumped from one state to another. 'You arrested a man already.'

Damn, thought Taffe—and he wondered how many other people who were stood on the perimeter thinking the same thing. He needed to damp that one down soon.

'No, Lynda,' he said, using her Christian name and not Mrs Bennet—keep it friendly and local. 'The man we've been speaking to is not the killer—he has been framed for the murders...'

'*Murders?*' she exclaimed. 'There's more than one?'

This was more than he should have given her but felt it was necessary to make headway.

'Two murders—same killer. But there is method behind the killings. And in order for me to get a start on Vonna's death, I need to know about her—about her movements. Her clients. Basically—everything you can tell me. Have a drink of your tea.'

Lynda Bennet dutifully drank her tea—in one gulp. She placed the cup down and stared at him for the first time.

'What did say your name was?' she asked.

'Taffe. Owen Taffe.'

She stared again. She was thinking. Slowly, her eyes opened and saw him for the first time.

'Swansea, three years ago—"Bully-Boy" Fletcher,' she said.

Colin Bullimore Fletcher—a Swansea hard man who ran a small Empire of girls—some of whom had been brought in by Eastern Cabals and had been sold as slaves. Taffe ran that investigation and brought it to a close. It ended hard for "Bully-Boy"—he and Taffe had had a real hand-to-hand set-to—and "Bully-Boy" was now a permanent fixture in a Prison Hospital, crippled for life. Taffe was subjected to another IPCC Inquiry from which he was eventually cleared and his reputation escalated upwards by some margin. Around twenty girls from Albania and Romania were found huddled in a large metal cabin inside the Fletcher Estate and were dealt with by Immigration. The world of the prostitutes were glad to see the back of the Fletcher Empire and while their misery did not completely leave them safe, they were living in a better place. What did come out of it was the name of DCI Taffe and the girls were grateful. Lynda Bennet now marshalled her thought and gave her fullest attention to the policeman who would probably solve her girlfriend's murder.

'What do you need to know?' she asked.

Taffe took out the notebook found at Greenacres. He showed it to her.

'These names—or codes—I need real names and addresses—or any information you have on these clients. Especially the last one—"The Preacher".'

She took the book and skimmed through the titles and handwritten expressions.

'We barely used real names—these codes are... how do I say it...? They're a reflection on the tastes of each of the clients. I mean—here, "The Cop"—he probably wasn't really a Cop. But he liked Vonna to dress up as a sexy WPC—and arrest him. Get out the handcuffs—furry ones so they didn't get hurt and a bit of hard cop/soft cop interrogating. Um... here we are—"Teacher"—well, that was someone who like a bit of Britney in a schoolgirl uniform. Most of them didn't even want actual sex—just the visual was good enough. Vonna would sing on that one—*Give it to me... ONE MORE TIME.* See?'

'The last one—"The Preacher",' said Taffe. Lynda looked at it and scanned her memory.

'Oh yeh—a real God-botherer. Wanted her dressed as a Nun—uh... doing her religious rant. She said he was a real creep—even by creep standards. Flagellation stuff—again, no real harm. I think she told me he was kind of old and pathetic, had a bit of knowledge of religion and liked to hear her singing that Monk type stuff.'

'Address?'

'Kind of a moveable feast some of these,' said Lynda, her thickness of voice now lightening up now that she had fluidity of speaking. Her crying was temporarily being held at bay as well—brave girl. 'Uh... Cardiff I think. She would always travel to a place provided the client agreed to pay for travel expenses on top of the session—if the place was too far enough away from home soil.'

'Regular client—once in a blue moon? How did he get in contact?'

'Semi-regular. Maybe once a month. And he would phone us. He had a phrase he would use and that always told Vonna who he was. He called… uh… the same afternoon she went to see him. That was unusual. He generally would give her a day or two notice.'

So, Taffe thought. That particular cycle was broken. *He* called Vonna, *he* wanted her that day. Was it "The Preacher" who called? If not, who else knew about their codes? Whose phone was used to book Vonna he asked Lynda.

'Mine,' she said. 'I was… like… her agent. The clients would call me, I would make the arrangements. She would go. We had our own safety arrangement. She would arrive at the venue, call me to confirm, then call me when the session was over. Give me an ETA on arrival home. She confirmed the arrival at the venue but didn't call at the end of it. I waited an hour then went looking for her. There was no-one at home when I got there. I waited till morning and then called the Plods—I mean, the Cops.'

'I need that phone, Lynda. I need to know where that call came from—and if it really was "The Preacher" who made the call. I want his address. I promise discretion.'

Lynda delved into her handbag and took out her mobile phone. She handed it to Taffe.

'Nobody has used that phone since Vonna's confirm call that night. Here's the address of "The Preacher". She wrote the address down. Taffe knew the Cardiff area and he would hand this over to DS Stone when this interview was done. Lynda told Taffe that Vonna had gone to Cardiff by train and from the station to the "Preacher's" address by taxi.

In the silence which followed as Taffe registered the information, Lynda resumed her crying. Not as gruelling as before but still as heartfelt. There was nothing more for him to get from her and he rang the buzzer for Officer Lambert to come in and take over.

And that was when Lynda Bennet dropped the bombshell.

'I know you got her personal stuff—what about the gun? Do I get that back?'

That stopped Taffe short. He slowly sat back down—the look of horror on his face all too obvious.

'Gun?' he asked—fear in his voice. 'What gun?'

241

'My gun,' she said, her voice calm. She said it as if she had just asked him about a compact mirror.

Taffe marshalled his thoughts now and kept his voice level. 'Tell me about the gun, Lynda.'

'I bought it years ago from a dealer. It is licensed and it's never been used while it's been with me—well, I mean it's never been shot. I once pointed it a client who refused to pay and Vonna pointed it at a Pimp who wanted to cut into our action. But it's never been fired. She took it to all the jobs—she kept it inside her brown bag where she put her clothes. There's a small pouch inside the bag and that's where the gun is. Or should be.'

'Make, size, calibre. Do you have a picture? Anything and everything Lynda.'

'Smith & Wesson. Model—uh… 317.22, LR 8-revolver.' She sat back. Then raised her hand and finger. 'Ooh—I do have a photo of it—but that's at home.'

Officer Lambert entered the room and Taffe stood up, taking Lynda by her arm.

'Right. Lynda—there was no sign of a gun found in Vonna's bag or belongings when we were at the house—which means it's either been lost, overlooked or… the killer stole it. Officers Lambert and Roberts are now going to take you to your home and you will give them the photograph of the gun…' Officer Lambert reacted with her eyes. This wasn't good. 'And on your way home, try and think of everything about this incident. Someone used the "Preacher" code to specifically target Vonna to get to her—for whatever reason—and there is your killer—but that means someone knows about your codes. Think back to everyone—and I mean *EVERYONE*… who you've had contact with over the past few years and write the names down. Friends, enemies, casual contacts, ex-Pimps—whatever comes into your mind. Get that info to us or Swansea Police as soon as. The killer is way ahead of us at this time and I need to catch up to get to them. Okay?'

She stood in front of him—all five foot four of her and stared up at his face. Slowly, she wrapped her arms around his body and buried her head into his chest and cried. Not the heart-wrenching sound she had made earlier but still affecting. Even Officer Lambert was moist-eyed.

'You got "Bully-Boy"—you find the bastard who murdered my Vonna,' Lynda said in amongst the heaving sobs. Taffe gave her a gentle hug—again against all the rules—and Officer Lambert turned away just in case she was compromised later on by someone asking a question. Taffe assured Lynda he was working on it.

Still sobbing, she was led out of the room by Officer Lambert and Taffe sat down.

Christ, he thought—a gun.

Chapter 43

The Investigation Begins

He had to move fast now. He reported the gun information to Superintendent Marsh—which sent up alarm signals straight away. The Armed Response Unit would have to be notified and every single police officer working the case, going from door-to-door asking questions to all the local Cwmhyfryd residents if they'd seen anything suspicious, would also have to know. If the killer *was* someone living there and they saw a couple of Cops walking up their driveway, they may make the assumption that they'd been discovered and decide to go out shooting. Such had happened before. This investigation had just taken a dangerous turn.

He gave the address of "The Preacher" to the desk sergeant and asked for uniformed police to go to Tyburn Road in Cardiff to talk to the man. The call to Lynda's mobile had been made on a land-line phone and Taffe had confirmed the address with BT. Uniformed police were sent out immediately.

He ordered for another search of Yvonne Shepherd's bag to be made—just in case the original search had missed the pouch. Unlikely, the weight of the gun itself would have caused suspicion as well the clumping sound when the bag was placed on the surface. But you never know.

He sat in his office compiling a list of the chief suspects the police would need to speak to. Taffe saw—as did Jack himself—that the man had been set up for the murders which pretty much localized it. Someone from the village. He took into consideration the list of the local ne'er-do-wells in the village—and the supposed hard knocks—but who the hell would be so insane as to commit such brutality just to implicate someone else—no matter how much they hated him?

He set the list of those people Jack knew and had history with aside and concentrated on the new people in his life—which thankfully, weren't so many. Vicar Redd for one—never take it for granted that just because we're dealing with a supposed respectable profession that the person involved is also respectable. So, a background check on *Mister* Redd was in order. Who else? Well, Peter Eddy, the Solicitor from Brangwyn. A good contender. Taffe knew of Eddy—but had never met the man. A small time and local personage who had been brought into this business by outsiders. An unlikely contender but he goes on the list.

Gibney Associates.

Now Taffe knew Allan J Gibney on a slightly social level and much of him by reputation. Both he and his father and other members of the Gibney family were hardly Persil clean and had tended to—how to put it—wander from the straight and narrow at least on the side of the Angels. According to Jack Farr, the Gibney angle had been extremely prevalent from the moment the Joe Farr inheritance had been written down by him and Sir Walter. As the Lord High Executioner sang in 'The Mikado', Taffe had *him* on the list.

After that very short entry—Taffe divided the list of names up and selected one portion to be given to DS Stone and the other to DS Morgan—and as if on cue, he then received a phone call from that officer.

'Good news, Sir,' said the enthusiastic DC. 'We went through the Quarter Haven area from the back of the Parry house. It's all very closely built and at night, there are no street lights. Anyone could walk through and wouldn't be noticed from the householders. Out of the area we walked up the pathway leading up to the mountain. Just a few yards up and you're already out of sight from the entire village. Trees and bends in the road and you can't be seen by anyone. Okay—you get to the gate leading up to the Vicarage but it's high up and you're just a dot—in the daytime—you certainly wouldn't be seen at night. Quarter a mile up and you come to the gate and the public footpath. Over the gate and we cross over to the forest. The ground is rock hard so no prints. But… and this is where we strike gold, Sir, we get into the forest and the ground is soft. Not actual footprints—but deep indentations in the ground, like the person is either heavy, or they're carrying something heavy—leading all the way across and down to the Farr house. Now where Mr Farr says he may have been photographed—by the big oak tree—there are a number of deep prints—nothing recognizable so the photographer may have been wearing boot covers—but they are there. There are other similar kinds of prints around the lower embankment leading onto the path. We can't get any more identifiable prints 'cause it's all concrete from there leading up to the house. But there is mud on the path leading into the kitchen door so maybe Forensics could match the mud from the area around the oak tree. Sir.'

Taffe smiled—so far, the best news he'd heard since the case had started.

'Well done, Constable,' he said. 'I'll arrange another trip for the Forensics Team to get back up to Greenacres. Stay there till they arrive and lead them through what you have seen. The killer would also have made his way back out—probably the same way—but that would have been in daylight. It's possible someone may have seen them walking through the forest. Soon as you're done, you and Sergeant Thomas get back down here. You all have a busy day ahead.'

Well, he thought as he stretched his arms upwards. The investigation had now really begun.

Ten minutes later, he was informed by the D.O. that Mr Farr had been given leave to leave the Station—his suit having been cleared of any DNA involvement of the murders. Jack was free to return to his home, though not his house. He would be visible again. Taffe wondered how that would go down with those who hated him—and possibly the murderer as well.

Chapter 44

Sour Victory

Malcolm Fisher had become a rare sight in the village after his very public dismissal from the café by his own daughter—which caused a great deal of mirth from those who couldn't stomach the man's precious pride, his superior-than-thou attitude and the constant boasting of how wonderful life was in this "close-knit" community that "we all love". Hah!

By mid-day, news of the two murders had been circulated all around the village. The continued presence of the police and their cordoned off area were still very much a source for discussion and speculation. And the Hyfridians just loved to speculate. Two murders—one of them in the house of old Joe Farr. So, the speculators concluded—that young rooster really came home didn't he? He'd been a source of so much unrest and violence (it did not matter that the violence had been inflicted *upon* him, but let's not let truth get in the way of a good speculation say the Hyfridians) and now he has reacted in the most heinous way. Not just a girl—*but a prostitute girl!* Young? Who knows, who cares? He killed her, that's the end of it. And what of the Parry murder? Well, we know Jack Farr went there a while back to have it out with the poor old sod—crippled in his chair—because of this supposed attack by two total strangers and we only have *his* word that such a thing happened.

Such is the nature of small-time talk running in a small-time village by small people who have never experienced scandal in such a way—actually, not since that wedding debacle twenty years ago and that involved the Farr family... and...

Oops.

Which was what brought Malcolm out of his early enforced retirement and back out onto the streets—just to gloat about the news that Farr—*that Jack Farr*—had merely continued his father's penchant for violence and it had now resulted in the worst form—the murder of a young woman. The shame it would bring to the name of Cwmhyfryd. We are all tainted by this man's presence and the sooner he is locked up and out of everyone's lives the better.

And the venue for this tirade was The Night's Tail Pub—pity the poor drinkers who had to suffer this man's eternal ramblings while they attempted to drink their beers, eat their lunches, just trying to relax and get away from the horrors of what they had learned that day.

'What did I tell you all?' crowed Malcolm Fisher. 'The man is Cain sent to us by the father who was evil incarnate. What did I say? If he comes back there will be trouble. He isn't here five minutes and already there is blood on the floor. He attacked me, he attacked one of my customers in my own café, he almost killed my son-in-law. If you people had listened to me, none of this would have happened. I told you. I warned you all.'

In fact, there had been no such warnings of impending catastrophe from Malcolm Fisher—just an inward groaning that the son of his greatest Nemesis was returning to the village.

'Do you wanna drink or are you just gonna prattle on all Goddam day?' asked the wearied Landlord whose heart sunk the moment he saw Malcolm enter his Pub.

But Malcolm was on a righteous roll and wouldn't tolerate any interference. The man is a killer now—all there for everyone to see—the police don't arrest people for no reason and Farr must be dealt with in the most extreme form by the Law.

God's Law? asked one of the drinkers who knew exactly where this particular tirade was headed.

'If necessary,' shouted a victorious Malcolm Fisher whose own personal take on his religion did not marry up to even those who attended Church. And where is Vicar Redd, he demanded, when we need him the most? Here in our midst helping get through the worst of days? No, he shouted, he is giving succour to he who has offended us all in God's eyes.

The silence which followed felt unreal in a place where there were at least thirty people drinking.

The door opened and Huw Evans entered. He took one step—and stopped. The silence from the full room confused him and he wondered if he'd just stepped into a private meeting. He waited and listened. Then he saw Malcolm Fisher at the bar and realized—the poor drinkers were getting another dose of fire and brimstone.

He joined a group of drinkers seated on the table the furthest away from where Malcolm was stood and said, 'What's he bloody on about now?'

The oldest of the group, Pedr Williams—in fact, one of the oldest living people in the village—leaned back in his chair and clasped his fingers together, forming a Spire and, adopting a sage-like tone as if he were a University Professor giving his students a final tutorial before passing their exams, said, 'According to young Malcolm, if we don't all line up to lynch Jack Farr, we are all going to Hell in an Asda plastic carrier bag.'

Huw Evans rolled his eyes and waited for Malcolm to end his next sentence.

'And I warned you—no-one can say I didn't warn you...' The tirade was fading and he appeared to be gearing up to take a second breath.

Malcolm was about to order a drink from a much relieved Landlord when Huw stood up and said, 'So, according to you, Jack Farr is death Incarnate and he's going to fry in Hell—yes?' And that stopped Malcolm from ordering his drink.

Bugger, thought the Landlord, who had hoped the rambling had come to a stop. Now there's going to be a bloody debate.

'Absolutely,' intoned the pompous café owner.

'And we're all meant to be grieving for the sad deaths which have happened here—yes?'

'The loss of any human life is a cause for deep sadness—yes.' Malcolm turned to the bar and raised his hand to address the Landlord.

Huw took himself to the centre of the Pub and addressed the drinking group, standing just a few feet away from the victorious Malcolm Fisher.

'In the first place, the girl was not a person from this village so we can't be sad about her—regardless of who she was and how she died, we didn't know her. In the second place, Hywel Parry used to be a notorious gangster and I remember, Mal, that yours was the only voice on the Community Council which objected to his coming to Cwmhyfryd at all. In the third place...' And here, Huw puffed his chest out, fingers in the lapels of his jacket, '...if Jack Farr is a wanted murderer...' Pause... 'How come he's walking about the village square with your daughter?' Pause. 'At this very moment.' He almost beamed when he said it.

The Pub became a tableau. No-one moved, no-one made a sound...

And then, like a flock of birds changing direction in the sky at the same moment, every last man leapt up and fled the Pub and into the beer garden—

much to the relief of the Landlord who moved quickly to shut the doors and locked them up, locking them out. He breathed out a huge sigh then went upstairs to join his wife who had gone into hiding.

From the beer garden, the Village Square can easily be seen. And sure enough, just as Huw Evans reported it, Jack Farr was strolling about the Square alongside Susan Tanner—both of them being watched by at least two dozen villagers.

At the head of the drinking group, Malcolm Fisher stared—in total shock and disbelief—at the sight of his own flesh and blood walking about, casually, with the man who he claimed had brought death, dishonour and shame upon his beloved village.

Shock gave way to red-faced fury. *'JEZEBEL!'* he seethed—possibly the worst insult he could dredge up to describe any woman—the one he had used against his wife, Moira, when she told him she was in a relationship with another man. He barged through the group and actually knocked a few of the more frail drinkers to the ground. He stormed down the steps and across the Square screaming *'NO,'* to everyone he passed, who looked at him with such fear upon their faces—as if they were about to witness maybe yet another killing.

'I won't have this—not from my own daughter—not doing this in front of people—not with... '

Jack had been back in Cwmhyfryd at least half an hour before he had eventually been seen by Susan who, he could see, was working inside the café. He deliberately didn't go there—in case there were customers inside who would be so reviled at the sight of this man accused of two grisly murders that they would clear off from the café, making Susan lose her clientele.

He had been brought back by two uniformed police officers who had been given very specific instructions from DCI Taffe as to how he was to be reintroduced into the village Community. They were to take him to the centre point of the village and—to all intents and purposes—parade their being with him in such a way as to suggest to all who witnessed the arrival, that they were in no doubt that he, Jack Farr, was not at war with the police or on the run from them. As it turned out, there were at least two dozen people milling about the Village Square when they all saw the police car arrive, the two officers getting out of the car, opening the back door and allowing Jack to step out of the car. The officers then conversed with him for a few minutes, even engaging in laughter, before shaking him by the hand and then getting back into their car and driving away—horn beeping. They may have felt a personal dislike for the DCI who had given them this order—but they knew exactly why he had given it. They left Jack alone and surrounded by a now very much confused populace—because they knew the police generally don't let murdering criminals free to wander about the shopping centre.

Susan was drawn to a number people outside the café who were pointing and expressing their doubts—so she stepped out to see what they were looking at—and saw Jack standing still and looking up at the café. She gasped and ran down the flight of steps and ran to him—tears from her eyes and it was all she could do to prevent herself from flinging herself at him and giving him a bear hug.

He told her everything about last night and the dead woman—his interview with DCI Taffe and up to the moment of his being brought back to Cwmhyfryd. Susan listened and was happy to hear that maybe her talk with the Inspector may have had some part to play in Jack's release. Now, she gave way to impulse and wrapped her arms around him—not passionately—but of gratitude that he was back and, for the moment, safe.

This heart-warming show of affection puzzled everyone who knew her—knew that she had jilted him once before and married the man she had jilted him for—and *he* was now in Hospital, it was rumoured, by the very man she was now man-handling.

The heart-warming gesture came to an abrupt and angry end when her father stormed up to the two of them and physically prised them apart.

Breathing out, heavily, Malcolm Fisher stood between them and glared at them both—apparently unable to speak a fluent language.

At the Pub beer garden, bets were being laid as to how this little scrap would end.

'This will be good,' said Huw Evans, 'the last time Mal had a go at Jack Farr, he got his tits squeezed.'

After a few minutes of glaring, Malcolm finally found his voice—strangulated to be sure but at least it was understandable.

'Evil,' he let out. 'This man is evil—and you are married. Your vows are sacred... Do not fornicate upon the streets with this...'

Susan ended it by taking Jack's hand and walking away, leaving Malcolm behind, bereft now of further speech and impotent rage taking over him.

Just a few hours ago, Malcolm Fisher had stood victorious in his own home, having heard the news of the terrible murders and that Jack Farr had been taken away. He had thus been vindicated—in his mind—that he had warned the people that they had a virtual Cain walking amongst them and the lives of two innocents had been taken by that man. He watched his daughter walking back up to the café he had run for so many years with that very man—knowing he was the subject now of close scrutiny from those he considered to be *his* people…

…and they were laughing at him.

Defeated, the taste of a sour victory in his mouth, Malcolm Fisher slunk away and retired to his home.

Chapter 45
The Investigation Progresses

In the following forty eight hours, progress continued with the investigation—slow but sure and important moves had been made. All the villagers living in and around Quarter Haven were now being questioned about their movements around the mid-evening mark on the night Hywel Parry was murdered and had they seen or heard anything at all that would appear to be suspicious?

The good news was Edgar Parry eventually emerging from his state of trauma and being able to give a sobbing but at least coherent telling of what happened to him that night. While the front door was heavily secured, the back door was opened for a small period of time while he took out the household rubbish and put it into the plastic bins located at the back of the house. He had already taken out two heavy bags—a two month collection—and was on his third when he was suddenly taken from behind—the smell of a heavy odour overpowering him—and he felt his legs collapse underneath him. In the time which followed, he regained consciousness a few times but was in a state of confusion, asking himself why he was so uncomfortable in his bed, but then falling unconscious again. It was only long afterwards when the effects of that terrible odour had worn off that he became aware that he was bound and gagged and crumpled up inside a small space that he began to kick and, within the ability to do so, scream—the mouth gag only allowing muffled sounds. By the time he was released by his concerned neighbour, his father had been dead at least twenty four hours.

Edgar did not see his attacker, had no sense of size, age or even gender. It was then he broke down and was unable to say anymore.

'It's called Associated Grief,' the Doctor looking after Edgar told DCI Taffe. 'In the past few years, Mr Parry has been... how can I say it—praying... for his father to die. Not out of malice, you understand, but simply for his father to be released from his terrible torment. Now that it has actually happened, Mr Parry feels a sense of guilt, believing he is responsible for his father's death. He wished for it—it happened. Now that it has happened, he has no one left to take care of—and he believes that is his fault. It doesn't help matters when you take into account of how his father was killed. Quite brutal I understand. He will feel this guilt for a long while to come, I'm afraid.'

So—the question of how the killer manage to get into the Parry house was answered. He simply walked in. But… was that just luck? Opportunity presenting itself and Hywel Parry's association with Farr just a coincidence or had the movements of Edgar Parry been kept under close observation by the killer?

It also didn't explain how the killer had gained such easy access to the Farr house—that house had been secured and no-one was at home to let the killer in. Still, one problem dealt with.

The uniformed officers found the house at Tyburn Road in Cardiff—and confirmed Lynda Bennet's claim that "The Preacher" was indeed old and pathetic—but more importantly had not been at home when Vonna Shepherd had gone there. Nor had he been in the three days previous to that. There was no doubt the phone call to Lynda's mobile had been made on the old man's landline—but it couldn't have been him making the call as he was away on an already booked excursion keeping him away from the house for at least a week, booked into a Holiday Spa for the over-60's at a Hotel based in Ross-On-Wye—according to the neighbours, a trip he had made this time of year along with nine other over-60 year olds in the Cardiff area.

What was very important was the fact that his car was missing. It would have been parked up inside his own garage and the keys secreted away in a bowl of fake sugar. The neighbours knew of his occasional forays into the world of Bondage and possibly Sado-Masochism—and some had even seen the young and attractive woman who had called there. But not this time.

Vonna Shepherd had been summonsed, had gone to Tyburn Road, was let into the house by…? Was she killed there? No, she had been rendered unconscious—don't forget, Dr Swain had found chloroform on Vonna's clothes—and was brought to Cwmhyfryd, possibly by "The Preacher's" own car, taken to the Parry house and was probably murdered there just after the killer had dealt with Edgar—and before the killer had dealt with Hywel.

Which meant the killer was either very lucky or had superior knowledge of the movements and the habits of the Parry's and of the "The Preacher"—but how did the killer know where to find the car keys? How did the killer know how Lynda and Vonna operated? No, thought Taffe, not lucky—very well planned, actually. Informed even.

DC Morgan's footprints find in the forest was a wonderful break for him. Forensics had gone back up to the mountain and worked around the area surrounding Greenacres. The soil around the great oak tree was of a different type compared to the mud and earth found in the rocky alleyway leading up to the mountain above the house. They found elements of the forest soil on the paving stones leading to the back door of the house which meant the killer had indeed walked through the forest and had possibly waited for Jack Farr to leave the house before carrying the dead Vonna into it through the back door. Again, the killer knew of someone else's movements.

But how the hell did the killer get inside the house? This business of so many people having had access to the house and its keys even before Jack Farr had come back home rankled him—so many possibilities to tie down.

There were no soil samples inside the house—primarily the kitchen area, the first place the killer would have walked into—which meant the killer had taken off the shoes and their covering before entering. Taffe thought about the killer and how he or she had behaved. Very careful planning had gone into this and his opinion was this killer was no beginner so Taffe wondered if there were similar killings recorded in the files—or maybe the killer was new to the area. He sent out the details off to other police Forces around the UK setting out the nature of the two murders and the killer's Modus Operandi and enquired if he or she had been active elsewhere.

The paperwork so far had been impressive but now he needed to be out in the field asking people questions—about their movements, their feelings for Jack Farr and just how much did they hate him?

He decided to begin with the Phillips Family.

Chapter 46

Families at War

'DAD!'

DCI Taffe sat in the living room of the Phillips' house and wondered if he hadn't wandered into a war zone, such was the unbridled animosity on display between father and daughters—while a shame-faced Sara sat away from him in a corner armchair wishing her husband would just, for a few moments, shut the Hell up and stop digging himself into a hole where, she guessed, was exactly the place the DCI had wanted to put him.

Taffe had to take into account he was sitting a private dwelling owned by the people he was speaking with and so was, to a point, constrained by how he could deal with it. But every time he asked a question to Mr Phillips, it was met with such vitriol and spite—anything to do with Jack Farr just led him onto the next venomous rant. Taffe had asked Adam Phillips if he had any kind of social intercourse with either Hywel Parry or the dead prostitute and instead of answering the question, Adam went off on a completely different tangent which ended with him saying the two murdered people would have been justifiably killed if it meant Jack Farr being lynched. This resulted in the elder daughter remonstrating with her own rant at her father.

Taffe was sat at least five feet from Adam Phillips but the smell of alcohol was heavy in the small room. And it was only two in the afternoon. He looked at the man's face—ruddy in the cheeks, and a nose which had the beginnings of a pickled look about it. If he isn't already an alcoholic thought Taffe, he's well on the way.

Eventually, Taffe got the reasons for Adam Phillip's anger from Catrin herself—which only reinforced what Mrs Tanner had already told him—about that small period of time after Mrs Farr had died when Jack had laid siege to those who had oppressed him—but he hadn't recalled all the names but now he knew he was in the company of a man who had been soundly beaten by Farr twenty years ago—and was still carrying the scars to show for it.

When he'd arrived—DS Stone in tow—he assumed the three teens in the room were all the children of Mr and Mrs Phillips—but no, the boy Tommy was in fact younger daughter Claire's boyfriend who had more or less moved in with them though he still had a place of his own in the village but was originally from Stone wall Mountain. Sara announced to Taffe that Tommy was a Fleminganese citizen which Taffe didn't understand so she explained to him the history of those people. Oddly enough, he now lived in the apartment one floor above Sion Edmunds—who was to be the next interviewee on Taffe's little list.

'Ha,' shouted out Adam, 'you think *I'm* bad—just wait till you get a load of *his* bile. If his spit could kill, he'd spit at Farr. He's in the chair for life 'cause of that bastard...'

'*DAD!*' from the two daughters in chorus paused his rant but didn't fully stop him and he carried on in full flow. 'Farr damn near killed him and now he's a permanent cripple. Always in pain he is. Poor sod.'

Tommy Leeming piped up his little contribution. 'I hear Mr Edmunds every night—coming up the stairs with his sons—always in agony. Always crying. It's very hard to listen to him, Sir.'

'Don't call him "Sir",' said Adam, 'he ain't a fuc... he ain't a Knight of the realm.' The emotion of the subject at hand was getting too much for Mr Phillips thought Taffe and so he decided to move onto something else.

He'd already established Sara's movements on the night Jack found Vonna Shepherd—she was at the Heath Hospital with Mrs Tanner trying to get a duff car on the road. Catrin was in the house all evening having finished at the café at six o'clock and stayed in mostly on her computer while Claire and Tommy were tucked up together on the sofa. Tommy was currently employed in the same factory Adam worked in and they came home together. Tommy was yet to pass his driving test so he relied upon Adam to get him back and forth to the factory which was some miles away from Cwmhyfryd.

'You drive to work, Mr Phillips?' asked DS Stone—no doubt looking for a drink-driving offence. 'No,' he retorted, 'I bloody swim across the lanes—it's easy this time of the year 'cause the lanes are always flooded.' DS Stone was getting to dislike Mr Phillips very much and if one good thing was going to come out of this interview it was the possibility that she may arrest him for drunk-driving. Given the amount he's tucked away, I'll bet he's still over the limit by six tomorrow morning, she thought.

Taffe didn't care about the DS's ambitions and arrest record—he wanted answers and he wasn't getting them from Mr Phillips.

At last, Sara spoke. 'I saw Jack in the village yesterday. Does that mean he's no longer a suspect foe the killings?'

'It is highly unlikely he killed those people, Mrs Phillips,' said DCI Taffe, hoping to get that message out to as many people as he could—if only to provoke a response of some kind. 'We had nothing to keep him in custody with so we had to release him.'

Adam Phillips snorted. He confirmed he was at The Night's Tail the night Jack came home but as he'd tied a few drinks together with good friends that night he couldn't remember what time he'd left—'You were here by eleven,' said Catrin who glared at her father—and as they were all slightly pissed he doubted the others could give him accurate times either.

This interview was over.

Sion Edmunds was the next to be seen. Taffe and DS Stone left—shown the door by a most apologetic Sara and Catrin who told them he wasn't always like this which DS Stone doubted very much.

As Taffe and Stone walked away from the house, they heard more shouting and screaming coming from within.

*

'Loog at be, I'm a fuggin' cribble,' sobbed Sion Edmunds when the issue of Jack Farr was raised. 'He did this to be,' he garbled as snot poured from his nose, mixing with the saliva pouring from his mouth and both elements being washed down his face by the tears which poured out from his eyes.

Seated at least six feet away from Sion Edmunds, DCI Taffe received the full whiff of whiskey and gin mixed with, he guessed, a few pints of the brown stuff. Sion Edmunds was another man headed for the alcy grave—though in his case, it would be a preferable state compared to the life of utter misery he was now living. Farr had really done a job on this man, thought Taffe—but given the vile comments he'd made to a grieving son just a day or so after the death of his mother, what else could this drunken oaf have expected? Any tinge of sympathy felt by Taffe was tempered with the opinion that Mr Edmunds had deserved his lot and had only made his physical situation worse by excessively imbibing on alcohol to the point of near oblivion.

DS Stone rolled her eyes to the ceiling, she having a poor opinion of any man who cried as hard as this one was doing. The ceiling was a dirty brown—similar to the heavy smoking Hywel Parry's home—and was festooned with spider-webs and dust—in fact, a spider was currently engaged in creating a brand new web as she stared. DS Stone doubted the dusting mop saw much action in this apartment. She sat, gingerly, on the edge of the armchair not wanting to sit back and relax as she had seen the stains on the cushion seat.—God knows what that lot came from and she didn't want to ask.

Seated by the open window, possibly breathing the fresh air, the younger son, Ryland, was looking out into the village and then back at his distraught father who was sitting deep in his own armchair—a result from a broken spring—that couldn't be helping his injured back, thought Taffe.

Ryland was himself obviously holding back his own tears as he heard his father describing exactly what Farr had done to him all those years—a rant he had heard so many times over the years and he couldn't bear to hear it again. He begged his father to calm his temper down because of his heart condition but once on a roll, Sion Edmunds never let go.

Well away from the central action, Steffan Edmunds skulked near the kitchen area, his head turned away from the questions and answering business. He had never met DCI Taffe before but he knew the man's reputation and the very last Copper he'd ever want in his home was now sitting a few yards away. He hoped Taffe didn't know about him—or the company he kept which was currently in the process of planning a venture that would make them maybe richer than they were now. This man Taffe was a known puncher and while he and his fellow would-be "mobsters" were tough men in their right, Steffan knew they wouldn't want to be crossing swords with this DCI.

'How you doing, Steffan?' shouted out Taffe quite suddenly. 'Still on Community Service? Learning how to dispose of rubbish? Hope that'll include some of your friends.'

Bugger, thought Steffan. He knows me. That's the end of *that* venture.

This interview was proving to be even more difficult than the one Taffe had with Adam Phillips. What he had ascertained—through Ryland mainly—that Sion and his two sons had been in The Night's Tail on the night Jack had come home and found the dead prostitute. There was no apparent relationship between

259

them and Hywel Parry though the Edmunds did know of the gangster's past. Ryan confirmed they had never met the McGregor twins and to his knowledge they had never stepped foot in Cwmhyfryd before the day they attacked Jack Farr.

'What a pair of tossers,' cried Sion, 'two of 'em, a bloody knife and they still couldn't kill the bastard.'

Taffe stood up and DS Stone joined him—with a look of relief on her face. The stink of this hovel and the three men contained within had offended her nose and she wanted out of it *NOW!*

'Your sons didn't exactly fare particularly well against him, did they, Mr Edmunds?' said DCI Taffe and he walked to the door. He could feel the hatred against him and DS Stone as they walked out—and heard more disrespectful noises about them from father and sons as they walked across the landing floor.

He and Stone got out into the fresh air, cleaned by a fall of misty rain and they made their way to his car.

'Who's next?' she asked.

'Mrs Tanner,' he said and they got in.

*

DCI Taffe gave no impression to DS Stone that he'd actually been inside Susan Tanner's home before today nor that he'd spoken to her at length about Jack Farr. He had knocked her door and when she answered, he introduced himself and DS Stone and told her they were making general enquiries about people who knew or had known Mr Jack Farr. Susan, taking the hint, was equal to the task and allowed them in—even asking the DCI for his name again. He confirmed it and she asked if it was after the river in Cardiff. Same pronunciation, he told her, different spelling. Masquerade confirmed.

Susan gave them the same details she had given the Inspector the day Jack had been taken to Cardiff Police Station. But now she added to the details. Jack had been dropped off by the police the day he'd been released and had come to her looking for temporary housing—which she provided not less than an hour before this visit. Jack was now situated in an old abandoned farm-house just a few miles out of Cwmhyfryd. It was a place which had just recently come onto the market and her Agency was given charge of selling it. It didn't possess much in the way of furniture, she told them, but ideal for someone who only required a temporary location.

At last, thought DS Stone—someone who could speak clearly and concisely and didn't reek of booze. This interview will be very interesting—not least because she knew they were dealing with someone who had played such an important part in Jack Farr's life. Reading about the man, she had learned about the Wedding Day and that Miss Susan Fisher—now Tanner—had jilted him at the altar. How curious then that of all the people in the village, she was the one who was giving him the most assistance. She kept that little piece of information to herself—just in case and wondered if DCI Taffe knew.

The hitherto session of the interview came to an abrupt halt when they heard the front door being opened and slammed shut—and Malcolm Fisher barging into the lounge room.

Not quite drunk but certainly heading that way, Malcolm came inside and was already delivering his rampage speech before he'd seen Susan had visitors. It was meant to be along the lines of: *I'm not having this. You and that man Farr are making me look like a laughing stock in front of my own neighbours and I am telling you not to have any more to do with him.* Or something along those lines. He'd reached the 'I'm not having this, Susan—you and Jack Farr...'

He saw the company and froze—odd face expression, thought DS Stone. Like a rabbit in the headlights of an oncoming artic lorry. Very red-faced as well. Another one.

'Oh,' he stammered. 'I didn't know...' He stared at DCI Taffe and guessed who he was. He pointed his finger at Taffe and said, 'Are you the two police officers asking questions about Farr?' he finally got out. His ruddy complexion had seemed to fade into a pale white.

'I am Detective Chief Inspector Taffe, this is my colleague Detective Sergeant Stone—and yes, we are asking questions. Not just about Jack Farr.'

His manner was polite—Susan, however...

'What do you think you're doing—coming into my house when you know I am at home? That is not our arrangement.'

His face turned red again—it didn't take much. He addressed Taffe again. 'You released him—why? He was in this village yesterday. A killer has been allowed to walk around, free as a bird, in my village.'

'Mr Farr did not kill anyone, Mr Fisher—unless *you* know for an absolute face that he did.' He let the statement linger for a few seconds, and then… 'Do you?'

Fisher blustered. He was only ever in command when in his own territory—and even though it was his daughter's house, the company she was keeping made it not his territory.

'The girl,' he stammered. 'In his own house. There's your proof. The axe—his own father's axe—in that poor man's head. There's your proof.'

'Proof of what, Mr Fisher?' asked DS Stone, to Taffe's delight. 'Do you think it likely that Mr Farr would kill someone in his own home—then call the police? Or that he would kill someone with his own father's axe—and then leave that crucial piece of evidence behind where the police could easily find it?' Well done, Sergeant, thought Taffe. On my side at last.

Malcolm was about to reply—but now his capacity to speak appeared to desert him. His mouth opened and then closed. Susan walked over and spoke to him, almost nose-to-nose. 'If you ever come into my home like that again—when you know I am here—I will take that key from you. Now—unless you have something worthwhile to say—and I know you haven't—please leave.'

He paused. Yet again, defeated by the girl who should defer to him at all times. So much like her mother. He backed away, staring at the two police officers who, he felt, had betrayed his world. Slowly, he slunk out of the room and this time did not slam the door. Quiet resumed. Taffe decided he needed to know more about this odd hatred of Jack Farr so violently demonstrated by so many people in the village.

It isn't Jack, she explained. It had been his father, Joe, and over a long time ago. This man had been a native of Cwmhyfryd even before the village had been given its name—his family maintained the forestry and the farming communities when the village was still being built. They were seen as poor relations by the newcomers and were kept apart from the burgeoning community. Then Joe was gone from their lives and the young bucks of the village began to spread their amorous designs on those young fillies who were now approaching the ripe period of their lives. The most attractive of those fillies—the most desired by every man bar none—was Theresa Phelps—and the man who wanted her most of all? Her own father. It never even got off the ground—not with anyone else either as she was far too sensible. But it was Joe that Theresa had run to. Within months, they were married, within a year she was carrying their first born—the twins. It rankled every man in the village that such a beautiful girl could fall for such a rough-house like Joe Farr—and worse, even live in that bloody tin shack on the mountain and away from them. In the years which followed, a number of men had made futile attempts to rewin her affections—to the point of physical challenges against Joe—to which he responded with vigour and success. The only man who hadn't challenged him was her own father—never a fighting man. The man Farr, his out of control twin boys, the gentle younger son Jack. Resentment by proxy if you like, she finished. Nothing more.

Taffe was clever enough not to ask her about her relationship with Jack—or why it had ended so oddly at the Wedding day. DS Stone was also quiet—that part of Jack's history she was not aware of—and hearing it put the way Mrs Tanner had explained it made her feel sad. DS Stone understood prejudice and isolation—her own family, descended from the days of the *Windrush* period, had suffered from a similar prejudice. Jack Farr suddenly went up a few notches in her book.

End of interview. They thanked her for her help and left the house.

*

'What an odd bunch,' said DS Stone. 'So much anger—even against themselves. Who is next, Sir?'

Before he had a chance to tell her, the phone rang. It was Sergeant Thomas calling from his police car.

'Sir—we have found the car belonging to Ralph Jones,' he said. For Ralph Jones, read *The Preacher*.

'We're on our way,' Taffe told him.

Chapter 47
Background of a Cop

'Why didn't you call me when they took you down, Jack? I would've been down there like a shot.'

'I thought about it—especially when that Sergeant Stone pretty well accused me of the murder—but I decided to wait until the formal questioning started up. Just as well—he seemed to have believed in me even before he came into the room.'

Jack was sitting in a deep plush armchair at Allan J Gibney's Cardiff office as Gibney made them both a pot of tea. He brought the tray over and Jack settled in. Camomile tea. He'd never drunk camomile before. Quite tasty. He took four chocolate biscuits and dunked them into the cup. To his amusement, Gibney did the same thing. A man of taste.

Gibney had been informed of the murders by Arthur Ellison who had then instructed him to get to Jack's aid the moment it became necessary. DCI Taffe's role had made it unnecessary and Jack had contacted Gibney to update him about events and the temporary change of address. Now they were having posh tea inside Gibney's own office in Cardiff.

After two mouthfuls, Gibney continued. 'You drew Taffe. You were lucky.'

'I know it. He didn't try to intimidate me into giving a story. Didn't try to fluster me.'

'Owen Taffe is... let's see how I can put it... something of an enigma even within the Force—and I mean the UK Police Force—not just South Wales. He's a known puncher—he's knocked quite a few criminal thugs about—those who got in his way and those didn't co-operate with his investigations. He is very methodical about his work and protects those who have been accused—or even charged—with crimes. He *looks*... doesn't jump to any final conclusions. Managed to get a few seriously accused criminals off from crimes they haven't committed—much to the anger of the Cops who originally arrested them. He isn't very popular amongst his own people—and...' Gibney let the next comment float while he dunked more biscuit into his tea. '...and, he is Cop-killer.'

That last statement paused Jack in mid flow of drinking his tea. The look of surprise on his face made Gibney smile.

'Something which occurred when he was in London and serving in the Met. He discovered a senior ranking police officer—his own DCI—was on the take and had actually planned an abduction of a child—a ten year old boy—Father was a wealthy German Industrialist living in London. Taffe worked it out somehow, confronted the bent Cop—who decided to shoot his way out and it resulted in the death of a uniformed officer, with Taffe himself getting shot in the shoulder and him killing the DCI. From that time on, he became a pariah inside his own Force. Curious business. The DCI was a criminal of the worst kind—but Taffe had killed him and in the lexicon of the police, taking down one of their own was more unforgiveable than the crimes the DCI had committed. They gave him a hell of time after that. He couldn't remain at the Met and was transferred back to where he started—at South Wales Police.'

'Ah,' said Jack. 'That explains some of the comments I heard when I was waiting in my cell. Quite a few were very disrespectful of him.' He dunked another biscuit.

'He has a story before that though. He had been abandoned as a baby, he was found in a big shopping basket next to the River Taff. A Nurse, I think, name of Sian Owens, found him.

He was taken in, given the names of Owen and Taffe—but the Registrar spelled the surname wrong so that's how he is called today. He was fostered out to quite a number of families—all giving him back to the State because he was... uh... unmanageable. Eventually he was placed into a sort of... Borstal Educational Complex... not because he was bad or anything but simply because that was the only place they could find for him. No details on record but I do know he was ill-treated there. And then... here's where it gets important... a man came into his life and served as a kind of mentor. Now this man was a known drunk—possibly a full-blown alcoholic—and *he* used to be a police officer. Thrown off the Force because of his drinking. Thing is, there was just enough of a physical likeness to suggest that this man may have been the boy's biological father. That was when Owen was thirteen. The man... seemed to... *instruct* young Owen... not just in the three R's or in basic education, but in other things as well. Life, I suppose. That lasted till Owen was about nineteen and then he found the old man dead one morning in his own bed-sit. There was a photograph of him getting married to a young valley's girl—and she was known to the police as well. Both of them were heavy drinkers. She died... get this... giving birth. But nobody knew what happened to the baby. '

'Taffe...?'

'Who knows—but the way it looked to everyone, was the woman died giving birth and maybe the father, drunk, incapable, simply couldn't face raising the child by himself and he puts the boy somewhere safe where he would be found and taken in. And then, when the child is thirteen, his life slightly out of control, the drunk father gets *his* life back together by doing his parental duty.'

'Wow,' said Jack. 'Some story.'

'There's more. He went to live in a small village in a small valley—not there now—it was mostly an industrial area and the main form of industry was controlled by a family called Grace. Uh... Philip Grace, if memory serves. Now he had a son—Peter—and he and Jack both had an interest in a young valley girl called Rhiannon. She was the daughter of the factory's foreman who was a good friend to Grace Senior. It was kind of an agreement that the daughter and Grace Junior would eventually marry—an agreement between the two fathers—and they became engaged. Now Owen didn't take to this as he knew the girl didn't love the Grace boy. But she rebuffed him purely on account of the fact that Peter Grace was rich and he, Owen, wasn't even employed. So the girl and the boy were engaged. Lasted two months.'

'And then she ran to Owen Taffe,' said Jack.

'No. She was killed. The result of a car crash and then her freezing to death. The boy, Peter, was the driver—but he'd done a runner and stayed out of touch for three days. The police couldn't prove if he was over the limit or not. Grace senior insisted his son had been injured in the crash and had temporarily lost possession of his senses. The Law couldn't prove anything against him and he was released.'

'And Taffe...?'

'Who knows exactly what happened but this is what *is* known. Young Peter and his out-of-control friends went out on bender one night—exactly one year after Rhiannon was found dead—and they got completely drunk. On their way home, Peter became separated from his friends and he ended up walking through a Communal Park. He went to sleep on a park bench—and was found the next day by a dog-walker—dead from hypothermia.'

'Same as the girl,' said Jack.

'Same as the girl,' confirmed Gibney. 'Within a few months, the valley industry went bust, Grace senior appeared to have given up on life, and the valley itself folded as it was wholly dependent on the industry led by Peter Grace. The majority of inhabitants left the valley, almost a ghost village now. Grace still lives there in his mansion—but he's a broken man. Here's a peculiar thing though. Two months after the boy had been buried, someone desecrated his gravestone. Same thing happened twice each time after it had been repaired. Young Owen eventually joined the Police Force. He rose in the ranks fast as well. He... *sees*... things. He doesn't just look, he sees things. He says his father taught him—well, that may have been the old drunk, who knows?—but he's a damn good Cop. Has quite a formidable arrest record. If you're guilty, he'll get you.' He dunked another biscuit. A worthwhile lecture, Jack thought. If Taffe was on his side, he could get out of this—maybe intact.

Chapter 48

Backstepping

DCI Taffe sat back in his chair and studied the sheet which had been placed before him. Ralph Jones' car had been found on a scrap dealer's premises about ten miles east of Cwmhyfryd. It was parked in the middle of the area amongst other cars and the lucky break was the owner knew exactly how many cars were meant to be parked there. Clever killer, thought Taffe—from the old game "Where's the best place to hide a tree?" Answer? "In a forest." The killer did the same thing by hiding the car along with other cars. They had even trashed it a little so it would blend in with the other scrap cars but the owner was sharp and he knew it was a new car the moment he clapped eyes on it. A simple call to the Brangwyn Police—just in case—and once he'd given them the car's registration plate three police cars were there within ten minutes. Once the plate had been confirmed as the missing car from Tyburn Road in Cardiff, possibly related to a killing in Cwmhyfryd, the information went out fast and DC Morgan picked it up immediately, then passed it onto DCI Taffe.

As a day of learning and getting things done, it hadn't been a disaster. An important part of this kind of investigation is eliminating people from the enquiry as well as confirming that such and such a person *is* involved. Again, without prejudging his case, Taffe pretty well took Adam Philips out of the equation and Sion Edmunds the same. Morgan had interviewed the remaining members of Jack's violent rampage twenty years ago and they each had alibi's.

Malcolm Fisher was a revelation though. That man had a big temper and clearly he hated the Farr family. Taffe had heard that this man was a devoutly religious individual which didn't gel with his treatment of Jack—no turning the other cheek here, nor of forgiveness for those who had trespassed against him.

Enough to commit a murder though? Or hire someone to do it for him because Taffe didn't figure the aged Malcolm Fisher to be able to steal a car, render a woman unconscious, kill her and another man and then carry the dead woman two miles up a steep hill and across country. Not for the first time, Taffe did wonder whether there was more than one pair of hands involved in this matter.

No—not the actual murders themselves—but was he capable of hiring someone to do it?

The name of Malcolm Fisher was added onto the list of possibilities in Taffe's notebook.

Back to the car. Allan J Gibney's assessment to Jack of the mysterious drunkard who had entered Taffe's life at the age of thirteen was indeed correct. The man *was* Owen Taffe's biological father though he had never admitted that to the thirteen year old Owen Taffe. Guilt, fear and uncontrolled bereavement had caused him to do the thing he had done—depositing his baby son by the reeds of River Taff—like the baby Moses—in a large wicker hand basket to be found by the Nurse curious about the mewling she had heard as she cycled her way to the Hospital. All witnessed by the father who then walked away from his son's new life.

The father had dragged his own personal hell along with him in life—but had still maintained a watchful eye on the institutions which raised his son. When he saw the boy was possessed of a mind older than that of his peers—and was inclined to use it—the father stepped back into the boy's life and had instructed him accordingly. The boy had never asked him why or who he was—or maybe he didn't want to acknowledge the shambolic man in front of him was his own blood but he listened to what the man was teaching him—and he learned an education you could never find in the place of academia—the best teacher...*LIFE!* The best classroom... out there in the big bad world. The old man took the boy to the seediest places of the cities where crime was rife, where the worst orders of life ruled despotically and were allowed to rule by the iniquities of the system which dictated over all. The old man directed the boy as to how he had failed—but how the boy could succeed—in changing things around and make a difference. But that it could not be done by honouring the written system all police officers in law sign up to. The boy observed, he listened and he learned. When the old man was found dead, he swore he would do this thing—that he would put himself in the position of making a difference. The best way was to become a part of that system—but not allow it to dictate that which he felt was systematically and morally wrong. Owen Taffe *appeared* to swallow those dictates—but would not allow himself be subjected to those dictates when he knew they were wrong.

Here in his office, he read the report on the finding of the car. DC Morgan had been thorough in his findings. Ralph Jones—*The Preacher*—had been more than helpful. Confirming his physical whereabouts at the relevant times and giving a list of persons who may have been able to gain access to his house and knowing where the keys to the car would have been secreted.

The most important part of what Mr Jones had given them was the odometer reading in the car—it having been given a MOT just a few days before he had parked it in his garage. Compared to what the original reading had read—and what it read when it was found at the scrap dealer's place—a total of forty eight miles had been added on. Taffe worked out it would have involved a single journey from Tyburn Road to Cwmhyfryd and then the ten miles from there to the dealer's premises. So how would the killer have returned to...?

That was the problem. There was still no evidence as yet that the killer was a resident of Cwmhyfryd. Brangwyn was actually nearer—but the killer may have brought his own car to the area and had driven home—or cycled—as neither village was so far away that even a walking hike home would have been impossible. Taffe finally concluded one issue however. The killer would have had to have been strong and fit. That trek up to the mountain from Quarter Haven, carrying a nine stone dead weight body and then through the forest would have tasked anybody who was not fit or strong. Had he seen anyone in the past few hours who would fit that criteria?

He decided to put himself in the shoes of the killer and retrace the journey they had made by employing another instruction given to him by the old man—which he'd called "Back-stepping".

The car was garaged at Tyburn Road—where its owner was away for a period of time and so he, the killer, would not be disturbed. The killer had gained access to the house—how? The killer knew the keys were hidden in a sugar container—how? The killer knew of the sexual assignations delivered to Jones by Vonna Shepherd—how? The killer knew how to make those arrangements become a reality—how? Arrangements made and completed, Vonna arrived at Tyburn Road, entered the house and was incapacitated by the killer. Dr Swain had confirmed chloroform was found on Vonna's face and inside her nose and around her clothing. There was no blood found at Jones' house so Taffe decided Vonna was not killed there.

Tyburn Road was a Cul-de-sac—dark at night, with few people up late, most of whom were as old as Jones so they would be in bed. They would not hear or notice a car being driven out of a garage and out of the street.

Taffe made a note of tracking down any region which held CCTV cameras that the killer may have taken as a route to reach Cwmhyfryd. He doubted it would yield any positive ID's—the killer was too clever to be caught out in such a way. So—the travel towards Cwmhyfryd. The killer would have had to have been there before ten o'clock which was the time Edgar claimed he had taken out the rubbish. Taffe noted the theft of Jones' car might have taken place a day before the killings—there was nothing to suggest all these things happened in the same single night.

The killer drove the car to the back entrance of the Parry household and waited. Perhaps he was waiting for an opportune moment or maybe he had the wit and the skill to break into the house and do his thing. He noted there was ample car space in the back garden of Hywel Parry's home and the killer could well have parked his car inside it without drawing too much attention to himself. There was even a large green canvass on the ground which could quite easily cover the parked car.

Edgar takes out the rubbish and he leaves the back door open—the killer lets themself into the house and disposes of Edgar Parry by use of the chloroform—simple enough, the puny man was no fighter—then brings in the unconscious Vonna and carefully places her on the floor. The killer has already taken possession of the Farr axe—Mr Farr probably never even noticed it was gone—and had brought it with them to do the foul deed on Hywel Parry.

The deed is done. Who was first? Hywel was first. Hywel Parry's blood was found under Vonna Shepherd's clothing—meaning the killer had struck the luckless Hywel Parry a number of times and his clothes or coveralls were drenched in the old man's blood. When the killer raised Vonna to a position where he could do his vile work on her, Parry's blood was transferred from his coverall and onto her clothes. He then carried Vonna up the mountain trail taken by DC Morgan and then across the mountain into the forest surrounding Jack Farr's home. There, he waited till Farr left home. (Was that just luck or was he waiting for Farr to leave?) Did the killer know that Farr was not only going out early that day but would be away for the rest of the day? Taffe made a mental note to enquire as to how many people knew of his day's arrangements that day?

Question: How did the killer gain such easy access to the house? Taffe knew he had to pin down everybody who had the keys leading up to Jack's return to Cwmhyfryd.

So, the killer gets inside the house. There was no forensic evidence anywhere belonging to Vonna on the outside of the house which could mean she was also wrapped up in some kind of anaesthetic clothing, laid on the floor very gently, was then unwrapped and left. The killer exited—probably immediately—the same way they had entered and back across the to the village in the same way he'd gone up. Where did they go then? To their own place, if they live in the village. To the Parry house? That morning or later on in the day when no-one was about? Jack didn't get home till late and the police didn't get to his place until two hours later. If the killer *is* a resident of the village, they may have spent the entire day inside the Parry house just waiting for the opportune moment to get into the parked car and drive it away from Quarter Haven—head towards the scrap dealer's premises and then get back home. To Cwmhyfryd, to Brangwyn— to… wherever.

After that, it was simply sit back and watch the real fireworks go off—the moment when Hywel Parry's body is discovered—and the screaming starts. After that, it was pure village pandemonium. Taffe wondered if the killer had watched it.

He sat back. So much for Back-stepping. It probably did happen the way he'd set it out but the analysis had not furthered his investigation by one inch and the relevant questions still had yet to be answered.

He looked at the wall clock. Eight thirty. A long day and the investigation, though on track, had stymied somewhat. He was grateful his Superintendent was not one of those who demanded an arrest upon demand from the populace or the Media. Time to go home. He had a life as well.

And then DC Morgan entered, a file in his hand.

'You're working late,' said Taffe.

'Yes Sir,' answered the young Constable. 'You asked for background checks on everybody who is new to the village or new in Mr Farr's life. Barely anybody from the village and they all pretty much check out as clean. There was only one that really proved interesting.'

He handed the file over to Taffe who opened it. As well as documented notes on the individual, there was also a sheet—an arrest sheet—on that person. A prison sentence, serving fifteen years—for a killing. In Romania. Taffe stared at the six by four photograph of the individual. He read the first few paragraphs and then put the file down. 'Do we still have a cordon around that area?'

'Yes Sir.'

Taffe paused. This was too important to deal with now, especially as he was tired and he didn't want to louse it up through tiredness. This could wait till tomorrow—but alert the police at the village to One: check that the person was still at home and Two: make sure they don't leave. Don't forewarn them. He wanted at least the element of surprise when he confronted this individual tomorrow morning.

'Back early tomorrow, Constable,' he said. 'We have to interview a Mr Jona Rezinski.'

Chapter 49
Mr Jona Rezinski

Every man has a story, son—and some even have backstories.
Joe Farr (1935–2018) to his son, Jack

In the small village of Jaroslav in Romania, the neighbours paid little attention to the constant crying of the small child who lived with its parents and who were situated on the outskirts of that village. They had little to do with the family— they were not part of that village and were looked upon with dislike by the people as if they were thieves in the night awaiting the opportunity to take other people's belongings. The father was a nomadic traveller, named Josef Rezinski, who had offered his services to the locals as someone who could provide assistance in their struggles. He could chop wood from the nearby forest, he could carry water for them from the nearby stream—which many of the womenfolk did when the menfolk were away sometime for days on end. These services were rebuffed by all the locals. They did not trust that which did not attend their Church and did not look like them.

Likewise, the Nomad's woman—whose name was Eriz—who claimed she could cook food for those who were too old and infirm to do such a task, she could wash their clothes at that same stream for those too weak to carry the large containers—but she was also refused immediately. How could they, the locals, trust such a person to even return with their clothes washed clean or even to return at all?

The Rezinski's then, resigned to exile, parked their horse-drawn caravan at the edge limit of the village so that they could not offend those proud Romanians—nor be accused of committing any kind of offence which would prompt the arrival of the Authorities.

Occasionally, Eriz Rezinski would take the babe in arms down to that stream and would join the other mothers who were either washing their clothes or feeding their own children. She was looked upon askance from the mother's—

274

in lust from the father's for Eriz was a woman of great beauty in spite of her obvious youth. She would smile at them, in need of friendship, and would show them her baby Jona who she stated was just four years of age. Her entreaties of friendship fell on deaf ears and she would always return to the caravan a little sadder and still alone.

It was a cold November morn when the neighbours complained of the constant wailing of the Jona child—couldn't its parents keep it quiet, or fed, or warmed? A week after the mewling had alerted them to its situation, a neighbour walked over to where the caravan was staked and he saw hell.

Josef and Eriz lay inside the caravan—their bodies mutilated by knives or swords—dead at least a week according to the Physician who was pulled from his own village of Jadu and had to announce their fate. The child had been left alive but in the week which followed hadn't been fed or clothed. Sat in its small home-built play-pen, the child screamed—blood from its parents covered its body.

There was a diary which announced the lives of Josef, the son of a woodcutter from Bucharest, and Eriz, the daughter of a housemaid living in a rich man's home, from Arad, and their only son—Jona—born out of wedlock and they, the young parents, turned away from their own shamed parents who would not lay kinship to a bastard child.

From shame, given their treatment of the newcomers, the people of Jaroslav took the orphaned child into their homes and their lives and raised him as a member of their community—Jona became the child of the Jaroslav village people.

This was to prove fortuitous for the people as their own lives were threatened by the Officials of the Court who were as corrupt as the local Bandits of nearby Jadu—who, it was guessed, were probably the killers of the boy's parents. Jona grew tall and strong and even by the time he had reached his teens, was able to demonstrate a physical presence to deter all outsiders who would demand monies with menaces from the now aged community.

Jona was instructed by the Elders of the village and gave his life accordingly to them. By the time he was twenty years of age, there was very little left of the village he had grown up in—or the people who had raised him for Communist Romania under the leadership of Nicolae Ceausescu in the 1960's was a place of great hardship.

Without being told anything about his natural parents or knowing anything about his own roots, Jona, through nature and not nurture, became a Nomadic Traveller—moving from one town and village to another—performing general services for the locals of those places—and occasionally performing a much harder service in dealing with those who would subjugate the lesser beings. Local gangsters who would operate a money-for-services-rendered service— protectionism in other words—would charge the small shopkeepers and self-made entrepreneur's a fee to keep them safe—from others such as their own kind. Only the worst kind of man profited from the hard sweat of honest men and women. Jona became a man known to defy those vile gangsters and was then employed by those who were oppressed by those who were violent unless paid off.

From this life, Jona found a way to make a living. On his travels, he learned that his reputation as a hard man had spread and he was challenged to backstreet brawls from which a great deal of money could be made. Disinterested at first, he was coerced into this lifestyle by people who could persuade others to do their bidding by the threat of something worse than just with-holding protection. Jona then duly complied—and quickly saw how easy much money could be made by this new lifestyle—and just how much he would be able to deter those who would oppress the weakest members of their society by winning enough money to take charge of his own interests. By the time he was in his early thirties, Jona was, by comparison of local standards, a wealthy man. Able to buy his own home and live in comparative luxury. Keeping to the honour of his own word, he slowly eradicated the protectionists from the societies they had cultivated and peace returned.

But, a reputation hardily won will always be a reputation to be challenged and a day came when Jona, no longer engaged in these professional backstreet fights, was challenged by a young Buck named Rojaz who wanted that man's unofficial crown. Time and again, Jona refused the demands made by Rojaz and his representatives to fight with him. Eventually, they chose the only path they knew which awaken the fighting man still contained within—they oppressed the people. Out of fear for their livelihoods, the people came to Jona for help and he knew there was only one way to go. He agreed to do one final battle. Which was exactly what those representatives were counting on—the "final" battle.

The time and the venue was set and the young buck trained religiously to fulfil the task set by his Masters for a great deal of prestige and money was at stake.

The day came—as did treachery—for the Masters who were confident their protégé would be equal to the mighty Jona also bought extra insurance in the vision of local police who were equally corrupt and wanted this foolish old troublemaker removed from their sight but without local recourse of protest.

The two men met and Rojaz—young and arrogant—asked Jona—older and more weary—where he would prefer to be buried and this told Jona this fight was not simply about the taking or reclaiming a crown. They both stripped to their trousers and the young buck was muscular compared to the now flabbier but still brave Jona. The fight was joined.

The fight was attended by many who were curious and many who had agendas of their own—including the pottage of winnings should the victor survive. What was not a part of the planned schedule was the duration of the fight as it continued from early morn to late afternoon. The young buck, for all his strength and agility, had not the power to keep Jona kept down to the ground permanently for Jona rose each time he was felled. Bloodied to a pulp, almost unrecognizable even to his closest companions, Jona suffered blows to his face and head and his body—and still he carried on.

When darkness was falling, the young buck resorted to using weaponry—a brick which cut open Jona's skull, a knife taken from a man who was whittling a piece of wood, used against Jona's body and he shed blood. The fight was seemingly at an end when it finally appeared Jona could sustain no more. He was bent over and breathing out hard and Rojaz, sensing victory, moved against him—to the screams of delight from his paymasters and friends—and as he raised his hand against the old fighter, Jona rose and drove his punch into the jaw of the young pretender. It sent Rojaz hurtling backwards and he fell against a wall, his head striking against the corner of stone. The young buck was killed instantly.

Consternation followed as the crowd suddenly ran when sirens from the observing police cars sounded and Jona was taken into custody.

Jona—bereft from the death of the young buck—offered no defence for what he had done, for though his chosen profession was of violence, he was not inherently a violent man. He refused to be defended in Court and pleaded Guilty to the crime he was accused of. In the entire time the Court sat against him, he did not speak once. The verdict was delivered even before the Court proceedings were completed. Jona was sent to a prison in Bucharest.

Jona had decided his own life was forfeit—regardless of the knowledge that the young buck had been sent against him, not only to rob him of his reputation but possibly even to take his life. Jona was aware of this but no words could prevail him to see the reality. He had taken a life and though he was not religious, he believed in the sanctity of the human life and he must pay the price for his transgression. He remained in his small cell, refusing drink and food and lay upon his bed awaiting death.

It was an Irishman who saved him—and restored his soul.

Father Liam O'Brien, a man of declining years, and a former Priest in the Catholic Church, was also an inmate of the very same prison having been jailed for preaching a religion which countered Roman Orthodoxy though he never claimed access to the Almighty having already been Excommunicated by the his own Church for teachings which were very much not of the Catholic Faith. He found the grief-stricken Jona, told him his life was precious in the eyes of the Maker of All Living things, resurrected his soul and gave him a reason to live. In the prison, Jona and Father Liam set about raising the spirits of those unfortunates, many of whom had been falsely imprisoned by the authorities serving Ceausescu's reign of tyranny. When that tyrant was finally removed from office in 1989 and the Romanian people rose against the corruption which had ruled them, many political prisoners were released from their captivity and re-joined the world they had been forced to leave behind.

In the case of Father Liam, he was given a stark choice—leave Romania or chance your luck with a new regime which also doesn't appreciate foreigners practising unorthodox religious dogma in its country. Age and infirmity and a new possible life elsewhere made his choice for him. He would return to his beloved Ireland, to beautiful Kerry, to his home in Killarney and live out his final years. And he would take Jona with him.

In the beautiful Country of Ireland, Father Liam was reunited with his old Church—though still not of the Faith—and he practised his teachings on those who were curious enough to hear another kind of message.

A new life in a new country made Jona become whole again. He learned to speak English—though he had problems with Gaelic Irish—and he found the strength to raise his voice—and arms—once again. In the years which followed,

278

he remained a constant companion to Father Liam as the latter found more good work for him to do.

And one day, Jona came to Father Liam with a request.

'Father—I have left behind my birth home, I no longer speak the language of my family. I would become a new man here in this new country. I ask you to Baptize me. To give me a new name.'

On a bright summer's day, Father Liam took Jona with a host of others who would learn a new doctrine, to the Killarney National Park and he entered the lake and became a latter-day John The Baptist, rebirthing those who had doubted their faith and beliefs. Jona was the last to be plunged under the water. He rose from the waters—a new man.

When he came ashore, Jona dropped to his knees and clasped his hands together, tears flowing from his eyes, thanking the Maker of All Things for the day he had met Father Liam. When he rose to his feet, Jona Rezinski was no more—the man who stood in his stead was John Redd.

*

It was early in the morning and Vicar Redd was eating his customary breakfast of toasted buttered buns when the door-bell rang. He answered to find the young DC Morgan standing there next to an older man—a man Vicar Redd knew to be Detective Chief Inspector Owen Taffe.

'Good morning, Inspector,' beamed the Vicar—and stood aside to let them both into the Vicarage. 'I've been expecting you,' he said. He stretched out his hand—and DCI Taffe took it. The grip was firm, his hand was dry and rough and powerful enough to… choke someone to death?

'Good morning—Mr Jona Rezinski,' said DCI Taffe. There was a brief pause and little more than a bemused expression on the Vicar's face as he gestured for both officers to enter the drawing room.

Chapter 50

The Kiss

And while DCI Taffe spoke with the former Romanian Nomadic Traveller who had protected his people from the corrupt Authoritarian State of Ceausescu's Romania, who'd killed a man in a bare-knuckle contest, served fifteen years in prison and then emigrated to Ireland with a wandering ex-Priest to become John Redd, Vicar of this Parish, Susan Tanner performed her charitable duty by taking clothes and food to the beleaguered and isolated Jack Farr living in a former farm so many miles away from Cwmhyfryd.

'Why's he living all the way out here?' asked a confused Claire Philips, snuggled in the back of Susan's car next to Tommy.

'Because his home is still a crime scene and the police advised him not to return to Cwmhyfryd as his life may still be in danger. Obviously they don't want him leaving town—even though he's done nothing wrong or illegal—and Cardiff is too near an Airport. Not that he would have taken off anywhere because he's done nothing wrong or illegal. Here, he's within grabbing distance if they need to speak to him.' Emphasis on the "nothing wrong or illegal" stuff.

Susan winked to Catrin, sitting next to her in the car as they travelled across the lanes and headed towards the temporary accommodation arranged for Jack by Susan. The whole move had been executed fairly quickly and it was only when Jack was in and settled that he realized he was still wearing the same set of clothes he'd worn on the day he met Gibney and they took off to Stroud. He called Susan and asked her to bring out a spare set of casual clothing that he could room around in. Susan called DCI Taffe who gave her permission to go to Greenacres, and in the full sight of the three patrolling police officers, found three sets of casual clothing Jack could be comfortable in. In case of an extended delay, she also brought out some basic foods which he could feast on without having recourse to use the present oven which hadn't been used for the better part of the past eight months.

It was Saturday and normally, Catrin would be assisting at the café but Susan had ordered a full stock report and that was way above Catrin's pay grade skills so Olwen Berry stood in for her and the café was closed for the day. She, at a loose end, decided to keep Auntie Susan company when she saw Auntie Susan loading her car with the necessary items to keep Jack comfortable. Of course, when Claire saw her sister going off with Auntie Susan, she had to be part of the trip as well. Dragging her boyfriend along, the three of them piled into Susan's car and off they went into the country.

When they reached the dilapidated farm, they saw Jack using an axe to chop wood for the open fire—which actually made the two girls wince.

'He knows how to swing an axe, don't he?' ventured Catrin.

Susan stared at her for a moment—then climbed out of the car. Jack was clearly happy to see her—and the provisions she had brought. He waved at the two girls who smiled and waved back.

'Thank you,' he said. 'I found this overall in the garage—it isn't too dirty and I can't chop wood in a suit. It got a bit cold out here last night.'

She placed the basket of food items on the large tree trunk and he sifted through it. All very basic stuff to suit his needs. Jack had a boring dietary system and Susan remembered enough to know of what he could eat without fuss.

'Did Taffe give you any idea how long you'll be out here?' she asked.

'No—but I think he's pretty much satisfied I'm not the local Cwmhyfryd Ripper and I don't think the police will be at Greenacres for much longer.' He paused and looked down.

'I want to go home.'

That jolted her. She didn't know which "home" he was talking about.

'Back to Oklahoma?' she asked, looking at him.

That jolted him. It was true that he'd already made his decision on that subject—but it was odd to hear someone else say it.

'No,' he said. Then he looked at her, the expression on her face confirming the decision he had made. 'No, Susan, I want to go home.'

And "home" meant Greenacres.

Holding back the tears, Susan moved a step towards him, her hand loosely touching Jack's without clasping it, and then she gently kissed him slightly to the left of his mouth. Not passionate, not pleading, no words at all actually. He didn't moved back or object or say "no" or look at her with revulsion.

That simple gesture had the two girls squealing in the car with unparalleled delight.

'Oh my God,' said Catrin, eighteen years of age, attractive and who had never had a true romantic moment in her life.

'Oh my God,' said Claire, sixteen years of age, vivacious and had never been without a boyfriend since she was four.

Tommy stared at the pair of them, confusion on his face.

'That was so romantic,' said Claire—no advocate of Mills & Boon but a natural romantic at heart.

'How is that romantic?' demanded Tommy. 'She's married.'

'Yeh—but David's a dork loser and Uncle Jack is a real man,' she championed. 'Look at everything that's happened to him and how he's dealt with it.'

Susan parted from Jack, walked back to the car and got in.

'Everything alright, Auntie Susan?' chorused the two girls in unison.

She started the car and smiled at them both.

'Everything's fine,' she assured them and the car moved away from the yard and back onto the lane. In the rear view mirror, she saw Jack continue with the chopping.

Chapter 51

Advancing

At the very least, DCI Taffe's appetite had been sated. 'Haven't had toasted buttered buns made from an open fire since I was a child,' he told DC Morgan on their way home from speaking—at length—with Vicar Redd.

'I've never had them like that all, Sir,' said DC Morgan, he who had been brought up on radiators and gas fires.

The interview did not tell Taffe much more about John Redd than the full report he'd already read the night before. The move from Ireland to Wales was interesting as it had been proposed by an Ecumenical Authority not totally in step with the conformities of the Church. In the past few years, attendance of local Churches had dipped so low below an acceptable figure that the Leaders, the Elders, felt they needed to get their message out to the masses without using the more established routes. A number of Non-Denominational Churches had sprouted up around the UK and Cwmhyfryd's was one of them. Prior to Vicar Redd and since the halcyon days of the not very convincing sermons of the late Reverend Parminter,

Cwmhyfryd Church's attendances had declined to the point where one resident Preacher found himself sermonizing to a flock of sheep one Sunday morn—much to the amusement of three ramblers who had strode by.

To this end, the Local Cwmhyfryd Community Council decided their new Preacher did not necessarily have to *belong* to an established or orthodox religion—as long as the message was getting out there, the practise could be open to options.

This missive found its way to the many "off-beat" religious quarters around the Religious world of the UK and Father Liam was one of those who responded. His protégé had served the Kerry Community very well—and he'd built up a sizeable following. It was time, Father Liam felt, that the net must be cast wider. With the concessionary title of "Vicar"—and a move to a brand new location,

Father Liam proposed John Redd to take up the mantle at Cwmhyfryd for a period of six months to see how this new doctrine would serve the people.

Father Liam had no doubts that John would get the "message" out there—if there was one thing he'd learned about John, he had no problem selling what he spoke—*because he really believed in what he was saying.* The difficulty would be *how* he would sell it—for sure, it wouldn't simply rest at the spoken word. And that was exactly how his mission turned out. No-one at Cwmhyfryd had ever met a Vicar who was so "physical" with his manners. When Vicar Redd demonstrated his pugilistic abilities to the local trouble-making youths of that village, the people knew they had a different Preacher in their midst.

Beyond that, the only other thing to come out of the interview was the certain knowledge that, bluff and physical as he was, John Redd was *not* the killer of Hywel Parry and Vonna Shepherd. Absolutely certain, thought DCI Taffe—but keep it on the back-burner, just in case.

Back in his office, he'd settled back to work out his next step when DS Stone rushed in, a broad smile on her face. It was always gratifying to Taffe to see his officers so energized in their work—and DS Stone was looking particularly excited. He sat back and waited.

'You asked for a background check on all those who'd come into contact with Farr—so I took it a step further and checked if any of them had contact with each other—I was looking for the single common denominator to connect *them* to each other.'

'And what did you find, Sergeant?' asked Taffe who had already started down that road.

'Vonna Shepherd and the two McGregors—they've all been arrested at one time for their respective crimes. I backtracked and found this.'

She put a sheet of paper on his desk. It was dated two years ago, in June, 2016, Vonna Shepherd had been charged with an assault against a man who was a Swansea pimp who had tried to muscle in on hers and Lynda's patch—of course, Taffe recalled—Lynda had told him about that man but hadn't mentioned it had ended in an arrest. It went to court and was thrown out by the Judge in the same session—the gun wasn't brought up in the charge and the Judge felt the pimp had deserved the bruising he'd got from Vonna. Case dismissed.

The McGregors case was barely worth getting a Judge out of bed for. A small matter of thuggery at which both the McGregors took a beating from their intended victim. They were fined £150 each and released.

So far, so mundane. But then Taffe noted the dates of the cases and the name of the Solicitor who had represented both Vonna and the McGregors in their respective cases. Both cases had been in Court in the same week. The Solicitor was…

…Peter Eddy.

Chapter 52

Peter Eddy

DS Stone did the driving and DCI Taffe did the maths while sitting next to her. DC Morgan was sat in the back calling Jack Farr to give him the happy news that his home was no longer a crime scene—the Forensics Division had cleared the house for all clues attaching Vonna Shepherd to the place and nothing was found implicating Jack Farr to the crime. Jack was free to return to his home at his leisure.

Taffe worked furiously to join the dots. Eddy had represented Vonna Shepherd *and* Lynda Bennet on similar charges involving prostitution. Their cases had been dismissed. The McGregors cases were a lot more involved. Eddy had represented them on at least five occasions in the past eight years, the last one leading to their present domiciled situation at the Brangwyn and Pentre Haf villages.

Both cases had happened at Court in the same week. Eddy knew Vonna— her life, her method of business, possibly her way of communication to her clients, possibly the fact she carried a weapon, maybe even the identifications of her clients. He had all her details on record—contact with her while pretending to be a client would have been simple enough.

Eddy knew the McGregors much more closely. Their criminal history—for example, their involvement with Hywel Parry—their whereabouts, practically living on his own doorstep as far as one of them was concerned, their abilities in the "tough-guy" department—or lack thereof as it turned out.

And of course, Eddy had intimate knowledge of Jack Farr—his movements before and after coming home—possibly the nature of the Joe Farr inheritance. He had held the keys to Greenacres before passing them onto Vicar Redd. He had all this information on all the relevant participants—and he could have operated these things from his own office.

What are the chances, he thought? Too many to be all coincidence.

He'd called Brangwyn Police to check on Eddy—to verify his presence at the office as Taffe didn't want to be trawling all over South Wales looking for the man. He was quite busy defending those who required it.

And the man himself? Too puny to do the actual killing—or was that just good cover? How often in his professional life had the miscreant involved in the crime been the person the least likely to be suspected. Back to Father's advice of keeping that mind wide open. No judgements made just because of appearance or professional status.

Eddy was currently engaged in his own office confirmed Brangwyn Police— and Taffe told them to make certain he stayed that way.

*

Peter Eddy was understandably miffed to find himself under the scrutiny of the police in his own office and being watched by his own people as the police made their enquiries about his involvement with the McGregors and the late Vonna Shepherd. At least the DCI had been polite which was more than could be said for his over-zealous Sergeant.

'Really, Inspector—I only ever represented Miss Shepherd once and that case was thrown out of Court before I even made my representation. I think His Honour may have had a prejudice towards her—and a very big prejudice against the man who tried to harm her. As far as the McGregors are concerned, I have washed my hands of them—they simply do not know how to stay out of trouble. I'm amazed they haven't received longer sentences than the ones they have served.' Small man, thought DCI Taffe, needs to talk big to maintain authority. He didn't carry a dead woman a couple of miles up a mountain either.

'Are you aware they attacked Mr Farr a while ago? Both of them. They attacked him and he threw them over a wall. If I am informed correctly, they were then chased out of the village by an old man on a bicycle.'

'Goodness,' said Peter Eddy.

'The point of my being here, Mr Eddy,' said Taffe, 'is the connection between the McGregors, Miss Shepherd—the fact you represented both of them in the same week two years ago and the fact that you have played a small part in Jack Farr's personal business. Now it may just be purely coincidental—or these events may lead to a connection to the person I'm chasing. So—not now as you say you haven't seen either for some while—but then, two years ago. The connection would be two years ago.'

'But in what way…?' protested Eddy.

'Well—maybe the people who worked with you two years ago for instance. Who is working for you now that was working for you then? Everybody and anybody—full time, part time, passing through—everything and everybody who would have been involved with you two years ago. I presume you have records of employment.'

'Well of course—and as far as present staff are concerned, the only three people who were with me two years ago are Miss Daly, Mr Jameson and Mrs Worthing—all of whom have been employed here since before I assumed seniority at the office—they were employed by my father. Everyone else you see here today are relatively new.'

Taffe looked at the newbies—youngish and all looking like they belonged here in such a place. He discounted them. As far as the three nominated elders were concerned, they were too old and Taffe dismissed them immediately as well. So—who was working for Eddy two years ago and isn't here now?

Eddy went to his files and looked up the Employment dates from that period. He stopped at May 2016.

'Ah—now this may be of some interest to you, Inspector. A small experiment which lasted for just two years—concocted by my late father's business partner at the time. A local Government notion of opening up such a place as this to Apprenticeships. *Are you interested in a career working in the legal profession?* kind of thing. We had quite a few people who showed interest. I mean, obviously, they did not undertake any of the actual legal activity—so far above most of them—but they were included in the preparations of certain cases, provided they weren't of a certain kind of nature—no confidentiality barriers were broken. Many of them decided they didn't like the amount of written work which went into the cases to be worked on and left after a such time. I ended the practice nine months ago'

'The McGregor and Vonna Shepherd cases. Who was serving apprenticeships and were involved with them at that time?'

Eddy sat down and scanned the files and wrote names down. After twenty minutes he stopped and scanned his list. Then he went to the computer, looked up the personnel files from that period, selected the names he had scanned and printed the names off. There were twenty names. Thirteen of them were female.

He passed the list to Taffe and DS Stone and waited. The silence inside the office was almost oppressive and Eddy could hear his own heart beating.

Taffe and DS Stone perused the list—hoping to see a name which would leap out at them and provide them with the answer they were looking for this enquiry—but neither of them recognized any name on the list and after ten minutes of scanning and rescanning the names, Taffe handed the list back to Eddy.

'Nothing,' he told the Solicitor. 'I was hoping I'd recognize a name which tied the McGregors and Miss Shepherd to Mr Farr but I don't know anyone there.'

'I should hope not,' said Eddy, 'We are not in the habit of employing criminals to assist us in our work to put criminals away.' Which made both Taffe and DS Stone laugh. They knew many Law films who would employ precisely such people. Taffe thanked Mr Eddy for his co-operation and walked towards the exit door.

But now there was something rankling Taffe. The peculiar feeling, that he'd seen something which didn't... *gel.* Something... he'd seen on the list... which was kicking into the deepest recesses of his memory. Not a name... if it had been a name, he would have known it straight away. What had he seen?

As he walked away, with DS Stone apologizing to Mr Eddy for the disruption, Taffe suddenly jerked back. He marched back to where Peter Eddy was standing, the list still in his hand and demanded, 'Give that to me.' He practically snatched the list off the Solicitor and scanned through it again. What the hell was he looking for? What had he seen which had pricked his memory? Name, Date of Birth, Gender, Nationality, CV to be included.

Names. Twenty names. Thirteen females, seven males, over a two year period. Most of them were from Cardiff, many were students of Law, with green ticks next to their name if they showed promise and red crosses if they were definitely not future legal eagles. Three from Cwmhyfryd but they weren't involved with the Eddy office until after the June period in question and Taffe concentrated on...

Not names of people—names of where they came from. And that was what brought him back. There was one place, isolated in its way because it was the only one of its kind. Under the heading of *Nationality*...

And there it was—one word. *Fleminganese.* Where had he heard that name before?

He prowled the room, his face almost distorted as he searched his memory. He knew he'd heard the word before—a place... an isolated Community, founded by an ultra-religious man who created the Community after a long march from Portsmouth—his name... his name was...

FLEMING. JOSHUA FLEMING!

And the apprentice's name on the list was... Fleming. *Thomas* Fleming. His nationality? Not Welsh, not English—but Fleminganese. And the Community existed... above the village of Cwmhyfryd—on one of the four mountains which overlooked that valley. And where had he heard this story? Again, he searched his memory.

The Philips house, Sara Philips had told him of this Community when they were questioning her husband about his whereabouts the night Jack Farr found Vonna Shepherd.

But why had she told him?

Back to Eddy. 'Do you have pictures of any of these people—for ID purposes?'

Of course he did. Mr Eddy was a diligent representative member of the Legal Profession and all servants of the Law would require ID badges to prove who they were should they find themselves in a certain environment.

Back to the computer and Peter Eddy went immediately to the aforementioned dates, and found the files where the pictures of each of the students or would-be apprentices were stored. He went straight to the name Taffe was signalling when he showed him the list. Up it came...

And Taffe stared at the image on the screen.

DS Stone, who had been confused by her DCI's sudden urgency, peered into the computer screen. Like her DCI, she stared.

'Oh my God,' she breathed out.

Taffe referred to the list. 'This says he was twenty four years of age when he served here.'

Eddy looked at the list, looked at the date of birth and confirmed the age. 'That was the age he gave us. We have a copy of his Birth Certificate if you would like to see it.' They would. Eddy had that document scanned as well. Up it came. Proof of age confirmed.

Taffe stood away—he looked at DS Stone—who looked back at him in shock. Then he walked away and out of the office. DS Stone thanked Mr Eddy and followed her DCI out. Peter Eddy went back to his computer screen, confused at this exchange as was everyone else in the room. They all stared at the image of the young man on the screen and wondered why it had caused so much urgency. Good looking boy as well. He stared at the face…

It was the face of Tommy Leeming.

Chapter 53

Lover's Assignation

He had the face of an Angel—so said Claire Philips and just about every other girl who was aged between fifteen and seventeen—but only Claire carried on with those thoughts when every other girl found out that Tommy Leeming was a Fleminganese boy and therefore not to be trusted with their souls. This they had been taught by their parents and grandparents who were old enough to remember the Fleminganese tribes who came down from Stone Wall Mountain to barter their goods with the villagers—and then sell their religion into the bargain—and the most vocal and vociferous of these religious peddlers was the old man, long white hair, unruly and out of control, cascading down his back, with an equally long scraggly beard which reached down to his navel, always dressed in the same unwashed black suit which appeared to be handmade and sewn with branch twigs judging by the size of the thread weaved in and out of the jacket and trousers. The man's name was Josiah and he claimed ancestral kinship with the founder of the Fleminganese people and their Community. He was loud and verbally violent—if you didn't follow his teachings, or the teachings of his great ancestor, Joshua Fleming, then you were damned to the pits of eternal flames and never to rise in the New World promised to us all by the great Saviour.

Boy, was that man scary. After hearing a few sermons from that man, the children did not need the advice from their parents to keep clear of the Fleminganese tribe.

When, a few years ago, Tommy was found crouching in a shop doorway, frozen and sobbing, saying the Elders of that Community had expelled him from their lives for "not having the true Faith"—he was taken in by the Hyfridians and was given comfort and work. First at the local Collier's Quarry situated miles away from the village and then, later, was placed in the solicitor's office based in Brangwyn by the Vicar Lennard who was related to the man who ran it—Peter Eddy.

When the Quarry was closed, Tommy became "involved" with the Cwmhyfryd village beauty—Claire Philips—and from there, was a permanent fixture in her and her parents' lives. It had been that way ever since that day and Claire rarely let a day go by without seeing him.

And so it was when Claire came running up to her sister Catrin and Susan who was just returning from her working day at the City, excited and out of breath. Susan Tanner, who always found Claire to be the breath of life she would have wanted in her own daughter and was never gifted with, stood by and watched the panting teen assail her elder sister.

'Tenner,' she breathed out.

Catrin paused for one beat and timed her answer perfectly.

'Right, in the first place you are a contralto, not a tenor—and in the second place there is no way Vicar Redd is going to let you sing in the choir 'cos you can't carry a tune in a bucket.'

Claire was equal to her sister in the timing. One beat.

'Not tenor—tenner. Ten quid you div.'

'Why do you want ten quid?'

'Taxi.'

Catrin looked beyond where her sister stood and scanned the street.

'What taxi?'

Claire stamped her foot—a tiny response but as she was begging for money she felt she couldn't overdo it.

'I haven't booked it yet, have I? 'Cos I don't have the money yet, do I?'

'Why do you need a taxi?' Where could she go? Mam had already driven to Cardiff and had asked Claire to join her for a day's shopping but she refused, saying she had homework to do which was untrue—Claire never did homework at home. Always in school.

'Tommy,' came the reply—and nothing else as if that name was quite enough to explain or justify her actions—but then decided that a further explanation might expedite the passing of money. 'Come on, he's waiting for me at the Quarry.'

This time, Catrin had to think about what Claire had said—and then the penny dropped.

'For God's sake,' she groaned and so brought out her purse. The ten quid note was not in her hand a second before it was swiped away by the teen sister who then ran, hot foot, towards the taxi rank.

'You owe me a tenner,' called out Catrin as Claire sprinted away.

'Pay you back when I get paid,' came the breathy reply as Claire disappeared around a corner.

Catrin sneered. 'Hah, you have to be working to get paid in the first place.' And that was the end of the most recent Claire episode. So many since she learned she had a personality and Catrin knew there would be many to come until Claire decided she was too old to have one.

She and Susan entered the house.

'And what was that all about?' asked Auntie Susan. Catrin stopped and looked a little embarrassed.

'Well,' she said, 'when you and... Mr Farr... uh... were with each other at that farm and then you both... uh... kissed, Claire went into romantic overdrive. Since then, she's been dropping mass hints to Tommy... to get... uh... romantic. And this might be the day.'

'To do what?'

'You know. Proposal.'

Susan was astonished. 'Proposal? She's only just turned sixteen.'

'Mam and Dad were engaged when they were seventeen.' Not true, thought Susan but say nothing.

'And the Quarry? I didn't get that.'

'It was when Tommy was working at Collier's Quarry just before it was closed down. Well, when the announcement came, everybody—well, all the men, went out to see the place. Dirty loud and disgusting but they all went out to see it.'

Of course they did, thought Susan—possibly 95% of the male population of Cwmhyfryd had at one time in their lives worked at the Quarry. Time and a lack of funding to keep it safe had ended its viability as a workplace and so it was closed—but Susan recalled the day when practically the entire village populace went out to look the place over.

'Anyway, Claire's school organized a special trip to see the place over as it was now an historical remnant of old Cwmhyfryd—I mean, that place was working even before this village was built—and that's when she met Tommy. He was helping clear the place out with the few bits of machinery that still worked. Claire saw him—and whoosh—she went dippy over him. So did all the other girls—till they found out he was Fleminganese child.'

And that was when Tommy was introduced to the family properly, to the consternation of both Adam and Sara. Up till then he had been looked after by the Vicars—first Lennard and then, when he arrived, John Redd. Then Cwmhyfryd Community Council located an empty apartment into which they placed young Tommy Leeming—and then Claire demanded he be allowed into the home for her to mould into her newest boyfriend—much to the ire of all her previous boyfriends and the possible future boyfriends because Tommy was, by designate, a non-person, of the Fleminganese tribe which made him, by their local standards, almost an alien.

But today, it looked as though he had arranged a lover's tryst—in a most unromantic setting to be sure but maybe the memory of their first meeting was enough to begin the relationship proper. Catrin peered out of the window to see if Claire had caught her taxi. She had. She saw it driving it out of the Rank.

And then, on the street, Sergeant Cenydd Thomas suddenly sprinted past the house and ran straight to the end of the road. A car suddenly sped into view and he jumped in. The car sped away, leaving behind rubber marks on the road and a cloud of dust to follow.

Catrin and Susan were startled—both confused.

'Now what was all that for?' asked Catrin.

Susan's phone rang. She answered. It was Jack. She listened—and then broke into a broad smile. 'That's wonderful. Do you want me to come and pick you up?' She listened a little more and then said, 'I'll see you later then.' The call ended. She smiled broadly. She seemed to be doing that quite a lot recently, thought Catrin.

Catrin looked at her, quizzically, and Susan realized she hadn't explained.

'The police have finally released Greenacres—it's no longer a crime scene so Jack can move back home. He'll be coming back later today.'

They reached the house and Catrin turned to Susan.

'What's going to happen with you and … Uncle Jack?' *Uncle*—the bi-part Colloquiallism used by every teen to describe their peers' parents along with *Auntie*. If Jack was earning that soubriquet then maybe there was hope.

She smiled and said, 'I honestly do not know, my dear.' They went inside.

*

295

Claire reached the outer limit of the path leading to Collier's Quarry. The road had been blocked off within a month of the Quarry closing down. It was still private property and the County Council did not want it or any part of the Quarry being tampered with—in case of accidents which would lead to litigation claims.

The taxi reached the edge of the path and parked. She paid him the ten quid and got out. The taxi drove away and Claire looked at the ten foot high, twenty foot wide metal gate which was topped with barbed wire. There was a sign which read:

PRIVATE PROPERTY
DO NOT ENTER. DANGER
TRESPASSERS WILL BE PROSECUTED

And in spite of the sign, many intruders had dared to enter, had become injured as was feared by the CC and legal actions were in progress.

Claire did not climb the gate—instead, slight as she was, she was able to crawl between the space of the base barrier and the ground. Through the space and standing up, she dusted herself down and then began the three mile walk to the remains of the Quarry building. Between where she walking was and that building, the CC had also laid boulders in the middle of the path to deter any bikers or car speeders as well as three other less troublesome gates.

Autumn had now waved her majestic wand over the countryside and the trees were a myriad colour of green, red and purple. The air smelt sweet—even though she was in the middle of what had been a putrefying industry—diggers excavating wet earth and dredging articles from beneath the ground which had been buried for centuries. Now, the air was clean and the birds sang their happy songs—a cacophony of sounds of happiness—which added to the way she was feeling today. If, as she hoped, this was going to go the way she was thinking it would, she would be wearing a ring—nothing expensive or grandiose—just the significance of it would place her way above the stations of her peers.

The three mile walk tired her—I love you, Tommy, but why couldn't we have met at the local Supermarket?

She reached the huge space of where the original industry had taken place. Here, years ago, there would have been multitudes of huge plant machinery, covered in dirt and dust, soaked in wet remains of whatever history had deposited under it and across the top centuries before. Skeletons had been found in this place in the late fifties—which scared the workers who discovered them—and such was the degradation of their decay nothing was ever learned about their lives—or deaths.

The only building still standing from the old days was where the hand machinery and explosives had been stored. There was no sign of Tommy but that front door was open and that was where Claire made for.

She entered—and walked straight into a cloud of dust, coughing and brushing it away, and taking care not to walk into the huge spider webs which criss-crossed what used to be the reception area, Claire entered the whole room and shouted, *'Tommy!'*

A footstep behind her and she turned and there he was, smiling. The face of the an Angel. She walked to him, her arms ready to embrace him. And as she reached him, arms still outstretched, he parried the embrace and stepped back, still smiling. Okay, she thought, not quite the warm reception I was expecting but…

He smiled and said, quietly, 'Whore.'

Claire was smiling as well—from hopeful anticipation—but then she realized what he just said.

'Beg your pardon?' she queried.

The smile dropped from his sweet face and was replaced by something… dark, sinister, angry, even frightening. Not Tommy at all. He moved one step aside and his face was then covered in shadows which gave it an even more frightening appearance. It distorted into something quite violent and his voice rose to a scream.

'WHOOOORRRE!'

Chapter 54

The Chase

DCI Taffe and DS Stone sprinted down the stairs, out of the building and then down the High Street, frightening every pedestrian who stood in their way—even to the point of running out into the road without checking to see what kind of vehicle might be about to run them down. They reached their car and DC Morgan saw them coming—and saw the looks on their faces. This was urgent.

Taffe climbed in to the driving seat and barked out his orders as he started the car. He was speaking in frantic mode and Morgan had to write fast just to keep up.

'We've possibly met the killer,' Taffe breathing out hard, 'it may be Tommy Leeming who we saw at the Philips' home a few days ago. Either that or it's someone named Fleming who looks very much like Leeming—maybe related—but I want the two officers based at Cwmhyfryd to get across to the Philips' home and check if he's there—be warned—he may be armed so no actual confronting him. If he isn't there, check the block of flats where we spoke to Sion Edmunds—that's his actual home address in the village. If he isn't at either address, call Vicar Redd and ask him if he knows the whereabouts of the boy—and he isn't a boy either, if it is Leeming he's lied about his age.' He paused and remembered. 'Did the mother say he was courting the younger daughter?'

DS Stone, making her own calls, nodded and Taffe swore.

The car sped away from its parked position and out of the village, a blue flashing light running across the front and back of his car to signify any other driver to clear out of the way. It took just two minutes to get through the High Street—it was packed—until it reached the lanes and then Taffe went into Grand Prix mode.

'I want uniformed officers in attendance by the time we reach the village,' Taffe continued. 'Keep a low profile. Also, see if you can latch onto that Sergeant, the one you went up to the mountain with…'

'Sergeant Thomas,' said DC Morgan.

'That's the man—he used to live at the village and he knows the area. He will be useful'

The car swerved around the lanes and Taffe only relaxed when he saw a straight road ahead of him. It would take at least forty minutes on a good road to reach Cwmhyfryd and he needed every minute.

Taffe also ordered a Police Unit to go to the workplace used by Adam Philips because he recalled someone telling him the Leeming "boy" was working with his prospective father-in-law—it was still early in the day so possibly they may be at work.

Morgan did the calling on one part of the list Taffe had barked out, Stone did the calling for the other—the results were the same. No-one was at the Philips home. Someone checked out the Leeming address—in fact, Taffe drew a lucky break here because Sergeant Thomas was actually in the village at the time as it was his day off and he was visiting his mother before going home to Swansea. PC Taylor had, by luck, bumped into him, informed him of the calls made by DS Stone bringing him up to speed about the most recent development. Sergeant Thomas was a very good police officer—but he knew when to bend a rule or two when it was necessary and here, he had a personal interest to intervene as his mother was living in a house just across from the block of apartments Sion Edmunds lived in.

He raced to the block, entered, ascertained exactly where Tommy Leeming lived and knocked the door. His neighbour confirmed to the partly dressed policeman that the occupant was a young man who hardly ever lived in the flat and he certainly wasn't in at the moment. Sergeant Thomas did not hesitate, lives could be at stake, and against the rules, he kicked the front door in and entered the apartment—much to the shock of the neighbour.

It was hardly a lived in apartment. One chair, no carpeting, a microwave oven, no TV, a bed with a single duvet and just a few sets of clothing. Not much in the way of personal items and the most basic of needs. No photographs, no mail, nothing to latch onto—until he saw a large green marker pen on the table. Something stirred in his memory.

The writing on the murder weapon used to kill Hywel Parry—the axe belonging to old Joe Farr had been made with green ink. Not enough to prove anything but it galvanized Sergeant Thomas. He rushed out of the apartment and back onto the street. PC's Taylor and Harris were stationed outside the Philips home and confirmed there was still no-one inside.

And then Vicar Redd arrived, having been called by DC Morgan to answer questions about Tommy Leeming.

'Tommy hasn't been with me for a while,' the Vicar told the officers. 'He told me he was having problems with his Family up... there...' He pointed up to the one mountain which mostly overlooked the village—Stone Wall Mountain. 'He said he had to deal with an outstanding domestic matter so he's been a bit withdrawn of late.'

'Does the Philips girl work in this village?' asked Sergeant Thomas. Vicar Redd confirmed she did—but Catrin was not working today as the café was closed for stocktaking. Catrin was with Susan Tanner for the day and she had to go to Cardiff to complete a late housing query—and Catrin had gone into the City with her.

'Claire?' he asked, but no-one knew where Claire was—altogether, a dead-end. The questions worried the Vicar and he saw the worried expressions on the face of the three police officers so he knew something terrible had either happened or was about to—and somehow, it involved Tommy.

'Perhaps he's gone up there,' ventured the Vicar, pointing to the mountain which suddenly looked quite foreboding from this viewpoint.

Left standing impotent, Sergeant Thomas called DCI Taffe and reported their findings and then he, the two officers and Vicar Redd left the area. In the car, Taffe pressed the accelerator and chanced the winding lanes and the oncoming traffic. And then they were in sight of the village.

Chapter 55

Hell on the Mountain

It is, of course, the curse of bad timing that in the space of time when Sergeant Thomas, PC's Lloyd and Harris and Vicar Redd left the street in their search for Tommy Leeming that Susan and Catrin had come home from the City, had been assailed by Claire for the borrowed tenner and all three had moved out of view by the time DCI Taffe had screeched into the village and Sergeant Thomas ran full pelt to the car while the other officers continued their search, unaware he was being observed by both Catrin and Susan from inside the house. Under guidance from Sergeant Thomas, Taffe steered the car back out of the village and across another set of winding lanes, heading towards the base of Mynydd Fach and then up that mountain trail towards Stone Wall Mountain.

Thankfully, the mountain trail leading up to the top was relatively smooth—no boulders or deep holes to traverse. It was not very steep either so their trek upwards was made without too much fuss. As they ventured upwards, Taffe saw in his rear view mirror two more Police Units speeding behind him. Good—can't have too many reinforcements on a job like this.

They made it to the top and all four officers climbed out to peruse the scene.

DS Stone confirmed the first statement. 'I ain't climbing *that*,' she said.

It was Sergeant Thomas who said she didn't need to. He pointed to the cave which was now covered by trees and rocks—but was still negotiable by foot.

'You been here before?' asked Taffe.

When Sergeant Thomas was a younger man and before he had joined the Force, he had a village girlfriend who he found crying her eyes out one day. A Fleminganese Elder had seen her in the village and had made a comment about her appearance—an insulting reference about her choice of apparel and make-up. This incensed the young Cenydd Thomas and he strode up the mountain and found the cave—not so hidden then as it was today as it was still used by the

Fleminganese to come off their mountain home and go to the village below—to either barter or sell their religion.

It was a hard and almost perilous climb through the mountain cave which would lead up to the escarpment and the Fleminganese community. He would confront the Elder and warn him to steer clear of the village—not a difficult task as many of the Elders really were elderly and would not therefore present a problem to the much bigger and stronger Cenydd.

The climb was made—he broke through the entrance and the first thing he saw was the horses and carts they used to make their journeys downward. He entered the community—and what he saw shocked him. No-one, to his knowledge, from the village had ever come up here before and so no-one had ever seen what the Fleminganese dwellings looked like.

It looked like something out of the medieval days of England when she was ruled by the Stuarts or the Tudors. Or even something out of the African mud huts.

The domiciles—if you could describe them as such—were made from mostly trees and branches, with joined together planks of wood, all tied together with rope or even tree bark. They looked like wild versions of the Wigwams made by American Indians although nowhere near as well constructed. Cenydd could barely believe his eyes at the dilapidated hovels these people lived in. He was grateful his parents had never forced *their* religion on him. He walked around the village—he supposed that's what they called it—and saw small camp fires either in full flame or dying down. In one area, he saw a number of slaughtered—and probably stolen—sheep being made ready for shearing, skinning and then roasting. The stench of dead animals filled his nose and he had to hold his breath as he walked through the village.

He saw a few of the Fleminganese residents attending to their own duties—and shuddered.

They were all dressed in black—their clothes barely functioning about them—and when they saw him, they all backed away, fear and trauma on their faces.

A hand was laid upon his shoulder and he turned…

…and screamed.

The man was huge, tall in height, wide in breadth—a face from the Bible stories of Moses as he came down from Mount Sinai holding onto the Ten

Commandment Tablet and screaming he had brought with him, *The word of God.* Cenydd backed away, his stomach rising to vomit.

Josiah Fleming.

The man was the very visual presentiment of the Biblical Prophets Cenydd had always read about from the days of the Old Testament—the visage of every God-thumping Preacher he had seen in his nightmares after listening to the sermons from some of the more rabid Vicars who had occasioned through the village.

The man's voice was as deep as his appearance was terrifying and he loomed over the young Cenydd.

'What dost thee want, *sinner?*' asked the man, with fire in his voice—and that was enough for Cenydd. Girlfriend or not, he didn't love her that much and she wasn't worth the pummelling he knew he would take from Josiah Fleming if he told him he was looking the Elder who had frightened her.

He staggered backwards and fell into a dying fire. This resulted in a scorched arse and him using language he would not have used on purpose given the company he was presently keeping.

Cenydd scrambled to his feet and dodged the huge man who he knew was going to convert him—one way or another—and he raced towards the cave entrance and was through it without a backwards glance. The distance between the two entrances was about a quarter of a mile and Cenydd counted every step, hitting every rock and tripping over them, crashing into the sides of the cavernous walls until he was out the other end and was able to sprint down the hill.

Once on Cwmhyfryd ground, he looked down at himself. Dirty, bloodied, burned, his face seemingly etched in a permanent expression of fear. It took him three hours in the bathroom to scrub that visit off his person.

His girlfriend dumped him that same day.

*

The memory swept back into Sergeant Thomas' mind and he hoped he would give a better account of himself today.

He dragged the trees away from the cave entrance and they all entered— himself, DCI Taffe, DS Stone, DC Morgan and eight police officers from Cardiff Police.

The cave was an aspect of natural design but had been worked on by the original Fleminganese dwellers from when they'd arrived in this valley hundreds of years ago. It was now big enough to allow a horse and cart through without difficulty—up and down—and certainly big enough to let through a small coterie of police officers.

What was very obvious to Sergeant Thomas, however, was the seeming lack of present use of the cave. This place hadn't been trodden on in some time. He wondered why—and wondered what they could expect to see above ground.

One quarter of a mile later, his wondering was satisfied. The Community was all but deserted and the domiciles pretty well abandoned. But there was something else which was much more alarming. And it was felt by every officer standing there.

'God,' said DS Stone, 'what *is* that stink?'

For some reason, all eyes went straight to DCI Taffe as if he, out of all there, would know the answer.

And as it turned out, he did.

He took out his hankie, brought out an aerosol canister and sprayed it onto his hankie and pressed it to his nose. He removed it after taking a breath and said, 'That, Sergeant, is the smell of death.' He then generously offered the canister to the other officers and all there copied his actions.

Smoke rose from those small abandoned fires and wafted around them. Taffe looked at the domiciles and noted nothing came from within those buildings and he guessed that all works needed to be done requiring fire, was done out here in the open—probably to ensure that none of the dwellings themselves would ever go up in flames—a definite maybe given that all of them were primarily made of wood.

From behind, someone screamed and they all whirled around—each officer as antsy as could be. Taffe smiled. The scream came from one of the male PC's and it was a very small woman who had scared him.

Upon secondary glancing though, Taffe could see why the officer had reacted the way he had. She was tiny—around four foot five inches, her hair, what was left of it, was straggly, matted, filthy and steel grey. Her face, legs and arms were uncovered and browned from aged and ingrained dirt. Her eyes bulged out of their sockets from her gaunt face—clearly the woman hadn't eaten a good meal in some while—and her teeth were reduced to tiny black stalks inside her mouth. She wore a thin, black one-piece dress which, like her body and face, hadn't seen water in a long time. She could have been any age between thirty and sixty. Her arms were outstretched, as if pleading for aid—which certainly didn't come from the frightened PC who backed away from her, a look of horror on his face.

The scream had brought others out from their tree-like abodes, all female and all similar to the woman standing in front of them now. A WPC moved towards her and tripped over an upraised mound in the ground. She took the woman gently by the shoulder and spoke softly to her.

'Please, don't be frightened. We're here looking for someone. Can you help?'

The woman groaned—and then pointed to her mouth, signalling she could not speak. She opened her mouth wide and the WPC could see why.

'Oh my God,' she said. 'She hasn't got a tongue.'

Taffe moved forward and spoke gently to the woman who stared at him as if he were a physical representation of something she had never before seen in her life—which, he considered, was probably the case.

'We are looking for...' how to put this, 'we are looking for the home and the family of... Tommy Leeming, or Thomas Fleming.'

The benighted woman staggered back as if she had been scalded. She began to wail, dropping to her knees and pounded the ground with her bony fists. She clutched her chest and moaned—only the intervention of the other similarly clad females gave her comfort.

Another woman stepped forward and gazed up at Taffe—again, with a curiosity of someone who could not comprehend what they were looking at. Taffe concluded these people had been so heavily closeted on this plateau, the outside world was as alien to them as another completely different species would be to ordinary people—if they'd happened across a UFO and little green men.

But this new woman had a little more savvy than the one on the ground. Again, with no apparent ability to convey speech, she indicated towards a house set further apart from the other abodes.

This arrangement was slightly different from the others. It was bigger, made from both strong wood and large stones. There was also a door which clearly had been purloined from a scrapyard—none of the other abodes owned one like it. Taffe brought the hankie back up to his mouth. Being helpful was good but the woman stank to hell and back and he guessed proper toiletry functions were also something not indulged in by the present crop of the Fleminganese people. He gestured for everyone to keep their wits about them and to keep back as he made his way to the house. Accordingly, the other officers kept their eyes peeled for any activity around them. DS Stone noted aloud that so far, they hadn't seen any males.

Taffe paused at the doorway. Strictly speaking, he should have waited for Armed Back-up to come up—if Leeming or Fleming was his man and the killer of Hywel Parry and Vonna Shepherd—he may very well be lurking inside the house, waiting to kill the very first intruder who stuck his head inside. He gently pushed the door open—and the stench assaulted him like a wave of hot foul smelling affluence from a cesspit.

He looked around when he heard a noise. One of the PC's had tripped over another raised mound. Breathing into his hankie—and even the clinical aroma of Vick's did not counter the stench from within—he cautiously moved into the house.

No horror movie film-maker could have done a better job if they'd really wanted to scare the living hell out of a person. The room was as oppressive as a torture chamber in current use and hadn't been cleaned from the previous victim. Much of what he was looking at was purely antiquated—the furniture, or what remained of it, was from the seventeenth century. In the middle of the room, there was a deep hole, surrounded by stone and what remained of charred wood from a fire. Taffe guessed this home may have belonged to someone of a superior rank amongst these people—a door, a fire, furniture which could be used—he'd bet his Superintendent's life pension that none of the other houses would own such privileges.

There was no glass in the window frames and a breeze wafted the slight fabrics about. The room was small by contemporary standards—big enough to house, say, two people—provided they were close knit.

But unless the owners were completely devoid of cleanliness, it was apparent no-one had lived here for some time. On the mud floor, there were no carpets or wooden beams to walk on, there were signs of animal droppings—probably rodent—and all around the walls, large spider webbing practically covered the interior.

There was another room. Bedroom? Kitchen? Both? He passed through a tree-made alcove and saw a rocking chair. An old rocking chair—old by some margin as well. He stared.

There was someone sitting in the rocking chair and he walked to it, then in front of it, not taking steps to be quiet—he didn't want to frighten the chair's occupant.

No chance. He looked at the person sitting in the chair and vaulted backwards—for a man who had barely experienced fear in his life, DCI Owen Taffe was scared now.

The occupant was female—quite dead. Had been dead for some time. She appeared to be almost identical to those he had seen outside. Similarly clad— though her dress had been ripped apart, probably by the rats or other animals because she had been feasted upon. Her face, her eyes, her stomach, arms and legs had all been eaten by… The sight was repulsive to Taffe. The bites were large—too large to have been made just by an animal.

The dead woman had been cannibalized.

He stifled the urge to vomit—but he had to get away from this hell. As he stumbled back towards the door, he saw the single concession to modern day living. A row of photographs standing on a tall cabinet. The pictures were mostly ancient—and they weren't all taken in the UK—one man and a boy were clearly dressed in Army uniforms—American Army, and they were taken from around the American Civil War period.

There were other similar pictures—but it was the one which looked the most recent which took his attention. A woman—possibly the one he had just seen— and a boy. The boy would have been around thirteen judging by his surliness and apparel—and he was the child version of the same boy he had seen at the Philips house.

Tommy Leeming.

He flung open the door and scrambled out of the place. He was now breathing in and out what passed as fresh air in this place and clasped the hankie to his face between gasps. He looked up and around.

The PC's were now surrounded by at least fifteen women—all identical to those he'd already seen. All of them clamouring to the arms of the PC's who, understandably, really did not know how to handle this atrocity.

He stood upright—and strode towards the group. The women all then moved back, in fear of this man who was clearly the Master. Even in their pathetic state, these women knew how to gauge who was the superior amongst the newcomers.

Taffe drew up to DS Stone—his face a mix of anger and bewilderment.

'Call Dr Swain—I want her entire team up here...'

Before he had the chance to finish what he was saying, DC Morgan called out to him. Morgan was the only officer of the group to have wandered away. Now he was standing on an slightly upraised hill and standing beneath a tall man-made monolith which had been covered by trees. It was around fifteen feet high and its single adornment was a large Cross which hung down from the top of what appeared to look like a battlement. He called Taffe again and beckoned him to come up the hill. Taffe duly obliged and climbed the hill. He stood next to his excited DC—and they looked down over the escarpment and the domiciles and the people.

DC Morgan said, 'I tripped over the damn things twice—so did some of the others—and I noticed there quite a few of these mounds so I came up here to get a better look... and...' Taffe could barely believe what he was looking at. The upraised mounds which he naturally believed were just parts of the ground on the plateau actually formed a pattern. They were long—about six feet in length, three feet wide. They were scattered all over the plateau—and all pointed to where they were standing now.

Graves. Over a hundred of them.

Taffe stared, aghast at the implication of what he was looking at. He could see DS Stone—equally appalled—giving him the thumbs up sign—she was calling Dr Swain. This place was just about to become one of the greatest crime scenes in Welsh history.

Chapter 56

The Horror of Stone Wall Mountain

DS Stone had never seen the Inspector so agitated—or angry—but he stalked around the area giving out instructions to the other officers to make a search of the whole grounds, going into the tree domiciles to find any other people who may be either dead or unable to move. He had told them all of the dead woman in the bigger house—and in what state he had found the body—and he wanted to be certain just how many people there actually were on this mountain. One mystery: where the hell were all the men? He hoped the explanation wasn't something like they were out hunting for their next meal.

He posted a young Constable on the door of the big house and they all went in search of other evidence. Situated some distance away from the living quarters—he didn't know what else to call them—Taffe found what used to be a large garden allotment—no longer in use as all the aids of such a place were either broken or lying flat on the untilled ground. What was useful, however, were some of the gardening implements, all man-made, many from another age. He handed the heaviest of these implements to the most burliest of the uniformed officers and instructed him to locate the most recent mound of upraised ground—the one which had the least amount of grass growth on it—and dig it up. The constable stripped away his upper tunic and tie, rolled his sleeves up, located what he was looking for and began to hack away at the proscribed ground.

The sound of wailing brought his attention back to the big house. All the women they had encountered had now prostrated themselves in front of the house and were moaning—were they speaking in some language?—stretching out their bony arms and bowing their heads in chorus. The Constable stood her ground. Judo taught, she could take out any or all of them, Taffe thought—but hoped it would not come to that. He wasn't sure if the wailing women were mourning the death of their neighbour or complaining about the fact that their food supply had been cut off.

No results were to be found at any of the houses—but the searches were cursory. SOCO would dismantle the houses and look much more closely—*under* the ground for instance.

The digging Constable yelled out and they all rushed to where he was now standing, leaning on the large hoe-like implement—a look of shock on his face. He turned away from them once they had reached him. As Taffe had feared, there was a skeleton buried there—no, two skeletons—and the burials had been recent. The bodies were mostly skeleton bone—but there was still flesh on both—and one of them had either been a small adult or a child. The smaller skeleton had been placed on top of the larger skeleton and their hands were clasped in each other's.

Natural deaths or something more sinister, wondered DS Stone. This case—which started out as just two grisly murders—had elevated into something beyond a Gothic nightmare.

And that was the way Taffe felt about it. This had once been a thriving Community—from hundreds of years back—now there were just a small handful and there was something clearly wrong with those they had found. There was no information, to Taffe's knowledge, of any of the Fleminganese being buried at Cwmhyfryd Cemetery—so—where did the dead go? Obviously this was the graveyard of the Fleminganese but just how recent were the burials and what were the causes of death? And again, where were the males of the Community? Taffe pondered the notion that the Community, under the gaze of the Fleming Patriarchy, had been provided for in one way or the other. Sergeant Thomas had told them of the day he had come to this place years ago and he'd seen the dead sheep—probably stolen or bought by bartering from the local farms—which had sustained the people. But—as time had passed and the Fleming line had maybe petered out—who had assumed leadership of the Community and how did they provide for them? If, as he was now thinking, the male population had died out and the women had been left to fend for themselves, had they taken to cannibalism to survive?

There were now even bigger questions which related to the case at hand: Tommy Leeming—or was he Thomas Fleming? And if so, why had he left this Community, under what circumstances, abandoning those who remained to fend for themselves? Who was the woman in the house? Mother? How had she died and was she cannibalized before or after her death?

The burly Constable asked if he was required to dig up another grave—for that was clearly what all these mounds were—and Taffe told him to stand down.

'Get dressed, son,' he said, without patronizing him, 'And no more digging, we have seen enough of hell for one day.' Grateful, the Constable redressed himself and Taffe ordered two Constables to stand alongside their colleague by the house—just in case the women got too hungry.

DS Stone received a call and she ran to Taffe.

'SOCO and Forensics are at the base of the mountain, Sir,' she panted, and for the first time, respect was in her voice as she spoke to her Inspector. This business had turned out to be more than she had bargained for when they'd set out on this expedition and she was, for once, glad to have the Inspector next to her. 'They're making the climb into the cave now.'

Sergeant Thomas also received a call—and he raced over to DCI Taffe. 'Sir,' he panted, with fear and anxiety in his voice. 'My mates down in the village have just confirmed Catrin Philips and Susan Tanner are home. They haven't spoken to them yet...'

Taffe shouted to Morgan and the DC ran to him. 'Wait for the teams to come up and apprise them of what we've seen. When Dr Swain arrives, lead her to that house and tell her what she's likely to find. I hope she hasn't had lunch. Stone, Thomas—we're going back into the village.'

DC Morgan felt slightly cheated that he was now out of the more active angle of the investigation but he confirmed the order and waited for the SOCO and Forensics teams to arrive. The other uniformed officers milled around, awaiting orders.

With some urgency, Taffe, Stone and Sergeant Thomas entered the cave and ran, as best they could, down the dark and boulder strewn cave floor until they passed the SOCO and Forensics teams and were, gratefully, back out into fresh air and brightness. The cloudy mist which had descended over the escarpment while they were searching the houses seemed to belong to that area, merely complementing the mountain's air of eeriness.

Into the car and they sped down the trail. When he saw Dr Swain approaching, Taffe screeched to a sliding halt and gave her a brief summary of what she could expect to find up there. She nodded and drove on. Taffe continued down the mountain, too fast, and was grateful when he drove onto firm concrete.

He drove through the village entrance gates and towards the Philips home.

Chapter 57
The Hunt

And while DCI Taffe was uncovering the grisly findings of Stone Wall Mountain, Jack Farr came home. He arrived in Cwmhyfryd by taxi, and got out of the car near the Philips' home. Susan happened to be looking out for him when he was wandering about and she ran out to greet him. Luckily, he had very little in the way of baggage so getting up to the house would not be difficult and he wanted to do the long walk just to stretch his legs.

Catrin watched from inside the house as she saw Auntie Susan standing next to Mr Farr. Body language is important to someone who doesn't usually speak it and Catrin's detachment from social skills was, by choice, obvious to every boy in the village who had asked her out on dates. She had seen enough evidence of grown up relationships to know this was an area of growing up she should avoid until she was properly prepared to engage in it. This relationship between Auntie Susan and Mr Farr was the most oddest to her bearing in mind their shared history. A love life growing up as children, an engagement—of sorts because there was no ring, no engagement party for him—and an almost marriage which was not completed because…

…Auntie Susan had jilted Mr Farr.

And now, she was standing next to him, gently resting her hand on his arm, not clutching it, and they were standing almost face to face, almost nose-to-nose and talking—about what God only knew—but the look in her eyes told Catrin that this was the real thing. This was love, unabated, unadorned, focused, more powerful than anything she had ever seen before, including her own parents' marriage—the state of which was one of the reasons why Catrin had steered clear of relationships.

Tactility is a curious thing between lovers—not a clamouring of touching or fondling—but a gentle touch with a finger, the brushing off of a hair upon the other person's shoulder, a barely grasped holding of a collar—anything of a minor nature seemed to have the most tender intention. Catrin watched—Auntie Susan was laughing, not something she did a lot of when she was with Mr Tanner—and in parts, sometimes she and Mr Farr did not even speak. And yet— even that silence spoke loudly.

Eventually, after ten minutes, Auntie Susan nodded her head and Mr Farr picked up his baggage. She leaned forwards and gave him a gentle kiss on the side of his mouth—nothing more than a gesture people would give each other when meeting in town unexpectedly and yet, this briefest intimacy electrified Catrin's mind.

Auntie Susan remained at the gate, waving to Mr Farr when he'd reached the end of the street and was out of sight. She turned around, seemed to sigh, and was about to come back into the house when...

The two village PC's ran up to where she was standing and spoke to her— clearly with urgency. One of them made a call to someone and Susan turned to Catrin—and the expression on her face made Catrin run out of the house.

*

Ten minutes later, DCI Taffe came speeding through the village street and brought the car to another screeching halt, just outside the house. The car was still in motion when he opened his door and he had to sit back to put the handbrake on. He stood in front of Catrin first.

'Tommy Leeming,' he said. 'I want him.'

This was not the pleasant spoken DCI she had been with a few nights ago— this was business and it was urgent. Before she spoke, Taffe brought up the name of Thomas Fleming.

'Are they related?' he asked, 'or is Tommy Leeming really Thomas Fleming?' Catrin said she had never heard of Thomas Fleming but that name was quite prevalent amongst the Fleminganese people—'Like Jones' she said.

Taffe broke cover and told Susan and Catrin about what they had learned at Peter Eddy's office—and the resemblance between Tommy and Thomas.

It was Vicar Redd—who had just run up to join them who filled in the gap.

'He told me,' said Vicar Redd, 'they are the same. Leeming was the name given to Joseph Fleming's right hand man when they came to this valley. I asked him about the Fleminganese people after Jack had told me about the Community on Stone Wall Mountain. Tommy then told me he was actually one of them—or

313

had been until they kicked him out for not being devout enough. The Leeming name is… as important to their faith as say, Peter was to Jesus and Christianity. Tommy often referred to himself as being more Leeming than Fleming—and here's what he said—"like his father", Josiah.'

Susan said Josiah was a Fleming—not a Leeming. That answered all the questions Taffe had about Tommy's real identity.

Catrin suddenly remembered Claire and was now distressed. 'Why do you want Tommy?' she asked.

The expression on the DCI's face was enough—Catrin spoke quietly and said, 'Oh my God, Tommy's the killer.'

'I don't know for sure, Miss Philips,' said Taffe, 'but I need to eliminate Tommy Leeming from my inquiry if he isn't.'

And then, Catrin's hands went to her mouth. She cried out, 'Claire.'

Susan shouted out. 'Tommy has made an arrangement to meet Claire—at Collier's Quarry. That's where he will be now.'

'Where the hell is Collier's Quarry?' asked Taffe. It was Sergeant Thomas who answered that question but then remembered, 'We can't reach it. The Council put up gates and left large boulders in the path to stop roadsters speeding up and down.'

Vicar Redd grabbed his phone and dialled. 'Ben,' he shouted out. 'Vicar Redd here. Listen to me—this is life and death important. You know the path leading up to… where?' This to Susan who shouted out Collier's Quarry to him. He continued. 'Collier's Quarry. I'm with a policeman who has to get to the Quarry but the path is blocked off. Do you still have your JCB?'

He waved DCI Taffe over to the phone. 'Ben,' he continued. 'this is an official sanction from DCI Taffe—he has to get to the Quarry and I promise you, it is life and death important. Can you get through the gates and remove the rocks?'

He brought up his thumb and DCI Taffe along with DS Stone and Sergeant Thomas piled into the car and sped away. Susan watched the car leave the street and she moved to a tearful Catrin who buried her head into Susan's body. Vicar Redd stood by—not certain how to comfort his charges.

And then, Susan clicked her fingers. '*Jack,*' she said.

*

314

Jack had just arrived at the house and was about to open the front door when his phone sounded. It was Susan. He smiled. He'd only just left her so what could she want. He was happy when he answered.

'I'm home, safe and sound,' he said.

The urgency in Susan's voice was enough to alarm him. 'Listen,' she said, 'it may be that Tommy Leeming is the killer.'

'Who's Tommy Leeming?' he asked, still not completely au fait with all the new names at the village.

'Claire Philips' boyfriend. He just called her a while back to meet her at Collier's Quarry. She left in a taxi so I expect she's there by now. DCI Taffe has just left to chase it down but they have to go the road way... whereas you...'

'I'm on my way,' Jack replied knowing exactly what Susan was about to say. The geographical advantage Jack had was from the old saying—"*As the crow flies*". The Inspector would have to drive miles out in the opposite direction to get to the entrance to Collier's Quarry whereas he could hot foot it across the mountain—Collier's Quarry could be reached quicker this way as it was situated at the back end of Mynydd Gabriel.

He ended the call, dropped his baggage and ran as fast as he could up the rocky pathway leading up to Mynydd Gabriel. The run was hard, for as well as watching his footing, he had to dodge the tree branches which still hung down, covering the upper part of the tunnel. His face was badly scratched even before he was halfway through the tunnel.

He made it through the tunnel and carried on his run up to the top of the mountain range. The physical requirements of this run were very taxing—it was such a steep climb—and by the time he'd made it to the level of the mountain, he was already exhausted. But...

Claire Philips.

Her safety was paramount and more important than the aching stitch in his side. After a bit of breathing out, he strode across the range, watching his footing from the many pitted holes in the mountain trail. He ran as fast as he could and ignored the perils of the terrain below him.

*

Ben Galloway, 85 years of age, former farmer from the days before the villages of Cwmhyfryd and Brangwyn were the larger corporate states they are now and was long since retired from the farming industry, did not hesitate when Vicar Redd gave him his instruction. That gentleman did not indulge in the games of exaggeration and so when he said the removal of the gates and boulders blocking the path to Collier's Quarry needed to be removed, he meant it. Life and death important he said—he meant that as well.

He jumped into his JCB, practically the only working piece of big machinery on the farm now, and drove out of his farmyard and across the field. The field itself was now operated by a small Corporation serving the County Council of this area doing pretty much the same job Galloway used to do when he was a younger man only now in half the time and with bigger results. The agreement between him and the Council was based on produce storage for a stipend fee at the end of the farming year. It suited him—and Mrs Galloway—who did not miss the 4am rising nor the everyday washing of his mud-soaked clothing.

The distance between farm and entrance gate was a quarter of a mile—and he drove at speed. Ahead of him was the gate which he would have to get out of the JCB to unlock—so, because it was an emergency situation—he drove straight at it and knocked it flat. The County Council would take care of its repair and costs. The distance between where he was now and the entrance to the Quarry path was a little over 250 yards—and he took that at speed as well, mounting the opposite embankment when he reached the large entrance area, turning the JCB into the gate and driving straight at it with such speed, he took both the gate and the concrete pillars out of the ground and dragged them for another 100 yards before it came to a halt and he drove the JCB over the gate and beyond. Then, towards the first boulder.

*

DC Morgan wondered who was having the most excitement—him or DCI Taffe's team? The SOCO team had taken a good look around the plateau—and were fairly horrified just looking at the place at first sight. When they entered the tree domiciles and began their work, there was much to find—mostly from the past ages of the Fleminganese people and their ancestors.

Something the original search had not discovered was the larger burial ground which held over it, a large monument which proscribed the memory of the Community's original Founder—Joshua Fleming. This would need to be dug up as well—for one thing, it was clear that a recent excavation had taken place here and Morgan needed to know who—or what—was buried here apart from the remains of the big man himself.

Dr Swain worked on the late remains of whoever Taffe found in the house. And her initial discovery indicated more than one set of human teeth had chomped into the body. As to the cause of death—that was yet to be learned.

An Ambulance had arrived at the base of the mountain and was ready to take away anyone who needed it—and Dr Swain decreed that every living remaining member of the Community needed to be immediately transported to the Hospital for a complete check-up—a problem that was considered to be quite big, given the possibility that none of these women had ever travelled beyond the Communal barriers in their lives. What they knew of life beyond the Community was whatever they had been told by their Patriarch and what they could see looking over the edge of the cliff and down into the valley. Another problem would be identifying the women. Legally, none of them existed in the eyes of the law. The Fleminganese Community had been so cut off from the outside world, that none of them had birth certificates, official registrations of identity, no National Insurance numbers of NHS references—to the officialdom of the outside world, these people simply did not exist. Talk about negotiating the first rung of the ladder—these unfortunates weren't even on the ladder.

It was certain they would require more than a single Ambulance.

The wailing women had been shepherded away from the where they had congregated around their late neighbour's big house and stared at the activity engaged in by the SOCO and Forensics teams as the burial mounds—for that is what they were—were dug up. And what they found buried there appalled everyone who witnessed it.

It was the discovery of a cache of weapons which caused even greater alarm. Rifles, pistols, from the USA—and from the age of the Civil War—had been found, and all of them in near pristine condition.

DC Morgan got onto his mobile and called Taffe immediately.

*

En route to the Quarry entrance, Taffe ordered calls to be made to the Armed Response Unit—a possible shout relating to an armed criminal who had killed twice and was possibly armed with a Smith & Wesson pistol. He also ordered an Ambulance to be attending a possible injury or death and gave out the Collier's Quarry address as the scene of crime. When DS Stone received the call from DC Morgan telling her of the arms cache found under the grave of the late and unlamented Joshua Fleming, Taffe's worries escalated and his driving became even more dangerous—in fact, in passing an oncoming car, there was a definite clash of side-view mirrors resulting in the a stream of a horn beeping and the other driver swearing.

'How far?' he shouted to Sergeant Thomas.

'Two miles,' replied the Sergeant who had never been so scared in his life as he was now watching the trees bypass him at such a speed. Assuming we are still in on one piece when we get there, he thought on.

*

Catrin was beside herself and it was more than Susan could bear, thinking that the vivacious Claire was walking to her possible doom. She ordered Catrin to hold on and she ran to the Agency where her car was parked and drove back to the house. Catrin climbed in and they sped away—highly unlikely they could make a difference and doubtful they would even be allowed to get near to where the scene would be active—but anything was better than waiting in a vacuum for bad news. God only knows what I'm going to have to tell Sara when she gets home tonight was pretty much dominating Susan's thoughts right now.

They entered the lanes and Susan drove as fast as she was able—not comparable to the eminent DCI's abilities but as best she could. Catrin did the best she could to stifle the tears.

*

Claire didn't know what day of the week it was, she was so disorientated. She lay on the floor where Tommy had just thrown her, clouded in dust and wooden splinters, her face a mass of bruising from where he had punched her.

In all her life, no man had ever laid an angry hand on her. Even as a child, when she was being naughty, her father refused to rebuke her with a physical hand—telling her off was as much as this doting father had been able to do. If it required anything more stringent, he left it to Sara—but he had never once laid a rebuking hand on his youngest daughter. No boyfriend had ever physically remonstrated with her even after she had broken up their relationship. That she should be in sufferance now at the hands of her precious Tommy was the ultimate betrayal—that it should be in the manner in which the blows were being delivered was even worse—a physical punishment followed by the religious rants of the most deluded sort. Tommy had raised Heaven and Hell, brought both to planet Earth and had set them on top of the fragrant Claire. Her eyes were swollen, unable to see at all out her right eye, her nose possibly broken and even now misshapen, her lips had been cut and blood flowed from her mouth. He had choked her—and then swung her around in mid-air by her hair and thrown her to the ground. In between blows, he would pound the floor and the remaining furniture and scream—really scream—the word of Joshua Fleming and his fight against the Un-Godly who had dragged this once demi-Paradise into the sewers of Purgatory where he had announced all sinners would end up.

And it was his screaming voice which scared her, even more than the beatings, for the voice came with such a change of a facial appearance that he was barely recognizable as the boy she had known, had met here in this very place when it was an industry coming to its end, and with whom she had fallen in love in the same week. Perhaps it was the shadows playing tricks with her now one good eye, with the dust and dirt swirling around from the activity which had been thrown on it, but he didn't even look like Tommy. The shadows across his face, under his now bulging eyes, had distorted his appearance to such a degree it simply wasn't her Tommy.

And the screaming raged on.

'Thee have SINNED! Thee have broken the covenant with our Maker who we have all signed for permission to exist here on this planet for the period of borrowed time we all have as the sons and daughters of the Maker. And YOU...' he turned and jabbed his finger towards Claire and screamed again, *'YOU... are the misbegotten spawn of the very JEZEBEL! Converging with the SINNERS who have broken their promises to the Maker—you who have sinned and copulated with the Infidel in front of our very eyes—in front of HIS! You are the vilest of all his creations for you have coerced those adulterers with a smile upon thy face to commit their SINS—under his very eyes!'*

Claire tried to sit up and she begged for mercy but this merely brought herself back to his attention and her pleas were met with yet another stinging slap and she was back on the floor, rolling in the dirt and dust.

In all her life, no man had ever laid an angry hand upon her—but today that angry hand was raised and was being delivered by Tommy—and Claire knew she was going to die.

He stood in the doorway and in her tear-stricken eyes, she saw the silhouette of his body arch back and he screamed…

'WHOOOORRREEE!'

*

Jack thought his heart was going to burst. The run to the Quarry seemed to be longer than he remembered it, there seemed to be more hillocks and holes and it was more uphill. Memories play tricks on you when you least want them to.

He ran through rough patches of terrain and there were many areas where he could not negotiate a track at all—the bush of that terrain was so firm and intransigent that it could not be run upon. He was forced to circumvent such areas and this took him away from his desired direction.

And then he heard the squeal of laughter.

He stopped—he had to, he was so out of breath—and he whirled around to see where the sound was coming from. Some distance away, judging by the minor decibel. And then he heard it again and was able to pinpoint its direction.

And when he was able to do that, he saw the most peculiar sight. A bicycle, standing upright and there in the middle of the mountain. And then came another squeal. Forced to go in that direction anyway, he diverted to where the bike was standing. When he reached the area, he peered into a small gully…

Two people were lying in the gully and were in the frantic throes of sex.

Where had he seen this…? Oh yes, the day he first came home and was walking across this mountain area with Vicar Redd heading back to Greenacres. Yes, of course, the two people who were making love that day as well. The Vicar had commented upon it, claiming they had even invaded the sanctuary of the Cemetery and had made love to each other amongst the gravestones and only the dead kept watch on their passion.

Jack stared, not quite believing his eyes, for the male on top was dressed in a blue 'T' shirt vest, his arms naked, wearing biking shorts so was bare-legged, socks pushed down to the trainers. He was even still wearing his safety helmet. He couldn't see his face—yet—but the flabby wrinkles on his arms and legs told Jack that this energetic ramrod was clearly in his dotage. And then, Jack remembered where he'd seen this village Casanova before. Ianto Evans—the septuagenarian who had been cycling underneath the wall the day Jack had battled against the McGregor boys—and one had landed on top of him as he cycled past. Jack recalled the moments when the old rampant had belaboured the unfortunate McGregor with a stream of verbal platitudes and then set about him and his cousin with his safety helmet, chasing the pair of them out of the village.

Whatever Ianto was putting in his porridge, Jack wanted some—but that was for another day. For this moment, Jack needed the bike. He was about to interrupt their coital endeavours when he decided their activities would not entertain any kind of interference—and so he merely took possession of the upright bicycle and purloined it.

He rode the thing, as best he could across the course ground until he reached the rocky but level path—and then he sped down the incline at breakneck speed, coming close to being thrown off, possibly ending this rescue attempt at a premature point.

*

DCI Taffe spun the car in a wide arc and drove straight to where the gates of the Quarry path had once stood—and right over them when they saw the gates were down.

'Thank you, Mr Galloway,' Taffe said aloud.

At least a hundred and fifty yards ahead of them, the path was clear.

*

Ben Galloway had removed four boulder obstacles and three closed gates from the path and he knew there were just two more. One large boulder and one more fixed gate. He gunned his engine and carried on.

*

Susan was driving faster than she had ever driven—nothing had ever been as urgent before. Catrin was offering possible scenarios to offset what the DCI had told them. Perhaps there *had* been a mistake in identification. Perhaps there *was* a Thomas Fleming, a man who bore a resemblance to Tommy. Susan said nothing. Such diversion gave Catrin comfort—the hope that her beloved sister was not in danger and all was well. She passed a road sign which told her the Quarry path was still two miles away. She hoped Jack had made good progress.

*

In fact, Jack had reached the point where the mountain trail veered off to the left which meant the Quarry was just a quarter of a mile away to his right. The ground was less certain from here on but he had covered a lot of rough terrain in quick time, courtesy of Mr Evans' borrowed cycle—all in a good cause, of course.

It was this final stretch which almost put paid to Jack's endeavour. He had been forced to slew the cycle across the ground because he had unaccountably run out of mountain. Susan had failed to notify him of the geographical changes which had been made, for some reason, in this area. The last time he had come this way, the mountain ended in a less steep incline which led down to the actual Quarry area. The ground was of a grassy make, with small brush trees that one could get a grip on should one decide to make this trip—as, of course, many Hyfridians did when they were employed to work at the Quarry as many of them, back in the day, did not own cars and a public transport system had not been invented for the new born village.

But now, the final stretch of the mountain had been blown away, removed, bombed to hell and back as far as Jack knew for it stopped way short of its original trail by a clear hundred yards or so and was now more of a direct vertical drop. Worse, there was nothing worthwhile to grab onto to make the descent. Had he not seen the geographical change in time, he would have cycled straight over the top and landed very hard, at least a two hundred yard fall, on top of large, jagged rocks.

He got to his feet and scanned the area ahead and below him. From this vantage point, he could see the remains of the Quarry building. What was directly below him was excavated mud walls and tree roots. There were ledges and points which jutted out and Jack's only recourse was to jump down and land on them, hoping they would not break and send him tumbling over the edge. Luckily, each level was not so high from the previous so the jump being made did not involve too great a distance and did not dislodge the ground he was jumping on top of…

…until the last jump.

This jump would be the hardest as it was at the steepest part of the former mountain and at least twenty feet below the level he was presently standing on. Below it, there was still yet another fifty feet or so to negotiate and that included jumping free of the rocks. He held his breath and jumped. But the muddy jutted-out placement was not as firm as he wanted it to be and when he landed on it, the impact was too much for its soaked foundations to withstand and it gave way the moment he landed.

He grabbed for anything to prevent the fall but the muddy wall was weak and he found himself toppling over and down, out of control and blinded by the mud which covered him. Jack landed hard on the rocks—and he was then covered by the mud and stone which followed him down, crushing him on top of the rocks he had landed upon. The avalanche was considerable and substantial. When the final pieces of mud and stone had settled, there was no sign of Jack Farr.

*

Susan had to bring her car to a sliding halt to avoid the two black speeding cars which had driven into the Quarry path just a few seconds after she had entered it. They, whatever they were, were each blaring a siren, and she had to pull hard right on the steering wheel to avoid a collision and drove into the remains of the gate fence. The cars did not stop to check her but sped on, over the remains of the gate and forwards to the Quarry. She had turned the car off and checked Catrin to see if she was compos mentis. Just about, but the scare was enough for Susan to calm it down and gauge her thoughts. She started the car up again and reversed out of the fence she had driven into. She was about to resume her direction when an Ambulance rushed past her. She and Catrin looked at each other and the possible scenario that there had been a mistake about Tommy's identity receded. Again, she brought the car back, and with greater care, drove over the fallen gates and towards the Quarry.

*

Ben Galloway was just a few minutes away from the next boulder when a car shot past him at a hell of a speed and was suddenly out of sight.

'If you be the Inspector,' he said to himself, 'I ain't got there yet.'

*

Taffe screamed the car down the rocky path—and asked again for the distance to the Quarry. Sergeant Thomas assured him they were close…

And DS Stone screamed. Ahead of them was a boulder just too large to negotiate around. Taffe brought the car up as near to that rock as he could and stared at it. No way could he bypass this monster. Was the Quarry near? Could they run it? No, said the Sergeant, mopping the sweat off his face with his sleeve. Taffe screamed in frustration and depressed the horn which he maintained purely out of anger and impotence. And then, from behind, the rumbling JCB came into view and he reversed out of its way. The boulder was the largest and therefore the hardest to remove but Ben did it manfully and had completed the job in five minutes.

Taffe gave another burst of his horn—in gratitude—and sped past the JCB. They had lost time—but how crucial was that loss?

Sergeant Thomas was almost too afraid to mention it—but he did anyway. 'Sir,' he yelled over the roaring car engine, 'there is still another gate to get through—and it's some distance away from here. It'll take Mr Galloway ten minutes to catch up with…'

And there it was—the last gate.

A quarter of a mile ahead—wide, maybe ten yards across, high about five feet up and made of metal, attached to two metal posts which had been rammed into the ground. And Taffe was speeding towards it like it was the finishing line in a race.

'Sir,' said a now worried DS Stone.

'*HOLD ON,*' yelled DCI Taffe.

Taffe pressed that accelerator to the floor and they all saw the gate coming towards them like a missile. Some blasphemous language was used.

The sound of metal crashing into metal at 90mph is a truly frightening sound and both Sergeants were holding onto their heads as if their very lives depended upon it—which they probably did. The car lurched forward and all three were considerably thrown around inside—only the seatbelts prevented any serious harm though Sergeant Thomas—all six foot plus of him—banged his head on the car roof a number of times. Taffe brought the car back on to the path and it continued onwards though a strange whining sound gave cause for concern—smoke rising from the bonnet didn't help.

*

Two police cars, sirens blaring and horns beeping, sped past Susan's car as she pulled as far over to the grassy embankment as she could. A second Ambulance was in the distance so she remained where she was. Catrin's face was now in a state of near trauma. Breathing out, Susan started the car up again and drove off—a little more slowly this time.

*

Claire had been flung onto her back on top of what used to be the receptionist's desk. All fight had been taken away from her—she had nothing left to use against Tommy—her mouth was so badly swollen and filled with blood it was useless to even try to talk to him. He leered over her and screamed again.

'Oh Father—give me the strength to do thy bidding—to cleanse this worthless life and wash her free of her sins so that she may meet thee, pure and unsullied, in mind and body—look upon her with charity and pity and forgive her—allow into your House and let her serve you in your Majestic Home. I send her to you, this pitiful Being, make her thine.'

He placed his huge hands around her tiny throat and squeezed and Claire knew this was death. The pain was excruciating—at first—but then the darkness seeped in from around Tommy and crowded around her until she saw the last thing with her eye—his face, distorted, angry, shaded—not Tommy at all but something which had taken over him and was controlling his actions.

The darkness swallowed her. The pain—still palpable—lessened. The screams which had frightened her so, faded into the distance and they became almost an echo which receded with each second. And then... silence.

So this was death. It had replaced the pain so that must be a good thing. She relaxed which is the way it must be if you're about to pass over. She wondered if she would see the "light" as she made the journey to her final destination. And as she travelled there, a number of final thoughts entered her mind. Even in her present state, she was able to give them consideration.

She gave thought to her life—had she behaved according to her rights? She had never knowingly hurt another person—not even the many boyfriends from whom she had parted, their crying protestations ringing in her ears, to give them another chance. Only one boy had reacted differently—Connor Williams—who had merely shrugged his shoulders and said "Okay" then walked away. The next day, she saw him holding hands with Betsi Jones and he didn't even look upset— which, curiously, upset Claire.

She had always tried to be fun around her friends so no-one would ever complain that she was dull or boring. She attended every birthday and always took a present so no-one could ever accuse her of being a "tight-ass". She had never smoked, never drank too much alcohol and had never sworn in front of her parents.

Which brought her to Mam and Dad—and Catrin. She had been the dutiful daughter—never giving Mam a reason to regret having her, never shaming Dad with course humour or making fun of him when he danced at the *Blooz* Club on a party night. She had worried about the state of her parents' marriage—were they as happy as they should have been? Was Dad drinking too much? Why was he so angry about the smallest of things?

Finally, her thoughts of elder sister Catrin—she who had taught her so much when they were children—so much more than she'd learned from school or from Mam and Dad—always so patient with her and giving her attention when only her vanity demanded it. Catrin had been the most wonderful elder sister any younger sister could have wanted—and Claire promised herself that she would try and send her messages from the Afterlife just to let her know she was safe and happy. Finally, and most oddly, the regret she felt that she would not now be able to repay her the ten pounds she had borrowed from Catrin which had brought her to this place—and her death. How ironic that it should have been her elder sister who had facilitated that moment.

At peace, in a state of serenity and relaxed. Just how it should be when you are about to depart this mortal world and meet something that is far greater than anything you have ever known…

Except the screams were coming back, loud, louder, louder again. The pain—which she thought she had left behind—was seeping back into her mind and she wondered if she were going to the wrong place. She could breathe again—and gulped at the feisty air and dust as her lungs took back control. Her eyes opened and she could see Tommy—still standing over her but no longer pressing himself against her. He was screaming—not words now but out of pain. His body was upright and his hands were clamped to either side of his head…

No, not his head, they were clamped onto… another pair of hands. A pair of hands which had grabbed a handful each of Tommy's long and curly hair and was pulling him off her body. His face was now a masked distortion of pain, not anger, and he was being pulled completely away from her and dragged across the room. The swirling dust prevented her from seeing who the hands belonged to but then her vision slowly returned and she saw…

Mr Farr—Jack Farr. Uncle Jack. Auntie Susan's friend.

She was able to throw herself from the desk and crawl to the exit door and she saw Mr Farr pull Tommy away to the far end of the room—putting distance between her and him. And then, Mr Farr pushed Tommy to the wall—and brought his hand back to give Tommy an almighty wallop to his face. Tommy yelled out in pain and he crashed to the dirty and dusty floor which sent up clouds of more dust and everything was hazy again.

Mr Farr was breathing hard. She looked at him. He was absolutely drenched in mud, totally covered in it. His hands and head were matted with blood and he seemed to stagger around, as if his leg were damaged.

Tommy lay still for a moment and Mr Farr came to her and picked her up. He asked her if she was alright but she was unable to speak so she wrapped her arms around his neck and held onto him. For a brief moment, there was silence in the room…

Until she saw Tommy getting back up to his feet. And she moaned, pointing her hand towards him. Mr Farr turned to face Tommy—and then he gently ushered her through the exit door and told her to run. As she left through the door, the bright day causing her to duck her head from the sun which ruled above her, she heard a scream—Tommy again—and she ran for her life.

Tommy launched himself at his opponent and the fight was joined. It was uneven from the get-go. Tommy, younger, taller, a man devoid of any conscience and was, therefore, not constrained by any false ideology of not harming another person because he was *human* and therefore his life was *sacrosanct*—a sociopath borne of a congenital insanity which had not deformed his body in the same way that disease had deformed his fellow Fleminganese but had instead warped his conscious mind to the point where he saw no value in the life of any other human and its opposition to his mission simply justified its own extinction. Tommy was thus beyond physical pain and without doubt about his duty here—this man, Farr, was an impediment to helping the girl Claire—*his girl*—go to a better world, she who had betrayed him when he'd seen her speaking with this man in the forest near the death well, had defended him when she had heard about the way her own parents had revelled in his pain the day he had been jilted by the adulterer Susan Tanner—*and she was the next to be dealt with*—and then, finally, had claimed how romantic it was that these two fornicators would probably soon be married themselves.

This man, Farr, is the seed of the Great Deceiver's own Dark Angel and his life must not be spared. He must die as surely as others have had to die in the service of my father—the omnipotent Joshua Fleming—who had discovered this paradise land and had brought his people to serve their Lord. The woman—Vonna Shepherd who had prostituted her body and sold her soul—had been a means of destruction to bring this man down and the older man—Hywel Parry—a criminal in the eyes of the Great Maker—was yet another method delivered to him by his father's word to complete this man's fall. But the Law of the land had failed. It had failed him and the society it is sworn to defend and protect from the likes of Farr, from soiled women and criminals and so he, Tommy, an agent of the Righteous had been sent to do his father's bidding, to rid the world of the spawn of Jezebel and this affront to all that was good and decent. He would not fail nor betray his father by human weakness or false compassion. His own Earth Father had taught him—the man called Joseph Fleming who had entered the village to barter with those people—and he would honour his father.

Tommy's strength was borne from something deep within the bowels of hate and Jack could not equal it. The race across the mountain had taxed his energy, the fall off the mountain had left him almost crippled. His leg, both his arms and hands and his head had all received damage in the fall and the fear he had of this man had also weakened him. Tommy was, therefore, able to land harmful and telling blows on Jack and the fight went very much in his direction.

But Jack also possessed an inner strength—one that he had barely required of late—one that he had first discovered years earlier and had lain dormant inside him in his youth, only to be awakened when he experienced the loss of his mother. When those men had challenged him, he found it and they had been dealt with accordingly. Now, he needed to reawaken that dormant combatant and fight for not only his life but for young Claire's.

And then the fight became truly equal.

Blows were traded. Their bodies suffered as did their faces, their hands bruised by the many contacts against flesh and stone and wood, and the fight between young versus old was determined by wisdom and experience.

And it was youth which suddenly prevailed. Jack's injured leg gave way at the worst possible moment and his body buckled to the ground. Tommy saw victory and clamped his huge hands around Jack's throat and dragged him up and over the desk table. His strength, weight of body and, of course, his insanity, drove him to the moment of winning the fight. Jack, like Claire before him, felt his senses leaving him and he tried and failed to rise.

Darkness surrounded him. The sounds of Tommy's heavy breathing faded and he knew he was going to die.

Fade. Fading. Fading...

Blackness.

And then, in that blackness: memory.

He was fifteen. He was in the forest in the mountain about a mile from their home, when he and his father had been walking through the rough patch of bushes which led to Farmer Rowland's land. This man had been a test against Joe—the only man who had objected to Joe Farr from being the protector of the forest, a position decreed to him by birth-right and then confirmed by the Farmer's and the Forestry Commission. It had come to Joe's attention that the Farmer had been laying animal traps in the forest which was against the rules of the land and the Commission. It had, inevitably, trapped a human, a sixteen year old girl who had been walking her dog—quite legally—in the forest. The Commission had laid the law down against Farmer Rowland never to repeat this act—but the man was stubborn to the point of callous and had continued this vile business. It was left to Joe to deal with the man face to face. As he and Jack trekked across the forest to find and deal with this arrogant man, Joe suddenly walked into another trap and was brought down. The blade saws were powerful and Jack was not strong enough to prise them apart. Joe—in agony—took his son's hands and moved them away from the trap. Then, slowly, he placed his own hands on either side of the jaws and gripped. Without even appearing to strain at them, he slowly drew them apart and pulled them back to their opening position. He dragged his foot, which would have been almost severed had it not been for the powerful army boots he was wearing, away from the trap, placed a branch into its maw and it snapped shut again. The branch was snapped in two.

Jack had to near carry his father back to the house where Theresa tended his foot. Later that evening, Jack asked his father how he had been able to prise those blades apart when he had barely been able to force them apart. The lesson he learned that day remained with him for the rest of his life.

'You think about the thing which opposes you,' his father told him. 'It is in your hands. You think about its size, its strength, its dimensions. You then think about what you must do to withstand its power, to weaken its grip, to lessen its hold. I have to pull this thing apart in order to save my foot—and your mind takes over. It sends the message to your hands—about what you have to do and your hands obey that message. It starts with your mind, Jared.'

Tommy's grip around his throat had increased and there was no time left. Jack placed his hands on either side of Tommy's wrist and gripped them—not pulling or squeezing—but just gripping them. He felt their power, he appraised their position and he told himself what he had to do to remove those powerful hands away from his throat. Slowly at first, slowly—and then…

The grip lessened against his throat.

Jack's own grip took effect as he slowly prised Tommy's hands away from his throat. As the choking hold became less effective, Jack then brought his legs up and around Tommy's, forcing him to buckle and then to lose his balance. As he fell aback, the grip around Jack's throat was lost and Jack pulled both hands away and outwards. He squeezed his legs and Tommy fell back altogether. The momentum brought Jack to his own feet and he stood up against the taller man. He drove a punch into Tommy's midriff which was cause enough to bring Tommy down. Jack then pulled Tommy back up to his full height and he dropped his right hand to the floor—and from that position he suddenly straightened up and caught Tommy with an uppercut which took him off his feet and sent him hurtling backwards into a wall which caved in behind him. He fell to the ground—unconscious.

Still. Silence. Only the dust was alive and it spiralled around the room as though blown around by a hurricane.

Jack dropped to the floor. He had not an ounce of strength left in him. If Tommy rose to his feet now, there would be no way Jack could prevent him from finishing him off, going after Claire and doing something even worse to her.

But all was still and Tommy lay supine on the floor. Jack breathed out and rested his back against the desk.

*

Claire had made it beyond the walls of the Quarry building and was lurching forwards, aided only by the brightness of the sun to guide her towards the path which would take her out of this place and to safety. And then she heard a noise. A loud noise. Whining. A motor. She rubbed her eyes—itself a painful thing to do—and stared at a shape which seemed to be heading towards her. And then, a loud bang and a small puff of smoke rising from the front of whatever it was that was coming towards her. She saw silhouettes of people leaping from the shape and yelling her name. when one of the people reached her and asked her if she alright, she found her voice, hidden in the thickness of her swollen throat, and she collapsed.

From behind, an even bigger vehicle came roaring into view and it drove past them.

'Look after her,' ordered DCI Taffe and a woman took his place. The woman was soft and her words so gentle—such a contrast between now and just a few moments ago.

'It's alright, honey,' comforted DS Stone as she held Claire in her strong arms. 'You're gonna be okay.'

DS Stone looked up and saw two ARU vehicles screaming to a sliding halt and their occupants leaping out. Armed police would now take over this operation and she, for one, was relieved.

The Commanding Officer from the ARU saw DCI Taffe running towards him.

'Are you Taffe?' Attack Advisor Sergeant Ross Whelan said, his voice all authority as his officers all awaited to hear his instructions. 'You called this?'

'Yes Sir,' confirmed DCI Taffe, looking behind to see if Claire was being attended. She was and so he paid attention to the matter at hand. He took Sergeant Whelan by his arm.

'I am in pursuit of a man who has killed twice—and I believe he is here and probably armed.' Taffe looked at the ensemble in front of him. Six armed officers ready to do their duty. Behind them, an Ambulance drew up to where his car was smoking black fuel out of its bonnet. Good, he thought, that's Claire being dealt with by the experts.

Now to deal with the matter at hand.

*

Jack practically had to crawl up the desk to get to his feet. He thought he'd heard a vehicle arriving and he hoped it was the police. He really needed an Ambulance as well.

And then he heard the click.

He turned and saw Tommy, still lying in the dirt, looking up at him, his right arm stretched towards him—with a pistol in his hand. A revolver. A Smith & Wesson.

Vonna Shepherd's gun. He'd heard the police officers talking about it when they held him at the Station. For the first time, Jack noted Tommy was wearing a thick belt around his waist, with a holster which was strapped to his right leg—and in the holster there was another kind of gun. He saw the butt of it.

Jack tried to silence his movements and his breathing. His ears pounded at him—partly from the physical exertions he had just gone through and partly from the fear of being shot. The heartbeats sounded like bass drums—he needed to control their movements and to concentrate on the sound of the gun pointing at him.

He had fired such weapons in Oklahoma. In shooting competitions against the real fast draws of the area. One man had told him he had faced down another gun shooter who had, through drugs abuse, pointed a revolver at him. In the silence of the situation, the victim listened to the squeeze of the trigger—which is quite loud in a closed environment—it squeaks like an un-oiled machine being brought to life. That action saved the man's life.

Jack heard the squeaking of the trigger being squeezed. In the confine of this building it was as loud as fingernails being dragged down a blackboard. He listened. And when the squeaking reached a certain point...

Jack moved:

The gun exploded.

*

Sergeant Whelan was about to advise all unarmed personnel to get away from the Firearms group when they heard the explosion from inside the building—and they all reacted by reaching for their own weapons.

Whelan shouted, '*EVERYBODY...*' But he didn't get the chance to finish his order. Tommy came out of the building, kicking the doors wide open and firing two revolvers as he stepped out onto the bridge which led from the compound and into the building.

As he did so, he was screaming—ranting religious dogma as he fired at the group.

'THEE ARE SINNERS—REPENT YOUR EVIL—COME TO THE BOSOM OF HIM, MY FATHER, AND LIVE THY LIVES IN INNOCENCE! MY FATHER, THE MAKER OF ALL THINGS, IS YOURS TO LOVE AND CHERISH!'

The firing was wildly put out but it had an immediate effect. One of the ARU officers was hit in the face, through his visor, and he fell. Another shot clipped the right shoulder of Sergeant Whelan and he also fell, struggling to reach a place of safety. Taffe rammed into the female officer who had stood nearest to him and pushed her across the compound and behind the remains of plant machinery which gave them cover. More firing continued along with Tommy still screaming his head off. Taffe heard the bullet rounds bouncing off other broken down plant machinery and he wondered just how much more ammunition Tommy had. Another bullet clanged against the machine behind him and ricocheted into the ground where he lay missing him by inches.

The officer he had pushed had banged her head against the machine and was dazed so he grabbed her Glock and took position. He tried to scan the area with jutting glances and it seemed that none of the ARU officers were in a position where they could return fire without jeopardizing their own position.

Sergeant Whelan was safe behind his own cover but the bullets were bouncing all around him and he felt the heat of one as it scorched his left arm. He tried to draw his own Glock but realized he couldn't move his hand. Blood seeped down his arm and he knew the bullet had maybe severed the nerve in his shoulder. His arm dangled down—rendering it useless. No matter. He had been shot before and pain was something he could indulge in—*after* the task was completed. He reached over with his left hand and pulled his Glock out of its holster.

As Tommy made more ranting incomprehensible shouts about those sinners before him being accepted by his father—whoever the hell he was—the Commander made his own move. He reached over the rim of the cover and fired twice, both missing the target but forcing the young man to duck back.

And while Tommy was avoiding the Sergeant's shooting, Taffe made his move. He couldn't fire from where he was placed so he ran two steps, dived forward, over the body of the dead ARU officer, completing a forward roll into another discarded pile of machinery and ducked when two more rounds slammed into the metal. Then he stood, aimed the Glock and fired.

In mid-rant, Tommy was lifted off the ground by the impact of five rounds fired by Taffe. His screaming was replaced with a pathetic whimper and his body hurtled backwards, off the bridge and into the stream gully below.

The whole compound echoed with the reverberating shots as it was, in effect, a man-made constructed valley for the use of the industry which built and used the Quarry, creating it into a purpose-built stream. The natural mountain which overlooked it had been added to by the stone mountains made from the earth piled up by the years of industry. It brought about an echo chamber and the firing from Tommy's revolvers, the Sergeant's and now Taffe's had a deafening effect on all. It took a while for the echoes to die down during which time, nobody moved.

After a few moments, Sergeant Whelan emerged and Taffe saw his right arm filled with blood, dripping onto his hand and onto the ground.

'EVERYBODY—STAY STILL! DO NOT MOVE!' Whelan's voice was firm and gave no indication to any of his officers that he had been shot. The man moved cautiously forward and Taffe stood, ready to join him.

When he saw the DCI standing, his weapon poised, both hands holding it in the proscribed manner, Sergeant Whelan was about to order him to stand down but then paused. Taffe. DCI Taffe… *Where have I heard that name… before?* And then, his memory clicked. *Detective Chief Inspector Owen Taffe. Oh yes. I remember. Cop-killer.*

Both men moved forward, one careful step after another until they both reached the concrete bridge. More cautiously now, in case the perpetrator was lying there, not quite dead enough, his revolvers pointing up at them ready to shoot their heads off.

Standing on the bridge, they both peered over and into the dry stream.

Tommy lay there, his face peaceful and serene. Both his hands were at his side and the weapons, still smoking, still gripped by his hands.

Taffe and the Sergeant stood rock still and stared at the dead man.

Chapter 58
Tragedy at Collier's Quarry

He had the face of an Angel.

In life, Tommy Leeming—or Fleming, it scarcely mattered anymore—had the sweetest face a boy could possess. Its look of pure innocence had always won the hearts of all the women who had ever known him and those Fleminganese women who had wailed over the death of the woman in the big house—saw him as the future leader of this Community—one they could be joined with, physically and spiritually—and maybe one who would not abuse them in the same brutal way his father, and the fathers before him, had done.

In that belief, those poor unfortunates would have been seriously betrayed.

Of course, to a young teenage girl, such a face was appealing upon first sight. If the owner of such a face had a nature and personality to equal its physical beauty, that girl would be the envy of all her friends. And in truth, Claire Philips, had been the first girl of his own age with whom he had had any kind of consenting relationship. And by age comparison the definition here is determined by the standards of Fleminganese Law, for he was not eighteen years of age as he had announced to the family—but a man very much in his mid-twenties as had been confirmed by Peter Eddy's records when Tommy had been employed at his office. Of course, as no Communal records of birth dates were ever made by the Fleminganese, there is no positive way of knowing for certain exactly how much older Tommy really was.

In death, now that the fury and anger had been destroyed, his Angelic countenance had returned to him, even though his face was still a mask of bruising. Taffe wondered how that had come about. Here, as he lay in the rocks, a thin stream of water weaving around the body impediment, Tommy looked as those he was querying an answer to a question he had asked and hadn't understood the answer.

Taffe and Whelan remained still. They were both watching for movement. They both stared at the body—which was now filled entirely with blood—Taffe's bullets had found their marks without doubt. But no movement came and so the Commander—still in charge of this operation—made the first move.

'Cover me, Owen,' he said. DCI Taffe confirmed it with a 'Sir,' and he moved slightly to the right side, his Glock pointed directly at Tommy's head as the Sergeant slowly scrambled down the rocky embankment and made his way to the supine body, his own Glock also pointed directly at the perpetrator's head. He gently lowered himself and observed the man's chest. No movement. No breathing. He placed his Glock to one side, away from any possible last second grab by the perpetrator in case he was feigning death and placed his hand on the man's chest, feeling for a heartbeat. Then he moved to his jugular and waited to feel a pulse.

'This man is dead,' he said. 'I am going to take the gun from his left hand.'

DCI Taffe adjusted his position again. This time, he pointed the weapon at Tommy's lower regions—away from where the Sergeant was placed. Nothing happened as Whelan removed the weapon—a Colt 45—from the dead man's tight grip. He took it and stared at it. 'Jesus,' he breathed out, almost in admiration. 'It's a Colt 45—and from what I'm looking at—an original model.'

Taffe then recalled the last phone message given to him by DC Morgan—a cache of weapons found in a crate—with lettering which indicated the weapons had been brought to the UK from the USA. When? What year?

Defying the Sergeant's orders, the surviving members of the ARU had now moved up to join them—each of them pointing their own Glocks ahead—not necessarily at anyone in particular but in case there was someone inside the building who hadn't announced themselves yet.

Sergeant Whelan then removed the second weapon from the man's right hand—also gripped tightly. He looked at it, almost curious. 'Smith & Wesson. Is this the weapon you reported stolen, Inspector?'

'Yes Sir,' confirmed DCI Taffe. 'Belonging to the dead woman found in Mr Farr's home.' Which confirmed Tommy as the murderer of Vonna Shepherd and probably of Hywel Parry as well.

An officer ventured down to where the Sergeant was squatting and helped him to his feet. He then took both guns and would then place them inside the Evidence bags. Sergeant Whelan, rather awkwardly, then made his way back up onto the bridge and joined Taffe. 'Thank you, Inspector,' he said and held out his left hand to take the Glock which Taffe had obviously purloined from one of his officers. He called one of his other officers over and said, 'Bag this—state it as the weapon which killed this man—append the name—log it as Officer Collins' personal weapon and confirm it was used by Detective Chief Inspector Owen Taffe in the course of his duty.' The officer took it, automatically—and then stopped. He stared at Taffe, in shock, and said, 'Owen Taffe, Sir? DCI Owen Taffe?' Sergeant Whelan smiled and nodded and the officer moved away.

Suddenly, Taffe asked, 'Who was he shooting at?'—which confused them all. Clearly the man had been shooting at them. But Taffe said, 'The first shot was fired *inside* the building—before he came out at us. Who was he shooting at?'

This galvanized the officers who were still standing by. Once again, potential danger threatened and their weapons were raised. As they stood, ready to enter the building, one of the officers came racing up to them, almost in tears, and said, 'Bryant is dead, Sir.' But Sergeant Whelan raised his hand and ordered silence. The late and soon to be lamented Officer Bryant could be mourned over later—for now the danger is still with us.

Two members of the ARU took up point and stood by the shattered entrance doors. One of them shouted, *'ARMED POLICE! IF THERE'S ANYONE IN THERE, THROW DOWN YOUR WEAPONS AND SURRENDER!'*

Still, no movement—and then they kicked the doors open. One officer went low and the second officer stood flat against the outside wall.

Nothing. No response. No sound, no movement. They signalled and entered the room. The Commander followed and Taffe went in behind him.

The dust still swirled around the room in a spiral and they could see the damage was recent. Cobwebs had been disturbed and the furniture—what was left of it—had fresh breaks in them. One of the officers prowled around and then shouted, *'SIR!'*

Taffe made it to him first—and he saw Jack Farr lying in the dirt, unconscious and bleeding heavily from the upper left breast.

'WE NEED AN AMBULANCE,' he shouted and one of the ARU ran out of the building. Taffe placed his own hankie against the hole in Jack's chest and held it there.

'Who is he?' asked Whelan.

'Jack Farr—he had been the accused man before we cleared him.' How the hell had Jack become involved in this, Taffe couldn't fathom. The last he'd heard was Taffe was residing at an abandoned farm some miles away from here. How did he get here...?

And then, he put that two-and-two together: Susan Tanner.

The officer returned with two paramedics who told Taffe to move. The officer stood forward and confirmed SOCO and Forensics had been called and were en route—they've had a busy time on this issue thought Taffe. The same officer then said, 'Sir?' Sergeant Whelan, who was being assisted by one of his own people working on his shoulder, looked across and the officer said, 'Not you, Sir,' and he nodded towards Taffe. He repeated, 'Sir?'

Taffe looked at him and the officer said, 'Your Sergeant, Sir.'

Taffe paused for a moment and looked confused. 'Is she alright?' The officer gave a small shake of his head. Sergeant Whelan resumed his Command, stood forward and said, 'Go Inspector, we'll take care of your friend.' Taffe rushed past them all and out of the building. When he got out, he looked across the compound and saw what was happening two hundred yards away.

DS Stone was on her knees and Sergeant Thomas was sitting on a small rock looking at her. The Paramedics from one of the Ambulances were working on Claire. Taffe sprinted towards the group.

When he reached the area, he could see Sergeant Thomas was red-faced and in tears. He slowed down and saw DS Stone was not moving.

When Claire had been taken by Taffe he ordered DS Stone to look after her while he dealt with the ARU. Stone scooped Claire up in her arms and saw the Ambulance coming up behind them. She walked towards it—and when they all heard the first gunshot from inside the building, they all ducked and hurled themselves to the ground, looking around to see where the shot had come from. A moment's pause had given them the chance to get up and rush from the area— but then Tommy came out of the building, both guns blaring. Sergeant Thomas shouted out to the emerging Paramedics to get down to the ground and they didn't need telling a second time. He ran towards the Ambulance as DS Stone ran behind him, still carrying the now unconscious Claire. A bullet round zinged into the door of the Ambulance, just inches from where Sergeant Thomas was standing. He looked back—and saw DS Stone slowly crumble to the ground, Claire still gripped in her arms. Blood flowed from her neck and onto Claire's clothes. Stone dropped to her knees and looked up at Thomas. He ran back to her and saw immediately she was already dead. He pushed her hair away and saw the hole where the bullet had entered the left side of her neck, passed the jugular which had been severed and exited the left side of her throat. She had bled out immediately and was still bleeding even as she carried Claire.

Courageously, the two Paramedics went to where Claire had fallen and even though more bullets were whizzing past them, they both pulled her away from the area and set to work on her.

Sergeant Thomas looked across the compounds and saw Taffe commit himself to the forward roll, standing up and fire his own shots into the ranting Tommy. The boy was lifted off the ground and sent flying backwards. And then the silence as Taffe and the Commander moved towards their opponent. The firing over, Sergeant Thomas started at the face of DS Stone. It was blank of expression. Not even a look of pain—mercifully, her death had happened so fast, she could not possibly have been aware of it.

Sergeant Thomas had, in his professional life, attended many funerals of fallen comrades in the Force—he had, himself, faced down a number of dangerous situations and had witnessed many of his colleagues being harmed— but he had never before seen a death like this. Such a death, under such circumstances had left him bereft of verbal expression. He had barely known her and now she was dead—in the service of serving the public. Unable to emote, he simply sat on the rock and placed his hand on her shoulder as if that would be enough to comfort her.

He saw Taffe rushing towards them and now he could not hold back the tears.

Unashamedly, he lowered his head and cried. Taffe reached them and from a short distance from where they were, he could see the lie of the land. His voice spoke for them all.

'Ah... hell...'

Sergeant Thomas felt he had to say something. His voice croaked as he spoke up. 'She was protecting the girl. Just protecting...' But then he could speak no more and bowed his head again.

An unlucky shot—she had been standing in the wrong place by just a few inches and a few seconds. Alive—and now dead. Her eyes were still open and to Taffe, it looked as though she was staring around and wondering why everyone was looking at her.

As he stood, helpless to give aid to the two Paramedics, he heard a car arriving and saw Susan Tanner and the elder sister, Catrin, getting out of the car. Catrin screamed as she saw Claire being worked on by the Paramedics and ran towards them. Taffe moved and stood between them and her. He gripped Catrin tightly and held her against the side of the Ambulance.

'Listen,' he told her, 'your sister has been badly beaten but she'll live—do you understand?'

But such words of comfort—as well meaning as those words are intended to be—are of no consolation to the grief-stricken sister of someone who is lying on the ground, clearly unconscious and being worked on by medical staff. Catrin struggled with him, against him, and his strength withstood the scratching and the pummelling of blows she inflicted upon him, until she broke and buried her head into his chest and sobbed. This duty was then assumed by Susan who had reached them and nodded to Taffe that she would now take over.

Taffe returned to his own Sergeant and sat down next to the Uniformed Sergeant, still grieving for the dead woman. He looked across the compound. It was a war zone. The whole fight, from beginning to end, had lasted less than two minutes but the price had been high. An ARU officer dead, DS Stone dead, Tommy dead, The ARU Attack Advisor wounded, Claire, so young, physically traumatized and beaten. And Jack Farr?—well God only knew what would happen to Jack Farr.

The emergency of the situation did not acknowledge the grief being felt by those who had seen their colleagues killed and wounded and now it was in the hands of the Paramedics who issued their own instructions. Both Ambulances were moved, ready to drive straight back out and towards the Hospital in Cardiff. Claire was placed in the first Ambulance and a now cared for Jack Farr still being stretchered out of the building.

Taffe told the Paramedics that the crying girl was the elder sister to the one they were transporting to the Hospital and they agreed Catrin could travel with them in the back of the Ambulance. He assured Catrin he would make contact with her parents to let them know where she and Claire were going to be taken. He walked up to where the second Ambulance had been driven—parked right in front of the building so the stretcher-bearers needed only to traverse the bridge.

Susan watched as the first Ambulance sped away from the scene. Then, as she walked up to where DCI Taffe was standing, she saw the stretcher bearing Jack being placed into the second Ambulance. She bowed her head and began to cry. From this point, there was no way she could tell if Jack were alive or dead. Taffe joined her.

The Ambulance started up and pulled away from the area—once it had reached the edge of the compound, all vehicles now moved out of its way, it sped up, siren blaring and was soon out of sight.

The female ARU officer whose weapon Taffe had taken came to him.

'Sir,' she said, and her expression was one of awe as she stared at Taffe, 'Inspector Taffe? I need to take our Sergeant Whelan to the Hospital. His shoulder needs tending.'

Taffe, who was now the senior officer on the scene, realized his ARU colleague needed treatment as soon as possible. He acknowledged her request and the Sergeant was placed inside one of the ARU cars and was driven away, leaving their colleagues behind who said they would not be abandoning their dead friend.

Which left Taffe, Susan, the ARU and Sergeant Thomas who was still sitting on the rock near DS Stone.

Taffe held Susan's hand—it seemed appropriate. 'I am curious, Mrs Tanner,' he said. 'How Mr Farr became involved in this? Last time I saw him he was ensconced quite neatly at a farm some distance from here.'

She looked down—an expression of guilt on her face – and told Taffe that Jack had arrived home a short while before he and his team had come down from the mountain and wanting to know where Claire had gone to meet Tommy. It was an afterthought, she told Taffe after he had left the village when she called Jack.

'His home, you see,' she explained. 'It's just a few miles away from here across the mountain. You would have driven miles to get here—Jack could run across the mountain and get here in less time.

Taffe considered her motive—and nodded. When he had arrived here, he saw Claire running from the building—say, a distance of a hundred yards and she was in state of near unconsciousness and all over the place—so a period of time had passed between Tommy beating up on her and his meeting her. Take also into account that she might not have left the scene the moment Jack had arrived and took Tommy on and you could be talking a long period of anything up to ten minutes.

How long does it take to kill a person? Claire, small, physically fragile, Tommy, big and powerful—he had already inflicted much damage to her, Taffe could see that just in the brief time he held her. In that period of time, he could have continued the beatings…

342

…or just kill her with a single blow.

Jack Farr's intervention, instigated by Mrs Tanner, had probably saved young Claire's life. He told Mrs Tanner so. She looked up, eyes filled with tears, as though she were seeking affirmation of her action.

'Jack saved Claire?' she asked. Taffe consoled her. He asked if she wanted to go to the Hospital now, and if so did she need his officer to take her there or could she drive? Grateful for the release—and his words—Susan said she would leave now—and drive to the Hospital herself. Sara and Adam would need her to be there.

Which reminded Taffe. He called DC Morgan, whose voice was still so enthusiastic concerning what had been found on Stone Wall Mountain in his reply that Taffe had to order him to calm down. Were the uniformed police who had come with them still on the mountain? Morgan replied in the affirmative. Taffe ordered one of the units—with a female officer—to go to the village and pick up Mr and Mrs Philips to escort them to the Cardiff Hospital—but to assure them that nothing serious had occurred—a lie but then he had no truth to give them as yet. The second Unit was to make their way to this place and meet with him. No more questions please, DC Morgan, who wanted so much to tell his superior officer what they had found on this dreadful place, you can tell me later and he ended the call.

Taffe then wandered about, aimlessly. He looked over to the remaining ARU officers who sat near their dead colleague. An officer's tunic had been laid over the dead man's face and all conversation had stopped. How does one speak when sitting next to someone one has served alongside and who has died such a pointless death? Officer Bryant—travelled all the way up from Base of Operations, a journey which had lasted, say about forty minutes, emergency situation confirmed, and Taffe knew they were all hyped up to do the thing they had been trained to do—possibly shoot someone to death. There may have been a form of gallows humour inside the vehicle—jokes, personal commentary— anything to not think about the possibility that they may become embroiled in a gun-fight, to kill someone, maim someone, watch one of your own take a bullet—or be killed yourself. And you leap out of the vehicle, awaiting instructions, scanning the area, and then—out of nowhere—the reason you have come to this place comes bursting out of a building and before you know it, *BANG*—you're dead, without even getting the opportunity to do the thing you've come here to do.

Hard to draw on any kind of conversation when something like that happens to your mates. The ARU officers, sitting by Officer Bryant, did not even try.

He took one final glimpse at the dead Tommy—the cause of so much hell and misery—trying to fathom what motives had driven him to commit such atrocities. As far as Taffe was aware, Tommy had not even met or known Jack Farr so how could all of this—Vonna Shepherd's death, Hywel Parry's, this bloody hell-hole—could be laid at the feet of Jack?

He walked away and saw Sergeant Thomas still holding his head as he spoke to the late DS Stone. No doubt, feeling guilt that he had not done more to prevent this tragedy—it was common amongst officers under such conditions. There was no answer to it. Sergeant Thomas, he knew, would go into Counselling to expel the guilt—asked how he thought he could have done any more than he did? He would postulate—this method, that action. The Counsellor would listen, then tell the truth—that nothing could have been done to prevent the unforeseeable—that death in this profession was a reality and no-one should blame themselves when something like this occurs. No consolation to the officer being counselled but…

He found himself staring up at the mountain. He scanned the entire area behind the Quarry and there was no way down. No trail, no pathway, and the mountain drop was quite steep.

How the hell did Jack get down…?

He stopped at one place and saw what was obviously a most recent rock fall. He looked up to the top—at least two hundred yards—almost a sheer drop. But there were areas jutting outwards from the side of the mountain—and Taffe stared. Yes, he realized, that was how Farr had done it. He had jumped from one jutting piece of earth to another—all the way down. But he could see, about fifty feet up and from there all the way down, there were no more jump points, so…

…how did Jack get down?

Yes. He could see now. Jack had landed on one area, it had collapsed under the weight of his movement—and he had toppled all the way down, landing on the huge boulders on the ground, the rest of the jutting area falling down on top of him. It would explain why Jack was so muddied up on the floor inside the building. There was blood on the boulder which more or less confirmed his hypothesis.

Lord, he thought, Farr smashed up against this, having run across the mountain at, Taffe knew he would have done just to save the girl, full pelt, then fighting against a younger and bigger man, one who was probably insane and therefore many times more dangerous, taking a hell of a beating—and then getting shot. If Farr survives all this...

Sirens were heard in the distance and Taffe saw the rescue crews rushing to them.

Chapter 59

In the Evening, Hereafter...

By the evening, practically everybody in the village had learned of the Quarry incident—not the full details but most of them knew that one of their own—a child—had been beaten, almost killed—by one of their own. Enough people saw the police car speeding into the village and picked up both Mr and Mrs Philips on the street where they had been arguing—again—in full view of their neighbours, the police talking to them, both of them then clutching onto each other, in tears, then bundled into the back of the car which then sped away, sirens blaring.

Why were they arguing? Well, Adam had tied on a few extra bevy's—again—probably with his loser mates, that one who complains all the time about his back and legs—at The Night's Tail and Mrs Philips had remonstrated—*again*—about his lack of decorum in front of her, his family and their neighbours. This rowing in the street was now becoming a more common occurrence. Odd the police turning up so quickly—and only over a row as well—wonder what that was all about? By early evening, everybody knew.

As Claire had made her way to the Quarry, she had phoned practically every one of her friends bragging about this assignation with Tommy—"He's going to propose" she gloated, only seventeen and the first of her group to become engaged. Big party, people, she boasted. On their phones, all her friends screamed their excitement and best wishes etc and when the calls ended all of them put their hands in their mouths and regretted the day they had spent at Collier's Quarry on that school trip. Even after all this time, they still had not accepted Tommy as potential boyfriend material for any of them never mind someone as picky as Claire.

Two and two make four—and that was how these teens put Claire's beating into something they could believe. Tommy had beaten her. Why? Who knows? He's from a deeply rabid religious Community and Claire—God love her—is a fly-by flirt. No way is *this* going to be a marriage made in... whatever that place is they want to go to when they die.

But by the time the regulars had congregated at The Night's Tail, more disturbing news had filtered down to them. There had not only been a beating, but people had died. Shot to death. And somehow, that... *pariah*... of the village, Jack Farr—was involved. This gave rise to the regular haters that their suspicions about the man had been confirmed. Jack Farr, Claire Philips, in the same locale, her now a Hospital case—well what else do you need to know? The likes of Sion Edmunds and Malcolm Fisher would be blaring their trumpets and telling everybody how they had told them so. Nobody listened—now look.

It was Vicar Redd—courtesy of Susan calling from the Hospital—who set the whole situation straight. He had heard the news, from someone who had actually been there, that Claire had indeed been attacked and badly beaten—but that it was Jack Farr who had saved her life—no exaggeration—and, get this, had been seriously wounded in the effort. No names—though the Vicar knew—as to who the beating came from, and he left it to the speculators to arrive at their own conclusions. When the teen brigade heard just how serious the beating was, to a teen, both male and female, they resorted to their true vulnerable selves and took refuge in the bosoms of their parents. Later, when the Vicar opened the local Community Hall, where all those who were Claire's friends could meet and be with each other, they repeated the act, hugging each other, crying and praying with all their telepathic skills that Claire would survive whatever had happened to her.

In The Night's Tail, the full pub was like a mausoleum. Nobody spoke—nobody ventured any opinions as to what happened, or what *may* have happened, at that place. All they knew was, one of their most precious darlings was now in a place she shouldn't be in, having suffered something nobody that age should ever have endured.

This business about Jack Farr though...

Sion Edmunds and his sons gave the Tail a wide berth this night—choosing to go *The Blooz*—which was all but empty and was closed by nine o'clock anyway.

Vicar Redd took his parochial duty to heart and stayed with the teens at the Community hall—as did some of the parents—while they grieved for Claire. A few asked him how could something like this happen and Vicar Redd made no pretence of knowing. This, he told them, had been an act of pure evil—but that

347

evil had lived within this happy Community for some time. The parents then worked out just how long Jack Farr had been back in Cwmhyfryd. For sure, nothing like this had happened before he came back, so…

Two and two make four.

Quite a number of people stood in The Square and stared up at Stone Wall Mountain and enquired as to what all the light on that mountain was all about. Many took photographs and reported the phenomena to as many of their neighbours as they could. And it was a truly awesome sight. As the night had turned really dark, the whole of the mountain overlooking the village was lit up, the strength of the lighting streaking up into the sky which almost turned the night sky into day. Naturally, the villagers wanted to know what it was all about and those who lived near the entrance to the village gates had seen the many police vehicles streaming up to the mountain—and only a few coming back down. Whatever had taken place up there, was still going on.

Life continued at Cwmhyfryd—but at a more cautious pace than usual and with questions being asked everywhere—and no answers from anyone.

*

Susan Tanner walked, almost trance-like, towards Sara who was sat in the waiting room—Catrin was near asleep on her Dad's lap and tears streamed down his cheeks which he tried to hide from both his wife and daughter. Sara looked up and saw her friend walking—almost wobbling—towards her, her face ashen, her mouth open as if she were trying to speak but had forgotten how. Sara stood and met her as she was halfway across the waiting room floor.

'Sue?' said Sara, unsure what to say to say under such circumstances. Her husband was lying in a bed just two storeys up from where they were standing and her… lover…? was in a nearby Theatre being operated on by the Doctors.

'Sue,' she said again. 'What's wrong?'

Moments, which felt like years, went by and Susan—not even looking at her—opened her mouth but nothing came out. Sara tried again and this time, taking Susan by her cheeks, forced her to look directly at her. 'Susan, what is wrong?'

Susan then looked at her—into her eyes, a blank expression on her face as if she had seen nothing at all in the past few hours and was surprised to see Sara here at… where the hell were they?

'Jack,' she breathed out. 'Jack...' A pause and then she broke. 'Jack... is dead.'

Jack is dead. Jack is dead. Jack... is...

And all was darkness...

Susan suddenly awoke, feeling her shoulders being gripped and her body being tugged about. She opened her eyes and saw Sara standing over her—her face was one of concern and her voice was one of alarm.

'Susan, wake up.'

Susan almost jumped off her chair and screamed, 'Jack'. Sara just grabbed her and held her in a bear hug—no inconsiderable effort as Susan was much taller than her—and held her tight.

'You were moaning,' Sara told her. 'You kept say something about Jack.'

Time passes by so slowly when you have dreamed so deeply and so precisely and then you are pulled away from that dream by reality and for a while you are unable to distinguish the truth between that dream and this reality. It took Sara quite a while to convince Susan that Jack was still undergoing the operation in the Theatre—that he was not dead.

Susan's legs wobbled underneath her and it took all of Sara's strength to keep her upright—an effort which was now aided by Catrin who had seen the distress Auntie Susan was in and ran to assist her mother.

Mother and daughter then pulled Susan along with them to where they were all seated and placed her in a chair while Adam went to the cafeteria to get them all fresh cups of tea—with hot chocolate for Catrin—and wait until they saw an actual Doctor or Nurse to update them about the conditions of their loved ones.

They waited a long time.

*

DCI Taffe sat at his desk, the report of the Quarry incident still on his computer and still unfinished. The after effect of the day's events had now sunk in and he was weary of how the tragedy had put a heavy hold over him. It was now nine thirty at night and he had not the strength nor the inclination to write this report up. For the second time in his professional life, he had killed—the circumstances demanded it of course but the taking of a life—no matter how justified—plays odd tricks on a person's psyche. It stems from the condition-built mantra, instilled in all of us when we are children, that all life is sacrosanct—truly a myth in reality—but even when it is justified, there are those, even after being trained to kill, who believe the prospect of killing another person just seems... *wrong!*

And Taffe was no different.

As he sunk into reverie, the door opened and Detective Chief Superintendent Olivia Radford sauntered into the room. Taffe saw her and was about to stand but she waved at him to settle back, went to the side-table, located the kettle, switched it on and chose two large mugs and two tea bags. Taffe didn't have the heart to tell her he'd already drunk two mugs of tea but this was an unaccustomed act of kindness from his Superintendent so he elected for silence. Five minutes later, she sat opposite him, brought out two packets of biscuits from inside her coat and placed them on the table. McVitie's chocolate biscuits and Jaffa cakes. When he saw them, Taffe realized for the first time that he had barely eaten today and salivated at the sight of them.

'Help yourself,' she said and Taffe took three from each packet. He dunked each biscuit in his tea—as did CS Radford—and he swallowed the Jaffa's in one gulp. The tea was too sweet but somehow it helped his mood. After ten minutes of welcome silence, CS Radford spoke.

'You still on the report?'

'Yes Ma'am.'

'Not getting far?'

He smiled. 'Slow going anyway.' He hoped she hadn't come to lecture him—but Radford was one of the few senior police personnel who had never chided him about his own brand of methods which he had employed to solve crimes. He had garnered good results and the real perpetrators were dealt with and put away. Taffe's methods of investigations had saved lives and there was no doubting his courage in the field of battle—today's spectacular being a marked example. She leaned forward and placed her hand on his which lay on the computer mouse.

'Look,' she said, 'Let it go for the night. You already know the Official Procedure for the discharging of firearms so you don't have to fret about the IPCC Inquiry. I have spoken to Commander Garrison from the ARU and he has commended your action today. He says it would have been a hell of lot worse if you hadn't taken point at that moment. You saved lives today, Owen. Ours, and the young girl who took a savage beating. Don't let the boy's death bring you down. Let this go for tonight, go home, come back tomorrow—choose your own time—and finish it then. Inspector Crew will be in and you can go through with it with him. It will look different in another climate. Promise.'

And he really needed to hear those words. He smiled, finished the last of the Jaffa's and drank the tea in one gulp.

'Besides,' she added, 'You've got the reports from SOCO, Forensics and the Pathology Department to see through yet. You don't know what that lot found on the mountain, do you?'

Christ, he thought. I'd forgotten all about that. DC Morgan's probably still up there. Radford told him to hold his water and she confirmed that she'd brought DC Morgan off the detail and another senior officer was now attending. But Morgan would give him the full report on their findings tomorrow. And, she told him, it is a real doozy.

She stood and went to the door, looking back at him with sadness in her face. 'I'm sorry about Stone, Owen'.

He thanked her and then she left the office. He locked his computer and went to the door.

He looked back at his office and reflected, not for the first time, that one day he would leave this room and not come back. From duty? Retired?

He turned the lights off and exited. The Station was not so active at this time of night and so not as many officers on duty. The nine he met on the way out all said the same thing. "Well done, Sir" and shook his hand. Detective Chief Inspector Owen Taffe—hitherto the pariah of the UK Police Force—was now, apparently, a hero. He didn't feel like one but gratefully acknowledged their words and exited the Station. The night was cold—rain in the air—and he sucked it all in as he made his way to his car. The fresh air revitalized him. He got into his car, waited five minutes before he set off then did so, driving at a sedate pace.

*

At midnight, such an ominous time to see a Nurse walking towards you, the Philips family rose to their feet ready to speak with that Nurse. Susan remained seated—if this was bad news they would band together as a family and she was not a part of that. The Nurse led them out of the waiting room and took them into an office some way down a corridor. Susan's breathing increased out of fear for

Claire. How much damage had Tommy inflicted upon her before Jack's intervention?

Time passes so fast when you're enjoying yourself—the same period of time is morbidly slow when you're living on tenterhooks, awaiting bad news. Susan was now the only person left behind in the waiting room which had been filled throughout the evening. She needed the silence. Listening to the hard luck stories of some of the people who had been in the waiting room had not been good for her—not in her present frame of mind. After an hour had passed by—rather ashamed of herself for not thinking about it earlier—she took a trip down to reception and enquired about David. She proved her marital identity to the Receptionist who explained she could only speak with relatives or spouse and, once identity had been confirmed, the Receptionist updated Susan as to the present state of her husband. Not out of the woods yet, she said, but slowly mending. He would require constructive surgery around the jaw-line and his ribs would take a while to mend. It felt odd that his beating he had taken from Jack had only occurred just a few weeks ago—so much had happened in the time since then. No other relatives had visited or called. Susan had messaged his parents about his situation. Either they didn't care or they were away. They hadn't called her to find out what had happened to their son.

Sara returned—alone—tears in her eyes but a smile on her face. She wrapped her arms around Susan's body and hugged her as tightly as she possibly could.

'Oh thank God,' she gushed, her throat thick with emotion. 'She's going to be alright. A lot of bruises, her face is badly swollen. That bastard really beat up on her. But nothing long-term serious. Nothing broken. Bloody miracle. She bit her tongue—that's why there was so much blood in her mouth. Her nose is swollen as well—but not broken. The Doctor told us she would be back to normal—physically anyway—in a few weeks but she's going to be staying here for a while so they can keep checks on her. Any blows to the head is a cause for concern, she said, but otherwise…'

And then she broke down into full blown crying. More out of relief that her daughter was not going to die—plus the fact that the injuries, though considerable, were not life-changing or life-threatening. Claire would be back to her vivacious best in weeks, Sara assured Susan.

Not likely, thought Susan. She'll mend in the body for sure—but how her mind will assimilate this incident will be another matter. But that was for another time—for this time, Claire was still with them and now at rest.

Adam had broken down when he saw his baby lying on the bed, her face a mass of swelling and bruising. There was a compress wrapped around her throat where Tommy had strangled her. Thankfully, she hadn't lost much blood. Superficial loss only, the Doctor had told them, and it all looked worse than it really was. In a few days, they would see a marked difference in their daughter—but for Adam, no such words comforted him—his precious baby was lying in a Hospital bed having been savaged by a man he had allowed into his home. He had not taken the trouble to find out about this man who was courting his girl and it should have been his fatherly duty to do so. And now, this. He was inconsolable. Sara couldn't bear to see him weeping and gulping over the sleeping Claire and she had to leave. Catrin—poor lamb—had to take up the role of comfort-bearer. Too much for one so young.

After ten minutes of soaking her tears into Susan's jacket, Sara eventually looked up into Susan's eyes. 'Jack,' she cried, 'Jack saved my baby.' Susan nodded and smiled. She had called Jack, he had risen to the danger and he had saved Claire's life. Even the DCI had told her that. The man she loved, had never stopped loving, had performed this service because…

And then Adam, assisted by Catrin entered the waiting room. His face was bloated from the amount of crying he had done. Catrin, out of all of them, had held herself together admirably. Susan reflected she would prove to be a fine product in her future to come.

The Philips family banded together again and Susan walked away. She called the Vicar, because he had demanded she do so the moment Claire's condition was known. It was now after one in the morning and he answered immediately. She told him Claire was going to be alright and he screamed a victorious yell—shouting out loud Claire was going to be alright and in the background, Susan heard screams and cheering. He explained to her that he had opened the Community Hall and the families of teenagers had been with him all night. None of them would leave until they knew their precious friend was safe and alive. Susan smiled. At least, some elements of Cwmhyfryd would be going to bed happy this night.

Which left Jack. And her.

Adam, Sara and Catrin left Susan to get refreshments from the cafeteria. Their pain was now at least held at bay. Hers was yet to be decided and she hoped to hell and back that the dream she had earlier was not a portent.

She asked permission to view Claire—and the Nurse in charge was doubtful she could do so until Sara had come back and confirmed to her that Susan was pretty much family—that Claire's life had been saved by an action instigated by Susan. The Nurse allowed the viewing but it was to be brief and no noise. Claire was asleep under sedation but still could not to be disturbed.

Susan stood over Claire as she slept and tears filled her eyes. It may have been only a matter of minutes, seconds even, between being where she is now and possibly lying on the morgue slab. If Jack hadn't reached her in time...

If she hadn't called Jack.

If...

She left the darkened room and enquired to the Nurse about the condition of Mr Farr. No, she wasn't a relative but she was the only close friend he had in this country. The Nurse confirmed the operation had only just come to an end and she would contact the Doctor who had operated on him as soon as he was available and he would speak with her.

An hour later, the Nurse escorted Susan to the Doctor's office and she sat down. He was in his mid-forties she guessed. A man used to speaking to people who were anxious about their loved ones. His voice was a deep and smooth baritone and had an almost hypnotic ambience about it. Susan, now beyond exhausted both physically and emotionally, wasn't sure if he was going to assure her that Jack was going to be fine or if he had not won his fight on the operating table.

His first foray was to ask who she was in relation to Jack and Susan did not stint in her reply. Their childhood, their romance when so young, their engagement and the marriage that did not happen. She declared Jack's present permanent home was in the USA—but that he was currently domiciled just a mile and bit from her home and where he had, in fact, spent some time with her. She also declared, un-necessarily, that she was still in love with Jack Farr and the part she had played in the reason for his being here tonight.

As she ran through that story, the Doctor's eyes widened. So much more than he had been expecting—and so exciting as well. He then gave her the glad news that the operation itself was a success. He had removed the bullet from Mr Farr's chest, and that the wound itself was not fatal.

'Mr Farr has taken a considerable pounding to be sure,' he continued. 'He has a hairline fracture in his skull, his left knee has been smashed, possibly from landing on something quite hard. His hands are badly damaged—probably from the fight he was involved in which I have been told about—and his body has sustained a terrible beating. The wound in his shoulder has been dealt with—it was a difficult retraction as the bullet was still in his shoulder, lodged up against his shoulder blade. If Mr Farr hadn't been wearing a thick leather jacket at the time, the wound could have been so much worse. He required a transfusion which, thanks to a Mrs Tanner's information on his personal blood group—A RH Positive—he has received quickly. Three of his ribs were broken or cracked, his spine has also been thrashed about and there was strangulation. The strangler had large hands and had gripped a wide area around his throat and neck.'

Vonna Shepherd had been strangled. So had Claire.

'He will be with us for a while to come, Mrs…' Susan confirmed her name and his eyes widened again. So this is *the* Mrs Tanner who gave us the information on Mr Farr's blood group. He looked at her and after a few seconds of close scrutiny, as if a memory had just turned on, asked if she was the wife of David Tanner who was on St Catherine's Ward. She confirmed she was—and he looked at her in a curious way as if not understanding exactly how she appeared to be more interested in the condition of Mr Farr than she was of her own husband—his curiosity notwithstanding, he said nothing and smiled. Barring any unforeseen circumstances, he told her, Mr Farr's recovery would progress— slowly to be sure—but it would progress.

It was enough to know Jack was—so far—going to be alright.

She made a second call to the Vicar and updated him on Jack's condition. This time, there was no scream, no victorious yell and no background cheering. The teens and their families had gone home—they had still not been told of the full circumstances of how Claire had been rescued and no-one knew the exact details of the part Jack had played in her rescue. The sigh of relief from Vicar Redd was audible enough to tell Susan that he was as nearly emotionally spent as she was. He thanked her, told her he was just locking the Hall up and going home. Tomorrow was going to be an eventful day. When the good people of Cwmhyfryd would learn more of the truth about what had happened to one of their own—and how her life had been saved by the man they had scarcely hidden their hatred for. The call ended and Vicar Redd locked up the Hall. He had another matter on his mind, which had been made known to him by a police officer from Cardiff.

A Chief Superintendent Olivia Radford was coming to Cwmhyfryd to give the Hyfridians a partial explanation about the day's events. Good. It would counter the rumours which were flying around and, hopefully, set their minds at rest, he thought.

But then, the Vicar did not know of what had been uncovered on Stone wall Mountain. The discovery of that hell would turn Cwmhyfryd into world-wide news.

Chapter 60

...And of the Morn Which Followed

For the second time in as many weeks, Cwmhyfryd was a village under siege.

Or at least, a part of it. Nye House—where Tommy Leeming had lived—was now being evacuated and the third storey floor completely cordoned off while the police searched his room. The residents naturally complained and the biggest complainer was Sion Edmunds who let rip on this intrusion and told the officers who were standing there but had stopped listening after his umpteenth gripe that he was an old and crippled man who shouldn't be treated like this.

What the residents couldn't understand—but what nearly everyone else knew about because it was all happening in plain sight—was why Mynydd Fach had been cordoned off. Clearly, something else was going on because everyone knew the assault had taken place in the other direction at Collier's Quarry—miles away.

But what they saw—especially those early shift workers leaving the village at six that morning was the road leading to the mountain was cordoned off and a sizeable contingent of police were guarding the gate. Immediately, they called their sleeping spouses to tell them which went down very well with those who had just gone back to bed.

And now the buggers were *inside* the village as well. It was becoming like old-style Soviet Russia shouted Sion, trying to get at least *some* kind of reaction from the Coppers who stood nearby and were still ignoring him.

A large Daimler entered the village, escorted by two police cars and they headed straight towards the main shopping centre. The people who had congregated near the main entrance or lived near Quarter Haven were all advised by the police to make their way to the Community Hall where an announcement—of sorts—would be made.

What kind of announcement asked a curious bystander? Nothing momentous he was told—more of an explanation of yesterday's events and the possibility of what was to come. This sparked interest and the bystander and his group hurried along.

Cwmhyfryd Community Hall was a multiple designed infrastructure to cater for as many different events as could be dreamed up by those who created events. It had a dance hall, a small utilities room which doubled up for a number of events, a kitchen, a theatre with four dressing rooms for either the resident drama group or visiting entertainment acts which even a backwater village like Cwmhyfryd occasionally paid lip service to. No-one would ever claim this village was a hive of high entertainment. Bingo, birthdays, the odd Karaoke night and that was pretty much it.

Today, for the first time in its near thirty year history, the Hall was filled to capacity with the curious and the "didn't-care-a-damn-but-it's-better-than-Jeremy-Kyle" residents with nothing better to do. A bit of excitement—it will last about ten minutes then it will be back to the humdrum life we all have come to know and despise. Some Hyfridians were that cynical.

It took a while for everything to be set up. The physical presence of the Vicar told one part of the story. If he's here, said those who knew the man, it must be important. He wasn't speaking to any of the residents either, which was most unusual. Instead, he assisted the woman Cop who stood by doing nothing except being very gracious to all and allowing her officers to do their thing, the Vicar parting the way for every move made by them to get the Hall set up.

After an hour of much arranging, and after much grumbling from the likes of Sion Edmunds and other thirsty members of the Tail clientele who wanted very much to sate their thirst but also wanted to know exactly what the hell was going on in their tiny village—why couldn't they hold the damned thing at The Night's Tail?—the meeting was brought to order. Chief Superintendent Olivia Radford took centre stage and Vicar Redd sat to her left. No-one else was on the stage.

She smiled. To those who did not naturally take to the police, she reminded them of a predatory animal who had been starved of food for a long while and then had been presented with a banquet to sift through. She coughed and began...

'The purpose of this meeting is by way of a courtesy—from my Force—to inform you that this village will soon be in the eye of a very heavy storm. In a short while, you are going to be invaded by a Media Blitz, local, national and international, who are going to be asking a lot of questions about you, this village—and... your upstairs and next door neighbour.'

Barely one person who had not already been apprised of the full facts knew what she was on about. Vicar Redd of course, knew about Claire, Tommy and Jack—but surely to God this would not warrant an international invasion from the media. Something else had occurred here that he was unaware of. He leaned back and looked up to the Gods—the theatre Gods of course, not the one his profession answered to.

'Most of you—probably all of you—are now aware of the incident which occurred at Collier's Quarry involving a young lady from this village—and a young man.'

Murmuring abounded around the Hall and the names of "Claire" and "Tommy" were spoken and heard. The Superintendent expected as much and smiled, holding her next speech back until she once again had their undivided attention. The lady was calm in such an environment having delivered so many police statements with hungry journalists bating her for more information and why had the police so signally failed to capture the miscreants which had resulted in deaths, injuries, this crime, that crime.

Silence returned to the Hall and she smiled. Some were calling for more details. Names and places.

'No names...' she said, 'not yet, not until all our facts are fully reported, but what I can tell you is although the young lady sustained a serious assault, resulting in a severe beating, she is now on her way to making a full recovery at the...' she paused, no names. 'At the Hospital. Her family are with her and are relieved to know their daughter is safe and well—considering what she has endured.'

More murmuring echoed around the Hall. Of course, she knew, because the Vicar had told her of their late night vigil the previous evening, that already many of the families seated before her were aware of the incident—and of the names of the principles who were involved. But not the next bit—which the Vicar himself had not been made aware of until after everybody had gone home, happy to know their friend and precious blood was alive. Vicar Redd had confirmed to Superintendent Radford that he had not told them of Jack Farr's involvement in this business.

'What I will tell you now is that another of your number was almost killed in the act of saving this young lady's life. He is now in the Intensive Care Unit at the Hospital recovering from the extensive wounds he received in the course of this heroic act.'

This time, the murmuring was loud and more pronounced. *One of their number?* Who the hell was that then? How come the Vicar didn't mention *that* at the party last night? Extensive wounds—what does that mean? How did that person become involved in the first place—was there some kind of jamboree at the Quarry or something? Sounds like there'd been a mass party or something.

Again, Superintendent Radford held her own counsel—naturally there would be mass curiosity and so she expected this level of interruption. Again, she waited, smiling. Someone shouted from the middle of the forum demanding to who that person may have been.

'The man who rescued the young lady, Mr Evans,' replied the Superintendent to Ianto Evans, 'has only recently moved back into this village, having left it twenty years ago. I believe his father died a while ago. He lives on the mountain.' She had addressed Ianto Evans by name—very clever thought Vicar Redd. This lady has certainly done her homework on the inhabitants of Cwmhyfryd.

Well—no names—but she might as well have just shouted out *JACK FARR*, because that's who she was on about. Jack Farr? Saved Claire? How? What was that about? Extensive wounds? Come on, Woman Cop—details.

More murmuring but this time, less audible and more out of disbelief than anything. How could a man so much hated be a hero and risking his life to save the of someone he probably didn't even know?

Vicar Redd looked down at his feet—partially to hide the tears which were welling up in his eyes. He had come to like, admire and respect Jack so much— his bearing when it came to dealing with the long-held prejudices of the people of this village—it felt odd that that it would take such an incident like this to, hopefully, change their opinion of him. Someone near the front—a girl—asked 'Is Tommy dead?'

Well that silenced the room completely. Superintendent Radford leaned forward and said, quite calmly, 'Yes Evie—Tommy is dead.' Again, thought the Vicar, another personal address to a member of the village. Very clever lady this Superintendent, thought the Vicar.

So—the Hyfridians were quick to put their own two's and two's together— Claire had been attacked, badly apparently if she is still in Hospital, attacked by her boyfriend Tommy—whom none of the teens had ever trusted anyway, and her life had been saved by the man everybody wanted out of the village and as fast as you can please, and he had almost lost his life in the process. This was a red-letter day for this village.

It would obviously be of great interest to the local news media—and by extension, the national body as well—but certainly not worthy of the international sons of the Fourth Estate. So, what's next?

'What I can now tell you—because you're going to be reading about in soon enough anyway, seeing it on the televisions—and just so you can stop speculating, is the man who attacked the young lady was also responsible for the two murders which took place in your village recently.'

Well—that was the real bombshell. Tommy—Tommy Leeming, their neighbour who had been living in this village for a long while—a privilege given by the common consent of the Community Council who had felt sympathy for his situation, having been cast out of his own Community on Stone Wall Mountain—or so he had claimed—had murdered two people.

I mean, yes, one of them was a prostitute so she wasn't one of us and the other guy was a known criminal so no loss there either but all the same... We took him in and this is how he repays us? He bumps off a couple of people and tries to kill one of our most precious darlings. What kind of gratitude is that? But again, after careful thought, how does this result in our little village being turned into a media circus?

'What I must tell you now—at least in part—is what the police found on Stone Wall Mountain yesterday.'

Ah—so *this* is what this meeting is really all about.

'As many of you already know, there is above you, the place called Stone Wall Mountain where a religiously based Community lived.'

Total silence. The congregation was now enraptured. Even the Vicar had shifted his seating stance. Up to now, he had been looking up to the people sitting in the rafters or down at his feet. Now, he was looking directly at the Woman Cop who was about to say something which had even more meat on the body than what we've already heard.

You could have heard a pin drop in New Zealand.

'My senior Inspector...' no name but they all knew anyway, 'as part of his investigation of the two murders, had cause to go to the Community on the mountain—I believe they were called the "Fleminganese"—to speak with the individual concerned. What he found was something quite monstrous...' everybody suddenly leaned forward, en masse, 'which necessitated the involvement of the SOCO Unit, Forensics and the Pathology Department. At this time, I am not at liberty to tell you exactly what they found…' damn, and the audience moved back, en masse. 'But what I can tell you is what they did find—and are still finding—will bring the world news journalists to this village—and they will be here for some while.'

BOOM! Now the questions flew out at her from practically everybody over the age of eighteen who demanded to know exactly what the police found living just a few miles away from where they lived. People stood up and waved their hands, pointed their fingers, angry, red-faced—were their lives still in some kind of danger? They wanted answers. They wanted the truth. You can't handle the truth, she would have told them but that sounded like a line from a Hollywood film so she kept silent.

She stood up. She moved towards them and her officers who seemed to be nervous moved in front of her. Anybody—anybody at all—getting to close to their Chief Super would have to get past them first—and that just about scared the hell out of them.

She raised her hands—which resulted in more shouting. Now they were getting out of control…

…until…

'*QUIET!*'

In just a few seconds, the entire Hall went from a screaming mob to near Church reverence—which was appropriate as it was the booming voice of Vicar Redd which had shut them up. Once that gentleman gave an order of such magnitude and decibel, you obeyed. Silence fell around the Hall and Chief Superintendent congratulated herself in her decision to have the good Vicar on the stage with her—having already been made aware by Inspector Taffe that the Vicar was the best man to have around if she needed crowd control. The officers led the way and she followed in their wake. When she reached the main doors she turned to face them all. Her placating smile had been dropped.

'In the next few days, I promise, all of you will know the whole truth of the two incidents which have occurred relating to your village. We will do what we can to keep media interruption to your lives to a minimum—but the next few weeks, maybe even longer, are going to be very difficult for you. If you require any police presence—I promise you—you will receive it. You will have noticed that Nye House has been cordoned off. For the residents who live in that block, you will be returned to it before the end of the day—but the third level of that block will remain cordoned off. Anyone caught on that level will be arrested for trespass. Many of you will also know that the pathway leading up to Stone Wall Mountain has also been cordoned off. I will tell you now there is still an on-going police presence and investigation on that section of the mountain and again, anyone caught anywhere near that mountain—and especially the Community itself, will be arrested and charged with trespass and the interference of police going about their lawful duty. Do not go anywhere near the place. You have been warned.'

She didn't smile when she said this and only the most foolhardy would even contemplate the notion of disregarding her words.

Chief Superintendent Radford left the Hall and her officers, grateful for the early release, followed her.

What followed, naturally, was the mass huddling of groups who wanted to know more than they had been told—and the only person who could fill this information blank in was the Vicar—and they crowded him at every available opportunity.

He fended them away as best he could with what he knew—though the revelation about the Fleminganese Community had taken him by surprise.

It was going to be a long day.

Chapter 61
Vigils

In the event, the media circus threatened by Chief Superintendent Radford did not immediately appear from story-hungry journalists—certainly the incident against Claire was reported on TV News and in local tabloids but so far, it wasn't the media explosion promised by the senior police officer.

But then, the whole truth of what was found on Stone Wall Mountain had yet to be released by the police. The promised explosion was from a bomb which had landed but had not yet detonated.

In the meantime, the residents of Cwmhyfryd sat silently on the news they did know about and contemplated the evil which had existed within its happy ranks. Any stranger from now on coming to Cwmhyfryd would be scrutinized as if they were a malicious microbe being studied under the strongest microscope.

Less than a week after the Quarry incident, Claire Philips remained silent in her Hospital environment—partly to recover from her beating, partly to maintain her sense of perspective of what had happened. At this point, she was still unaware that her once beloved Tommy was now dead. The bruising around her face had so bloomed out that she was almost unrecognizable as the lovely girl she had previously been. But this, the Doctors told Sara and Adam, was good. It showed the body was functioning the way it should do given the extremities of her injuries. It was her throat injuries which gave cause for concern. Her throat and neck looked like a black and large necklace, such was the size of Tommy's hands and the pressure he had placed on her. It too, had caused swelling and actively prevented Claire from speaking—just about able to mouth her words with a squeak. Initially, it was not a communicative problem as she spent much of that time asleep, kept under sedation while her body mended. But by the fifth day, she was awake, managing to eat—liquid foods to be sure but eating all the same—and was aware of her surroundings. In her private room, arranged by an outsider whom neither Sara or Adam knew, there was never a moment when

Claire was without a member of her family. Mostly, it was Catrin who had more free time to spare. Susan had kept the cafe open but it was now being run by Olwen Berry—the village stalwart who stood in for anybody and everybody when a body was unable to attend whatever an arrangement had been made.

Adam gave his circumstances to his employer and an accommodation was made. He would attend work—but a car was parked nearby, again, arranged by their mysterious outsider—to get him to the Hospital in the event of an occurrence demanding his time. Likewise for Sara whose situation was much easier to arrange. Susan brought in two of her stable-mates from Cardiff to run the Agency in the village while she spent time at the Hospital—ostensibly taking care of her husband but really making certain she was never more than a five minute dash to be with Jack who was making slow but steady recovery in the ICU.

Of the small group, Adam, Sara and Catrin, Susan was the only one who knew who their mysterious benefactor was. Through Vicar Redd and Peter Eddy, both Allan J Gibney and Arthur Ellison had become involved. They were given the whole story—first from the Vicar and later, the story corroborated by their contacts from within the South Wales Police Force—and they acted to assist the Philips' family, knowing this action would be exactly what Jack would have wanted. He had almost sacrificed his life to rescue Claire and so, by extension, his own benefactors continued this assistance. Claire was given a private room within the Hospital and her family were to be taken care of at the highest level.

Susan had visited David a number of times with little enthusiasm as his appearance looked truly pathetic. His face was still bruised, even after so much time had lapsed since the awful night when he had launched his hysterical attack on Jack which resulted in him being brought here, and now he was soon to endure reconstructive surgery to repair his injuries. Susan wished with all her heart that she could feel even an ounce of sympathy for her husband's plight but she tempered her feelings with the knowledge that he had been the author of his own misfortune and besides, Jack's situation was far worse. If *he* died…

On the sixth day, there was a minor breakthrough with Claire. She had managed to eat her first proper meal. A small offering, but a solid one. Simply, a jacket potato. She ate it and smiled at her mother and father who, eyes filled with tears, smiled back. And here, she managed to speak. It was barely more than a whisper and a squeak but it filled them with such hope.

'Uncle Jack… saved me.'

They stopped holding back their tears and both of them bawled their eyes out. Sara pressed a bell and two nurses rushed in to see parents and child holding onto each other. The nurses were given the empty plate along with Claire's minor verbal discourse and they were moved back while the Nurses executed their duties on Claire.

Uncle Jack, Claire had said. So simple but it meant she was aware of what had happened even though no-one had even spoken to her of that incident—and she referred to Jack as *Uncle*—which meant she saw him in the same way she saw her parents' neighbours who were all called *Uncle* or *Auntie*—family by proxy. And now, Jack was of that number.

Sara and Adam were moved out of the room while the Nurses—and later a Doctor—attended on Claire. For some odd reason, it was Adam who was the more affected by the reference of Jack's name and now honorary title.

'After what we all did to him,' he sobbed. 'All those years ago and after he came back—all the things we did—and…' he sobbed so much he couldn't get the words out so Sara soothed him. 'He saved my baby… Farr saved my baby…' Husband and wife wrapped their arms around each other and held onto their selves as if their very lives depended upon it.

Later, when the excitement had calmed and Claire was asleep, Sara related the comment to Susan who, like they, broke into tears. Sara returned to her daughter's room and Susan went to the ICU.

She watched Jack as the machinery around him did its work. His chest was seen—the padding around the bullet wound area was still in place. From where she stood she could see the extent of his injuries. It was of little consolation to her when it had been explained that some of his injuries had not come from the fight with Tommy—but from the fall from the mountain which the new Forensics team had put together after Inspector Taffe told them how Mr Farr had descended the mountain. Along with the debris, they also found a bicycle which also had Mr Farr's fingerprints on it. Underneath the seat, there was an invisible Post-code stamped into it—put there by the local Cwmhyfryd Police. The bike belonged to Ianto Evans who had already filed its theft with those same officers. Taffe concluded that in his run across the mountain, Jack had purloined the bike while Ianto and his un-named paramour were engaged in another kind of physical activity. The explanation given to the healthy octogenarian was accepted and Ianto was proud that his bike had played such an important part in the rescue of that lovely girl, Claire Philips.

Susan read—again—the list of Jack's injuries. Jack's perilous fall from the mountain notwithstanding, Tommy had really laid into him. Broken ribs, strangulation—which seemed to be almost a trademark with Tommy—his face swollen by the punches, his hands bruised by his retaliatory action. The bullet wound which, if it had entered his chest by even so much as a degree elsewhere, would have proved fatal. She stared into the bruised face of the man she had never stopped loving and smiled. If the people of Cwmhyfryd could now see the man they had so hatefully chastised for so long…

A sound behind her made her jump—and she saw the sad face of Vicar Redd who stared past her and through the window of the ICU. Instinctively, both slowly wrapped their arms around each other and cried.

The sound of silence.

Here, in the Hospital, Sara, Adam and Catrin maintained their silent vigil looking over at Claire. In another part of the same Hospital, Susan and the Vicar kept Jack under close watch—with Susan now telling the Vicar that before this week was out—she would tell her husband she would be divorcing him. Sad, but not unexpected, the Vicar nodded and asked her if she would be marrying Jack and his question was met by silence.

In the village, as the night assumed the day, the many residents kept their own vigils. Parents of teens were now more cautious about where their children were going to be that night when they told them they were going out. But not a single teen was braving an unknown element. Safety in numbers was the order of the day—and all of them always in full view of their *Aunts* and *Uncles*.

*

In another place, another kind of vigil was in motion. DCI Taffe and CS Radford were huddled together in the same office, studying the now most recent updated and near full report submitted by the SOCO Division, the Forensics Team and the Pathology Department—all of which were still encamped on top of Stone Wall Mountain—and still discovering the latest truth of the Fleminganese Community.

Chapter 62

The True History of the Fleminganese

While Chief Superintendent Radford studied the preliminary reports submitted by SOCO and Forensics, DCI Taffe pored over the huge tome found inside the large house where he had seen the dead woman. The tome was a curious mix of diary and a self-created Bible—but not one which linked to the orthodox religion of that period. Taffe noted it made no reference to the standardized Deity—God—there was no mention of the now familiar stories of Genesis, the Garden of Eden, the first Man and Woman, the first murder, nothing about the Great Flood, Noah and his story, Lot and his wife, Moses and his great journey across the desert—no parables spoken by the man who was called the "Son of God". No. Joshua Fleming was as single-minded a man as ever there was and his own take on serving "The Great Maker" was a new turn for a man like Taffe who had been raised on strict religious teachings. The creation of this tome had been prepared very carefully. Its two covers were made from the hides of a bovine animal which were then placed over a firm piece of thin wood which had been shaved to an almost paper thin parchment. The same form of parchment was also used as writing paper for the diary. The instrument used for the writing was probably a feather from a large bird—what passed for ink in that day Taffe couldn't guess at but there must have been a plentiful stock in supply for there was a great deal of writing contained therein.

It took Taffe quite a while to decipher the words—they were of course the parlance used in the 15th and 16th centuries. Once he had read through a few of the pages, he managed to pin down the flow and read quite easily.

The whole tome was prefaced by a loose version of the Lord's Prayer. It ran thus:

JOSHUA'S PRAYER
FATHER JOSHUA, WHO ART AROUND AND WITHIN US
HOLIEST IS THY NAME
THY KINGDOM IS COME, THY WILL BE DONE BY THOSE WHO GIVE
SERVICE TO THEE
GIVE US THIS DAY THE SUCCOUR AND WISDOM OF THY WORDS
FORGIVE US OUR TRANGRESSIONS THOUGH WE DO NOT FORGIVE
THOSE WHO TRANSGRESS AGAINST US
LEAD US FROM THE TEMPTATIONS OF THE FLESH FOR WE ARE
WEAK AND SINFUL AND YET WE YIELD
THEE ARE OUR KINGDOM FOREVER AND FOR ALL TIME

...Though we do not forgive those who transgress against us; Taffe read that passage twice and realized that the Fleminganese were led by a very strict leader—today, it would be called a religious cult. Once that prayer page had been read he continued—with great care—to leaf through the rest of the tome. The Forensics team had already cleared the book for reading but he still wore anaesthetic gloves as he carefully turned each page.

Possibly the only fullest and accurate passages of this tome—which had been exclusively written by Joshua Fleming—covered the period of time of his own life. Probably, and Taffe only speculated here, Joshua Fleming was the only man amongst this disparate group who then possessed the intelligence to actually write such words and in such a descriptive flow. His details included times and dates—since they had come from the outside world, there was plenty of reference to draw from. In the later passages, after Joshua's death, the detail became less fixed and time periods disappeared completely from the writing.

To begin with, there was plenty of detail of the original journey Joshua and his Followers were to make on *The Mayflower* ship, transporting the Pilgrims to the Americas. It detailed the mass falling out Joshua had with the other leaders of that journey and how, after a long fight, he was abandoned by Standish and the ship sailed away leaving them stranded on the harbour.

Then the trek across the young Island to find "The Promised Land"—led by Joshua who, Taffe noted, listed his age then as being 49, one of the few real dates and numerical notations contained in this massive book. He took them to many places where they lived temporarily and then moved them on again—either because they had been run out by those who already occupied those places or because he had been directed by "The Great Maker". This trekking continued for a long period of time—until they reached the Middle of Wales—and the valley.

The valley was exactly what Joshua had been searching for and he screamed their search was over, for "The Great Maker" had delivered unto them the fruits of their efforts. His Followers set to work on the valley, using the forestry to build homes, channelling the flowing river which ran from the overlooking mountain into building a well—drinking water and cleaning water, water he could use to cleanse the sin out of those who had followed him. Nor did he stint upon himself—for he was as flesh as they and therefore a sinner to be cleansed by the waters delivered unto them by… "The Great Maker".

*

Later, of course, as Taffe had discovered in the Cwmhyfryd library, the history section, Joshua went up to the top of the largest of the four mountains—like the very Moses—and returned a long time after to tell his people he had found their home—that they were to abandon the valley and to go with him to the escarpment where they could be nearer to…

Taffe was tired of the expression and set it aside.

It was here, from this passage on, that the history books differed in the retelling of the Fleminganese—but then, those historians only had word of mouth from the descendants of that original tribe to write their stories.

The reality of the Fleminganese story ran thus: Joshua led his people with the strictest of hands and dictated their every action. Initially, many of the men had to make repeated trips back down to the valley to bring that which did not grow on the escarpment. These trips were very difficult—the cave Taffe and his team had run through had not been excavated back in that day and the passageway was not easy for horse and cart to traverse. These journeys took time and they spent the energies of the menfolk who made them. A tragic consequence of these journey's resulted in many injuries and a number of deaths. This led to a peculiar arrangement on the mountain.

By the end of the first generation, the female population outnumbered the male population by almost three to one, sickness taking up many of them as there were no skilled apothecaries within the group. Another aspect was the age of the menfolk—considerably older than the females. In his final years, Joshua decreed the only way the Community could survive was for it to become a polygamous society—he decreed the men were to take as many of the available women as there were. Since the physical communions were not based on love, sex or intimacy, the unions did not breech the essential meaning of their religion. The whole purpose of these unions was to continue the population—and, by extension, the word of "The Great Maker" for the Followers of Joshua Fleming had long since been leaving the actual escarpment to spread the word amongst the settlers in the valley below—which had now been usurped by newcomers—and many other places beyond the valley.

The last written date was 1660—Joshua had written it in and it signified one great event—his final entry and his death. The penmanship which followed was of a different calibre, and the continued telling of the Fleminganese from this point took a completely different path. Joshua's entry noted the depletion of young men in the ranks of the people and how rebellion had risen while he was too old and sick to counter it. The rebellion had been led by his own son, Joseph, who had assumed the mantle of leader and his decrees took the people away from Joshua's teachings.

1660—in the year of the Great Maker
My son is become leader of the people I have saved and served. His life is of
the dissolute and the perverted. I fear he will lead them to the home of the
Brimstone and into the pits of Perdition. We have become the same of that from
which we fled. I fear for my...

The pen—or quill—slid down the page at this point. What is recorded on a later page however is the Fleminganese became a populace out of control, beyond education and a society which effectively damned itself to extinction. By the age of the fourth generation—there were no more recorded dates—the Community had over two hundred living members—and every last one of them was related to each other.

Because no records had been made or kept of who gave birth to whose union partner, no one knew who they were having physical relations with. Fathers/daughters, mothers/sons, brothers/sisters. The flesh had become all and lust was now the driving force. Deformities of the grossest natures crept in, mentally and physically, and still they continued to procreate amongst their own. A natural consequence of these deformities reduced the numbers—and it was the menfolk who were the greatest sufferers.

One single constant remained however: The blood-line of the original Founder continued. Every single Patriarch was the natural living descendant of Joshua Fleming. This was understood. It was the way of things. That Patriarch would lead and direct their every action which would guarantee their survival and the word could still be spread. Except, by now, the populace no longer left the escarpment to preach their word—fear of the outside world kept them isolated to such a point that by the seventh generation, not a single living soul had ever left this small closeted world. As far as they all were aware, this was … *the world.*

There was one curious departure from this arrangement. Two brothers—both Flemings—claimed leadership of the Community and the eldest, Jedidiah, maintained his age should be observed as the reason. However, his younger brother, Job, was, by nature, the stronger of the two and was possessed of greater intelligence. He, out of the pair of them, owned the greater force of power and he ran Jedidiah and his son, Jakob, out of the Community. When, many years later, Jakob returned to the escarpment to find Jared, son of Job, was now the new Patriarch, he told the Community of the New World outside which existed beyond the mountain range. He told them how they had found their way to the Americas and how he and his father had played a small part in what was called the *American Civil War*—where one half of the nation had waged battle against the other half, resulting in the deaths of millions.

He even produced a picture—called the *Photograph*—of he and his father, dressed in a strange garb called *Military Uniforms*, carrying weapons called *Rifles*—which had caused so much devastation in that benighted land. Jakob had—by some miraculous journey—brought with him a crate of such weaponry. He showed them to the Community but to their eyes, these weapons were strange and unearthly. Jedidiah had died on the return journey and Jakob was now a man in his mid-fifties and too sick to show the Community how these weapons were used. When he died, just weeks after his return, he was buried in the huge grave which contained his Fleming ancestors—and the crate of weapons, unused, along with him.

And so, life for the Fleminganese continued on the escarpment. Their incestuous congress continued unabated until the latest of the Fleming Patriarchs—Joseph VI—rose and took his people down into the valley below. The valley had long since become populated by infidels and unbelievers and were not to be involved with beyond the bartering of their wares and, by Joseph alone, the spreading of the *Word of the Great Maker.*

Here, the diary faded from one passage to another—none were completed in any comprehensible manner, the writings were as blurred to read as if they had been spoken by one drunken man and recorded by another. Taffe concluded that Joseph VI had, in some way, been contaminated now by that same form of deformity as had affected the others.

The final entry from Joseph—and indeed of the great tome itself—described his angry displeasure of how his youngest son, Thomas, had grown. His eldest, Joshua V11, had died in infancy. Thomas—he who possessed the countenance of the "Great Maker's" own Angels but was possessed of the "Great Deceiver's" blood—had become his very Nemesis. Thomas challenged every command he, Joseph, had uttered, and turning the remaining few survivors against him. Thomas—(*Tommy?* Taffe wondered*)*—led the rebellion which signalled the end of the Fleminganese way of life and Joseph's last sentence ran thus:

We are ended—our ways have become finished. The creature I have sired is not the produce of the Great Maker but the bastard child of the Great Deceiver who has stolen the child's innocence. He has used the weapons against me… I am to meet…

There was nothing more. Whether he expired by natural causes before he was able to write more or was assisted into the next world by an unseen hand, will not be known until an autopsy—if there is one—can determine cause of death.

And while Taffe read that incredible history, CS Radford digested the more clinical words of the early reports submitted by the SOCO, Forensics and Pathology departments. It made for frightening reading.

They had unearthed at least 200 graves, all of them containing more than one body. Most of what they had found were skeletons which were clearly centuries old—but there were more recent additions and this drove the teams to keep digging. Evidently, a burying process had been devised—probably because space was now becoming less and less—where bodies were being placed on top of already built burial mounds. In a number of cases, there were three or four separated layers of burials. Whether this was the Fleminganese attempt to keep blood families united it is difficult to say as there were no records stating which body belonged to which family. What was particularly disturbing was the physical forms of the dead—many of them clearly and seriously deformed. Another disturbing aspect related to the more recent burials. From the state of the bodies, it was evident that not all of them were dead when they had been placed inside their graves. Were they being punished or were they so sick or so much in pain that burial alive was a kinder act to follow than allowing them— after all they were related, they were all family—to live in pain? Or could it be something conceivably worse? It was the continued discovery of the children clinging to their fellow adult buried which caused the greatest upsets. Many of the officers—all of whom had seen real hell in their jobs—were reeling from these discoveries and CS Radford fancied many of them would be requiring possible therapy when this chaos was eventually closed.

Taffe closed his book, Radford did the same. Sweat streamed across their brows and they leaned back in their chairs. They stared at each other.

In unison, they both said, 'Bloody hell.'

Chapter 63

Tommy

But how did Tommy... *become?* From the Fleminganese Community, he had come down and somehow joined the world below—though he never entered through Cwmhyfryd village. The eventual answers came, partially by joining lots of dots, and putting a number of jigsaw pieces together, by taking statements from Father Lennard, John Redd's predecessor, and Peter Eddy—which still really didn't explain the whole picture. But, finally, that picture was the only one which made sense.

It began some years ago when the Church was run by Father Lennard, long before the introduction of Vicar John Redd. Father Lennard was taken to task by the questioning police officer as it was he who first met Tommy—and it was he who introduced him into this new life. The young man had arrived at the Vicarage one early day having just descended from Stone Wall Mountain and declaring who he was and how he had come to be here. Father Lennard, a pious and deeply thoughtful man, took the young man at face value and gave him a temporary home in the Vicarage. He did not declare this to his employers and it is a matter of fact that in the two years the young man remained at the Vicarage, that he did not once venture into the village below nor did he involve himself with the residents. It may not be inferred that Father Lennard kept the young man as... a secret... but he certainly did not alert anyone to the young man's presence.

The name. The young man claimed his name was Thomas Fleming. From there, Father Lennard went to the local Authorities with Thomas Fleming and he was given all kinds of friendly assistance based on the wishes and recommendations of this religious man from Cwmhyfryd. Within a short period of time, Thomas had a National Insurance number and a bank account—which had been set up by Father Lennard—its first deposits coming from him.

When the revitalized young man asked questions about the wider world, Father Lennard devised a scheme to get him integrated into society and contacted his cousin, Edward, who was a partner to the Solicitor Peter Eddy—a man of Law—who lived in the village called Brangwyn. At that time, Edward had introduced a form of apprenticeship to introduce people into the world of Law— and Father Lennard jumped at the opportunity to get his young man involved.

Thomas went to Peter Eddy's office—and studied the ways and mannerisms of the new communities he lived in. He watched as his employer set about defending people who had committed offences which required punishments— such people certainly would have been punished on Stone Wall Mountain for these transgressions—but here in this new community, no punishments followed. Thomas Fleming watched, observed, opined to himself at the iniquity of this perverted system but kept silent when amongst his fellow apprentices. After a period of time, and after Edward was no longer involved in the practice, Peter Eddy slowly brought the apprenticeship scheme to an end and allowed those who were in it to leave—Thomas being one of them. By this time, Father Lennard had been displaced by the Cwmhyfryd Community Council who felt his own peculiar brand of religion did not meet with the acceptable standards set by the Elders of the Council. Father Lennard was gone—and the place was left open—until the arrival of Vicar John Redd.

When Thomas returned to the village and saw his benefactor was no longer in a position of authority, he successfully found work at the local Quarry— owned by Reginald Collier. He was taken on even though he had been warned by its owner that the Quarry was doomed to close soon.

And so it closed. Afterwards, Collier required only a few strong people to help with the materials which were still serviceable and Thomas Fleming was one of them. The site foreman—Alec Leeming—took Thomas Fleming under his wing and they worked the site for three weeks before its gate was finally closed. On a day before that final closure, the local comprehensive school arrived with twenty five students and a tutor who told them all that this Quarry had existed even before Cwmhyfryd village had even been built and christened. Many of their fathers had found their first employments at this Quarry and it should be preserved for posterity and remembered with fondness. Many of the students took photographs and it was at the taking of these photographs where a fifteen year old girl saw the sweating, topless, "Tommy" who had been taking apart a large digger standing next to a man who called him "Son". When the working day was done and the students were ready to leave, the girl stared at the beautiful young man she had photographed and she asked where he came from—

causing the giggling girls with whom she was in company to observe "Claire's in love again".

Thomas told her the older man was his father—that his father was returning to his home up north and that he—*Tommy*—would be staying behind for one last day. Claire just stood and gazed upon him—again making the other girls giggle—they had seen this before.

The following week, when it poured with rain, a member of the Community Council found "Tommy" huddled up inside a shop doorway, sheltering from the downpour. He claimed he was now out of work because of the Quarry closure, did not have a home and was about to walk to Cardiff—a place, in reality he had never visited but had heard of from the other Quarry workers—to find employment and a place to live. The Councillor took pity on the poor wretch— after all, didn't *he* once work at the Quarry? A kindred spirit and a kind heart— he took the bedraggled young man in and learned that his name was Tommy Leeming—that he was just eighteen years of age and was desperate to find a home and make a living.

At the very next Community Council Meeting, the kind-hearted Councillor enquired as to whether the apartment in Nye House was still vacant and when it was so declared, he told them of the young industrious man he had found and, out of kindness, had taken him into his own home and maybe a further act of kindness could see this poor unfortunate housed and from there able to find employment.

And so, Tommy Leeming came to Cwmhyfryd. As no-one in the village had ever seen him when he lived with Father Lennard, there was no-one who could lay claim to knowing him at all. When he was discovered shopping in the village Square by Claire and her friends, he told her where he was now living and Claire wasted no time in getting him to meet her parents, Adam and Sara and "mouthy" elder sister, Catrin. And so it was, after a small period of time, though he kept the apartment going at Nye House, Tommy Leeming effectively took up residence with the Philips family—and love blossomed between him and the youngest daughter of that house. Everybody was happy. Tommy was given periodical work at the same Foundry Adam worked at and everything was sweet. To Claire, life was beautiful. One day, she told her friends, all of whom knew he was Fleminganese, that her Tommy would walk her down the aisle and they would be happy for the rest of their lives. Though he was included in many of their group excursions, the others could not put out of their minds what had been told to them by their parents—that the Fleminganese could not be trusted. They were a deeply religious movement and rabid in their ways. Claire saw nothing except the beautiful boy she would eventually marry. And that was how it was—until Jack Farr returned.

*

From this point, Taffe had just one source of relatively reliable information. It came from the poor women he found on the escarpment when he went looking for Tommy. After the SOCO, Forensics and Pathology teams arrived, the fifteen women were herded together and escorted through the cave—screaming as though they had been scalded—and when, eventually, the two Ambulances arrived, they were taken to a Hospital in Cardiff.

The first examination, made almost impossible by the continued frightened wailing from the women, established that all of them had had their tongues cut out. Their ability to communicate with outsiders was practically impossible but eventually, when food and drink was placed in front of them—a result of sorts was arrived at.

The women delved into the food as if they had not eaten for weeks, which, as it turned out, was pretty much the case. No food of any kind had been found on the mountain so how had they lasted this long…? And it was Dr Swain, still on the mountain, who gave the first inkling of the hell the Hospital was about to go through. There was no doubt that the dead woman had been cannibalized—and the chances were, the fifteen women had been the main feasters on her. Certainly, she had been nibbled at by smaller animals—like rats and squirrels, even carrion birds—but the large bites had come from something bigger and probably human. So—examinations were made to establish what was inside the digestive tracts of each of the women and after the results of the fifth test, the Doctors knew what they had in front of them.

By now, considerable time had passed between taking them off the mountain and setting them up in a place where they could feel safe. Instinctively, the women knew their lives were no longer in danger and a form of communication was attempted by the medical staff to come to an understanding. It took nearly two weeks before a the first breakthrough was made—and that was after Taffe suggested showing them a photograph of Tommy Leeming.

The result was startling.

In recent days, the women's screaming had died down to barely any noise at all—beyond their own particular methods of inter-active communication with each other which the medical staff kept a watch on just in case there was something they could pick up on and assimilate.

When they saw the four-by-four photograph of Tommy, they reverted back to their feral world and screamed the place down for a solid three hours—wailing, rocking their bodies back and forth, raising their hands to the medics as if to plead for them not to be punished. When a Psychiatrist, who had been apprised of the events on the mountain, took the dread photograph and ripped it to shreds, the screaming immediately stopped. They looked up at the Psychiatrist as though she were their saviour.

From then on, communications were made.

After three weeks, a number of facts were ascertained.

1. None of the women were above thirty years of age—though most of them looked much older.
2. DNA proved they were all blood related—though in what capacities it was impossible to tell at this time.
3. The clothes they were all wearing which had been taken from them when they came to the Hospital had all been carbon dated—as far back as two hundred years. Blood—of all kinds but mostly human—was found drenched within the fabrics of those clothes.
4. The eldest of the group, had a limited ability to speak English. After much time and patience, Sarah took the hand of the Psychiatrist—and told her of their lives on the mountain—and under the leadership of Joseph Fleming—and of his now only son, Thomas.

This is what she told the Psychiatrist:

Life under the Fleming Patriarchs had always been hard, a desolate existence under extreme and austere conditions. This lifestyle had been made worse under their last Patriarch, Joseph, and grew even more degenerated as he became older and physically infirm, his mind also losing all sense of proportion. When he died, the women and the few men who remained waited for Joseph's successor—Thomas—to assume the mantle of Patriarch and lead them—to anywhere away from here but hopefully to food and warmth and safety. Instead, Thomas completely abandoned them to their own perils and survival. What he actually *did* do—something he had been frequently and secretly had been doing since his early years—was to leave the Community and go down into the valley below where he would watch—surreptitiously—the activities of the demonized outsiders so vilified against by his father and the Fleming forefathers. What he saw opened his eyes to the wider world—and he had decided that when the time came, this was where he would come to continue his own existence—the Fleminganese Community could go to the "Great Deceiver"—whoever the hell that was. When that day did come and Joseph was so weak and demented he could no longer function in any capacity, Thomas dealt the fatal blow. He dragged the dead Patriarch across the ground in the full view of the living and deposited him on top of the camp fire—then ordered those men who were skilled with the boning knives to take their leader for meat—which they did. They feasted on Joseph Fleming for five days and then buried his remains alongside his ancestors in the "Leader's" grave. Thomas watched the feasting—if only to be absolutely sure his father had finally been taken—and then he left the escarpment—forever.

Sarah told the psychiatrist their lives changed for the worse from that time on. For the first time, the Fleminganese were without leadership—the evil they had lived under for so long was bad to be sure but at least it had worked to some degree. Now, they were expected to fend for themselves and this new life defeated them. Bereft of instruction, rudderless in direction, they reverted to feral Beings from another age. From being a Community of just over a hundred, they were reduced to a handful within five years. Many of the Commune simply died from sickness or as a result of their mental and physical deformities. They were used as meals by those who stayed alive. Their final meal had come when their sister—and the mother of their now absent patriarch—became ill and was unable to direct them. Still alive, the luckless mother was pounced upon by the starving women—there were now only women left in the camp—and was eaten. Not completely cannibalized as the women did not know how to start the fire—a skill which only the menfolk possessed. In the weeks preceding DCI Taffe's arrival, the women had been reduced to taking mouthfuls of their dead sister—but by now, her body was rancid and gangrenous and eating on her only brought on more sickness until only fifteen were left.

The arrival of DCI Taffe was first seen to be the most frightening day of their truly frightening lives—but then, much later, they recognized it as their day of salvation.

380

And now, here they were—dressed in clothes which kept them warm, not matted with the blood of their own, cleansed, their medical needs being addressed and being spoken to in soft calming tones, fed with food which did not make them puke and learning about a life they had never before believed could exist while under the harsh ruling of Joseph Fleming.

The sisters were kept apart from everyone who did not have a direct part to play in their future rehabilitation. The Psychiatrist would make certain these poor unfortunates would not become the 21st century equivalents of the 19th century carnival freak shows which would exploit dwarves, bearded ladies, lycanthropic imaged boys, giants, and the mainly physically deformed. This would not turn into a Barnum sideshow.

A single concession to that limited list of observers was made for DCI Taffe who had sat in on the story Sarah had told the Psychiatrist. After all, he had played the most important part in bringing these women down from that hell on the mountain and had, indirectly, given them a new life. Assimilation would be slow, for sure, but the process had begun. Taffe, lauded by the medical staff for his heroism, took what he needed for his own investigation and left. He would never see the women again. When he stepped out of the Hospital wing, he drew a long breath and saw life in a different kind of light. It was raining—and he walked the three miles from there to the Cardiff Police Station in the pouring rain—just to be cleansed.

He left Hell behind.

Chapter 64

Advance of the Fourth Estate

The promised invasion of the media, as foretold by Chief Superintendent Radford, did not immediately appear in the small village of Cwmhyfryd. Many of the residents believed they had been misled for some peculiar reason. Some police tactic intended to misdirect actions taken by the locals.

The two murders of Hywel Parry and Vonna Shepherd had, naturally, made all the Welsh newspapers and even managed to find small spaces in some of the national tabloids. Likewise the attack on the young teenage girl but these stories were no great shakes as far as the possible media invasion was concerned. It was only after the link between the two separated incidents was made did the media interest grow. The man who committed those grisly murders had also throttled the young girl—aha, went the media world—a possible serial killer in the offing, meat and drink to their kind.

When the story finally began to take shape in the form of police statements, the interest grew exponentially. First, the actual murders—now we know how the prostitute died—throttled—and how the old man had been constantly bludgeoned by an axe—all good juicy stuff, we can run with this for months. But then they learned that the man who had heroically saved the teen girl had also sprinted across the mountain, running nearly three miles (there was no mention of the stolen bike, much to Ianto Evans' chagrin) and that man had jumped off the side of the mountain, a height of over two hundred feet, almost killing himself into the bargain. Then there was the brutal fight between that man and the killer and the sprinting hero had been shot by the killer—almost killing him—who then went on to murder two more people, both Cops, and wound a senior officer before he himself was fatally slain. Whew!

But then they learned that the killer had been killed by a Cop who was himself a notorious Cop-*killer*. God-*DAMN*—this is just getting better and better—*and* that the same Cop also saved the life of the hero sprinter.

It was only after the full truth of how the hero mountain runner had even become involved in the rescue that the media interest became a full-blown media circus—and they brought everything except the elephants. The man—named locally as Jack Farr—was a village pariah who had once been hounded out of this small place called Cwmhyfryd by the other residents and had left the UK to go live in the States. He was now back—the very prodigal—to lay claim to a great deal of money which had been left him by his late father, who had *also* been a rebel shunned by the good people of Cwmhyfryd. But it was the next bit which was the best—Jack Farr had been called upon to save the teen girl by— and get this—*the woman who had once jilted him at their wedding twenty years ago.*

WHOOSH! This was latter-day Shakespeare. Love, romance, tragedy, action, murder and damn near sacrifice. This story had *everything.* But it was the love bit which took off. Those wonderful journo's made huge capital on the relationship between Jack Farr and the woman who had jilted him—Susan Tanner—who was now possibly in the throes of ditching her own hubby still lying on his deathbed—such an exaggeration—to attend the deathbed of the man she had jilted—*who was lying in an ICU Ward in the same hospital!* Romeo & Juliet, Macbeth, Hamlet—you name the Shakespeare play—we got the latter day equivalent, buddy. Hollywood will be crawling all over the story to find out who's got the rights to whatever interviews are going to be given by the principle actors and will pay *zillions* to get the rights and the film made.

The story went universally viral when the discoveries of what had taken place on Stone Wall Mountain. Although the whereabouts of the surviving women were kept a closed secret, there was no way the authorities could keep the history of the Fleminganese existence quiet. The official history—to be found at Cwmhyfryd's Library—was certainly referred to but the real truth was laid out in minute detail by the subsequent police investigation. It was after all, relevant news. No names of present day people were given—Thomas Fleming/Tommy Leeming was not mentioned though every living soul in the village knew exactly who had been involved.

The reactions of many of the residents were understandably mixed. The elderly of the village resented the Press intrusion—especially from those hungry hyenas who wanted to promote their own by-lines. There was money to be made for the first Journalist who could get the exclusive whammy on Jack/Susan/Claire/Tommy. It was then, a credit to all the residents of the village that while they were happy to speak of their own experiences relating to the Fleminganese Community, whenever they came from that place on the mountain and into their village to sell their wares and religion, that they collectively said nothing about the personal lives of the principles who had been mentioned in nearly every questions-and-answers interviews aimed at them—for the trade of money. No-one—not one—spoke about Jack, about Susan, about their once-upon-a-time relationship and certainly not about the once nearly wedding. Nor would they feed the hyenas on whatever the current state of their present day relationship was. Yes—there had been minor conflagration between Mr Farr and Susan's husband, Mr Tanner (David's Christian name didn't even get a mention) and that Mr Farr was indeed responsible for putting Mr Tanner in the Hospital—but that was almost as far as they went. The hyenas went hungry on that story. Mercifully for the Philips family, there was closed protection given to them by the police, the medical staff at the Hospital and their Cwmhyfryd neighbours. Typically, some Journalists of the more sordid variety managed to sneak into the Hospital. One took a sneaky mobile picture of Catrin, Claire and Sara when they were speaking with each other in a communal area and another, braver Journalist had successfully breached the ICU ward and managed to get one picture of Jack lying on his bed, strapped to the wires and other medical paraphernalia, with Susan sat next to him, before a resolute Nurse bowled him out and literally kicked his ass out of the Ward.

None of the pictures were allowed to be published.

Eventually, the whole media had to settle for what were the bare facts of the stories and not much more. The story behind Vicar Redd's former life also made the pages for some bizarre reason—and all of a sudden, his profile ascended amongst those who had previously sought to challenge him. It was also established that the Church Elders who had brought him to this village had already been made aware of his former life before his arrival and had supported him accordingly. Their faith in him had been redeemed and repaid a thousand-fold. His role in this story was also written about and he gained a greater degree of respect from many more people than he had known since arriving here in the village. The same week of the media invasion, the Church was filled with the village's residents for the first time in, say, twenty years. And life continued.

Chapter 65

After...

And so life continued on in Cwmhyfryd.

'I know many of you got a grievance against Jack Farr—I was one of them. But I got to tell you now—if ever I hear anybody saying anything against him or doing something against him—you'll be dealing with me. I know most of you think I'm a joke—but I can still swing a punch and I don't care that you my buddies—from now on, you leave Jack Farr alone.'

Adam Philips then lurched out of The Night's Tail, bumping into two of the regulars and still having the courtesy to apologize. He had already consumed a smaller than usual portion of his usual tipple before addressing the small company with just a little Dutch courage inside him. But the company understood the reason why he felt it was necessary to say what he said. His daughter was alive because of Jack Farr and there was a moral obligation to be observed.

In fact, the subject of Jack Farr and the whole incident relating to him had not even been mentioned. After weeks of media intrusion which was still going on as the police continued to find other things on Stone Wall Mountain, the residents had more or less returned to their humdrum lives. There was still talk that a film company from Hollywood was going to make a movie about the whole incident, starting with the wedding from umpty umpty years ago to present date. It was the rumour of the movie which made Adam stand up and state his position.

The thing is—hardly anyone in Cwmhyfryd was making any kind of unpleasant comment about Jack anymore. Possibly Sion Edmunds and his sons—but they were just loudmouths anyway and barely anyone paid attention to anything they said. Maybe Malcolm Fisher still had that bee in his bonnet—especially since his daughter had clearly staked her claim on her former beau and had made it known she was intending to divorce her husband. But neither Sion nor Malcolm had been seen very much since the revelations of what exactly had taken place at the Quarry and the part Jack had played in the rescue of young Claire. When honesty was to be taken into account—who in the village could have done what that man had done? In truth—none of them. In the media press and TV, Jack Farr was declared a national, and now, international, hero. No-one in the village was going to say anything to disrespect that. Adam, probably, still thinking he had let his daughter down by not being the man to save her, was merely assuming a macho position in order to fly his own flag.

Some of the pub regulars watched him as he lurched out of The Square and towards home. They all doubted they would see him here so often from now on.

*

Sion Edmunds sat in his broken armchair—in agony and almost in tears from his constant pain—and read the same newspaper which had carried the whole story relating to Jack Farr's entire life history—including some fairly unpleasant incidents which had occurred in Oklahoma. The newspaper story made him out to be some kind of latter-day adventurer who had railed against the Ungodly, rather like the Saint had done from the Leslie Charteris novels and the many TV versions. This was not what Sion wanted to hear about the man who crippled him. He had even given an interview to a Journalist—and the whole article had made him look like some kind of neutered buffoon. Worse, everyone in the village now stared at him and saw him, possibly for the first time, as a nasty waste of vilifying bile who used his small infirmity as a weapon to get attention he did not warrant and sympathy he definitely did not deserve.

Both his sons sat in their own armchair and watched their father seethe with fury as each paragraph continued to laud Farr as some latter-day Knight errant, saving the life of some pathetic love-struck teen who had behaved in such a state of wanton abandonment. They sighed, waiting for the moment when his medications would kick in and he would fall asleep and they could leave without him bewailing how bad his life was, being left alone and deserted.

When, eventually, the meds had done their jobs, they both stood and, without speaking, quietly closed the apartment door and went out.

Snoring, griping, Sion Edmunds lay in his broken armchair and his bladder let flow.

Vicar Redd sat alone in his Vicarage lounge and read the same newspapers the whole village had been reading. As some of it included himself, they made for interesting reading. The remarkable thing was the amount of positive feedback he had received from the residents—not at all judgemental from the main mass though he was aware of some adverse commentary from some of the more pious members of the Community Council. Nothing official had been passed to him and the Authorities to whom he answered had not called for his resignation. His minor role in the incidents leading up to the Quarry scrap had been noted and his general behaviour was to be condoned. This suited him. He had taken a personal lead in letting Peter Eddy know where things stood after his own participation dealing with Jack Farr and it was Eddy who made contact with Gibney Associates and updated them. Academic of course—Allan J Gibney already had his own personal pipeline in knowing exactly what had happened and the latest updates regarding Jack's recovery progress were furnished to him almost immediately.

In the meantime, Vicar Redd had slow time on his hands. He sat in front of his customary roasting fire and indulged his one guilty pleasure with toasted rolls and lashings of butter. These he ate while rereading the one line sentence message from his one-time mentor, Father Liam which read:

Proud of you me boy. Fr Liam

More than anything else, the one thing Vicar Redd needed, wanted, was the approbation of the man who had saved him, redeemed him and made him the man he was today. The single sentenced message, along with the toasted buns, warmed him inside and out. It was going to be a lovely day.

*

At Peter Eddy's office, life continued undisturbed. The police had made a thorough check on the period of time Thomas Fleming had spent at the office while serving as an apprentice to Peter Eddy's ex-business partner.

With his experience during his time of employment there, Tommy had had access to Eddy's clients and had gleaned a great deal of information on many of them. He had also purloined information of some of the worst or the most regular offenders and had stored that information—to be made good use of when and if the right time came along.

Eddy's involvement in the whole business was purely incidental. Nothing he had done had brought about the incredible events which had occurred and he could not possibly have known about the incursions upon his office made two years earlier.

It was a more thorough police search of Tommy's address at Nye House which uncovered that piece of knowledge.

*

So why? Why did Tommy... Leeming now... want to hurt Jack Farr so much? As far as everyone knew, he had never even met Farr. The answer was found in a diary—very similar to the tome found on Stone Wall Mountain composed by Joshua Fleming and inherited by all his descendants. Clearly, Tommy intended to continue that tradition. The diary was home-made—not as concise as the Community Bible but just as interesting for the police to read.

Tommy's despising of Jack Farr stemmed from two sources. First: the day he spied Claire and Farr talking with each other in the forest a few days after Jack had come home. He had been making his way to meeting Claire through the forest having just left the Community from above—he occasionally ventured up there to see what was happening but always in secret. He watched Claire talking with this new man—laughing and looking at him. To Tommy, this was as great a sin as sexual infidelity. He wrote about what he'd seen in the diary:

She has sinned against the law of fidelity with an infidel.
The Great Maker will direct my hand and I will act upon his Word

The second source against Jack Farr effectively came from the stories trumpeted about the village by its residents about this man Farr. Had he not heard, from Adam Philips himself, the man who would become his Father-on-Earth, that Farr was a danger to all that was decent and should be lynched by the villagers? Had he not heard the constant and painful words from the man living below him that Farr was evil and should be put to death? Had he not heard from Malcolm Fisher—the most religious of all the residents that Farr had been sent

388

by the Devil himself and should be delivered to his grave? Subsequently, Tommy elected himself to be that deliverer.

Claire's fate was sealed.

Hywel Parry's life was, automatically, forfeit. He had been a sinner all his life and the Law of the land—so weak—had allowed him to continue his sin and so his selection in the grand plan was easily made.

Vonna Shepherd had sold her body for the purposes of financial advantage and used her bodily Temple in the service of lust for the flesh—she also served the Great Deceiver. Her life was therefore forfeit.

The participants chosen—it only required the time. Tommy had maintained a vigil watching Farr as the man continued to wage war against those who lived in the village. He saw Susan Tanner sitting next to him at his house—just a few short hours after this man had almost murdered her husband. Sara had told her whole family she had seen the fight and Tommy had listened. He went there, watched her entering his house to, no doubt, enjoy carnal relations with him, Tommy broke down in despair. This woman—this whore—was a friend to the family he was engaged to and her continued influence he had witnessed when it came to discussions relating to Farr. The elder daughter, Catrin, had openly defied her father challenging his authority within the family ranks. This surely meant the man Farr had to be disposed of. Using the sinners, Shepherd and Parry, as the instruments of that disposal was merely functionary. The Great Maker directed his hand—and he had acted.

*

Malcolm Fisher had all but become a recluse. Those activities which had kept him alive and serving as a primary functionary within the village had now been taken away from him by his own friends after he had made an unpleasant comment about Jack Farr's heroic rescue of Claire Philips. One of the members of the Community Council—no doubt bating Malcolm because of his known hatred of Jack Farr—had stated loudly that the Council should consider putting up a statue of Jack to commemorate his heroism. Malcolm blew a fuse—not difficult and certainly not rare—and exploded the rescue stories as being nothing more than idle tittle tattle and the girl involved had received little more than a justified slap from a decent young man who had objected to his girlfriend enjoying time spent with the man who had so disrupted the well-being of the village.

Even those who were used to Malcolm's occasional rants were taken aback by this incredible version of the events. "A justified slap, Malcolm?" ran Mrs Lewis' shocked retaliation. "Nothing justifies any kind of physical abuse on a young girl—and this was more than just a slap." Malcolm was unperturbed—he repeated his claim that Claire had had it coming and Farr's involvement in the so-called rescue was next to pointless. In his opinion, Tommy never had any intention of really harming Claire—a bizarre statement to make in the light of what had happened to Vonna Shepherd and Hywel Parry. No-one there had ever pretended to understand Malcolm's continued hatred of Joe Farr—long after those events of yesteryear had passed by—nor of his unabated bile against a man no-one had seen in over twenty years—but this rant was extreme even by his standards and the same night, the entire Council quickly decided Malcolm could no longer serve them or the village and he was dismissed immediately.

He sat alone in his lounge, in the semi-darkness, staring at the switched off TV, a letter in his right hand which had been sent to him by a now nearly recovered David Tanner. It read:

Dear Father,

I have just spoken with Susan and she has informed me that she intends to divorce me on the grounds of irresponsible behaviour. She has directed me not to challenge this claim or charges will be pressed against me resulting from the fight I had with Farr. As I am the victim here, I am completely at a loss to understand her motives. I am in no present condition to fight from my hospital bed and I ask you to intervene on my behalf and persuade her to drop this nonsensical claim—when I am fully recovered I know we can run our lives as before without the continued interference from that man who, I hope, will be returning to his home in the States.

Your loving Son, David.

Malcolm did indeed broach the issue with Susan—even showing here the letter her husband had written—and Susan delivered her reply in short shrift. Their marriage was over years before Jack had returned and she no longer loved David as a husband. He had no right in involving her father in what was private business. She had already seen her own Solicitor to bring about divorce proceedings and that he, her father, had better mind his own business from now on. When Malcolm asked if she was considering marriage with Farr Susan replied if that was possible, yes. Malcolm stormed away and vowed never to speak to her ever again.

So now he sat in his own home—alone. Friendless, with no useful part to play in the village, Malcolm Fisher effectively gave up that night. The coal fire was dimming in front of him. He reread his son-in-law's letter one last time, ripped it up and threw it on the fire. Its flare parodied David's. A small outburst—and then nothing but smoke.

*

In the time which followed, David Tanner's surgery had come and he was made near facially presentable again. Released from the Hospital but with treatment still to come, David made a single attempt to ingratiate himself back into Susan's life. It failed mere seconds after he made it. Then, later, and from his wife's Solicitor, he was told in no uncertain terms that he was to have no further contact with her and it would be wise for him to leave the marital home. Unlike his father-in-law, David, at least, had the sense to see the wind had blown in Jack Farr's favour. Susan allowed him one final access to their home where he could pack all his belongings and leave with at least a little dignity. This he did, relocating, temporarily to a Cardiff bed-sit and he attempted to continue his time at the Bank. But the Managers at the Bank had now been made aware of the fight which he had instigated against a man now recognized as a national hero and of the axe-throwing incident which had nearly killed that man and they decided such behaviour reflected badly on their branded image. He was advised to transfer to another Branch.

Divorce in the offing, his reputation shattered, his masculinity totally destroyed while at the same time, his Nemesis was constantly being spoken of in such heroic terms, David decided to return to his home in Cheshire—back to live with his confused parents who had failed to understand how he could have ruined this previously wonderful arrangement. He was taken back at the same Bank he had first found employment with—but at a junior posting and at a lesser rate of pay. His star had once shone high elsewhere but it had reached its Zenith in the Welsh Capital and would rise no more.

And what of the Clay twins? What of that pair of no-hopers, those third rate bandits who aspired to run a Gangsters Empire but truthfully didn't possess the personality to run even a fruit stall. They couldn't even beat a man they'd attacked from behind without blowing it big time. After their abortive attack on Jack and their ignominious defeat at his hands and the bottle of milk thrown by Susan—plus the absolutely humiliating sight of their being chased out of the village by a man, more than twice their age, waving a biking helmet at them and using language only ever heard in Quentin Tarantino films, they managed to escape the ranting pensioner and didn't stop running until they hit countryside where nothing except birds and rabbits were the only living creatures to witness their humiliating retreat. Andrew and Sean McGregor made their way through the forestry and carried on running until there was nothing but silence around them. No sirens, no shouting, nobody chasing them. When they were both satisfied they were safe they collapsed onto the ground and breathed out like their very lives depended upon it.

They both decided they could not return to their respective safe houses—there was no doubt both of them would be arrested for breaching their probationary boundaries and equally no doubt that their names would already be lit up for the attack on Jack Farr. Their clothes were rank from the sweaty run they had endured and now—to cap it all for a really wonderful day—it began to rain.

What was most urgent for them were the injuries they had both sustained in the fight. Andrew had taken a really serious blow to the face and his nose was now a great cause for concern. Too many blows breaking it had already brought about respiratory problems and the latest from Jack's punch just added to the list. Sean's own nose woes were not much better. They needed cover from the elements and time to recover from this dismal day. What they did have to their advantage was the £500 given to them by their mysterious employer who wanted to harm Jack Farr which they could use for food and other items—but first, they needed to get out of the rain.

Ironically, they secured refuge in the one place they were certain the police would not come near. Twenty years ago, when the police were advancing on Hywel Parry's final stab at criminal activity, the Clay twins cowardly took refuge in a tin shack where the owner of the large building stored his equipment, now long since abandoned as the small industry which had thrived for so long had become bankrupted and the larger building had been torn down after months of non-use had rendered it unsafe for it to remain standing. The only thing still standing and of any use at all was the small tin shack they had once cowered inside when all hell was breaking loose elsewhere.

Sean—the fitter of the two—made his way to a small village where he purchased a sizeable chunk of tinned food, many boxes of matches, a tin-opener, blankets, some weather clothing and a couple of battery operated lamps. They would hole up inside this shack and wait it out, wait until their wounds mended and they could brave the harsher elements which were due to hit them—winter wasn't far away now. Once they were able to stand without feeling the pain, they would escape the area and try their luck, bad as it was, somewhere where they wouldn't be so easily recognized—which probably meant England.

In the event, things did not pan out even that way. Andrew's injuries were obviously worse than they had first believed and his physical constitution fell way below par. This, with the now colder weather and their inability to function even to the level of the most basic Boy Scout level, seriously jeopardized their safety. When it came to a point where Andrew really required the need of a Doctor, Sean had no alternative but to walk to Brangwyn, some eight miles from their current position and to alert their situation to the police—which he did.

Both men were arrested for the breaking of their Probationary Boundary rule and for the attack on Jack Farr—even though he was the one who had come out of the scrap with victory on his lips. Both the McGregors were immediately taken to the nearest Hospital and Andrew was admitted to the ICU ward—suffering from diagnosed double pneumonia as well as body damage sustained from the fight which had not mended correctly. Both men were in considerable agony and even the police—royally fed up with their antics—felt sympathy for their pains.

Long after other events which have been recorded here were memories in the minds of all those who had witnessed or participated in them, and with no kind of ceremony at all, Andrew McGregor died from his illness aged only forty eight. Sean wept at his bedside. A sad epitaph for two men who had started their lives in such a blaze of happiness and glory. Great things had been promised for them when they were mere babies and they had chosen to walk down a dangerous path instead. Sean was the only attendee at Andrew's funeral.

*

It is a natural consequence of police procedure that any officer who discharges a firearm, even in the course of their duty, must face a Tribunal to justify the reasons for its use—and to examine the events which followed. For the umpteenth time, Detective Chief Inspector Owen Taffe faced such a Tribunal. Was the shooting necessary? Could the officer have made another choice? Was it necessary to kill the victim, could the officer had shot to wound? Every facet of the said incident is examined and the verdict brought in at the most fairest level to all concerned.

By the time DCI Taffe faced his Tribunal, a number of facts relating to the Quarry incident had been established. The Ballistics Department and the report from Pathology were vital items of evidence in the Tribunal case. When Tommy had come out of the building and started firing, his first two shots came from the Colt 45. Both these rounds, just by sheer fluke, found targets. The ARU officer had been hit full in the face and was killed instantly. DS Stone, her back facing Tommy's firing, was struck on the left side of her neck, the bullet entering at the jugular and exiting an inch beyond. It was found, spent, in the bonnet of the Ambulance parked nearby and facing Tommy. There was blood, confirmed to be that of DS Stone, on the bonnet and the spent round also had DS Stone's blood on it.

The Pathology Department had performed its autopsy on Tommy and had discovered his right hand and wrist—that which was holding the heavy Colt 45—had been broken, probably from the fight he had just had with Mr Farr. The scale of his injury plus the weight of the Colt and its very powerful kick back when firing it, had prevented Tommy from using the pistol further as he continued his attack.

DCI Taffe smiled when he heard that aspect of the report—he reflected that Jack had indirectly saved more lives from Tommy's wayward firing, being unable to use the Colt because of his wrist injury and was forced instead to use only the lesser powerful Smith & Wesson in his left hand, the weaker of the two—by which time the officers had all taken safe cover.

The Tribunal duration was, by its own previous standards, a relatively short entry. With the evidence presented and the commendation of DCI Taffe given by Commander Garrison of the ARU, taking into account the murderous actions already conducted by Tommy and his attempt on the day to kill Claire Philips—plus the successful killings of the two police officers on site all added up to a justifiable homicide committed by a police officer in the course of his duty to protect. DCI Taffe was declared innocent and cleared by the Tribunal.

*

The full truth and history of the Fleminganese will probably never be known.

The police operation on top of Stone Wall Mountain took months to get through and even after the operation was finally closed they were never really certain if they had truly completed their task.

What eventually became the full report of their findings and what was officially released to the story-hungry world media ran thus:

Three hundred and fifty graves were found—though many of them had more than one burial level. Some of the graves had been dug down at least twelve feet and had only been prevented from being dug deeper because they'd hit solid rock. There were multiple levels and on each of those levels, multiple bodies. Nor were the graves consigned solely to the upper level of the mountain. Some graves were found on the two sides of the mountain in places where there was very little stone impediment. Even within the cave trail which led from the escarpment and down to Mynydd Fach, bodies wrapped in heavy hessian blankets were found—the skeletons so badly degraded it was almost impossible for the Pathologists to determine what gender they were. In at least 90% of the skeletal remains, the bodies were found to be seriously deformed in some way. It was impossible to determine the manner of their deaths. In total, five hundred and thirty five skeletons were recovered. The experts all agreed there must have been more than that number living on Stone Wall Mountain in the period of time since its founding so what happened to the other bodies remains a part of that hideous mystery. It was agreed by everyone who took part in this gruesome task that this operation had been one of the worst discoveries in peacetime history.

The fate of Stone Wall Mountain resided now in the rebuilding of it. As no vehicle of any size above a Mini car could ever make its way through the many caves, large excavators were helicoptered onto the mountain. They razed the entire Community to the ground and salted it until it was totally physically absent of any of its previous history. The area was—and now probably always will be— cordoned off by the many authorities who laid claim to it and it now resembles, if such a description could be applied, a latter day reminder of a War-time Concentration Camp.

Six weeks after she had been admitted, Claire Philips left the Heath Hospital in a blaze of media attention, with Journalists photographing her from every available angle and many attempting—and all failing—to get any kind of comment from a sixteen year old girl who could still barely speak. Once the whole family had secured refuge in their tiny village, the residents closed ranks and no Journalist, or anyone carrying a camera bigger than a mobile phone, was allowed anywhere near the street. The word was out—*KEEP CLEAR—OR ELSE.*

Claire's recovery was slow but sure. Her physical bearing was remarkable given what she had been subjected to. Her throat was still painful and it hurt to speak at any length so the families and friends made certain vocal conversation was kept to a minimum. Much of the communications were made via their I-Pads—writing down basic questions of how she felt—every day that question would be asked—and tons of other less important queries. When the families congregated at the Community Hall for birthday parties or this celebration or that event, Claire was always surrounded by a coterie of teenaged bodyguards who made certain she never became too taxed by the innocent enquiries of friends or people who may have felt spurious curiosity. Absolutely *NO* stranger ever made it to with a six yard grasp of her. Another consequence of her experience was sent out by all the parents relating to the relationships status of their children. From now, they declared, you can have friends, you can have dates—but only when in the company of other people—from now on—*NO-ONE* will ever have a… *serious* relationship—not until they are fully adult and have left home. No parent will ever make the same mistake Adam Philips made.

And everybody will live happily ever after.

Which left only Jack Farr.

The extent of Jack injuries meant that he had to be kept sedated and secluded while his body slowly repaired itself. Nothing but time would help him. Mercifully, DCI Taffe's early intervention in slowing the blood flow from Jack's bullet wound undoubtedly saved his life. Had there been no other people at the Quarry after the fight, it is left to the curious to divine what may have happened next. Tommy—beaten and wounded by Jack to be sure—was clearly still active and able to cause more hell and would have done so if not for Taffe's heroic actions. Had there been no police presence, there is no doubt Tommy would have caught up with the dazed and confused Claire and finished off what he had already started. Equally, there is no doubt he would have left the area and Jack Farr would have bled to death inside the building. It was by pure luck that Claire had announced to her sister when begging for the taxi fare that the right people had been alerted to that geographical position.

So Jack lay upon his hospital bed—attended only by the Doctors and Nurses—though kept watch over by Susan who spent her every available moment situated near the ICU Ward. In the time which followed, Susan was introduced to Allan J Gibney—she knew of him by reputation—and Arthur Ellison whom she knew of through Jack's meeting. Ellison assured her that once Jack was out of the danger zone he would be transferred to his own Pharmaceutical Business in the Cotswolds where he owned a Private Hospital. It was in that very place where Joe Farr received the completion of his hospital treatment. Confident that Jack would receive the very best of treatment, Susan relaxed. There was also an established relationship between Ellison Pharmaceuticals and General Hospitals around the UK and provided Jack's condition was deemed to be in a safe position, the sanction for his transfer was given. Arthur Ellison assured Susan that she would be made welcome to be in attendance to Jack whenever she chose—in fact, Ellison assured her even further—probably necessary. The first face to be seen upon his awaking really should be hers.

It was enough for Susan to know Jack's life was now no longer in danger. As for his long term recovery, only time would tell. She accepted Ellison's offer—and was gifted with the aid of helicopter travel between her work at the Agency and the trips to the Hospital in the Cotswolds.

Susan had now become accustomed to the fact that her life story—or at least, the parts involving Jack—had now made the local and national newspapers. The main thrust—inevitable really—concerned the marriage which did not happen. The facts were accurately reported though not a single soul from Cwmhyfryd ever gave interviews concerning that day. The fateful death of Theresa was only lightly touched upon and nobody gave a comment on that either. Given the many substantial offers of large money from the Media to induce free comment, it was quite surprising just how tight-lipped the residents could be. It would be true to say that some had been tempted—but were possibly afraid of facing the wrath of their neighbours later on should they speak out of turn. After all, two people had been brutally murdered, one of their own Angels had almost met her end in the most terrible fashion and two police officers had also been slain—by, or as near as dammit—one of their own for that was how the residents of Cwmhyfryd considered Tommy.

Jack occasionally murmured noises from his sick bed—would now and then open his eyes and stare around his room inside the ICU—but would then fall back into unconsciousness and continue his recovery in the nether world. At all times, Susan would be alerted by the Medical Staff as she was pretty much the only regular person there. She had received her own visitations from Sara, from the Vicar and even, on one surly occasion, her father who had come to remonstrate with her for her decision to divorce David—which was bad enough for him but *to even consider marrying Jack Farr as well?*

Two months from the night he was operated on, Jack stirred in his bed. His voice growled and whimpered and his movements were agitated. Susan was there by his side and she immediately pressed the emergency button for attention. But this time he opened his eyes and stared—wide-eyed—at her. His eyes, his face, was all confusion. His breathing was heavily laboured as though he had been running—and for all Susan knew—may well have been in that nether-world of recovery. The Doctors told her it was entirely possible he could have been dreaming of his last moments fighting with Tommy—staring down the barrel of the gun, hearing the explosion and then reliving those moments in his sleep.

His face was fearful of his surroundings and Susan took his hand. She leaned in closer to him and prayed he could hear her voice, understand what she was telling him.

'You are safe,' she said, in slow, comforting tones. 'You are in Hospital recovering from a beating but you are going to live and you are recovering.'

She hoped that basic message would permeate his confused mind but said little more than that—too much information would be as a sensory overload. She waited, watching closely his confused face as he assimilated his position, staring back up at her, maybe not even knowing who this woman was.

He opened his mouth and the voice was barely a croaked whisper—but what he said was audible.

'Claire—safe?'

Susan's eyes welled up with tears as two Nurses rushed into the Ward. It was hard to believe she even had tears left to fall, so much had she cried over the past weeks but this time, they were the tears of unbridled joy.

It was alright. *He* was alright. Everything was going to be alright.

Chapter 66

Letter from Auntie Phelps

Hi y'all

I do hear tell that a nephew of mine is all set to get hisself married away to a beautiful red—all I can say is "about time"—man his age should be long down the aisle by now, paying attention to his li'l woman and makin' li'l babies who can take the family name forward to a new generation.

Well—you hear me now nephew mine—I ain't gonna be able to make it to the big do but you sure as hell can make it back here to sweet old Oklahoma and I do expect to be meeting the lovely new Mrs Farr any day soon—this ain't just a polite invitation if you know what I'm saying.

I also hear word on some kind of scrap involving you, nephew, and I want to hear the full skinny on that when you taking your honeymoon in my vineyard.

The farm is still running at a profit so you don't need to get your sweet ass back any time soon—but I will tell you I sure do miss you.

Home, soon.

Your loving Auntie Phelps

Only Jack knew the real humour of the author of that letter and just how misleading the humour in the letter was—Auntie Phelps was no backwoods "Okie"—she possessed a mind sharp as a blade and a tongue as pointed as a stake designed to impale anyone. *This ain't just a polite invitation* wasn't simply a quaint phrase, it was tantamount to a Royal Command.

Well, that decided where part of the honeymoon would be spent.

Chapter 67

The Right True End

'I do.'

The congregation had held its breath—the silence leading up to those two words was incredible, as though there were some people who were still almost in disbelief that those words would ever be spoken at all.

But Susan had spoken them—and she meant them. When she looked up at Jack, the tears filled her eyes and it had been a monumental effort for her to keep her emotions in check, not wanting to break down—at all—but definitely not at the wrong moment, the moment when she would speak the most important words in any wedding ceremony—the affirmation to all who witnessed the ceremony that she, Susan Fisher, formerly Tanner, was now marrying the man she really should have married twenty one years ago.

One year to the day of Jack's return to Cwmhyfryd, twenty one years to the week of their first abortive attempt to be married, both Jack and Susan officially did it. Once the words, the confirmation that they were now married, had been made public, the congregation let out a collective sigh of relief.

Standing in front of them, officiating at his very first wedding, Vicar John Redd—such an important player in this story from the moment Jack stepped foot back in his old home village—was equally as tearful. These two people he had come to love as much as if they were his own. Of all the services he had presided over since taking up the cloth, this was the biggest, the most important—and the most joyous. His face ruddy red, his hands clasped together, a smile which would brighten any misanthrope's day, Vicar Redd raised his arms out wide and shouted out the silence of the Church, 'EVERYONE—THIS IS THE HAPPIEST OF DAYS—CHEER!'

And everybody did as they were exhorted to by their Vicar. Such a strange chap, they all thought, compared to his predecessors who would never have allowed such a vigorous outpouring of emotion within the sacred walls of this old Church. The cheers echoed around the Church and filled it with the happiness that such a joyful ceremony demanded.

The Church was filled to capacity—such a statistic could only be found a handful of times over the last fifty years and then mostly for the most solemn of occasions. Outside in the graveyard, the remaining residents who could not all fit inside the Church, had been listening to the wedding ceremony on the huge speakers which had been placed around the front entrance of the Church. Nor were they cheated out of the visual splendour of the day—a wide monitor screen had been constructed over the front entrance and the clever photographer using the camera inside had been weaving around the Church in order to get the best angles for all to see. The man was an employee of the BBC, experienced in catching the best angles—and had been hired by Arthur Ellison to capture this day on camera. There would be a copy made for every single resident to gaze upon at their leisure in the future, all expenses taken care of.

Sara Philips held the position of best girl to the bride and Adam was Jack's best man—a role he took on with pride and enthusiasm and would boast on for the rest of his life. Catrin and Claire were chief bridesmaids and both sisters looked stunningly beautiful—in fact, little versions of the bride herself. They wore slightly off-white gowns and a red rose was pinned to their left upper breast—just like Auntie Susan's, who, this being her second marriage and not being a hypocrite, had decided not to wear virginal white down the aisle.

And who gave the bride away? This time, Moira, Susan's mother, had not shied away from this wonderful duty. Any scandal she had been involved in all those years ago had long since been forgotten or forgiven. She led her daughter down the aisle, her arm linked with Susan's, and brought her to the front of the Church where the groom was standing. And just to impress upon everyone who was watching that she thoroughly approved of *this* choice of husband, she then stepped over to where the groom was standing and kissed him on his cheek. A smile and a wink followed and a whispered "well done" could only be heard by those who sat in the first two rows. Smiling, proud and loud, Moira took her place next to her sister, Ruthie, who stood as proud of her Niece today as she had done at the previous attempt and had stood in for Moira all those years ago when Susan had made the only mistake in her life.

But not this time.

The cheers were followed by a loud and long-lasting applause as Jack and Susan Farr made their way to the front door. They passed by Arthur Ellison who beamed a genuine smile and Allan J Gibney who had never before attended a wedding outside of his own family unit in his life. Standing at the back, another guest of honour also joined in with the applause. Detective Chief Inspector Owen Taffe—a once deeply despised police officer within his own profession but now an acknowledged hero by that very same Force and was definitely the hero in the eyes of Susan Farr, saving, as he did, Jack's life at the Quarry. When they passed him, Jack shook the policeman's hand and Susan placed her hands on his shoulders, kissing him on both cheeks, saying, 'Thank you for being there for my husband.'

Finally, just before they made their exit, they passed by a small, smiling man, wiry to look upon, a beaming expression of pride on his sunburned and heavily lined face—but the proud look was not for them. Father Liam, now in his nineties and long retired from the religion he had loved for nearly all his life had made this special journey to see his charge engage with this, the most precious of ceremonies, and to see how he discharged that duty. It would be fair to say, Vicar Redd would never be the most conformist of Church Ministers—his own brash style of how a Churchman behaves would probably repulse many of his peers— but to Father Liam, it didn't matter. He *believed* in what he did and performed his duty with the utmost sincerity.

That young man he had found all those years ago in the prison, almost begging for God to release him from this life because he had taken another's, had more than redeemed himself in the eyes of those he served. Father Liam had been made aware of just how important a part his protege had played in this incredible story involving this man, Jack Farr, and his actions in this affair more than justified Father Liam's belief in that younger man, Jona Rezinski, reborn as John Redd, Vicar of this Parish.

The ensemble left the Church and they were followed out by everyone inside. In the area outside the Church the photographers did their work with great professionalism and speed and in no time at all the pictures segment of the ceremony was completed. Upon a signal from Arthur Ellison, the Ushers, hired by Ellison, then announced they would now be making their way up to the top of the mountain where a gigantic canopy had been installed and the celebrations and refreshments would continue up there. Accordingly, the whole village trailed up behind the helpful and smiling young men and women who ushered them across the pathways and through the huge gates—the tent standing just a few hundred feet ahead.

The whole village laughed and sang their way to the canopy—with the notable exceptions of Malcolm Fisher, Sion Edmunds and his two sons, none of whom had been invited—they being the only residents who continued to spit bile at the mention of Jack's name.

And as the villagers walked upwards the canopy, Jack and Susan made a small diversion to the four graves belonging to Joe, Theresa, Joseph and James. They stood over the now well-tended graves and, without speaking, both gave of their thoughts to those who had not physically been able to be with them this day.

For Jack, this was the most poignant moment. In their lives together, father and son had never been particularly close though they had shared some wonderful moments. As does happen, the son learned a truth about the father he had not been aware of in life. His father the hero—and how that act of heroism in saving the life of Ellison Senior such a long time ago had resulted in the meeting between their two sons who lived their own legacies passed down to them by their fathers.

It was also curious, thought Jack, at how his brothers had also played their own part in recent events. Unconnected at the time but their working for Hywel Parry, their meeting with the McGregors and the terrible consequences of both those relationships led to this moment. Almost a whole generation had passed between the two incidents and yet...

Of course, nobody could have foreseen the Tommy Leeming intervention.

Jack wondered if there was an after-life, and if there was, what would his father think of how his legacy to his son had turned out. That was some legacy, Dad.

Jack held Susan's hand and saw she was talking—to Theresa. He didn't ask about what—he didn't have to.

They promised the four graves they would come back and see them before leaving for the States and then left to join the party on the mountain.

*

Down in the village, sitting outside his café which Susan had allowed him to come back to, Malcolm Fisher washed, for the umpteenth time that day, the same table which had not been used by any Cwmhyfryd resident. He sat down and stared up at the mountain where a person could just about see the top of the

404

Church. From here, he could hear music starting up as well as the bells being pealed by some happy soul and he scowled. Right up to this moment, he had fervently believed, hoped for, that Susan would still see the foolishness of what she was doing and would repeat what she had done twenty one year ago—but the sound of the bells told him this belief, this useless hope, would now not be realized. He remained seated at the table until six o'clock when the café was officially shut for the day. Betrayed, he thought to himself, by his daughter, by the residents to whom he had given dedicated service over the years—and the final insult, his ex-wife had been given a place at the wedding. No values were left in this world for him to admire. He cleaned up the empty café, locked the door and walked home—disgruntled and alone.

*

With less ceremony and effort displayed by Malcolm Fisher, the Edmunds family remained at home, the father drinking beer from cans—The Night's Tail was closed for the day—and the two sons, in their own rooms, getting quietly high on skunk.

The party went through the night and into the morning when they all walked outside of the large canopy and, with glasses raised, bade a welcome to the rising sun. The night had been fun, exciting, new (to the teens anyway, they'd never seen their parents dance themselves into exhaustive oblivion before) and laughter was never more than a few seconds away from the last roar or the next to come.

Jack stood next to Arthur Ellison who had provided so much to this celebration. He had bought the services of the Night's Tail landlord and a sizeable amount of that pub's alcohol quantity. From the village itself a group of teens who had formed their own musical band were allowed to play an hour of their music. Another Hyfridian was an up and coming DJ and for an hour, she played the kind of music only people between the ages of thirteen and seventeen would appreciate and dance to—but the theme of the night was observed— *everybody* got a shout.

To cap it all, some of the parents showed their children just how *they* did it when they were teens themselves and for another hour, the children saw their own parents in performance—and then they all exhorted their Mams and Dads to apply for *X Factor*, *Britain's Got Talent* and *The Voice* shows. For more than twelve solid hours, the happy party raged on.

At one in the morning, DCI Taffe, who had already been active for more than eighteen hours, told Jack he had to leave as work was waiting for him in Swansea. How does a man thank another who had saved his life—and allowed him this chance to keep living? Susan again kissed the Inspector on the cheeks and told him there would always be a place for him at Cwmhyfryd should he ever be in the area—professionally or casually. The police officer took his leave and walked through the cemetery to get to his car. The drive down the lane was quiet and he opened the window to let the night air in.

When he reached the village, it was in near total darkness. He exited through the gates and stopped the car. He got out and stared up to the mountains—on the one side, the night sky was lit up from the lights surrounding the canopy. He could still hear the beat of the music booming over the speakers and maybe, if he strained his ears hard enough, the sounds of a happy throng in full flow. Over on the other mountain, a hell had existed right in front—or rather, above—the people who lived here in this village and no-one had suspected a thing. Life.

A man had once told him that all life was a comedy—not the funny ha-ha comedy which played on TV but the whole of life—the tragedy, the laughter, sadness and happiness, sickness and health, boredom, lethargy and thrilling excitement—it was all life and it was all comedy. Shakespeare wrote plays about all of it—and sometimes would include all the separate elements in a single play. "All the world's a stage…" he had written, and everybody plays their part. Well, DCI Taffe had played his part in this comedy. Tomorrow, the comedy would continue when he would attend the next victim of "life". He got back into his car and drove through the dark lanes, away from this comedy, and to home.

Susan was speaking with Arthur Ellison, another man to whom she showed gratitude for Jack's quick recovery. From the day Jack had opened his eyes and spoken, things moved. For another week, the doctors maintained their watch on him as he slowly regained his senses, his voice and, best of all, his appetite. The most promising aspect of his recovery was the clarity of memory with which he demonstrated by relating, in detail, how he had made his way across the mountain—and down it—to save Claire from Tommy's murderous onslaught. Such clarity pretty much effected the full police report on that part of the incident. No more putting pieces of evidence together—they got the whole story from the man who was there. From that happy week, the transfer to the Ellison Private Hospital was arranged and seen through. Susan was given a private suite and saw Jack every day without great loss to her own work, much of which she was able to do at the hospital.

Moira and Ruthie came to Susan at dawn and mother, aunt and daughter hugged—so long absent from each other's lives. Mother-in-law was effusive to the new son-in-law and all four took ages to say 'goodbye' as the two sisters left Cwmhyfryd—again—and travelled home.

After sunrise, the strongest of those who had strung out the whole night, gave up the fight and more hugs to the newly-weds followed. The clearance team brought in by Arthur Ellison began their work to clean the mountain of any evidence of a party and Susan bade her happy 'farewells' to the last of the stragglers. The last people to leave were the Philips family. Mostly, they said their farewells with silence—but sometimes silence can say so much more than words.

And then, it was just Jack and Susan. They both stood with a still beaming Vicar John Redd and made their farewells to him, with gratitude for everything he had done to facilitate this celebration. He, in turn, blessed them both, his giant hands covering theirs as he joined them together. He nodded to the small man who was asleep on a chair and told them, without any explanation, that the old man was his saviour. No more detail than that. Vicar Redd then gently lifted the old man to his feet and they entered the Vicarage.

Hand in hand, Jack and Susan walked across the mountain and towards Greenacres—the family home which would now, *not* be sold.

The sun rose and the new day began.

Chapter 68

A Gentle Breeze

One week after the wedding, Jack and Susan prepared to make their journey to London, Heathrow, and from there to the States and then to Oklahoma to visit the family matriarch—Auntie Phelps. Jack had already warned Susan about how the old woman could outperform Meryl Streep in any drama and not to be taken in by her generosity or to be scared of her vicious tongue. Forewarned, Susan prepared herself accordingly.

It was a wonderful sunny day on the mountain, very much like the day Jack came back to the village on. He lifted two heavy suitcases into Susan's car—the limp in his leg still slowed him up and the Doctors had told him the damage to his knee would probably require a knee replacement—something which he could easily afford now and would be done via the auspices of the Ellison Hospital.

Susan came out of the house, followed by the excited Philips sisters and Sara—all three staying at Greenacres while Jack and Susan enjoyed their honeymoon in the States. As Susan went over the final instructions with Sara, Claire ran to Uncle Jack with a small, carefully wrapped box and gave it to him— a belated wedding present she told him. She followed this gesture with yet another bear hug and held onto him as if her own life still needed it. And then— she whispered into his ear.

'Will you call your first child after me, Uncle Jack?' Without waiting for the answer, she then ran back to where her Mam and Auntie Susan were standing. Catrin—with less ecstatic energy—walked to Jack with her own carefully wrapped box and gently wrapped her arms around him. With Catrin, words were always at a premium and she said nothing about the incident beyond thanking him—again—for bringing her loud and always annoying sister back to her.

As she pulled away, she also whispered, 'Will you name your first daughter after me, Uncle Jack?' and stared up at him, almost imploringly, and Jack hoped the man she would eventually marry would realize just how lucky he was. When she walked away, he wondered if there was something the two Philips girls knew that he didn't. Susan was now talking to the two girls in near conspiratorial tones, before looking at Jack, a half-smile on her face. More hugs followed then they both got into the car, Susan driving, Jack in the passenger seat.

Sara looked at Jack as he strained his head to turn and wave at them and Sara waved back. No words could ever translate the way she felt about the man who had risked his life to save the life of her youngest daughter and Jack always squeezed her hand when they met—as if to tell her no words were ever necessary.

The girls—laughing—went back into the house and Sara stood by the front porch, still waving the car goodbye even after it was long out of her sight. Smiling, sad, grateful, she also entered the house and quiet around the house resumed. The removal of the human element allowed the sounds of the forest to assume command and now the animals and birds could sing, dance, howl and play without interference.

A gentle breeze streamed through the forest, weaving in and out of the trees until it escaped the many hurdles nature had placed in its path to find its way into the open area of the house and the garden where it too played and danced. The breeze enveloped itself around the house, sending leaves and small grains of dirt flying into the air—even creating a small tornado in the front garden. Not as big as its American-type cousins and nowhere near as intimidating but nature comes in all shapes and sizes.

Finally, the breeze entered the porch of the house standing on the mountain and it gently nudged a rocking chair which had been placed there. The chair had been built by the old man who had once lived in this house and it had always held pride of place on the porch—principally because it was too large an object to get through the doorway. The rocking chair gently rocked back and forth as though someone was actually sitting in it. It squeaked as it rocked.

Not bad, the old man who had once occupied the chair may have thought, maybe thinking about the legacy he had left his son...

Not bad at all.

The End